THAT DEVIL'S PROMISE

The bedroom had once been light and airy, even beautiful. The colors were a soft yellow touched with splashes of green, but time had dulled the tones and fabrics to an insignificant whimper of color. The gray daylight merely highlighted the nicks in the simple furniture and the stains on the coverlet. Though she detected no dust, the simple ravages of time made the room seem forlorn.

Still, it was much better and larger than any room Lynette had yet enjoyed in her life. She turned to her guide. "Is this my room alone? Or do I share?"

She detected a slight shift to his lips, but Adrian's eyes remained remote, his tone distant. "It is yours alone." Then he gestured to a doorway half hidden in shadow beside the bedpost. "That leads to my bedchamber. I will thank you to knock before entering."

She stiffened, turning to him in shock. "I shall not enter at all, sir! I am to be married, and I shall enter that state with my purity and my honor intact."

This time he did smile, though the expression seemed hard. He stepped into the room, folding his arms across his chest as he leaned negligently against the bedpost. "Your honor is not my concern. Your purity, however, shall be grossly torn."

Devil's Bargain

JADE LEE

LEISURE BOOKS NEW YORK CITY

A LEISURE BOOK®

July 2004

Published by

Dorchester Publishing Co., Inc.
200 Madison Avenue
New York, NY 10016

ISBN 0-8439-5372-1

Printed in the United States of America.

Visit us on the web at www.dorchesterpub.com.

Devil's Bargain

Chapter 1

Lynette ran her fingers along the dark, black lines of Admiral Lord Nelson's tomb. She held her breath in awe as she imagined the hero, his voice echoing through the crypt of St. Paul's Cathedral as he said his most famous words: *"England expects that every man will do his duty."*

Every man, of course, included the women. And so she was doing her duty—to her father, who was now dead; to her family, which could no longer feed itself; and to her uncle, who did not want one more dependent relative than he absolutely had to have.

She clutched her bag tightly, feeling the tiny lumps that contained all her worldly possessions: two dresses and underclothes, two shillings, thruppence, and her Bible. If only the Baroness Huntley would appear, then Lynette could go on about the business of getting a wealthy husband.

Abandoning the spacious crypt floor, Lynette

climbed the stairs to the main cathedral. She had thought to be inspired here and so had arranged with the Baroness Huntley to meet at St. James's. In truth, beyond Nelson's tomb, the great building intimidated her. The soaring lines of massive stone weighed down, making her feel dwarfed and small.

It did not bother her overmuch, or so she told herself. Her father had been a tall and massive man, well used to booming his sermons from the small parish altar. She was accustomed to feeling tiny beside him. She just had not expected the feeling to follow her here, to London, as she at last took matters into her own hands.

The baroness had promised her a Season in London, and a rich husband to boot. And so Lynette had stolen away from her family on the very day they were to pack up and leave for her uncle's tiny estate. She had written a note to her mother, claiming to enter a nunnery so as not to overburden her uncle. And then she had come here, to begin this quest despite the misgivings in her heart, despite the nervousness that even now made her limbs shake.

Lynette climbed the last steps to the main floor, skirting the edge of the pews, trying to stop herself from hiding in the shadows. She apparently succeeded, for a broad, imposing woman stood in the aisle between the last pews and cleared her throat imperiously.

Lynette hurried forward.

"You are late."

"My apologies." Lynette stammered, doing her best to quiet the rapid beat of her heart. "I was viewing Lord Ne—"

"Come along, then." The baroness—for surely that

was who this woman was—didn't look at Lynette, but let her gaze skim along the pews, nervously skipping past the altar.

"Where are we going?"

"Out of here," the baroness snapped. Lynette recognized the symptoms: Obviously, the woman was uncomfortable inside a church, or at least one as large and awe-inspiring as this one. But the baroness's discomfort was Lynette's gain. Lynette had taken an enormous risk coming to London in this manner. She would not go further until she had a few of her questions answered.

"Before we leave," she began, pretending to a confidence she did not possess, "I wish to know the details of our bargain. I was told you could find me a rich husband."

The baroness's eyes pinched down over her nose. "Nothing is for free, girl. I get a quarter of your marriage portion."

Now it was Lynette's turn to frown. "But I have no dowry."

"Don't be stupid." The baroness practically growled as she turned toward the door. "Your husband will pay for you." She stopped to glare at Lynette. "And it shall be a tidy sum if you do as you're told."

Lynette wanted to hear more, but the baroness had clearly reached her limit. The woman was leaving, her tall form covering distance fast. And yet Lynette hesitated. She had left her home in Kent full of confidence. She was going to London on a grand adventure, with no one to naysay her and everything to gain. But now that she was at last faced with her future—in the guise of a statuesque woman with beautiful skin but a sour expression—she felt all her fears rush to the fore. Her hands actually trembled, and she could not make her feet move.

Then she saw him: a man leaning with negligent grace against a column. He had dark hair and a brooding air, and when he noticed she was looking at him, he pushed away from the column, walking with a stride that seemed sinful, though Lynette could not say why. Perhaps it was the way his lips curved with feline cunning. Or perhaps because his steps seemed to stalk more than walk, prowl more than approach. And when he came near enough, she looked into his eyes and saw a blue so piercing she thought of morning sunlight through stained glass.

Her throat went dry, and instinctively her gaze skittered about her, looking for a minister or altar boy—anyone who might protect her, for the baroness had already pushed through the front door.

"You had best hurry," the man said, his voice deep and low. It was musical, but in the way of a distant chime that one had to strain to hear. "She hates the church and will not wait long."

"The baroness, you mean?" Lynette's voice came out weak and high, and she swallowed, trying to calm her fears. This was just a man, she told herself sternly. And they were in a public place. A church, no less. And yet, for all her admonishments, her nerves still skittered and made her skin feel prickly.

"The baroness," he acknowledged. "My aunt."

She jumped as if pinched. "Your aunt?" She bit her lip, not knowing what to say but finding words nevertheless. "She is to find me a husband." Then, for the oddest moment, she wondered if this man was her future bridegroom.

He smirked, as if reading her thoughts. "No, I am

not the one for you. Your husband will be old and wrinkled with bad teeth and even worse breath. He will remind you of a shriveled prune, but he will be rich. And he will die while you are yet young."

She stared at him in silence. Then she made her voice cutting. "I do not know you, sir, nor do I wish to." And with that she meant to walk away, but his chuckle stopped her. It was low and warm, despite her coldness to him.

"You have spirit. Good. You will need it in the years to come."

She wanted to leave, but her desperation to know her future overcame her anger. She could not stop her question. "Years?" she echoed, hating the quaver in her voice.

"Six months to marry. Another ten years for him to die."

"Ten years," she whispered softly. "I will be thirty-one."

"An excellent age to be a rich widow."

Suddenly, it was all too much. Grief welled up inside her. Unbidden, the tears came, spilling over her cheeks to drip silently onto her gloved, clenched hands. She tried to stop them, but the grief was too raw, the change in circumstance too new.

How could her father do this? She knew he had not intended to die. The sickness came upon him quickly, tearing through him in barely more than a week. But how had he not made provisions for them: his wife and three children? Why had he left them destitute and dependent upon a pinch-penny uncle?

It wasn't right. It couldn't be what God intended. And yet it had happened, and Lynette was here now, doing the only thing she could to restore the situation.

Then she felt the stranger, his touch warm and reassuring as he gently led her out of the church. "Come," he said softly. "The baroness is waiting."

He guided her until they stepped out into a gloomy London afternoon. The baroness had already hailed a hackney, and all three of them climbed in. The baroness's nephew sat beside Lynette, his arm a firm, hot presence against her side. Rather than look at him, she turned to the window, watching the streets of London to block the flow of questions in her mind.

In the end, they came to a respectable neighborhood with modest homes that seemed dull in the gray light. They stopped in front of one, striking only in its absolute sameness to every other house on the street. As Lynette stepped out of the hackney, she couldn't help but think of what all that sedate sameness was meant to convey: moral correctness, wedded bliss, glowing children, and the contented veneer of a happy, wealthy family.

Was all of it a lie?

Of course it was, she answered herself. The house, the neighborhood, even the stiff-necked baroness herself could not hide the truth from Lynette. What they were doing—this buying of a husband—was immoral. Marriage was for love, not commerce. Lynette had assisted her father in dozens of marriage ceremonies. She knew the liturgy by heart. And a common business arrangement was not what God intended.

And yet it was so common as to be expected. So typical, in fact, that she—a parson's daughter who knew better—was already enmeshed in a devil's bargain to buy herself a rich, old man. She would not have joy in her marriage. She would have to be content with wealth.

Her hands shook at the thought, but her back was straight and her shoulders square as she entered the baroness's home. The interior looked much like the exterior—sedate and gloomy. The baroness did not stop, but went directly down a hallway to the back of the house. To her right, Lynette caught a sight of a large, ugly butler, quickly introduced and just as quickly disappearing into a side parlor.

Unsure what to do, Lynette moved to follow the baroness. She was stopped by the nephew—she had no other name for him—who touched her arm and gestured upstairs.

"Let me show you to your room," he offered.

She nodded, agreeing only because it would be rude not to. She followed him to a bedroom that had once been light, airy, even beautiful. The colors were a soft yellow, touched with splashes of green; but time had dulled the tones and fabrics to an insignificant whimper of color. The gray daylight merely highlighted the nicks in the simple furniture and the stains on the coverlet. Though she detected no dust, the simple ravages of time made the room seem forlorn.

Still, it was much better and larger than any room she had yet occupied in her life. She turned to her guide. "Is this my room alone? Or do I share it?"

She detected a slight lift to his lips, but his eyes remained remote, his tone distant. "It is yours alone." Then he gestured to a doorway half hidden in shadow beside the bedpost. "That leads to my bedchamber. I will thank you to knock before entering."

She stiffened, turning to him in shock. "I shall not

enter at all, sir! I am to be married, and I shall enter that state with my purity and my honor intact."

This time he did smile, though the expression seemed cold. He stepped into the room, folding his arms across his chest as he leaned negligently against the bedpost. "Your honor is not my concern. Your purity, however, shall be grossly torn by even the most lax standards."

His words shook her. He spoke as if it were a foregone conclusion that she would be dishonored. But what were her alternatives? She could not run. She had no money to return to Kent, and even if she did, her family had already left for her uncle's. They thought her safely ensconced in a nunnery. What would she say to them? That she had decided to take a jaunt to London? Alone?

Her reputation would be in tatters. She had to make the best of her situation here. So she lifted her chin, deciding to salvage her pride if nothing else.

"Sir, you are offensive," she said stiffly.

He nodded, as if that, too, was a foregone conclusion. Then he abruptly sketched a mocking bow. "Please, allow me to introduce myself. I am Adrian Grant, Viscount Marlock, and this is my home."

"Your home," she echoed weakly. Her mind whirled. Had she heard tales of the Viscount Marlock? Even in Kent? Was he the one with a reputation for debauching young girls? She could not remember. So she took refuge in good manners, dropping into a demure curtsy.

"Perhaps you were told that I shall be assisting in your education," he drawled.

Her gaze hopped to his face, seeing his lips curve into a sensuous smile. There was no doubt what he was suggesting, and yet it could not possibly be true. "I have been told nothing," she said slowly. "Perhaps you could explain exactly what your duties will entail."

He was silent as he stepped closer. She wanted to shy backward, but there was no room. She was already backed against the door. So she stood firm, holding her breath as he extended his hand and touched her cheek in a slow caress. "You were told nothing? But I understood that you arranged for this meeting."

"Yes, my lord. A family friend recommended the baroness, and so I wrote to her." In truth, he had been a friend of a member of her father's congregation, visiting from London. The elderly man, the Earl of Songshire, had approached her quietly one evening as she performed her cleaning duties in the church. They had spoken at length, mostly about herself, her father's death, and her family's destitution. Then he had pressed the baroness's address into her hand, urging her to inquire—secretly—into the woman's services.

"What you do not know," said the viscount, his smile growing, "is that all that the baroness does, she does at my bidding."

Lynette was trembling. She did not know why, but she felt weakness in her limbs and was powerless to stop it. If only she understood what he intended. "You will not find me a husband?" she asked.

"Oh, yes. You will have a bridegroom, and a rich one at that. But it is I who shall be in charge of your education. Not the baroness."

"But why?" she cried out. Then she hastily moderated her tone, dropping her gaze until she appeared appropriately modest. "I mean, why should a gentleman of your obvious breeding concern yourself with my education?"

His sharp bark of laughter startled her, but when she lifted her gaze, the traces of humor were already fading. "You will find, little Lynette, that breeding, as you put it, does not fill one's belly." He made an expansive gesture indicating the house. "This and a moldering pile of rocks are all that are left of the family fortune. I cannot wed an heiress; my reputation is too unsavory. And so I market young brides instead."

Lynette gasped in shock. He *was* the evil viscount. And she was here. With him. And if that was true . . . Her thoughts spun away. Good Lord, this whole scheme was impossible!

"You have a question?"

Her gaze lifted only to find that he was watching with the intensity of a cat staring at a mouse hole. "I . . . I have many questions," she stammered.

He raised an eyebrow, neither encouraging nor discouraging her to continue. In the end, she felt compelled to speak. "If your reputation is unsavory, my lord, then I, too, have fallen by association." She gasped, her gaze once more flying to the door that adjoined their two bedrooms. "My presence in this house has already ruined me!"

She had not meant to sound so dramatic, but if this scheme was doomed from the start, she had best do what was required to rectify the situation. She turned as if to leave, but he blocked her path.

"You are correct," he said, his tone conversational. "Your reputation suffered the moment you entered this house. However, I will still find you a husband. Indeed, my fortune and yours depend upon it."

She shook her head, denying everything he said. "But—"

He cut her off with a single raised finger. "Do you know what a courtesan is?"

She bit her lip, trying to decide how to answer. Her father would have flown into a rage if she confessed the full truth: that she had eagerly listened for any drop of gossip about such creatures. So, instead of a full confession she chose a partial truth. "I only know what little I have heard. I am sure none of it could be true."

"Of course it could be true. That, and a great deal more," he drawled, his amusement obvious. "No matter. You, my dear, will be educated very much like those wonderful creatures."

She gaped at him in horror. Her, a courtesan? "But I was told—"

"Listen to the rest, Lynette. You will become a Marlock bride. Like a courtesan, you will be beautiful, accomplished, and knowledgeable in a variety of pleasures. But you will also be loyal, gentle, and, of course, presentable. And for this, some man—likely an older, experienced man—will pay a great deal to wed you. So that you may grace his table by day and his bed at night."

"But, I don't understand. Why would he marry me? When a . . . a courtesan's pleasures can be had—"

"For a few gems? Until the man becomes bored? Or the woman unpresentable?"

She nodded. That was exactly what she meant. Why would a man wed what could be had for a few pennies?

"Because a smart man knows the value of paying once instead of monthly or at a lady's whim. Of tying a woman to him for the rest of his life—assuming she is the *right* woman—rather than for a few months. Of finding a bride who will nurse him kindly in his old age, rather than abandon him to seek her own pleasures."

"But you cannot promise that—"

"Of course I can!" he snapped. "Because you will. Because I have done it before and my reputation stands on that promise." He stepped closer, until he was looming over her, his breath hot on her face.

"My lord," she gasped, wondering what she could say to make him retreat.

"Will you be faithful to your husband?" he asked. "Will you please him at night, care for him in his dotage, even if he is a hundred years old with cold hands and rancid breath?"

She blinked, wondering why tears blurred her vision.

"Will you, Lynette?" he demanded.

"Yes!" she gasped, knowing that was the answer he wanted. Knowing, too, that it was the truth. For whatever reason she wed, she would not dishonor the man she married. "I could not break a vow made before God," she whispered.

He stepped back, his entire body suddenly relaxed, almost congenial. "Then I believe you shall be my best bride yet." He reached out, gently stroking her cheek with an almost paternal air. "You will fetch a high price indeed."

She jerked backward, drawing her face away from him. "I don't understand—" she began. But he cut her off.

"Enough questions. It is all too new for you." He

abruptly moved to the door. "There will be time enough after the initial evaluation."

That drew her up short. "Evaluation?" she asked.

But he was already gone.

Chapter 2

For an hour Lynette sat numbly on the bed, staring at the walls. Finally, weary of doing nothing, she unpacked her few belongings and stood in the center of the room, her mind churning uselessly.

Perhaps she should focus on making a good impression. She knew many great houses dressed for dinner, and though this was obviously not a great house, still she donned her best dress: a pearl gray gown with a lace collar. She also did what she could with her light brown hair, brushing it to a fine glossy appearance and despairing over her lack of curls. She had no cosmetics, so she contented herself with pinching her cheeks for color.

Finally, with nothing else to do, she ventured downstairs.

No one was about. The staircase deposited her in a dimly lit hallway as deserted as the upper floor. A parlor stood abandoned to the left, the grate cold.

Deeper in was a library with few books and a pockmarked desk. A smaller escritoire pressed against one wall, almost as if it were hiding. She thought to call out but knew that would be ill-bred. And, in truth, she had no wish to disturb the tomblike feel of the house. So she continued to wander.

Farther back she discovered the formal dining room. This was clearly the best room in the house. The table was a huge, gleaming block of mahogany, the chairs were tall and stately with thick cushions, and the linen was a crisp, blinding white. She noted candelabra, chandelier, and silver as well, and yet this room felt as devoid of life as the rest.

In fact, it gave her a chill just standing in it.

She heard a muffled thump. It came through the servants' door, no doubt originating in the kitchen. The thought that someone was preparing dinner made her stomach rumble hungrily. She had felt too nervous this morning for breakfast, but now she imagined food with great relish. She pushed through the door and rushed down the short, dirty stairway beyond.

The kitchen she entered was large by London standards, but even so it felt cramped. All manner of cooking equipment covered the walls and table space. Unfortunately, Lynette saw nothing that resembled dinner. Despite the prevalence of cooking paraphernalia, the larder was obviously empty. The only food she noticed was a hard loaf of black bread clutched in the fist of a massive man with dark hair and an even darker countenance. He was the same hulking brute of a butler who had opened the door nearly an hour before.

"Mr. Dunwort, isn't it?" she asked.

The man looked up, surprise lifting the scowl from his expression. "Aye, that be me. Good o' ye to remember."

"Please, sir, could you tell me at what time dinner is served?"

His eyes narrowed, as if taking her measure. "It ain't, miss."

She frowned. "I beg your pardon?"

"The new miss always makes the menus and stocks the larder. There won't be no food until ye decides wot I'm to buy."

Lynette shook her head. "But I couldn't possibly presume. I am sure the baroness—"

"Master's orders. The young miss plans the food and keeps the accounts. Learning about money is part o' yer training." He paused to bite off a hunk of his bread. "Ye won't eat unless ye works."

She looked about, clearly seeing the truth in his words. There were indeed no plans for any type of dinner. "Am I to cook it as well?"

Dunwort shook his head. "That be my job. Exceptin' fer the dinner party after ye be presented. You are to engage a chef."

"A chef!" Without conscious thought, Lynette sank onto a stool beside Dunwort. "But how—" She cut off her words, her thoughts spinning. At home, her mother performed the cooking and shopping duties. Lynette had always spent her time assisting her father in his many tasks as minister.

Dunwort leaned back, his gaze narrowed onto her face. "If ye asks, we'll help ye. Otherwise, we'll leave ye t' muddle on yer own."

She looked at him in surprise. "Well, then, I shall most certainly ask."

He smiled, abruptly softening his entire countenance. Obviously, she'd just passed some sort of test, so she returned his smile uncertainly before walking slowly about the kitchen. Unfortunately, the situation did not improve upon inspection. There was nothing by way of even the basics of eatables. She would have to buy everything.

But what that *everything* consisted of, she could only guess.

"Do you know how much I am able to spend?" she asked.

Dunwort had been watching her every move, his dark eyes frank and assessing. "Wotever ye spend comes out o' yer marriage portion. Wot you eat now is food out o' your family's mouths later."

She heard the cynicism in his tone and turned to study his expression. Though she did not like being reminded that she was just one of many girls brought into this household, she could not resist asking the question. "The other girls have spent freely," she guessed, "relying on their marriage portion to be large enough to carry them through."

Dunwort nodded, a slow, measuring movement that nonetheless conveyed a bit of respect for her deduction. "Some spent. Others pinched."

Lynette continued to wander about the narrow room, absently looking inside cupboards and poking into drawers as she mentally inventoried their contents. "Well, I am afraid I shall be more of the pinch variety, Mr. Dunwort. This entire day has been like a bizarre dream to me, and I cannot believe that the viscount's scheme will succeed."

"Oh, it'll succeed, all right. I seen 'im do it six times afore."

Now he had her full attention. Closing a cupboard, she returned to her stool. "Six times?" she asked. "Six other girls?"

"Aye. And all bed and wed."

She noticed that he had the expression backward. Did not one wed first, then bed? But she ignored his error, choosing to voice her deepest concern. "But I am a poor parson's daughter. All that commended me to marriage was my virtue. And now that I am here, even that . . ." Her voice trailed away on a sigh.

"Aye, it's tainted. No doubt about that."

Lynette winced at his frank tone. She had hoped for something much more reassuring.

"But he'll get ye a husband nonetheless."

She turned, studying the servant's face. In her years of assisting her father on his visits, Lynette had met many people of various walks of life. She had learned to assess not their clothing nor their surroundings but their expressions. In studying Dunwort's countenance, she realized he had a harsh face only in that it appeared worn and beaten. His brows were as thick as his dark curly hair, but his eyes were steady, and his mouth was neither pinched in disapproval nor pulled wide in a hungry leer. In short, he appeared honest, if a bit reserved. Until he proved otherwise, she would count him a friend.

Having decided that, she pressed her hands flat on the table and stood. "Very well, Mr. Dunwort, for better or worse it appears I am in charge of the larder. Pinchpenny I may be, but even a pinchpenny must eat. Therefore, unless you enjoy that black bread, I propose we find some better fare. Do you have the purse, or shall I get that from the baroness?"

His craggy face split into a grin. "I 'ave the purse,

miss. 'Is lordship sold sheep for it just yesterday. So, do we eat or shop first?"

She glanced about the room. Even the stove was ice cold. If she chose to delay her meal, it would be quite delayed. As if on cue, her stomach growled, reminding her that she was hungry now and had no wish to wait.

"I have had a very trying day, Mr. Dunwort. Though normally I would suggest we shop as best we can at this hour, tonight is different. Tonight, I say we eat. Do you know of an inn with a tolerable stew or meat pie?"

He nodded, even as he was reaching for his cap. "I know just the place."

"Then buy enough for you, me, his lordship, I suppose, and the baroness—"

"The viscount has chosen to dine at his club," Dunwort interrupted. "And the baroness will like as not drink her dinner."

Lynette paused. She knew many of her father's flock chose to drink themselves to death, but she refused to aid anyone in such an endeavor. "You shall buy meat pies for the three of us, then. I will bring hers to her myself."

"Very good, miss."

"Are there any other servants dependent upon this kitchen?"

"No, miss. Just me." Then he buttoned his cloak and prepared to depart. She stopped him, placing her hand on his arm.

"I could go with you," she offered. She knew many great houses where the housekeeper went on the shopping expeditions, but then she hesitated. "*Should* I go with you?"

"No, miss, ye can't. Yer t' be a lady, and it ain't smart t' be seen wit' me."

She nodded, understanding his meaning. "Very well," she said, relieved not to face London after dark. Kent was near enough to London that she had heard many tales of dangers lurking not more than a step outside one's door. "Perhaps I shall enjoy what is left of your black bread," she added without enthusiasm.

With a quick nod, Dunwort disappeared, slipping out the back door faster than she thought possible for such a large man.

She did try to eat the black bread, but hungry as she was, she could not stomach the hard crust. So, rather than sit and wait impatiently for Dunwort's return, she went in search of the baroness.

She found the lady upstairs in a sitting room across from her own. Though the room might once have been inviting, done in shades of blue and a pale yellow, it had fallen victim to the same ravages that haunted her bedroom. The furnishings were shabby, the draperies frayed. Even the fire hissed fitfully. The baroness sat next to the grate. She was wrapped in a thick rug, her hands curled around a glass of sherry as she stared dully into the fire.

Lynette stopped at the door, taking her time to study the room's occupant. When she had first met this baroness, Lynette had disliked the woman immediately. She had felt small enough in that huge church, and the baroness had made her feel even smaller.

But now Lynette wondered if she had been wrong. The person she saw now seemed old and frail, her slumped posture indicating a depressed spirit. And though the woman held a glass of sherry, she was not drinking it. The bottle that sat on a small table beside her was nearly full.

In fact, this particular sight suggested the baroness truly was the viscount's pawn. Certainly Lynette could not see this broken woman as being strong enough to countermand anything the viscount dictated.

"If you want food, you shall have to find it yourself." The baroness's voice was not so much cold as it was weary.

"I have already sent Dunwort for meat pies. He shall bring us ours directly."

The baroness's eyes flickered, lifting for a moment from the fading coals. "You bade him bring me food?"

"Naturally. I will leave no one to starve when there is money available."

This time the woman's gaze did rise, coming to rest on Lynette's face. "You understand that whatever you spend comes from your marriage portion?"

Lynette nodded. She was beginning to dislike everyone's calm assurance that some gentleman would pay a rich price for her. They made it sound as if a wealthy man would suddenly appear like magic. Lynette wanted a plan, and without one, she was prone to creating anxious questions. What would happen if no groom presented himself? Would her mother have to pay for what was spent? She didn't have the money. Would Lynette be sent to her uncle's home? She would be disgraced, possibly outcast.

Fortunately, she was not given time to dwell upon such thoughts, for the baroness continued, her gaze returning to the grate. "I am sure Dunwort informed you that I prefer to drink my meal tonight."

Again, Lynette nodded. She crossed to the coals,

warming herself as best she could. "He told me, but I am sure you know meat is better sustenance for mind and body." The words came without thought, because she had said them so often to her father's parishioners. Then, when she looked up from the grate, she was startled to see the older woman's watery gaze was steady on her. "Baroness?"

"You do not hate me." It was a statement, not a question, and it caught Lynette off guard.

"Why would you expect hatred from me?"

The woman's laughter was startling in the silent house. "You mean from a minister's daughter? I assure you, every girl he has brought here has hated me."

Slowly, Lynette settled into the chair opposite, understanding the meaning beneath the words. "Then it is true; you have only done as he bid."

The baroness chose to drink rather than respond, draining her glass with one swift motion.

Lynette looked away, seeing that as confirmation enough. "*You* are not my enemy, Baroness," she said softly.

"Have we drawn battle lines already?" came the harsh response.

Lynette shrugged. She had not intended to wage a war, but if she was honest, she had already begun to view the viscount as her enemy. He alone seemed to rule this household, and from all appearances ruled it to no good effect.

"You will lose, you know. You cannot fight him. He will not allow it."

Lynette chose her words carefully. She was new to this household. She could not afford the luxury of thoughtless speech. "I do not wish to create disharmony, Baroness."

"Ha!" Again, that high crack of laughter. "You are a minister's daughter. There isn't a soul on Earth more disharmonious to him than you." The baroness poured herself another drink. "You will fight him, and you will lose. Then he will marry you off, never to think of you again." The woman abruptly shoved her sherry glass into Lynette's hand. "Drink, girl. You need it more than I."

Lynette stared at her, then at the glass, finally letting her gaze slip to the fire. Nothing made sense. Nothing felt right. But one glance at the baroness told Lynette she would get no more information tonight. The woman was already folding into herself, shutting her eyes as if preparing to sleep.

Still, questions pounded at Lynette. What was happening? When she'd left Kent, she had been filled with hope, the Earl of Songshire's recommendation the only security she needed. If he'd recommended this woman, it must be safe. After all, wasn't he an earl? Didn't he know the ways of the world? Certainly better than Lynette.

But now she began to fear. What scheme had she embarked upon? Risking her entire future on a simple suggestion from a kind old man?

Lynette felt her spirit quail. Her gaze returned to the glass in her hand. She despised spirits. She had seen their effect all too clearly. And yet, even so, she lifted the glass and drained it.

Chapter 3

The viscount came into her room that night. It was late, perhaps even close to morning; she could not tell. She merely heard their adjoining door open.

Her eyes flew open, but she did not move. He did not bring a candle, and so she felt his presence more than saw him: a black silhouette, impossibly large, towering over her bed. She meant to scream, but the sound was locked in her throat. And even if she managed to give voice to her terror, who would come to help her? No one in this household, surely.

"Do not fear. I will not touch you tonight." His voice was low and strange. Not thick with drink, but neither was it a sibilant whisper. It was simply deep and dark, as if the sound came from the blackness surrounding her and not from a man's lips.

"Breathe, Lynette. I would not have you suffocate ere we even begin."

She took a shuddering breath because he commanded it. The bed dipped as he sat down beside her, and her throat froze closed. Oddly enough, her limbs could still move. Without conscious thought, she scooted to the farthest corner of the bed. Her hands clutched the coverlet to her breast, and she felt her eyes widen as she searched the darkness.

It was a ridiculous pose, she knew. He could easily overpower her no matter the corner of the bed or room in which she chose to hide. As for the coverlet, what protection was that? He could do as he willed with her.

And so, with a creeping sense of powerlessness, she allowed her hands to drop away. Her white, high-necked gown more than adequately covered her, even if he could somehow see her through the shadows.

He must have heard the movement, because he acknowledged it with another soft comment. "Feeling resigned, Lynette? I have not come to hurt you."

It took her three tries before she found her voice. But find it she did, and it came out steady, though pitched too high. "Why are you here, my lord?"

She felt him shrug, the movement rippling through the mattress. "To see if you slept. To accustom you to my visits." He sighed, a soft whisper in the darkness. "No, that is not true. I came to ask a question."

She closed her eyes for a moment, wondering if ever there was a more bizarre household. Why would this man come to her bedroom in the middle of the night to talk? Still, she was a clergyman's daughter. She knew what was required of her. "What do you wish to know?"

He laughed, the sound startlingly rich. "Are you always so polite, even when a strange gentleman enters your bedchamber unannounced?"

"Having never been in this situation before, I cannot answer as to what I would usually do." Her answer came without thought, her tone, thankfully, dropping into its normal register.

The viscount's laughter burst forth again, and she felt her fingers curl in annoyance. But then he was speaking, his humor fading quickly. "My question is simple, Lynette. Why are you still here? You were obviously unaware of the nature of this arrangement when you arrived, and yet you have not run screaming from my home. Why?"

She frowned, wishing she could see more than his dark silhouette. "I have come to be married," she stated. "To a rich man. As the baroness promised."

She felt more than heard him shake his head. "You are accustomed to living in genteel poverty. With your looks, you could have found some local man to wed you. And yet you have thrown off everything you know to come here, to the home of a libertine. Why?"

She sighed, oddly unsurprised that he was asking the very question she had been struggling with herself. There had been time, earlier in the day; she could have left and found some way to return to her family. The damage to her reputation would not have been so great.

"Is your uncle so very terrible?" he asked, his voice gentle.

She shook her head. "It would have been unpleasant. Difficult even, but I would have survived. Perhaps even been welcomed."

"Then why?" he pressed, and she bit her lip, struggling to answer.

"Do you know what it is to want, my lord, and not even know the reason?" She didn't wait for his answer, but continued, groping blindly for words to express the restlessness that churned within her. "I assisted my father with all his parish tasks. All of them, my lord. I know more than most what awaits a respectable girl from a country village. I have listened to the wives and mothers. I have heard their regrets and their dreams." She sighed. "They are not all unhappy, but . . ."

"But what, Lynette? You want more?"

She shook her head. "Not more, my lord, so much as . . . different. I will not find happiness there. Nor will it come in my uncle's village."

"So you sought my services out of boredom?" His voice held an edge of disdain, and she straightened.

"Not boredom, my lord. Simple logic. I will not find joy where I was. I could therefore accept a joyless life or search elsewhere." She shrugged. "The baroness . . . or rather, you, are the only *elsewhere* available to me."

"So you seek joy, then."

She felt her hands clench in frustration but kept her voice level. "I just told you, my lord. I do not know what I seek. I only know I will not find it at home."

"And if you do not find it here? Under my tutelage? What then?"

She sighed. "That is the risk of making any change, is it not? Sometimes it is for the worse."

"And what then?"

"Then I will live with the consequences, whatever they may be." She wanted to touch him, as if that could make him understand. "I will not find happiness at my uncle's. So I might as well find unhappiness with a rich man than with a poor one."

So saying, she fell silent, awaiting his response. But

he did not answer, and after a time his silence began to weigh on her, making her fidget. She was too uneasy with her choice to feel comfortable with his silent scrutiny. In the end, she stumbled into speech again.

"I intend to follow this course through to the end, my lord. I will not run away out of fear or intemperance."

He laughed, though there was no humor in the sound. "So you claim, Lynette. But understand this—I have already expended funds upon you, and a great deal more to come before I see any return. My future rests on your success, my girl, as much as yours. And so your course is set. Even if you change your mind, even if you manage to run screaming from this house, I will find you. And I will make you fulfill your commitments—to me and to your bridegroom."

She bristled at his tone, angry that anyone—especially a self-professed libertine—could so question her honor. "You cannot force me!"

"I can," he returned, his voice low and ugly. "Do not doubt that."

She swallowed, not doubting him for a moment. There were things men could do to disgraced, dishonored women. Ugly things, and no one would lift a finger to protect them.

"You made your bargain the moment you stepped into my house, Lynette. Do not think I shall ever let you change your mind."

She nodded, struggling to fit power into her tone. "I told you, I will not run." She took a deep breath. "Just do not forget your promise. At the end of all this, I shall have a rich husband and a new life. A man rich enough to sponsor my sister into society and buy my brother's commission. That is all I require." She said the words, but in truth, she quailed at her own bravado. What if her husband were brutal? Violent? Insane? What would she do then?

She was startled out of her thoughts by the touch of a hand—gentle and soothing—as the viscount caressed her cheek. "I shall enjoy the coming months," he said softly, a trace of admiration in his tone. "By God, I will."

"And what shall I enjoy, my lord?" She didn't know why she asked. In truth, she did not expect an answer. And yet he took the question at face value, answering it calmly.

"You shall enjoy whatever you choose to enjoy, Lynette. It is you who will decide if what comes is torture or joy, hateful or wonderful."

"Sinful?" she prompted, unable to resist lashing out in some small way.

Even through the darkness, she could see him nod. "Yes, sinful. Or"—he leaned closer, so close she could feel his breath lift the fine hairs of her brow—"heavenly."

She gasped, unable to control the frisson that drew her entire body tight. But he pulled away, standing so that he once again towered over the large bed.

"Enough for tonight, Lynette. I can see you are tired."

"You can see nothing, my lord. It is too dark." Why she persisted in fighting him, she could not fathom. But the words came out nonetheless, sparking another of his deep chuckles.

"On the contrary, I see excellently in the dark." He sketched a short bow and turned to leave. She heard him open the adjoining door and slip through. But he did not close it.

Instead, she heard his every movement in vivid detail. She caught the rustle of his clothes as he removed them, the soft clink of coins that he set on a table, even the splash of water and the creak of his mattress when he finally settled down.

Then there was nothing. It was silent, and Lynette imagined that he, at last, was falling asleep. It was only then that she consciously willed her body to relax.

"One other thing."

His voice startled her, filling the darkness so that she once again sat bolt upright, believing he was beside her bed. He was not. His voice came from his bedroom, no doubt from his own bed.

"In the future, Lynette, you shall sleep naked."

He was pushing too hard.

Adrian peered into the darkness surrounding his bed and chastised himself for moving too quickly. She was a strange creature, this Lynette. A minister's daughter, and yet she had come to him of her own free will, escaping everything she knew to risk all in London. Merely on the recommendation of a parishioner's relative.

He pushed up from his bed and began pacing silently about his room as he tried to analyze his latest charge. For the most part, she was no different from any of his other girls—young, pretty, naive—though clearly she possessed unusual strength and courage. Beyond that, she was clean and well-formed.

She would sell well on the marriage mart, assuming she did not lose her nerve.

"I will not run."

She had spoken the words firmly, loudly, and he believed she meant them. But she had chosen a difficult path. No one—least of all a minister's daughter—could walk this courtesan's path without doubts. It was up to him to make sure she did not change her mind, did not ruin both herself and him, for he had staked everything on her success. The price of outfitting her alone was enough to cripple him if she did not marry well.

But when she at last spoke her vows, his share of the marriage portion would free him from debt, free him of the burden his father had so casually dropped upon his shoulders. He ought to be thrilled, ought to be gleefully anticipating her wedding. And yet he wasn't. Why?

"Do you know what it is to want, my lord, and not even know the reason?"

Her words echoed back at him, filling the darkness with the very hunger she'd named. Yes, he knew want, the crippling need for something—he did not know what. He felt it eat at him late at night when a beautiful woman meant for someone else slept in the next room. He felt it when he looked at his barren fields and mangy flocks of sheep. He felt it chip away at his strength at the worst possible moments, and yet he did not know what he searched for. Only that he did not have it.

And neither would Lynette. He knew—as she did not—that her answer would not be found in her wealthy marriage. It would not come in London any more than in Kent. But at least she had a hope. In ten or fifteen years, after her husband died, she would have all she needed to search for her answer: wealth, status, freedom. The very things he had longed for while rotting away in debtor's prison. The very things he worked for now with the training and marketing of young girls.

So why was the thought so distasteful? Why did it leave him with an aching hunger for something unnamed, something out of reach?

He did not know. And without an answer, he could only persevere. He had to plan and think, manage and train, make sure Lynette became his best bride yet. And when he was done, she would embark on a wealthy future, and he could, at last, forge his own peace. He would leave London forever, devoting himself to establishing his own wealth, his own future.

And then, maybe one day he would find the answer. He would discover what he needed and fill the emptiness that gnawed at his soul. But until then, he would devote himself to training and selling Lynette.

Chapter 4

Lynette woke early out of habit. Her father had been an early riser, and she had always joined him at breakfast, enjoying the sound of his voice as he struggled with his sermon. This morning, however, found the viscount's house in silence.

She opened her eyes, missing the soft snores of her brother and sister. She heard nothing but the morning sounds of London. She might have gone back to sleep. Indeed, she had slept poorly after the viscount's nocturnal visit and was quite tired. But she could not close her eyes knowing the yawning black doorway was just a few feet from her head. That *he* was a bare few steps away.

As silently as possible, she eased out of bed on the far side, away from the opening. She grabbed her clothing and dressed quickly, her eyes trained on the dark entrance to his lordship's bedroom for fear he would appear. Then she tiptoed from her bedroom, barely daring to breathe for fear she would wake him.

No one was about on the main floor, not even Dunwort. Lynette slipped down into the kitchen, hoping the servant had thought to buy something for breakfast, as she had not told him to, or asked him about it last night when he'd returned with the meat pies. As she pushed open the kitchen door, she found the baroness sitting at the table, a hot bun in her hand. The room was pleasantly warm, and a kettle was heating on the stove.

"Good morning, Baroness. I trust you slept well." It was the customary greeting she gave her father. He just as religiously responded that he had slept the rest of the holy, and he hoped she had as well. Lynette wondered for a brief moment how she would have answered her father today, as her sleep had neither been restful nor holy. Fortunately, she had no time to ponder as the baroness glared at her through red-rimmed eyes.

"All the other girls slept late," the woman accused.

Lynette hesitated, suddenly missing her father desperately. "I have always risen at this hour," she said carefully.

"Morning is my time," snapped the baroness. "It's when *he's* asleep."

Normally, Lynette would have departed simply out of politeness. But she could not pass up an opportunity to learn more about her mysterious host. "The viscount? Does he usually sleep late?"

The baroness did not answer at first, taking refuge in her breakfast instead. But eventually she spoke, every word filled with sullen anger. "His time is at night. You will not see him before noon, and even then it shall be to growl. Best remember that, girl."

Lynette nodded. "Of course—"

"He leaves notes," interrupted the baroness. She dragged an envelope out of her pocket and shoved it across the table. "Orders that he writes the night before. These are yours."

Lynette stared at the pristine white envelope. For a moment, she felt an overwhelming sense of dread; if she so much as touched the missive, she would be irrevocably stained. But she threw off the feeling as ridiculous. She was already stained. The moment she'd walked into this household her reputation had been sullied. Had not everyone said as much? Touching an envelope could do no more harm.

Still, she delayed reading it with the only excuse at hand. She stood and pulled the kettle from the stove just as it began to sing. "Is there any tea?"

"None."

Surprised, Lynette glanced back. It was obvious the woman was lying. Why else would she have put the water on to boil if not for tea? But one glance at the lady's pinched expression stopped any comment within Lynette's throat. She had learned from watching her father that sometimes things, even tea, were not worth the unpleasantness of an argument.

So she dropped into her chair and stared at the viscount's message. Without another ready excuse, she had no choice but to open it.

You have this day to set the kitchen to order. I shall dine at home tonight.

M

She looked up to see the baroness's smug face over her shoulder. "He writes the same thing every time," she said with her sharp cackle of laughter. "Of course, you're the first girl to get it when there was still time to do aught about it."

Lynette looked around the bare kitchen, struggling with an overwhelming sense of panic. Where was Dunwort? "But what am I to do? I know nothing of setting a kitchen to rights." The baroness did not respond to her question, and in time the silence stretched between them. Mindful of Dunwort's stricture to ask for help, she turned and said, "Would you assist me, please? I have not the slightest idea."

"You asked for my help!" the baroness exclaimed, a smile beginning to spread across her face. Lynette watched the transformation in a state of shock, startled to see how handsome the woman could appear. Her straight brown hair perfectly complemented her tall frame and high cheekbones. It was only the baroness's red-rimmed eyes and sour expression that made her seem ugly. When she smiled, as she did now, she was beautiful.

Lynette was still reeling from this observation when Dunwort burst into the room, booming, "'Ere she is. She'll be awake, I says as I blew out me candle last night. I best sleep quick 'cause she'll be ready, and then it'll be my ears that'll be ringing."

"We have been waiting a long time for a new girl," explained the baroness. "Now that you are here, we shall have food aplenty."

Dunwort hefted a large purse. "I 'ave the blunt." Then both of them turned to stare at Lynette, waiting on her orders. She could only blink, her head spinning.

"H-how much may I spend?" she stammered.

The large man handed the purse to her. "You best count it. His lordship will want a clear reckoning."

"She has already asked for my assistance!" said the baroness, her glee apparent.

Dunwort clapped his hands. "I knew she was a smart 'un." He leaned forward and opened the purse for Lynette, lifting out a pound note. "We always starts with the menu first. Shall I find us breakfast?"

Slightly dazed, Lynette could only nod. Dunwort pulled respectfully at his cap and disappeared out the back door. Meanwhile, the baroness pulled out a tea tin she had hidden within the folds of her gown and calmly dispensed tea for them both. She produced paper and ink and settled in as if they were the best of friends.

And yet, moments before, the lady had acted as though Lynette were the most hideous of intruders, unwanted and reviled. She had even lied about having tea! What sort of household made guests an enemy first, then later mysteriously accepted them as friends? And how would Lynette manage in such a strange home? It was so different than all she knew.

"The future will watch itself. For now, do as he says and be content."

Lynette started at the baroness's words. Had her thoughts been so obvious? Flustered, she took recourse in a half-truth. "I'm sorry. I was thinking about my family and how I shall miss them."

The baroness's sharp cackle startled her. "Don't ever lie. We know what you are thinking. We have seen six other girls go through it."

"Then why are you suddenly so friendly?" Lynette blurted.

The baroness took her time responding, reaching for her tea and taking a long sip before she spoke. "Because you asked for my help. Remember, you are a lady now. No one will *offer* to assist you with these types of tasks."

Lynette could not restrain her laughter. "I assure you, Baroness, asking for help has never been difficult for me. In fact, given my responsibilities in the parish, it was most definitely a requirement."

The other woman nodded, her expression thoughtful. "Then perhaps there is an advantage to being the daughter of a clergyman." She cast a baleful eye at Lynette. "Though, somehow, I doubt you will think so."

The day flew by as if on wings. There was so much to learn! The baroness, it turned out, was a wealth of information. Add to that Dunwort's sometimes coarse but always amusing commentary, and Lynette found herself wishing the day would never end.

Together, they seemed to traverse all of London and bought all manner of foods. Lynette knew her eyes were the size of saucers, but she could not help it. She was fascinated by everything and tried to see and learn and remember it all. Better yet, her companions were friendly, helpful, and filled with mirth.

Until they returned to the house. Abruptly the other two sobered, and Lynette's laughter was not returned. They worked together to put the food away, but moved in silence, their occasional comments delivered in a hushed whisper. Frustrated and saddened, Lynette dropped her hands onto her hips and turned to her two companions.

"Does he hate laughter so much?" she demanded.

Both Dunwort and the baroness raised their gazes to her, their expressions a mixture of shock and wariness. But neither spoke.

"Lord Marlock," Lynette pressed. "Does he hate to hear laughter?"

The Baroness frowned. "Of course not. Whatever would make you say that?"

"You." Lynette crossed her arms on her chest. "We have been having such a gay day of it. Why must it end merely because we have come back to this house?"

"My dear," exclaimed the baroness, "that has nothing to do with Lord Marlock."

"Then what is it? Why do we suddenly speak in whispers with one another?"

It was Dunwort who explained, though he rubbed the back of his hands in nervousness as he spoke. "It ain't seemly, miss. I be a servant, she be a baroness, and you be a minister's miss." Then he stopped, as if that was all she needed to know.

But it was not enough. Not enough by half. "I know these things, but—"

"It simply is not proper," put in the baroness. "You and I should not associate with the servants."

"That be me, miss," inserted Dunwort.

Lynette sighed. "But we have been associating all day. And quite enjoying it."

"Aye, and right bad that was of us," said Dunwort. He cast a reproachful glance at the baroness. She returned it in equal measure before focusing back on Lynette.

"If you are to wed as a lady, you must act as a lady." Lynette would have protested further, but the baroness raised her hand, effectively cutting off all comment. "You became a lady the moment you entered this house. From now on, we absolutely must treat you as one."

"Best learn it now, miss," said Dunwort firmly. And with that he pulled on his forelock and stepped out of the kitchen through the back door. The baroness, too, headed out of the kitchen, but through the upper staircase.

"Come along, Lynette," she called over her shoulder. "You will need to dress before dinner."

Lynette did not move. She stood there, staring about the suddenly empty room with a feeling of dismay. Her father had always warned her that she was too familiar by half, but in the end he'd seemed to appreciate it. Especially as she spent most of her time consoling the poor who liked her easy manners.

Now, suddenly, she was supposed to transform herself into a lady? She wasn't sure she liked the idea. Yet it appeared she had little choice in the matter.

Lynette did not need to "dress for dinner." She had precious little to dress in, and certainly nothing that required hours to don before sitting down to table. So, after pulling on the same gray dress she had worn the night before, she left her room to wander.

He was downstairs; she knew it the moment she took the steps. The house seemed to convey his tangible presence when he was home, as if even the furnishings were waiting, anxious to find out what he would do. Or was it her imagination? Likely she had heard the rustle of papers in the library, or perhaps seen the flicker of his candle flame. But whatever the reason, she stood at the base of the stairs, her breathing suspended as she waited, not knowing what to do.

And then she was caught. He stepped out of the library and saw her. He held some papers in his hand, but he ignored them, choosing instead to smile lazily at her.

"Lynette." His voice was soft, his tone mellow, but she felt a shiver travel down her spine at the sound. She was not precisely afraid of him. She did not know what she felt, except that she had a sudden urge to run.

She did not. She squared her shoulders and gave him a steady regard. "My lord," she responded as coolly as she could.

"You do not seem to be dressed for dinner. Could it be that things are not quite prepared in the kitchen?" He had a slight sneer on his face. Apparently he had not expected her to accomplish her task.

"On the contrary, my lord, Dunwort is even now performing his culinary arts. Dinner will be served on schedule."

It was a good thing she did not expect any great show of surprise. Not by so much as a raised eyebrow did he betray his thoughts. He merely nodded, his gaze returning to her gown. "Then you should change. A lady is expected to wear her best for dinner."

"This lady is," she responded curtly.

This time, he did react. His lips pulled down in disgust, and he stepped away from the wall to inspect her. "A governess could not look more prim."

She lifted her chin, stung by his dismissal of a dress she had labored long hours creating. "I had thought to apply for a post as a governess."

"And why did you not?"

She bit her lip, wondering if she should tell him the truth. One look at his face told her that she would have to confess, for she truly believed he would spot any lie. She sighed, giving in with what she knew was ill grace.

"Understand, sir, that I have been assisting my father since I was very young. I am accounted most helpful in a sickroom." Her gaze slipped away from his face as she confessed her greatest shame. "But the truth is, my lord, that I am a most unnatural girl. I do not like children." She lifted her chin, anxious to explain. "I don't hate them as a general rule. If only they would behave. Children are always running about, getting into things that were just set to rights, always making noise or needing something. And whenever I scold them, the mothers are quite furious with me. But truly, how can they allow their little ones to behave so wildly? Yet they do, and the very thought of caring all day, every day, for someone else's children, of trying to make them mind when they have no reason to . . ." She swallowed, overcome by the horror of her strange feelings. "I could not do it. I simply could not force myself to do it."

He must have heard the bitterness in her tone, for his frown was quick and dark. "It is no sin to despise someone else's squalling brats. You are far from unnatural for that."

She looked down at her hands, relief flooding her that he did not despise her oddity. "I thought," she confessed without thought, "that an older husband would prevent the conception of children."

"You are a surprise," he said quietly. So quietly, in fact, that her gaze flew to his face, wondering if he mocked her. He did not. Indeed, if anything, his expression was pensive. Almost admiring. "That was well thought out, though uninformed. There are ways to prevent conception with any man, young or old."

While she was still confused by his accepting attitude, he reached out to touch her. With the tips of his fingers he stroked her cheek, and she felt his caress like a brand.

Abruptly, she jerked her head backward and would have stepped away from him, but he grabbed her arm and held her fast.

"Do not run from my touch."

His hand was like steel around her arm, and she tugged, but his fingers remained solid. "My lord!" she exclaimed. "You are hurting me."

He did not soften by the smallest margin. If anything, he seemed to grow larger, dominating her without seeming to move. "Then do not fight me."

"Then do not touch me!" she exclaimed.

He laughed. The sound did not warm her. "I shall touch you a great deal," he said. "Understand that now, Lynette. You may not shy away from me, turn from me, or so much as lift a hand to forestall me. You have much to learn, and I am your only teacher."

She glowered at him, her heart hammering. "You are not my husband! You have no right—"

"Quite the contrary," he interrupted, his voice low and threatening. Her struggles had pulled them close enough together that she could feel his breath heat her face. "It is time we came to an understanding, Lynette," he whispered. "Last night I was patient. Not today."

She trembled at his words, thrown by his methods. He did not bellow like her father. Nor did he stomp or crash about to make his point. Looking into the brilliant blue of his eyes, Lynette knew a moment of true fear. Where her father was like a hammer, large and brutal when defied, Viscount Marlock reminded her of a rapier blade. Surgically precise in everything he did, she feared he could cut much more deeply than her father ever had.

She trembled in spite of herself. Still, she did not give in. And he did not release her.

They continued as such for an inordinate amount of time: he gazing down into her eyes, she glaring right back. But eventually she felt herself weakening. His will seemed to beat upon her senses. He was stronger and more powerful in so many ways. How could she fight him?

At last she went limp, nodding her acknowledgment. "Perhaps you are correct. We should discuss our understanding."

"Good," he said softly, and then released her. Instinctively she rubbed the spot on her arm his hand had held. Had it only been one hand? Was that all he needed to bend her to his will?

Shame flooded her face with heat. Had she so little self-respect that she crumpled the moment he grew angry? No! She regarded him firmly, coldly. "You are not my husband. Nor am I your slave. You have no right to my person. I have set your kitchen to rights. I have stocked your larder—with my own money, by all accounts. These tasks I have and will continue to perform. But you have no leave to my body, and you will not touch me again." She paused to make sure he understood the level of her determination. "That is my understanding."

She had meant to walk away, but she didn't. She

lingered the merest fraction of a second to level one last haughty stare at him, and in that moment's pause, she was caught.

"Have you ever been kissed?"

She blinked, thrown by the question.

"I am still your teacher, am I not?" he asked before she could frame her own question. Then he began to walk around her, forcing her to turn to see him. "That is part of our bargain, is it not? That I shall teach you how to capture a rich husband?"

She nodded slowly, sensing a trap, but unable to fathom exactly where the danger lay. "Yes, my lord," she finally said. "You have been hired to instruct me."

He released an abrupt laugh. "How clever you are with words, student. So, I am a hired employee? Very well; I shall accept that characterization for the moment. And what, do you suppose, shall be the nature of my instruction?"

Lynette hesitated. Isn't that exactly what she had been trying to discover? What was to happen to her? How was she to ensnare a husband?

"You do not know, do you?" His voice was gentler now, but no less commanding. "Of course you do not know. Because you are the student, and I am the teacher." He leaned almost casually against the wall, but she was not fooled. His eyes remained dark and focused. "And as such, you are merely required to learn." He folded his arms across his chest. "I shall add one additional requirement: You must always be honest with me."

She glanced up, startled.

"Ah, I see I have surprised you. Most tutors merely require their pupils to echo back what they have learned. These students become parrots, mimicking their instructors' knowledge as if it was their own. Those are bad instructors." He was warming to his theme, straightening as he took a step toward her. "I require more."

He stopped and searched her face, gauging her reaction.

She held her tongue. Not for the world could she have spoken. Her mind was in too much chaos for her to form the words.

"In order for me to know if you understand your lessons, you must tell me what you think. What you *feel*." His voice dropped with that last word, taking on a husky timbre, as if it had special meaning. But she did not understand it, nor did she comprehend the tightening in her body, the pure physical reaction to his words.

"That is all, Lynette. I require your honesty, and that you allow me to teach you."

She nodded, her throat inexplicably dry. It made logical sense. But what did that have to do with his unconscionable liberties with her person?

"Say the words, Lynette, so I know you understand. Say you agree."

"I agree to be completely honest with you. I shall tell you my thoughts and express my feelings to the best of my ability." She had no fear of speaking her mind. If he wished for her honest and frank opinions, he would get them and suffer the consequences.

"And what of my instruction? Will you allow me to teach you as you need to be taught?"

She lifted her chin. "Of course I shall allow your instruction. It is my"—she searched for the appropriate word—"obligation to you. Because I want a wealthy husband." She swallowed. Indeed, the truth was that she *needed* to find a wealthy husband if her brother and sister were to have a chance at a real life.

He grinned. It was the first true smile she had ever seen on his face. It made him sinfully handsome. His features lightened, his eyes sparkled, and the curling disarray of his dark hair gave him an air of rakishness. "Well said, Lynette. Now, listen carefully. My instruction requires me to touch you, and you have just pledged to allow it."

"No—" she said, but then suddenly knew it was true. This was the trap she had sensed but could not see.

"Oh, yes." Abruptly, he softened. "But I do not wish you to fear me." He stepped near, once again stroking her cheek until she looked directly into his eyes. "I will give you this pledge: I shall never touch you in anger, and I shall never hurt you."

She saw the truth in his eyes, but still she felt cornered, trapped. Betrayed. "And will you also pledge to answer my questions truthfully? Whatever I ask of you?"

He nodded slowly, as if he was considering the question from all angles. She did not care how long he considered, so long as he agreed.

"I will give you such truth as I understand it. You will indeed have many questions in the coming days. Be assured I shall never lie to you, but know also that there are things that are . . . difficult to explain." A mischievous twinkle entered his eyes. "Perhaps you require a pledge?" He straightened, placing his hand upon his chest in a formal gesture. "I pledge my word as Viscount Marlock that whatever you ask, I shall answer truthfully."

That was exactly what she wished to hear. "So, if I ask if your touches are part of my instruction . . ."

"Then I shall answer honestly and in absolute truth that they are."

He looked at her, and she held his gaze. Eye to eye, they made their bargain, and Lynette knew that whatever arrangement had begun the moment she entered London, she had just deepened it, made it more binding.

Whatever came, she had given her pledge. She would allow the viscount whatever he willed so long as she got what she sought.

Chapter 5

"Very good!" the viscount exclaimed. "And since that went so well, I believe it is time for your first lesson."

Lynette blinked. She felt as if she had just run a circuit about London. She certainly did not feel prepared to learn anything just yet. "My lord—" she began, but he cut her off.

"Do not be concerned. It shall not be too difficult. I require you to answer a simple question. Have you ever been kissed?"

She should not have been shocked. Indeed, hadn't he asked that very question just a few minutes ago? Still, she *was* shocked, and confused and disoriented. "This cannot be part of my instruction," she stated firmly.

His smile abruptly faded, and Lynette was surprised by her own dismay at the sight. But then he was speaking, his tone more weary than angry.

"Have we not just established that I decide what constitutes instruction, and you are simply to comply?"

"V-very well," she stammered. "I have been kissed once. By my father's curate."

"Truly? Well, how did that kiss feel?"

Her gaze flew to his face. Surely he could not mean to ask . . . But apparently he did, because he raised a single brow in warning.

"Do not try my patience, Lynette. I will not have you constantly questioning my methods or my tutelage. Please answer the question."

She did not dare defy him again. But she still did not know how to answer.

"Think, Lynette," he prodded. "Remember how the kiss occurred. How old were you? Where did it happen?"

Her mind spun back to the moment behind the small barn, remembering the day, the hour, the very instant. "It was just last year. There was a farming family whose grandmother caught a summer chill. Father asked me to visit them."

"Did you often perform clerical visits for him?"

She nodded. "I visited the less distinguished members of his church."

"I see."

His tone was dry, and she could tell that he did indeed see. She sighed. Perhaps her father was not perfect, but he was her father. She might have defended her absent parent, but he did not allow her the opportunity. "You visited the grandmother," he pressed. "Was the curate there?"

"No. The grandmother and I were alone. We shared tea, and I gave her what comfort I could."

"You prayed over her." Clearly from his tone, the

viscount was not a religious man. Lynette stiffened at the implied insult.

"Whether *you* believe God hears or not, *she* most certainly did, and the prayers gave her comfort."

He bowed slightly. "My apologies. I am sure your visit cheered the woman immensely."

Lynette shrugged. "I am not entirely sure. She died three days later."

"Then no doubt your prayers eased her travels to Heaven." She studied his face, but Lynette could not detect any mockery in his manner. "Please continue," he urged.

"Very well," she said, rushing her words as she recalled what happened next. It was not difficult. She had relived the experience countless times, wondering over it, pondering it. "I was leaving through the back meadow. It was a shorter distance that way. The curate, Tom—he was just coming for a visit as well, and I'm afraid I was not attending because I was in a hurry."

"Fleeing the sickroom?"

She shook her head. "No. I went for a special tea to ease her cough. I had the leaves at the church, but I would have to run there for the herbs, deliver them, then return home for dinner."

"What a busy creature you were."

She shrugged. "Time hangs when one has nothing to do."

"That it does," he agreed. "That it does."

Lynette paused to study his blank expression. Did he sometimes find himself alone with hours stretching endlessly before him? It was such a rare event for her, she couldn't help but view it as a wonderful luxury.

"Come now." He interrupted her thoughts. "What of Curate Tom?"

Lynette folded her hands together to keep her fingers from worrying at her gown. "There is not much to tell. I fell into his arms. Literally. I tripped, you see. And as I was speaking my apologies, he leaned down and kissed me. I was so startled, I just gaped at him."

"Did you return the kiss?"

She frowned. "Return it? My lord, I had stumbled into his arms only to have his . . . his face swoop down upon mine. He was not quite on target, and his hair tickled my cheek. Then, suddenly, he disappeared into the parishioner's home."

The viscount's chuckle was a low, mellow sound, but it stung as smartly as a wasp. "He abandoned you?"

She stiffened. "He most certainly did not! I am quite capable of handling myself in such a circumstance."

"A first kiss?" His laughter had faded, but his smile had not. And she could still sense the humor rippling beneath the viscount's words.

"No! In my village." She shook her head. "My lord, you are deliberately confusing me. It merely seemed as if he disappeared, but in truth we looked at one another for a moment."

"And what did you see?"

She shrugged. Indeed, what else could she do? "I saw Tom—a man of God with an overly passionate nature. He has a handsome face, though it was quite red at the time. And he was trying to apologize."

"For kissing you?"

"I suppose. It likely was not because I had tripped and fallen into him."

"No, not likely," the viscount agreed.

Exasperated, Lynette rushed to end the conversation. "He was as embarrassed as I. One does not go about kissing the minister's daughter behind barns. Or anywhere, I suppose."

"And how old was young Tommy?"

"Twenty-nine."

"Older than you. Larger as well? Stronger?"

She nodded. "And broad. His shoulders, that is. Broad shoulders." She did not realize her expression had softened into a dreamy smile until she noticed the viscount's smirk. Then she hastily straightened, bringing her wayward body into a semblance of modesty.

"Did you see him again?" he asked. "Perhaps when you brought the tea herbs?"

She clutched her fingers tightly, trying to sort through her thoughts, her confusion. It had been such a wonderful kiss. Hard and wet and too fast. "I have seen him many times. He is my father's curate, after all."

"And how did he act?"

She smiled, remembering the next encounter. Unlike the moment of their kiss, that time she had felt in control, capable of managing the situation no matter how delicate it might appear. "He was naturally quite awkward at first."

"Naturally," agreed the viscount.

"He tried to say something, another apology no doubt, but I stopped him. I told him quite simply that I was to blame for tripping and falling on him, so to speak. Anything else that might have occurred was simply a product of surprise due to our awkward circumstances. I told him we need not think of the entire wretched event again."

"Wretched event?" the viscount prompted. "Was it that terrible?"

"Oh, no," Lynette gasped. "It was just clear that he was so very embarrassed. How could it not have been anything other than wretched for him? Especially if his wife were to misunderstand the situation."

If he had been laughing before—however quietly—the viscount's attitude abruptly sobered. "He is married?"

Lynette's gaze dropped, feeling that all-too-familiar mixture of excitement and shame. "As I said, Tom is a passionate man. He does everything with enthusiasm and often without thought. He told me he wished to travel to Africa to convert the heathens, but his wife would not allow it."

"And did you find him passionate?"

She bit her lip, trying for the thousandth time to understand her feelings toward her father's curate. "I admire him greatly, my lord," she finally said. "He is extremely well educated, and unlike so many of the clergy, he is deeply religious, deeply committed to God."

"Do you truly believe so? A married man who would kiss the minister's daughter?"

She lifted her chin, but she could not look at him. "I fell, my lord. And surprised him. And I did say he was often impulsive."

"No, Lynette," he drawled, "you did not. But I am beginning to understand why you were bold enough to write to us."

She looked up sharply at that, wondering—knowing—that he did indeed understand. She could not remain in the village she called home. Not with Tom always about. Not with the thoughts he inspired in her, and the fears as well. She had no wish to live at her uncle's. It would merely be more of the same: the same tiny village, the same gossiping women, the same restrictions for the minister's daughter until she felt as if she would scream. So, when the opportunity to escape appeared, she grasped it with both hands.

Meanwhile, the viscount was watching her expression much too closely for comfort. As she lowered her eyes, trying her best to appear demure, he asked another question. "Was that your only kiss?"

She nodded, unable to speak of the other things—the accidental touches, the way Tom often appeared wherever she worked, and worst of all, the way his wife forever watched.

"Did you ever speak of it again with this Tom?"

Lynette shook her head, the motion almost painful in her vehemence.

"But did you think about it? Wonder at it, perhaps? Spend long evenings by the fire reliving it despite its inappropriate nature?"

The blush that flooded her face answered the question eloquently enough, and she was glad he did not ask that she state her thoughts out loud. Oddly enough, when she looked up at him, he was smiling, his expression almost triumphant.

"My lord?" she asked.

"It is nothing, Lynette. I am merely pleased that my task may not be quite as difficult as I had thought."

"But—"

"Enough for now. The lesson is concluded." He stepped away from her, picking up the papers he had dropped on the side table and heading once again for the stairs. She stopped him with a cry.

"Ended?" she exclaimed. "But I have not learned anything!"

He smiled. "Actually, my dear, you have learned a

great deal. You have learned that you can be honest with me and I shall not curse you for it."

She had started to take a step toward him, but stopped at his words. "I do not understand."

He took his time answering, folding up his papers before addressing her. "Have you told anyone else of your experience with Tom? Anyone at all?"

Lynette looked away, shaking her head mutely. She had not even confided in her sister, whom she told nearly everything.

"And why is that?" he pressed. "Did you fear laughter? Ridicule? That perhaps no one would understand how inexplicably confused and yet exciting the whole tiny event had been? That perhaps you could never look at Tom the same way again, and yet you could not speak of it to anyone, least of all the man himself?"

She looked at him, shock reverberating throughout her body. He did know! "It seemed like so insignificant an event. Not worth mentioning at all. But it was all so very awkward."

"But you remember it, do you not? Every scent, every breath, every sensation is etched in glorious detail in your memory."

She bit her lip. "Yes," she whispered. "Oh, yes."

He lifted her chin. It was the slightest touch, but it encouraged her to look openly at his face and see that his expression held no condemnation, only brutal honesty. "It is that way for everyone, Lynette. Every first kiss, every first love is as heart-wrenching, as unspeakably wonderful and terrible and ridiculous and stupefyingly fabulous all at the same time. Yours happened to have an extra measure of complexity added on, but the essence is the same."

"Everyone's?" She gasped. She could hardly believe it. Had her mother once felt like that? Her uncles and cousins and friends—had they all sat by the fire and dreamed and remembered and wished and pretended until they felt as if they would crawl out of their own skin with wanting?

Had her father?

"Everyone," the viscount echoed. And with that final comment, he turned and hurried up the stairs.

Dinner was a stilted affair.

Though Dunwort had done an excellent job with the meal, Lynette could not stop thinking about what she and the viscount had discussed. At home, her silence would have gone unnoticed. Her father created most of the dinner conversation while his wife and children served as audience. But here she was expected to speak.

In fact, she got the impression that this was the "evaluation" the viscount had mentioned earlier. And that she was failing it.

Apparently she was expected to do everything as a lady would. Her table manners, her conversation, even the way she turned her head came under scrutiny. Surprisingly, it was not the viscount who dispensed most of the criticism. It was the baroness.

Though the viscount frowned at her when she did not wipe her lips after taking a drink of wine, and once he flicked a double glance at her when she lifted the wrong fork, he chose to say nothing. Instead it was the baroness, the very same woman who had laughed so merrily with her that afternoon, who was now the unforgiving source of discipline.

"You have begun to slouch," she snapped. "Do not do so.

"Do not grab your glass as if it was a mule. Hold it delicately. Gently.

"Really, Lynette, your conversation is most lacking. You must learn to exchange pleasantries, on-dits. You must say *something* at the dinner table."

That last was the final straw. Slamming down her larger fork, Lynette glared across the table at her tormentor. "You did not find my conversation lacking this afternoon at market."

The baroness stiffened, casting an uneasy glance at the viscount. "That was this afternoon. This is now," she said coldly. "And a lady never, ever loses her temper."

"I am not losing my temper! I am taking hold of it as one would a stubborn mule."

At that moment, the viscount began to choke, or so it seemed to Lynette as he coughed rather indelicately into his napkin. All eyes turned toward him, and so, after he had recovered, he slowly rose. "I believe I shall take my leave of you ladies."

"Now?" gasped the baroness. "But we have not yet had the pudding."

He bowed to his aunt. "Even so." Then he turned to Lynette, the reflected candlelight sparkling in his eyes as he sketched another bow. "If you would please bring your accounting to me directly after dinner, I would be most grateful."

Lynette gave him a curt nod, and he beat a hasty retreat. She was no fool. She recognized a man running from a storm. Her father had often disappeared in a similar manner whenever her mother and sister squabbled.

"Coward," Lynette muttered under her breath.

She did not say it quietly enough; the baroness heard her. The lady gave her a sharp look, then allowed her lips to form the faintest ghost of a smile. "I quite agree," she whispered. Then she lifted her chin and said, "But that does not change the fact that your manners require a great deal of work."

And so continued the meal. Thank God, there was only one course left. Any more, and Lynette would likely have reached across the table and, in the most ladylike manner possible, sweetly strangled the woman.

She knocked lightly on the library door and waited until she was bade enter. The answer came almost immediately, and Lynette stepped inside.

The room was most certainly a man's domain. The furnishings, though sparse, spoke of a man's determination and power. There were a modest number of books lining the shelves. A small fire sputtered in the grate. But the room was dominated by a huge desk.

This morning, Lynette recalled, the desk had been spotless—a gleaming wood surface polished to a brilliant and intimidating shine. This evening, papers littered the top. Behind it sat the viscount, his cravat askew, his hair curling in disarray. If possible, he looked almost . . . vulnerable.

And what a strange thought that was about the viscount.

She approached quietly, her neatly figured page of accounts clutched in her hand. He did not glance up at first. Instead, he simultaneously reached for his brandy and gestured for her to sit at the simple wooden chair opposite his desk.

"I see you survived dessert unscathed."

She settled primly onto her seat. "You were not there. How would you know what wounds I suffered?" Though her words were tart, they held no rancor, and he did not appear to take insult.

"Truer words were never spoken," he said. "But as you are not sobbing, nor do you appear to be bleeding, I shall assume that my aunt was thorough without being lethal."

Lynette nodded. How could she not? The baroness had indeed been thorough in cataloging her sins. By the time the meal was over, the lady had in fact given her a written list of tasks she was required to perform come morning: everything from walking with a book on her head to a hundred repetitions of the correct way to drink from a glass of wine.

"Suffice it to say," Lynette finally commented, "that I shall be adequately occupied tomorrow."

The viscount set down his glass. "Indeed you shall. Tomorrow there will be dozens of people here for your dresses, hair, boots, slippers, fans, and the like. If you wish to learn from them, ask as many questions as you desire, make suggestions even, but never, ever, seek to overrule their decisions. They have my complete confidence."

"Unlike me?"

She did not know what demon prompted her to say that, but the viscount did not so much as blink at her vulgar challenge. He simply smiled. "Most assuredly unlike you." Then he shifted the papers on his desk before pinning her with a steady regard. "Show me your accounting."

She passed forward the paper without comment,

then watched his expression closely. She was not disappointed.

His face lit with surprise. "Your figures are excellent. You are sure these sums are accurate?"

"Of course they are accurate!"

He smiled at her outrage. "Then you need have no fear of me."

She frowned. "Did the others . . . the girls that came before me . . ." She trailed away, unsure if this was forbidden territory.

"Yes?" he prompted.

"Was their accounting slightly exaggerated?"

He set down her page of figures. "Do you mean, did they try to embezzle from me? One did, yes, but I found out." He pinned her with his hard gaze. "Remember that, Lynette. I always find out."

She nodded, having no trouble believing his statement.

"Very good," he said. He pulled out a ledger from his desk. "Record the sums in this book; then you may keep your papers for yourself." She nodded as he gestured to the small, rather battered lady's escritoire in the corner. "You may work there."

Lynette took the heavy ledger and crossed to the tiny seat, sitting down to begin her task. Unfortunately, copying figures was tedious, and her mind soon began to wander.

She glanced back at the viscount. His head was bent over another ledger, and he moved through his stacks of paper one by one as he copied figures from bill to book. He looked very focused, and she knew she should not interrupt him. And yet a question burned in her mind.

He looked up, his eyes locking onto her regard with a suddenness that made her gasp. "What is it, Lynette?"

"What was your first kiss like?"

He stiffened, and his face grew cold before he bowed over his work again. "A lady does not ask such personal questions, Lynette."

"Of course not, my lord," she answered immediately—but some perversity in her character led her to pursue the topic, despite his clear displeasure. "Except you did say that I could ask anything during the course of my lessons."

"This is not one of your lessons."

"And you swore to answer honestly," she pressed as if he had not spoken.

"Your time would be better spent finishing the task at hand."

"The figures will be recorded, my lord. But right now I am asking you a question, student to tutor."

He frowned at her. She remained stoic, her most pleasant expression fixed on her face. His scowl deepened into a glower, but she remained unimpressed. She knew he was trying to intimidate her. Apparently her personal experiences were open to his most minute dissection, whereas his own past was to be shrouded in secrecy.

Well, she would not have it. And if he refused to answer honestly as he promised, then she would no longer feel bound by her own oath to attend his instruction.

Finally, he returned his quill to its stand. "Very well." He stood, moving around the desk and across the room until he towered directly over her. She did not have time to stand, so she sat there, craning her neck while he seemed to drop his every word on her like a stone. "My first experience was with a whore from Vauxhall Gardens. It was Christmas Eve, and I was home for the holiday."

She frowned. "Your parents took you to Vauxhall for Christmas?"

"My parents were dead. I was here. In this empty place." He waved his arm at the house. "And Jenny . . ." For the first time, he looked away from Lynette. His gaze wandered out the window, no doubt to the distant pleasure garden. "Jenny was my Christmas present to myself. I sold a silver candelabra, as I recall, and used the money for her. I suppose I was her Christmas present as well, because I was young. Easy work for a whore."

He wandered away, following his gaze to the window, where he stood almost immobile. "Lord, she was young, too. She could have done it quick and cold, but she didn't. We went to her room. It was in a dark, dank hovel, and the bed had ticks, but at least it wasn't here. She taught me what to do. Slow and easy, she said. Slow and easy."

He laughed softly at something in his memory, then turned, fixing his gaze on her. "Jenny was smart. She initiated me properly, tenderly, and for that she had a loyal customer for years." He paused for a moment, his eyes distant. "She was the one who got me out of debtor's prison. I owe her a great deal."

"Debtor's prison?" Lynette echoed. She knew there was a message there for her, but for the life of her she could not understand it. "Where is she now?"

His smile was lightning quick and full of pride. "As I said, Jenny was smart. In many ways she and I grew up together. She met my friends and did right by them as well. Now she's a rich woman, a well-paid mistress who costs too much for me. She even owns a bawdy house, runs it in her spare time. Every once in a while I see her and we speak. We laugh." He glanced down at her. "Perhaps you will meet her some day. She could teach you a great deal."

Lynette swallowed, not sure she could imagine what wholesome things she could learn from a whore turned mistress. "I think one instructor is all I can manage for now."

Marlock released a low chuckle. "In that, little Lynette, you are correct." And suddenly his face closed, and his laugh was strangled, as if it had never been. Without another word, he sat down at his desk and went back to work.

Lynette watched him a moment, not daring to speak, not knowing what to say. And so, after a time, she returned to her own task.

It was difficult, for she was constantly aware of him: the movement of his pen across the page, the shift of his body in his chair, even of the ebb and flow of his breath, though she swore she could not actually hear it. It was as if he were a lodestone, and she lead.

She heard him stand, crossing to the bookcase with quick strides before depositing a small and worn book before her. She looked up at him but could read nothing in his expression. In the end, she was forced to examine the book itself.

The title was a single word: *Investments*.

"It gives a review of the banking system and provides general guides as to what would be a sound investment or a foolish one."

She nodded, carefully picking up the small tome and riffling its pages. "I am to read it?"

"That is up to you."

"But I need not."

He shrugged, already returning to his chair. "It is not necessary to the getting of a husband. Indeed, I advise you to keep anything you learn from such a book a secret until after you are wed. The men who will offer for you will not be interested in your knowledge of England's monetary system."

She nodded, too aware of what her father would say. And yet the prospect intrigued her. "But you give it to me now. Because, when I am a wealthy widow, I shall need to manage my money?"

He looked at her, his eyes dark and intense. "Not necessarily. There will be many men all too eager to assist you."

"Even take the task completely out of my hands, I shouldn't wonder."

He nodded, the truth obvious.

She looked again at the book, her reason coming to the fore. She needed to understand money. She did not want to abruptly discover herself penniless. Not again.

Without another word, Lynette slipped the book into her pocket. She would read it. She would read every word.

Adrian watched Lynette leave his library, and he breathed a sigh of relief so profound he felt it all the way to his toes. Now that she was gone, perhaps he could concentrate on his work.

But even though his little bird of a charge had disappeared, thoughts of her remained. She was undoubtedly the easiest student he had ever had, and yet he had the distinct feeling she would also be his most challenging.

Imagine, her demanding to know about Jenny! Good Lord, even Audra, bold as she was, had not so much poise. What would she be like when her tutelage began in earnest?

It was too early to start, he knew. She had not the clothing nor the manners for the campaign. But *she* was ready. In fact, Lynette the woman was more than ready. All he needed to do was control the direction of her thoughts, turn her mind step by step to her sensuous nature, and the men would flock to her in droves. What red-blooded man—rich or poor—could resist a woman just awakening to her sensuality? Himself included.

When she had spoken of her first kiss, her face had been alight with hunger, a yearning that had heated his blood as no other woman had done since Jenny. But he dared not rush her. There was too much at stake. He had to play her perfectly, stoke the embers of her passion until the time was ripe for her to burst free. Then, with his percentage of her marriage portion, he would at last be free himself.

Free!

The thought was a joyous one. So joyous, in fact, that it nearly overrode his lust for his little Lynette.

He glanced again at the small escritoire where she had worked. There was no imprint of her body upon the chair, no scratch on the desk made by her hand. There was not even a lingering scent that he could identify. Yet he sensed her there as surely as if she had remained to stare at him in that provocative way just before pestering him with questions.

Tomorrow, he decided abruptly. Tomorrow her education would begin in earnest.

Chapter 6

He lingered by the door, staring into her dark room, and listened intently to her slow, even breaths.

She was not asleep.

He wasn't sure how he knew. He had a sixth sense about his girls that he never questioned. Still, he was shocked to find that it had developed so quickly with this girl. After all, Lynette had been here barely more than a day.

"You still wear your nightrail." He spoke softly, his words floating across the darkness. But she heard him. Even in the gloom, he could see the white outline of her gown twitch.

He stepped into the room, scanning her garment, which he'd forbidden. It was a prim thing, with buttons, no doubt, up to her chin. Perfectly appropriate for a clergyman's daughter. Sacrilege in his household.

"I will allow it tonight," he said, his voice still soft.

"But tomorrow you will burn it or I will tear it off your body myself."

She didn't answer. Indeed, he had not expected her to. She was still pretending she slept. He waited, allowing her the illusion of safety, letting her believe she fooled him.

He took another step closer. In truth, he had not intended to. He had merely meant to see her, listen to her, feel her. He often stood in the doorway between his room and his client's, especially at the beginning. It allowed both the girl and himself to grow accustomed to one another. Perhaps this was how he aligned himself with each girl's particular rhythms.

But not with Lynette. With her, there was no need to attune himself. He already felt like one end of a tight wire, inextricably connected to the other one. To her.

"Do you feel it?" he whispered into the darkness. "Do you feel me here?"

She didn't answer, though he knew his words were echoing in her mind. Again, he meant to leave. He had already given her enough to think on tonight. Timing was everything in this business.

But he did not. In sudden decision, he sat down beside her. The bed shifted beneath his weight, and Lynette should have rolled into him. She did not. Instead, she feigned a gasp of surprise and rolled backward, avoiding his touch.

"My lord! You startled me."

He smiled into the darkness. Virgins were so predictable. He kept his voice harsh and cold. He had to establish the rules firmly at the beginning.

"Do not lie to me!" He reached out and pulled her roughly toward him. He was careful not to hurt her, but he had to impress his will upon her. Leaning down, he whispered harshly into her ear. "Never lie. Not to me. Never to me."

He felt her fear in the fine tremors that shook her arm, but he also felt her control. She was appropriately terrified, and yet she kept it deeply buried, as though she dared not allow anyone to know what she thought. What she felt.

Had she learned this from her father? he wondered. Not the restraint. By all accounts, her father—and the uncle, as well—were singularly obvious in their emotional expression, as though they had the right to not only show their opinions but force them on everyone else. She must have learned early how to hide her thoughts from them. A bright girl would never be allowed to flourish near such heavy-handed arrogance.

He would have to choose her bridegroom carefully. Unless nurtured or at least allowed expression, her unique spark would wither and die.

And as all these thoughts flitted through his mind, he waited silently for Lynette's confession. Thankfully, he did not have to wait long. Soon her head dipped in telltale acknowledgment. "My apologies. You are correct. I was awake." A plaintive note crept into her voice. "But how could you have known?"

He released her, though his body was reluctant to do so. He saw her rub at her arm, as if trying to brush away his touch. Years ago, that would have angered him. Now he knew how to turn that emotion into instruction, her fear into passion.

"I knew you were awake, Lynette, the same way you knew I was here. You felt it. You heard it."

She was silent, but in the deep shadows he thought she bit her lip in contemplation. He wanted to see more. He wanted to see what kind of imprint her teeth made in her bottom lip. One of her front teeth was chipped. Did that part of her tooth touch her rosy bottom lip? Did it make a jagged line? The urge to light a candle was almost overpowering.

He resisted. There was much to learn in the darkness.

"Close your eyes, Lynette."

He knew she hesitated. He waited silently, knowing that in the end she would accede to his demand. After all, she was the student. Still, he had to hold his hand directly in front of her eyes to block her sight before she complied. And the slight brush of her long lashes against his palm was the most erotic sensation he had ever felt.

"Listen to me."

The silence stretched out. He heard the near silent whisper of her breath, felt the heat of her body skating across his skin, and knew of the faint tremors that still gripped her insides. He knew it as surely as he heard the blood rushing through his own body, pooling in his groin.

"Do you hear it?"

She shifted uneasily. "You said nothing."

"Correct. But what do you hear?"

Once again he let the silence wrap around them.

"I hear people on the street. A drunk."

"Inside, Lynette. What do you hear in this room?"

"The curtain in the breeze as it rubs against the chair."

"Closer, Lynette."

Again she shifted uneasily, unable to still herself as he pushed her to face what she was too frightened to acknowledge.

"Nothing!" she suddenly cried out softly. "I cannot hear anything."

He pulled his hand away from her face, letting it drop into his lap. It was too soon. He knew it was. And yet he could not stop himself.

"Do you hear your heart beating?"

She waited a moment, then her voice drifted to him, whispered in agony.

"Yes."

"Hear your breath as it comes in and out of your body. The movement is rough, harsh. Your blood is pumping, your body tightening."

"Yes," she whispered, though agony throbbed through the sound.

"Your skin tingles. Your breasts are heavy and tight." And her core, her woman's core, would even now be thickening, tightening. Trembling.

"Yes." Her word was a soft gasp that heated his blood even more.

"That is desire, Lynette. Awareness. Feel it. Remember it. Want it."

She shook her head in one simple, almost violent movement. "No!"

"Keep your eyes closed!" he ordered.

She obeyed instantly, probably not even realizing she had opened them. But now she squeezed them firmly shut, just as her body pulled taut with nervous tension.

"Years from now you will need to remember this. You will want to recall every little detail. You will relive it time and time again in your memory. Do you feel the weight of my body on the bed?" He leaned close, not touching her but bracing himself on either side so she knew she was surrounded. By him. "Do you feel me?"

She made a soft mewl of distress, but he continued, leaning even closer, allowing his breath to skate across her brow. But he did not touch her.

She gasped at his nearness but didn't open her eyes.

"Do you feel my breath touch your face? My body's heat mix with yours? My scent in the air?"

She stopped shrinking away from him. Indeed, there was nowhere to go. And then she spoke, wonder and fear inextricably mixed in her voice. "Yes."

Lust slammed through him. Its force caught him unaware, gripping him, cutting off his breath. He had no defense. It happened too fast, in the space between heartbeats, making him insane with desire like a mad dog. He had meant to touch her tonight, accustom her at least in part to the most innocent of caresses.

He could not. If he so much as pressed one finger into her warm, yielding flesh, he would explode in his breeches like a schoolboy.

He could not. And yet she was right here . . .

"Lynette." His voice was tight. Controlled. He could not move even an inch. "Lynette. Open your eyes."

He was so close to her that the shadows no longer obscured her face. He saw her eyes open, watched as they widened in surprise at his nearness.

"My lord?"

Her formal address gave him enough control to ease backward, taking much of his weight off his arms, but not enough to remove the cage they made around her.

"Leave, Lynette. Go to my bedroom. Where there is a lock on the door."

He heard her gasp in horror, recoiling as if he were about to attack her. Of course, he thought dazedly, that is exactly what she thinks, and understandably so. She did not realize that he was trying to protect her.

"Alone, Lynette," he continued, his voice hoarse. "Go. Go now!"

The urgency in his words convinced her. Or perhaps it was his clenched jaw or the rigid way he held his body. Whatever the reason, he was grateful. Still, she had to wriggle out from beneath him, her breasts jiggling as she moved.

He closed his eyes, not wanting to see, but the action did nothing to relieve him. He could still hear her as she slid away. He could still imagine the innocent lift of her buttocks as she crawled out from the bed. And then her hair, her long silken strands of bronze, brushed his forearm, and he was nearly undone.

"Shut the door," he rasped. "Lock it!"

She at last gained her feet, then paused, tempting him in ways she could not even imagine. "My lord?"

"Go!"

She fled, forgetting to shut their connecting door in her haste. But then she came back and he heard it shudder into place, the lock slamming as the impact reverberated throughout the entire house.

She was gone.

With a muted groan, he collapsed, face first into her bedlinens. Lying there, he could smell her. The scent was as clear and clean as a summer's morning after a rain shower. He buried himself in it. And then he closed his eyes, needing no extra effort to envision her beneath him, all purity and innocence. Her breasts filled his hands, her body arched in glorious revelry.

He gripped the sheets, his breath coming in short bursts as in his mind he settled into her, driving deep within her, surrounding himself with her.

But he couldn't, he shouldn't think this way. She was a Marlock bride—her virginity by definition given to someone else. She was not his, and never would be. All he could ever have of her was her scent, her touch, and—of course—her money.

With a curse that echoed through the room, he ripped her sheets from the bed only to collapse back onto the mattress and bury his face in her pillow.

It took her hours to stop shaking.

Lynette still did not know what had happened. It was true, she had heard him come to bed. She knew he was standing in the darkness watching her. He was there. And she was in her bed. Tense. Anxious. Too afraid to move.

What did he want? Even now, she had no idea. Good Lord, he hadn't even touched her. Except for that moment when she had pretended to be asleep.

"Never lie. Not to me!"

She couldn't. She hadn't. But to herself? Perhaps. She had been lying there, pretending that he did not frighten her. That his mere presence did not fill her with thoughts and feelings clashing within.

Then he had spoken to her, not in a whisper but in low tones. It was hard to describe his voice, and her thoughts wandered around it, trying to put into words what she had felt more than heard. His voice was not deep, like her father's. There was no holy zeal behind his words, no push of air from huge lungs that could fill the rafters of a church.

And yet when he spoke she heard him as no other. The sound filled not the room but her soul, slipping inside until she seemed to thrum with the tenor of his voice, rising and falling with the cadence of his words.

"Do you feel me?"

She had felt him. She had felt every part of him, as if his hands had indeed been all over her body. He spoke of heat, and the touch of her bedclothes against her skin had been like a fire.

He had whispered about tingling and her hands had clenched the linen as the fine hairs on her brow, her face, her entire body had risen in awareness.

Then he had asked about her breasts. She had nearly cried out as suddenly her body changed. Her father had told her breasts were sinful, gifts from the devil to tempt man. She had not listened. Her breasts were functional, serviceable, set there to feed babies. They were no more sinful than her legs or her hands or even her nose.

But not now. Not in her bed, with him poised above her. With him, her breasts became hungry things, aching for something. Anything. Him.

He had not touched them, and yet she felt as if they had been changed, molded somehow.

She was in his bed now, surrounded by his massive pillows, his dark sheets, and his heady scent. It had taken her a moment to gain enough courage to mount the massive edifice. But then she had heard a noise and, fearful that he was following her, had sought the dubious safety of his bed.

Somewhat like jumping from the frying pan into the fire, she thought ruefully. But there was no help for it. She was here now. In his bed. Surrounded by his presence, even if he was not with her in actuality. And she thought about her breasts.

"Your skin seems to tingle, your breasts are heavy and tight."

She raised her hand, lifting it almost without thought. Then slowly she acted, her every movement fraught with tension. But the urge was undeniable.

The bedsheet was pulled up to her chin, pressed tight against her neck as if that would somehow protect her from her wayward thoughts. But it could not. It did not. And so she pushed the sheet down, drawing it slowly to her waist until she felt its weight upon her belly.

She touched her nightrail. The fabric was soft from long use, the white dimmed to a gentle gray.

"Tomorrow you will burn it or I will tear it off your body myself."

He could not truly have meant that, she told herself. But in her heart she knew he meant every word. Tomorrow night she would sleep naked.

She touched the tiny buttons at her neck. She turned them beneath her fingers, feeling their pebbly weight, the tiny tug as she pulled the fabric away from her skin. She would burn this gown tomorrow. She would not even save the buttons, for they were too old and too worn to be used again.

Then she felt a button press into her neck as she slipped it free. The first button of her nightrail was undone. It was warm in the viscount's room, the air close and thick. Brushing the skin of her neck, she felt perspiration make her fingers slick.

A second button slipped free.

Once, as a child, she had looked long and hard at a man's neck. She had noted the bump of his Adam's apple, seeing the bulge as firm, hard, commanding. She touched her own neck now, seeking that same bump and exploring its contours with her fingers. Hers was small by comparison. Compressed. Withdrawn.

Buttons number three and four fell away.

She could now feel the hard ridge of her collarbone. There was a dip in the center where left met right, a small *V*, and she wondered if a man's Adam's apple would fit right there.

Would *his* fit right *here?*

Button number five caught and held on a tiny thread, but with a little tug the barrier snapped. Her nightrail fell open to her waist.

Her brother had once told her there were twenty-four ribs in the human body. She had always wondered if it was true. Abruptly, she decided to count.

One. Two. Three.

She whispered the numbers into the darkness.

Four. Five.

It was hard to feel them now. The rise of her breast prevented clear definition of each rib. She pressed harder. Then softer. She wanted to know the difference in texture, in feel. There seemed to be no clear place to define where there was merely skin over rib and where her breast interfered. She slid her hand lower, and suddenly she was holding her breast.

Shocked by her action, she pulled her hand away, locking her arm straight and pressing it tightly, rigidly, against her leg.

It was some time before she relaxed. But it was hardly surprising when she finally did. In fact, she thought with a laugh, she was being ridiculous in the extreme. She rested alone, in a dark room, in a bed that would dwarf a giant. So she had accidentally touched her breast. It was of no importance. She was being a silly widgeon. And more than that, she still wished to know how many ribs were in the human body.

Slowly, she once again raised her hand. She used her left hand this time, counting the ribs on the right side. She had no logic for this change except that her left breast still seemed sensitive, almost tingly from her earlier exploration, and she did not want to irritate it further.

She began to count.

One. Two. Three.

All was the same on this side as it was on the other.

Four. Five.

Again she felt the shift from hard rib to the softer curve of her breast. She hesitated. Then, feeling foolish, she quickly skipped six. But she wanted to feel the length of seven, and so she stretched her left arm as far as it would go, outlining the bone with her fingertips.

Rib number seven wrapped around her chest, underneath her breast, and down to where she could not reach any more. She retraced her movement, following the curve of rib number seven back. But as she moved, her forearm brushed against her breast; pulled it, in fact, and she shifted and turned, seeing if it felt better to press her arm tight against it as she moved, or if she preferred the lighter, more gentle tugging of the fabric against her skin.

It took her some time before she could decide. And in the meantime, there was something else that caught her attention. Above the breast, she could not find a clear line where the mound began and where it did not; whereas below it, the line was quite obvious.

Rib eight was there. A hard ridge with no softening. But between seven and eight, her breast began. She could feel the weight of it on her hand, and if she pushed in from the side with her other hand, her breast stood out starkly, formed into a tight cone.

She tested this from all sides. She could mold her breast up. She could press it down. She could push it inward. And, she realized with surprise, if she pressed the other breast in as well, she created a deep furrow of cleavage between them.

Thump.

She suddenly stilled, freezing in place as she strained her ears to listen. Where had the sound come from? It wasn't from within the room, was it? Had it been him? In her room? In her bed? Was he coming back to his bedroom?

She waited, her breath coming in short gasps as she tried to silence the loud hammering of her heart.

Silence.

Silly girl, she scolded. He could not come in here. She had locked the connecting door as he instructed. He would not come here tonight. She knew it in her bones. Indeed, she would not have begun counting ribs if she had thought she might be interrupted. Still she waited, not daring to move, listening to her own harsh breath in the silent house.

She looked down at herself. At some point, in the last few seconds, she had whipped the bedsheet up to her neck again. Beneath the coarse fabric, her nightrail was still open, her breasts still sensitized to the scrape of the coarse material. In fact, she thought, as she took a deep breath, both breasts were now sensitive.

How odd that she could feel every fiber in the material, every slight hitch in the fabric. And yet every night before she had felt nothing.

Another deep breath. The fabric pulled against her naked breasts, setting them tingling.

The bed smelled like him, she thought. With every deep inhalation, she remembered him, felt surrounded by him. She closed her eyes, trying to identify the scent more closely.

Bay rum. Yes. But mostly him.

With her eyes closed, she could picture him stripping off his cravat, unbuttoning his shirt, and then slipping into bed. She knew how a bed felt when he sat upon it. She remembered the dip as his hands settled on either side of her head. His heat as he hovered above her.

What if he had touched her?

She had felt surrounded, imprisoned by him.

She squeezed her nipple.

Lightning shot through her. She gasped at the sudden tightening of her entire body. Legs, stomach, breasts, hands—everything clenched. The movement was violent, shocking.

She could not do this. She should not do this!

Hurriedly, she flipped over, burying her face in the pillows. Her nightrail pulled against her body as she pressed into the sheets. Her hands went rigidly to her sides, clenched and immobile. In her mind she heard her father, his voice hammering into her. *"Tie your bodice tight,"* he bellowed. *"Lace it flat, lest the devil find an opening into your soul."*

Clenching her eyes shut against her thoughts, she turned onto her side, curling herself into the smallest, tiniest ball she could manage.

Hours later, she slept.

Chapter 7

She woke late.

At first she had no idea where she was. Then she took a deep breath, smelled bay rum, and knew. She was in his bed. In his room. She stretched out of her cramped position, burrowing her toes deeply into his heavy covers, oddly reluctant to leave. She was tired and achy from sleeping in a tight ball all night, but his bed linens were soft and warm, and most of all, she liked the scent.

Bay rum, she decided, was delightful.

Then she heard a street vendor. Opening her eyes, she realized it was midmorning, and she had promised to meet the baroness by ten. For what, she had no idea. But whatever the purpose, she was already late.

Scrambling out of bed, she was appalled to discover her nightrail hung open nearly to her waist. Heat flooded her face as she recalled her actions last night. Clutching the garment's edges together, she buttoned it as fast as her fumbling fingers could go. Perhaps this afternoon she would have to burn the thing, but for now she very much needed to button it to the very top.

Except . . . her hands paused on the last button. She needed to get dressed quickly. She ought to be stripping out of her clothing as fast as possible. But what would she wear? Her few dresses were all in her bedroom.

She glanced to the side at his lordship's wardrobe. Unable to resist, she pulled open the doors to reveal neatly pressed attire: pantaloons, trousers, coats, shirts. All were orderly, but far fewer than she had expected. Indeed, she thought all the gentry had drawers of clothing stuffed to the point of bursting.

Her father certainly did. But his lordship had only the essentials. Obviously, the viscount was as accustomed to practicing economy as she was.

Then she heard another noise, this time from within the house. The kitchen, no doubt. Which meant Dunwort, and likely the baroness, were awake and waiting for her. She had to get dressed. Yet she could not wear his lordship's clothing!

Closing his wardrobe, she turned back to the door between his room and hers. Her clothing was in there. But then, so was he.

Dared she go in? With him asleep?

Or worse yet, with him awake?

She glanced down at her bare toes. She would have to go in there. She couldn't very well meet the baroness while still clad in her nightrail. And yet . . . she hesitated, the image of the viscount's face slipping into her thoughts. He had seemed so . . . what? Frightening? Yes. And no. Urgent, perhaps was a better word. Different?

She shook her head, willing herself to think clearly. She had to get her clothing.

Glaring angrily at the door, she made her decision. She would just have to do it. She would creep in as silently as a ghost, grab her clothing, then slip back here to change. She could do it. She had tiptoed about her own house dozens of times, careful not to wake up the younger children or, most especially, her father. This would be just the same.

She put her hand on the latch, undoing the lock, and slowly, quietly eased the door open. She knew the hinges were well-oiled. How else could he come into her room so silently? Perversely, the very thought emboldened her. If he could sneak in on her unawares, then she could creep past him equally unnoticed. Still, her nerves failed her when she saw him.

He lay sprawled, facedown, crosswise, on top of the stripped mattress. His bare feet pointed toward her, his head nearly obscured by the broad expanse of his back. He clutched her pillow beneath him, and his bed jacket lay in a crumpled heap by his feet.

He was totally, completely, gloriously naked.

Never had she seen a more chiseled form, and she had seen many, to her shame, when she had made a secret study of Greek art at the age of fourteen. Her father had not known, of course. But she had found a book in the lending library and, while her other siblings busied themselves with their lessons, she had perused the sketches from every angle.

The viscount more than compared. He put the ancient Greeks to shame.

His legs were muscular. Even in their lax state, his thighs remained thick and corded. What did he do to keep them so fit? she wondered. His buttocks were small, tight, and so perfectly shaped that she blushed to be staring, and yet she could not tear her gaze away. They looked like two hot, golden loaves of bread. Shaped wrongly for bread, but oh so delightfully perfect for him.

Of course, his glory did not end there. Allowing her gaze to slip upward, she noted his trim waist and the smooth perfection of his back. Here, too, she saw well-defined musculature. In fact, she realized with a start, though she would not be able to count his ribs just by looking, she could draw quite a detailed sketch of the muscles that laced a man's back. His shoulders were broad, and, higher up, his dark, curling hair lay rumpled and sleep-tossed.

She saw only one side of his face, and it lay, thank God, slack-jawed in sleep. Still, she saw his high cheekbones, the slight dusting of beard, and of course, his lips, full and sensuous even in sleep.

Though he displayed nothing she had not perused before in her book of sketches, she still was overwhelmed by the sheer magnitude of seeing a man in the flesh. The naked flesh. Of course she'd expected that a living, breathing man would be more interesting than a statue, or in her case, a sketch of a statue. Still, she was unprepared for the sheer masculinity of the viscount's body. His flesh was almost golden, with intriguing areas of paleness over the lower half. There were crevices and dimples, mounds and bulges all over.

What would it be like to touch him? She was already stepping forward to find out when she suddenly came back to herself.

Good Lord, what was she thinking? Pressing her hands to her heated face, she chided herself for her sinful behavior. And yet she still stood, staring at him. Wondering.

Then he moved.

Where before he lay flat across the bed, now he shifted slightly, bending one leg up as he tilted slightly on the pillow. In fact, his hips were now canted slightly, enough to give her the slightest view of . . .

Good God! She gasped and spun away back to his bedroom, only belatedly remembering her attire. Moving faster than she ever thought possible, she snatched her clothing, not even caring what it was, and ran from the room.

Her heart was pounding, her hands were sweating, and it wasn't until after she had shut the adjoining door and completely dressed that she dared allow herself to breathe. She forced herself to take deep breaths, drying the palms of her hands on her skirt.

Still the image persisted. Closing her eyes, she moaned into her hands. The sight remained as if seared upon her mind's eye: A shadowy pouch of flesh nestled between firm, masculine thighs.

Abruptly turning, she rushed from the room, seeking someone, anyone, who might turn her thoughts in a safer direction.

The baroness was waiting for her. The tea was poured and already cold. A biscuit lay uneaten, while another crumbled in the lady's fingers. Lynette rushed forward, already voicing her apology as she hurried into the room.

The baroness did not even look up. She waved

away Lynette's explanations with a weary expression. Indeed, thought Lynette as she peered closer, the older woman appeared grim.

"Baroness?"

Without looking up, the lady pushed another one of his lordship's notes at her. Lynette accepted it in as composed a manner as possible, praying that the woman did not notice the slight tremor of her hand as she opened the pristine white envelope.

Be silent and learn.

M

Lynette stared at the note, her thoughts at least temporarily diverted. She read it again, followed the curve of Marlock's letters, the bold slash of his hand, and still understood nothing. She looked up to see the baroness shaking her head.

"We are to buy your wardrobe today."

Lynette brightened. Shopping! Exactly what she needed to take her mind off . . . other things. But before she could express her enthusiasm, the baroness quashed it.

"Your clothing is under my complete control. You may make suggestions, voice your opinion, but rest assured, you have no say in this matter whatsoever."

Lynette looked at her, shocked to her toes. "I cannot choose my own clothing?" It was the one luxury she had been allowed all her life. So long as her dresses were appropriately modest, her father had allowed her complete control over her attire. In fact, she had chosen so well that her mother allowed her to buy all her siblings' clothing.

She adamantly refused to relinquish that one freedom. "I have an excellent eye for color," she offered, hoping gentle persuasion would change the baroness's mind.

The older woman did not respond, seemingly completely focused upon her biscuit.

"I know many excellent ways to make a single dress appear like a dozen. It's all in the choice of laces and other accessories."

Again, no response.

"Truly, Baroness, I can be counted upon to buy appropriate clothing."

At this, the woman looked up and cackled. "Appropriate for whom? A minister's daughter? You forget, you are one of *his* girls now. And clothing for them must be entirely *in*appropriate!"

Lynette bit her lip, silenced by an overwhelming sense of shame. She had seen scandalous dresses before. Low-cut bodices, wetted underskirts. Was she to wear those? What would her family think? What would her father say?

She looked down at her hands where they gripped her teacup. They were trembling, and so she carefully set down the delicate cup onto its saucer. But for some reason, she could not release it. Try as she might, her hands continued to rattle the cup against the saucer.

She was supposed to be married in her father's church. She would wear white and hold flowers. But now . . . now she was counting her ribs and staring at pouches. What was happening to her?

She had not realized she was holding her breath until she suddenly had to exhale. She did so in a gasp that sounded more like a strangled sob. There was nothing she could do about it. It was as if she stood beside herself, silently cataloging her breakdown.

And still the teacup rattled in her white-knuckled grip.

Lynette watched as if from a great distance as the baroness carefully disengaged the cup, gently prying her fingers away. Then, with a gentle smile, she wrapped her hands around Lynette's, stilling the tremors.

"You came here of your own accord," she said softly.

Lynette turned, her movement stiff, her gaze unfocused.

"You chose all of this. Your wardrobe. Your future. Even your . . . evening discussions with *him.*" She lifted her chin slightly, gesturing upstairs where the viscount still slept. "That is what you started the moment you wrote to me." She paused, waiting until Lynette focused on her face. "Do not turn coward now. You have nothing to go back to."

Lynette shook her head, struggling to remember what she had thought, what madness had prompted her to begin this charade in the first place. "I am a minister's daughter," she whispered. "I am supposed to be pure."

The baroness didn't answer at first. Instead, she appeared to be thinking, her mind turning inward as her expression hardened and her hands slipped away. "You are supposed to be your own woman, making your own choices. Even if it is this life, this way." Her eyes focused outward again, capturing Lynette's gaze. "Many women do not have as much. Ever."

Lynette shook her head, anxiety making the motion tight. "I do not think I can do this."

The baroness sighed, the sound coming from deep within. "You will have to learn. As have we all."

If she was feeling more confident, more herself, Lynette would have questioned the baroness, pushed for an explanation. Clearly there was something here, a tale to tell that might explain the dark happenings in this household. But she found herself taking the coward's way out. She simply did not want to know the answers, and so she turned her thoughts elsewhere.

"But the clothes," she began. "Surely if I am to pay for them, I should be able to choose."

"You will choose nothing," the baroness snapped. "Be ready to leave within the half hour." Then she stood and, without so much as a nod, quit the kitchen.

Lynette watched her go, wanting to call her back but unable to form the right words. As the door clicked shut behind the older woman, Lynette at last found her voice, speaking the words as if in a litany. "I will be able to sponsor Amy. And buy a commission for my brother." Her siblings' images floated before her mind's eye.

Then, overwhelmed, she lay her head down on the table and cried.

Lynette looked pale.

Adrian shifted in his seat, turning his attention away from his charge. He was sitting across the table from Lynette, his aunt, and the modiste. He was supposed to be examining fabric. Indeed, he was supposed to be discussing dress designs, depth of décolletage, even the length of the tiny puff sleeves on this gown or another. But all he could think of was that Lynette looked pale.

He should not be surprised. After last night's debacle, he'd half feared she would run screaming from his home. Thankfully, she was stronger than that. However, that did not negate how shockingly he had abused her the previous evening.

He did not know what happened. One moment he had been speaking with her, accustoming her to his presence. The next moment she had been like a fever in his blood. He had wanted her more desperately than his next breath.

Never before had he been so consumed by a woman. And never, ever, had he allowed such a breach with one of his girls. But Lynette was different.

God help him, she was so very different. Little Lynette was more of a woman than he had even guessed. She used her mind, reasoning things out. She challenged his thoughts, his edicts, the very nature of his instruction. She listened and learned and then surprised him with her understanding.

Lord, when he had realized she was inspecting his body this morning . . . He had pretended to be asleep, but not one cell in his body had been resting. It seemed as if his entire soul had been attuned to her curiosity. What was she looking at? Did she like what she saw? Would she touch him?

Then, once again, he had been unable to resist testing her. He had wanted to know how she would react to a fuller view. How much did she want to see male flesh?

He had shifted on the bed. She had not screamed, as had two of the others. Nor had she stepped forward boldly to learn more. Instead, she had surprised him by simply rushing to gather her clothes. Indeed, it was a slight blow to his vanity. One might almost believe she had been fleeing the sight of his ugliness, so quickly had she departed.

But he knew differently. Indeed, looking at her now, he knew that it was herself she feared. She, too, was supposed to be interested in her clothing, anxious to offer her opinion as to her upcoming attire. Instead he found her watching him, her brow furrowed, a slight blush adding a rosy glow to her features.

She was thinking about last night; he was aware. She was pondering this morning. And she was wondering at the changes in herself. What was happening to her? What was to come?

He looked down at the pattern book before them. His aunt and the modiste were in earnest conversation about the cut of the waist. But his mind returned to Lynette's waist, her belly, her body. Did she realize what was happening? Did she know what indignities were to come?

Of course not. And he could not warn her. Neither could he prevent it. By this evening, Lynette's sweet air of innocence would be torn, and he grieved that it would be at his instigation.

"This gown is lovely," Lynette suddenly said. Adrian looked up, seeing that she pointed to a ballgown of simple, elegant lines. "The classic style is the most versatile, don't you think?" she continued. "With only a moment to add a ruffle or bow, it can be most functional."

The baroness and the modiste turned to her, shocked surprise on their faces.

"You are quite correct," said the baroness graciously.

"You will go far, girl," added the modiste. "You know how to economize."

Then both the baroness and modiste turned to him. He barely glanced at the gown, already knowing it would be suitable. He looked at the modiste. "You know the fabric?" Even as he spoke, he caught sight of Lynette admiring a dove-gray silk. Of course she would be drawn to that dull fabric. It was simple, elegant in a drab way, and most appropriate for the spinster daughter of a cleric.

But it would never, ever do for Lynette.

The modiste understood. With barely more than a flicker of her eyes, she acknowledged his requirements. Adrian had brought all his girls here. She was well aware of what type of clothing he purchased.

That accomplished, he returned his attention to his charge. Lynette appeared more confident, as if her venture into the discussion had restored some of her equilibrium. Good. He did not wish to see her broken. Indeed, she would need all her strength to survive the rest of the day. He only wished he could be there with her, somehow help her through the process. But he knew he could not. He had tried it with the other girls and it had only made the situation worse.

He pushed to his feet, nodding politely to the ladies as he said his farewells. It was only when he turned to Lynette that his demeanor changed. He felt himself soften, and he fought to keep an expression of regret from his eyes.

"This morning's work was well done, Lynette. Only a little more and the worst shall be over."

He tried to speak warmly, bracingly, but she couldn't understand. Still, he bestowed a kiss on her hand as gently as a suitor's. Later she would damn him for his actions, but he needed to touch her, stroke her fair skin, while he silently apologized for the abuse she would soon suffer. If he was lucky, she would eventually comprehend his actions.

If he was unlucky . . . His thoughts trailed away. Some things were too unhappy to contemplate.

He sketched a bow to the three women. "Good afternoon, ladies. I believe I shall go in search of a drink."

Lynette watched the viscount disappear, a frown knitting her brow. Something was happening. There was some subtle message in his touch, some extra stroke that had meaning. But she did not understand. Indeed, she barely had time to recognize the extra touch before he disappeared out the door.

He'd said the worst was almost over. Undoubtedly he referred to the interminable fitting to come. Hours standing still while every part of her was measured and pressed and pinned. But she was well used to such nonsense. Indeed, when her younger sister had been learning her stitches, Lynette had endured countless such afternoons.

How like a man, she realized, to focus on the body's inconvenience and completely ignore the soul's. It was not the hours of tedium ahead that bothered her. Indeed, the real problem was the loss of her independence. The shift from her father's household to the viscount's had been a change, but not a significant one. A man still controlled her life. True, she had different duties, new things to learn . . . Her cheeks heated before she could push that thought away. But all in all, much of her life remained the same.

Until today. Suddenly even the most basic of choices—what she wore—had been stripped from her. Could anything be worse?

She brushed away a tear, resolving to take the indignity in stride. In fact, it had not been so terrible. They'd listened to her opinions, even complimented her choices. If they did, in fact, use the gray silk material, she would be joyous.

With that thought firmly planted in her mind, Lynette turned her attention to the fittings, allowing herself to become a human doll. The modiste and her assistants went to work, the woman quite thorough in her note-taking, measuring everything from the width of Lynette's wrist to the length of her breast. More than once, Lynette found herself blushing, but the modiste was quite efficient and the ordeal was soon over.

They finished quicker than Lynette expected, and she felt her mood lighten. Perhaps there were worse things than losing one's choice in attire. Of course, she thought as she smiled sweetly at the modiste, she had not lost total control, had she? She had been able to influence the baroness significantly, she was sure.

She watched happily as the baroness shook the lady's hand. And then Lynette turned to leave, only to realize that the baroness was not following her. Confused, she turned toward the older lady. "Is there more we need to accomplish?"

The baroness smiled, though the expression was not warm. "Of course there is, Lynette. A great deal more. Come this way."

She gestured to a back room. In fact, the modiste was holding open the door to a darkened interior, and everyone was looking at her. For an absurd moment, Lynette felt like Daniel bearding the lion's den, but then she shook off the thought. This was a fashionable shop in the center of London. There could not be lions in there.

Nodding to the baroness, she calmly entered the dark hallway, wondering at the sudden, taut silence between her two companions. They quickly followed, as if blocking her escape, and Lynette felt a real stirring of distress. Especially when she slowed her steps only to be pushed rudely ahead by the baroness.

"We have an appointment to keep," was all the woman said.

Abruptly, the passageway ended. The door that confronted Lynette was simple. Plain. Cold to the touch, but sturdily built and extremely heavy. In fact, it took a great deal of her strength to push it open. Beyond she found a stark room, empty of decoration and barely heated by a weak fire. In the center rested a large table. To one side were a plain screen and a hard chair.

On the other side: a man.

He was a nondescript gentleman. Though well dressed with a round face and an impersonal smile, he nevertheless seemed to disappear. Even for Lynette, who had spent a lifetime noticing peculiar aspects of her father's parishioners, this man faded away. In fact, it was difficult to acknowledge him as he stepped forward, bowing politely over first the baroness's hand and then her own.

"You are Lynette?" he asked, his voice somewhat high and nasal.

She nodded, her questioning glance hopping between the man and the baroness. It was only then that she realized the modiste had disappeared, shutting the door behind her.

"My name is Mr. Smythe," continued the man. "I am the surgeon who will be performing the inspection."

"Inspection? What inspection?" Lynette addressed her question to the baroness, who did not deign to answer. Instead, the woman settled down beside the fire with a sigh. It was the small Mr. Smythe who continued.

"I am to check for diseases, weaknesses, any type of scarring."

Lynette turned to stare at him. Abruptly, it dawned upon her that he meant to look at *her* for those things. She stiffened, outrage pouring from her. "I assure you, Mr. Smythe, I am in perfect health."

"Of course," continued the man, nodding. "Then this should go quickly. Please remove your clothing behind the screen."

Lynette turned to the baroness, who was in the middle of a huge yawn and was easing her feet toward the fire.

"Baroness, surely you understand that this is not necessary. I am in perfect health."

The lady shrugged. "Of course you are. But you certainly cannot expect your prospective bridegroom to take your word for it. It must be authenticated."

"Authenticated?" she stammered.

"Naturally. Mr. Smythe is well respected. He is quite discreet and cannot be bribed."

Lynette turned her shocked gaze to the man in question. He merely bowed in an unassuming way. "I will, of course, be authenticating your virginity as well."

"No!" Lynette took a sudden step back, her eyes widened in horror. The thought of this man seeing her body was unacceptable. The idea that he would touch her . . . *there* . . . was horrifying.

"I assure you," the doctor continued, "the procedure is quite painless and can be accomplished speedily if you cooperate."

"Of course she will cooperate," the baroness said.

Again he bowed, this time to her. "Of course." Then, with a welcoming expression, he gestured Lynette to the screen. "You may ask as many questions as you like. I am quite knowledgeable on the subject of virginity."

"Questions?" echoed Lynette weakly.

"Come, come," inserted the baroness, "we haven't all day. Remove your clothing." When Lynette did not move, the lady's eyes grew hard and cold. "You have no choice."

Lynette stared at her, blinking back the tears that blurred her vision. Gone was the delightful companion she had laughed with so freely yesterday. In her place sat the witch: the woman who had stared at her so coldly when they'd first met at St. James's.

Lynette hated it. And she hated the baroness. Yet the baroness was right. She had no choice. Once again, she could not run. Even if she could escape the hideous Mr. Smythe, where would she go? Her uncle would not take her in. Not now. Not unless she were wed. As for other options: she had no money, no means of employment, nothing.

Nothing except the memory of Adrian's words: *"If you run, I will find you. I will make you fulfill your commitments—to me and to your bridegroom."*

"Come, come," Mr. Smythe coaxed. "I will make this as pleasant as possible."

Pleasant? Lynette turned once more, staring at the little man. Pleasant? She nearly laughed out loud. Not because the word was so opposed to what she was about to experience, but because she had just answered her own question. *This* was worse than losing her choice in clothing. And yet for all the irony of the situation, for all the naïveté she felt slipping away by the second, there was absolutely nothing she could do. She had to comply.

Moving stiffly, she stepped behind the screen. She began to unbutton her dress, her hands shaking as she did. The tears that had threatened only a moment ago began to spill down her face. She bit her lip to keep from making any sound. She did not want anyone to know, much less look in on her in her misery.

She continued, slowly removing her clothing until the cold pricked her skin and she shivered. But she did not leave the sanctuary of the curtain. She could not.

Instead she waited, feeling misery engulf her while shame seemed to pour down on her head from Heaven itself. But then, something happened. Oddly enough, it came as an image, the very image that had haunted her this morning: the viscount sprawled naked across her bed. Apparently he slept that way all the time. And his various girls had been able to come in any time they chose.

To see him.

She remembered one of her father's parishioners—the man every woman whispered about behind her hand. Lynette wasn't supposed to have heard, but she had. And she had wondered about it. This man, they gossiped, this miller by trade, had so many women, he was like a desert sheik. He had dozens of bastards, they said. And he walked about his home stark naked without a shred of embarrassment.

Lynette hadn't believed them at the time. What person—man or woman—could walk about completely nude? It wasn't possible.

But having seen the viscount this morning, completely undressed, and unabashedly so, it must be possible. Of course, he had been asleep. But apparently that was his custom. Every night. As it was to become her custom.

And if he could sleep naked, allowing any one of his girls to walk in upon him, and if the miller could prance about his home completely unclothed before his hundreds of women, then she, at least, could stand naked before this surgeon. She could allow him to touch her, verifying what she and God already knew.

She was a good girl. A wholesome girl with no defects. One whom any gentleman would be proud to marry. And now, she thought as she lifted her chin, now she would prove it.

So thinking, she took a deep breath and stepped out into the room.

Chapter 8

Mr. Smythe was waiting just where she had left him—standing directly beside the high table. The baroness, however, was pacing before the fire, clearly agitated.

"Well, thank Heaven. I thought I would have to go back and drag you out." She took a deep breath. "I know you don't understand this, but believe me, it is necessary."

Lynette didn't answer. She was too busy standing stock still, her hands by her sides. She was naked, and she refused to lift her hands in any feeble attempt to cover herself.

Apparently, that pleased the baroness. She came closer, nodding as she inspected Lynette from every angle. "Very good," she murmured. "Even your negligees can be simple. You don't need padding anywhere."

Lynette frowned, not understanding the comment.

Then all thought of clothes fled as Mr. Smythe stepped forward, his gaze much more penetrating than the baroness's.

"Yes," he murmured. "There is much to recommend this girl. She is clean." He looked up, pinning his pale blue eyes on her. "I find that cleanliness is not only pleasing to the senses, it is also an effective deterrent to disease. You would do well to remember that."

He waited, still staring at her, until she nodded in acknowledgment.

"Excellent," he continued. "I see your hair color is natural. I had my doubts at first. Your particular shade of auburn is quite rare. And pleasing, I might add. Your bridegroom should be quite happy." He paused for a moment. "However, if you wish to add a few more red tones, I am sure the baroness can assist you."

"My very thought," chimed in the baroness from the side. "But for the moment the viscount considers her hair color quite adequate."

The doctor nodded his approval, and all the while Lynette stood there, her anger rising with each comment.

"My God," the doctor suddenly whispered. "Her color when angered is magnificent." He looked at her again. "You are an exceptional woman, my dear. Exceptional."

"Harumph," snorted the baroness.

Lynette lifted her chin. "If you are quite finished . . ." She let her voice trail away as she began to turn back toward the screen. But the doctor leaped in front of her. Indeed, she did not realize he could move so fast.

"Finished? No, no, no! On the contrary, I have not begun my medical examination."

Lynette stopped. Indeed, she had no choice unless she wished to literally bowl over the small man. And above all other things, she did not wish him to touch her.

"Please. Lie down." He gestured to the long table in the center of the room. When she did not at first comply, he reached out to take her hand.

She jerked it away.

He stiffened slightly, but then bowed, accepting her rebuff. "Lie on your back, if you would."

She did as she was bid, though she was shaking by the time she stretched out. And as she moved, the comments continued.

"Her walk is most lithe, though I believe she needs to gain some weight."

From her place by the fire, the baroness nodded. "Her upbringing was most severe. She is a clergyman's daughter."

That apparently surprised the man, for he jerked around. "Indeed? And yet she is one of the viscount's women?"

The baroness inclined her head. "Her choice."

"Indeed!" returned the surgeon, his amazement obviously growing.

It was that last comment that undermined Lynette's calm facade. "My choices are not your concern," she snapped. "If you have a task to perform, then do it. I grow chill."

The doctor spun around. "Magnificent," he breathed. "I must again compliment you and the viscount on your choice."

At that moment Lynette would have gotten off the table. She would have stood, donned her clothing, and walked out the door no matter what the cost. Whether or not she was forced to live on the street, whether she had to steal to survive or even sell herself in the most humiliating fashion, she did not care. She would not lie here and be discussed like a piece of meat.

But at that moment the man strapped her to the table.

She should have expected it. She had noted the restraints on the table but could not imagine that they would be used on her. But before she so much as lifted her head, she found her body crossed with a leather strap.

"What—" she began.

He cut her off. "Merely a precaution, I assure you. I find that virgins are skittish about the more intimate aspects of my inspection. I promise I shall not intentionally harm you."

"Remove this bond immediately!" She used her most authoritative voice, the one she used to discipline her younger siblings. The one her father used when trying to terrify the sin out of his parishioners.

It had no effect whatsoever, except to make it clear that she could not break the strap restraining her. In fact, as she struggled, more leather buckles were snapped about her ankles.

She turned her head, her eyes pleading with the baroness. "Please," she whispered, tears slipping into her hair. "Please, make him stop."

Then she saw it. She saw the baroness's expression change. Where before the woman had been coldly assessing, almost cruel in her indifference, now she softened. Her eyes took on a regretful cast as she stood and crossed to the table.

And, for the first time since entering the chamber, Lynette began to hope.

The baroness laid a gentle hand on her shoulder. The woman's voice was soft and soothing, but she made no move to remove the restraints. "It is necessary, Lynette. Please, try to relax. It will be over quickly. I promise."

Lynette had no interest in promises. In fact, she had no interest in anything but the straps that bound her tightly to the table and the tears that dripped unchecked from her eyes. But she did not cry out. She stayed stoically silent, even as the hateful doctor began to touch her.

He started by inspecting her hair.

"No lice. Excellent."

He brushed his hand across her face.

"No pockmarks, but I suppose you were already aware of that."

His hands traveled lower, pushing at her shoulders, squeezing her arms, poking at her breasts.

"A pleasing amount of padding. No obvious deformities. Fine, pert breasts."

He paused, shaping first her left breast, then the right.

Lynette gasped and tried not to scream.

"Doctor?" the baroness queried.

Again, he pushed and squeezed her two breasts. "They are of different sizes," he finally said. "That is common, of course, but her left is a tad more full than typical." He glanced down at Lynette. "You must be left-handed. The muscles beneath your left breast are more developed than the right." He pressed into her rib cage just to prove his point. "You would be well advised to develop the opposite side to even out the difference."

Then he paused and frowned slightly. "Unless, of course, the viscount wishes to promote the oddity. I daresay there will be many gentleman who view this as an intriguing anomaly."

The baroness nodded. "I shall make a note to discuss it with his lordship."

Apparently that satisfied the doctor, as he returned to his task. Without warning, he took out a leather crop and slapped it down on Lynette's belly. She cried out, startled by the sudden pain and furious at the betrayal. She had almost convinced herself that they had not lied to her, that this was a simple physical examination and no more. How wrong she had been!

She surged off the table, feeling the straps bind her, and yet she still fought.

To no avail.

All too soon she exhausted herself, and the surgeon was once again inspecting her belly.

"I apologize for that," he said. "But it was necessary to see your reaction." He looked up at the baroness. "She is unaccustomed to being struck in her more vulnerable areas." Then he sighed as he pointed to the mark on her skin. "And she will bruise easily. Even tear." He shook his head. "Most unfortunate." He looked down at Lynette with what he must have meant as a reassuring smile. "But do not concern yourself. There are many ways of toughening up the skin. In fact, I believe you already know this. From the condition of your arms, I warrant that you have been hit before."

Shame flooded her face. Her father had not often been violent, but there were times. It was one of the ways he enforced a godly path at home. Fortunately, the baroness spoke, effectively diverting the doctor's attention.

"She has not been damaged, has she?" Her voice was filled with alarm.

"No, no," returned the surgeon. "Merely some old bruises."

He pointed at marks she had forgotten, an old injury from her father's lost temper when a wealthy parishioner dared criticize his sermons. His temper had been very short that day, and his cough had already started. But she was not allowed to dwell on the past, for the doctor continued.

"She will, of course, need to learn about cosmetics, depending on the proclivities of her bridegroom."

The baroness nodded and, for a moment, Lynette experienced a wave of terror that had nothing to do with her current ordeal. Cosmetics? Proclivities? Though young and a clergyman's daughter, she had heard whispers of depraved men. More than that, she had sat with any number of female parishioners after they had been beaten or injured. Some men, it seemed, enjoyed giving their wives pain. Was she to suffer the same fate? Would her groom delight in the bruises, the beatings, the anguish of his wife?

"No!" She spoke forcefully, startling both herself and her companions. "I will not marry such a man."

The doctor looked up from where he stood hunched over her legs. "I assure you, there are ways to minimize—"

"Hush," interrupted the baroness. "The viscount will choose an appropriate bridegroom."

"I will not marry such a man!" Lynette repeated, as forcefully as she could.

"And your wishes will be taken into consideration," soothed the baroness. "However, he can only choose among those who wish to marry you."

Lynette ground her teeth as she once again tested her restraints. "I will not—"

"Then you had best attract a large group of eligible gentlemen," snapped the baroness. And with that the woman turned her attention back to the surgeon, effectively ending the conversation.

Dr. Smythe was busy at Lynette's feet, separating each toe, prodding the arches, and flexing her feet in a most unusual manner. "Her feet are excellent. Small, yet strong." He ran his nail down her sole, making her foot curl in reflex. "Delightful," he murmured.

Lynette looked down, appalled by the hungry tone in his voice. He was practically drooling.

"That will be enough of that!" snapped the baroness, and to Lynette's shock, the doctor colored, quickly straightening and moving to the side of the table. Then the woman glanced back at Lynette, her expression gentle. "Dr. Smythe enjoys a particular fondness for feet. But I assure you, I shall keep you safe from his attentions."

Lynette gaped. As if she cared about her feet! He could happily do whatever he wished to her toes, if only he would allow her to dress!

Her thoughts must have shown on her face, because the baroness shook her head. "Ah, Lynette, you are so innocent. Believe me when I tell you, there are depravities that you cannot even imagine. Some things, no matter how innocent, cannot be encouraged no matter what the cost." She took a step forward. "That is why I am here. You must learn to trust me." She sighed. "This could be a great deal worse."

Lynette might have agreed. For the most part during this ordeal, she had only been severely embarrassed. All in all, she was beginning to think she might survive.

Then the surgeon grabbed one of the straps holding her ankles. With a fierce tug, he pulled her leg wide. She fought, of course, but she was no match for both his strength and the straps that assisted him.

Within seconds, her legs were pulled apart, her knees affixed open, revealing her most private parts to the hideous man's cool regard.

And then he touched her.

She could not help herself. She screamed. She cursed.

He continued undeterred.

"No lice. Excellent."

And as his fingers began an invasion she had not thought possible, he continued to smile and nod as if this were the merest social call.

"Tight. Very tight."

"But is she a virgin?" That was the baroness, her voice high with anxiety.

"Yes. Most definitely. In fact, her husband must be selected with care. She will be injured if he enjoys force."

He pushed his fingers in farther, and Lynette bucked against the table. Indeed, she might have hurt herself if the straps hadn't bound her so tightly.

"Yes, most definitely a virgin."

The baroness released a sigh of relief. "Good. We had worried. Sometimes clergymen's daughters are vulnerable to the wrong sort. . . ."

Suddenly it was over. The doctor pulled away, wiping his hands on a towel. The baroness unhooked the straps, quickly and abruptly releasing Lynette.

"We are done," she said. "You may dress."

Lynette stared at her in shock. She pulled her knees together, then curled her arms close, her angry glare encompassing both her torturers.

"That is all? No apologies?"

The baroness lifted her eyebrows. "I told you, Lynette, this was necessary. And believe me, it could have been much worse."

Dr. Smythe stepped forward. "There will, of course, be a written report, submitted to the viscount, signed by myself. Your bridegroom will wish to inspect it before your wedding day."

Of course he would, Lynette thought sourly. She was a bride on the auction block. Whomever purchased her would want a thorough accounting.

"You are despicable," she spat. "Both of you." And with that, she stood, brushing away her tears as she strode to her clothing behind the screen.

Behind her, she heard the doctor sigh. "Such magnificent feet."

She was in her room; Adrian knew she would be, but still he went over Dunwort's account of their activities. The two women had come home early in the afternoon, and Lynette had gone directly to her room. His aunt had chosen to skip afternoon lessons, pleading a headache, and neither woman had appeared for dinner.

But now it was late, the night gripped in a thick cloud cover that shut out even the moon. Yet when he appeared at Lynette's door, Adrian found her sitting beside her window, her eyes on the blackened sky.

It was a delicate juncture. This night's discussion could very well make or break his little Lynette. He had tread too harshly with Audra, his first, and had lost her completely. Perversely, she was the one who had been most successful, marrying the greatest catch of all his girls, and would soon embark upon her glorious widowhood.

Whenever he faced one of these nights, he remembered that time with Audra. He had spoken too plainly, his words too harsh, and she had turned cold.

He did not want that for Lynette.

Taking a step into her bedroom, he decided on a strategy. He had to start with the obvious. "How do you feel?" he asked, striving to keep his voice casual.

She kept her gaze firmly fixed out the window, but he noticed that she hadn't jumped when he spoke. She had known he was there.

He stepped farther into the room. "Lynette?" He infused a note of command into his voice. He had to keep her speaking to him. It would be disastrous for them both if she closed down, shutting herself away from everyone and everything. "How do you feel?" he repeated.

"Angry. Very, very, very angry. Angry as I have not been since my father first beat me. Angry as I have not been since my mother stood by and did nothing." She turned, allowing her glittering eyes to focus on him. "Angry as I have not been since you first walked unannounced and unwanted into my room."

He absorbed her emotion quietly, patiently, giving no clue as to the pain her words gave him. That she should have suffered so twisted in his gut. But it was necessary. He took another step forward, finally settling down on her bed near her.

"That is understandable," he said softly. "You were used abominably."

She did not remove her gaze from his face. She stayed immobile, her soft brown eyes hard and accusing. "You can say that, even though you ordered it?"

"Yes." He took a deep breath. He had married off three girls before he realized how important his next words were. It took his fourth before he'd understood that honesty was absolutely crucial at this time. "It was necessary."

"To verify my virginity to my husband." Her tone was steeped in bitterness.

"It was necessary so that you understand you are being sold. In marriage. To the highest bidder. He is interested in your body, first and foremost. And in your mind only in that you can conceive of clever ways to amuse and satisfy him."

She was silent, as he knew she would be. No histrionics for his little Lynette. She was made of sterner stuff. She would absorb what he told her, understand it, and then use it as a weapon against all who dared harm her.

He quite admired that in her.

"I could have been a governess."

"No longer." Her association with him had firmly closed off that avenue.

She looked away, her gaze drifting back out the window. "No," she echoed softly. "No longer."

They sat together in silence. Neither moving. Neither speaking. Then she had another question. Without shifting her gaze, she spoke, and for a moment he wondered if he had imagined her words. But he knew he had not, for who could have imagined that she would ask so perceptive, so important a question?

"Did all your other girls go through this?"

He swallowed. "Yes. Though Dr. Smythe has been available only for the last four."

"And how did they react?"

"They all wanted to quit this house and never see it or me again." Sadness welled up in him at the memories, but if he could not allow her to hide from the truth, neither would he.

"But they were trapped here," she said, her voice dull.

He shook his head, vehement in his denial. "No. They could have all left, as you can. And I will lie about your experiences here if that will help protect your reputation."

She turned to look at him more closely, and he could see he had startled her.

"Did you think I chained them here? Locked them in? Fed them bread and water until they succumbed?"

"You told me you would chase me. Force me to keep my commitments to you and my bridegroom."

He nodded. "I have to keep the girls here through the beginning. That usually means threats, but it is a lie. My outlay so far has been minimal." He took a deep breath. In truth, he had already committed a great deal of his funds to this enterprise; it would be a heavy setback if Lynette changed her mind. "Try to understand. Most of my girls come here unwillingly, brought by a parent or guardian. But I never keep them, never even begin unless I think it a good choice. A choice they can understand."

"That they are selling themselves?"

He nodded. "Because in the end they will have their freedom. A wealthy widowhood is worth a great deal of present unhappiness." He leaned forward. "What are your other options, Lynette? You said yourself you would not find joy in your old life."

"I cannot go back now. I have been too compromised."

He nodded. That was likely true. "But there are other options. A convent. General labor. Do you want that kind of life?"

She shook her head. No, she was not suited to be a laborer, even if the lower classes accepted her. As for a convent, she had discarded that thought long ago. Probably because she had too much fire in her to make a cloistered life appealing.

"So they all stayed?" she pressed. "Even after the surgeon?"

"They all chose to stay. I would not have kept them otherwise." He sighed, his shoulders slumping in defeat. "I know you will not believe me, Lynette, but I have never, ever kept a girl against her will. Not beyond the first few days. All of them chose this path. And I do everything I can to make it a smart one."

She was watching him, silently evaluating his words, and he squirmed beneath her regard.

"The surgeon is deliberately cold," he said. "Impersonal. Because nothing in this marriage business is personal. It is important that you understand that from the beginning. Otherwise, you will never be content in your marriage."

She released a most inelegant snort. "Can you imagine anything more personal than having a man's hands—having anyone's hands—in the places where he put them today?"

He looked away. No, he could not. But she would have to come to accept that much and more from her husband. And for many years to come.

"Lynette . . ." he began.

"Tell me about the other girls." Her voice was flat. Implacable. And he chose to allow it because, more than anything else, she needed to re-establish her sense of control over her life. "Tell me about their reactions."

"Audra cursed and threw things, but when her temper cooled we talked. Eventually she agreed to stay. She was illegitimate, you understand. She had spent her childhood being shunted aside, hidden away. She wanted a life of wealth no matter the cost."

He took a deep breath, searching Lynette's face for a reaction, an emotion. Anything that would give him a clue as to how to proceed. But she gave nothing away, and in the end he continued, "Suzanne cried. For two days and three nights. She was from a poor family—very, very poor. But she had an ethereal beauty that stole one's breath away, and her parents wanted to make the most of that." He glanced away, remembering the hurt reflected in Suzanne's crystal-blue eyes. "Her inspection was performed by a woman, a midwife who has since left London. But even with a woman, Suzanne felt hideously betrayed." He sighed. "She understood, I think, better than any of us what was happening. She was mourning the loss of her dreams. Then, two days later, she said she was ready. Just like that. And she was." He glanced back at Lynette. "Her husband is bedridden now. He probably will not last another winter."

He leaned forward, trying to impress upon Lynette his point. "This is the game we are playing. You are selling your body to an old man. In return, you will receive a wealthy old age. You'll be rich enough to sponsor your sister. To buy your brother's commission. You'll be rich enough to travel, to take lovers, to do whatever you wish."

Only by the merest fraction of an inch did she nod. Finally she whispered, "The other girls . . . they understood this? Agreed with it?"

"Each had her own particular combination of tears and anger, but eventually she began to see that it was her choice. Not her only choice, you understand, merely the best of a bad lot." He paused, seeing her study him even as he watched her. "You are the only one who has asked me such questions, though. Only you have admitted to your feelings and then gone about dispassionately assessing your situation." Again he paused, trying by his sight alone to comprehend her thoughts. "I knew you were smart from the beginning. But this . . ." He gestured weakly in her direction. "This is unusual."

"I learned early that emotions did not work with my father. Neither tears nor histrionics nor any type of pleading would ever change his mind. Only logic had the barest chance."

He nodded in understanding. But then he pressed further. Her father was such a significant figure in her life; he needed to know more. "Your father did not change his mind often, did he?"

"Do you? Does any man?"

He paused, then eventually sighed. "No," he admitted. "Or rather, none that you are likely to encounter. And certainly none who will marry you."

She looked away, and for a moment he was glad

she did. He could not bear the flash of pain that flared in her eyes.

"The man who will be . . . selected for me . . ." She paused, as if searching for words.

"Yes?" he prompted. Then, when she looked uncertain, he sought to reassure her. "Remember, I promised to answer any of your questions honestly."

She nodded. "The man whom I am to marry. He will likely have very specific desires of his wife. Perhaps even peculiar tastes?"

Adrian hesitated. She had gathered a great deal from her one experience. But he worried about telling her too much too soon. It was not an easy thing for anyone to stomach, much less a parson's daughter having just experienced the most humiliating event of her young life.

"You promised," she whispered. "I want to know the truth."

Taking a deep breath, he finally gave in. "Yes. Your bridegroom will likely know exactly what he wants, and occasionally those tastes are rather particular. But rest assured, I will make the best choice for you. I will weigh the assets of your suitors most specifically—"

"No."

He frowned. "I beg your pardon?"

"You will not decide this for me. I will decide."

He pulled back. Of all things, this he could not give her. But she was relentless.

She surged to her feet, towering over him as he sat on her soft bed. "I will do this," she repeated, her voice ringing with certainty. "I will sell myself for a title and for the money it will bring. So my mother can have her own home, away from men. So my sister will not have to suffer this same fate." She blinked back her tears. "And so my brother can buy his commission." To her credit, her voice did not even waver, but still she had to stop, taking a breath before she continued in a softer voice. "I chose this. I contacted you. So I will be the one to choose between my suitors."

He sighed. He should have known this was coming. He should have seen that she would insist upon it now. In truth, all his other girls had asked for it. But he had easily swayed them. Their resolve had crumpled under his steady regard, and eventually he had been the one to decide.

He did not think it would be so easy with Lynette.

"There is a great deal to consider," he began slowly. "The marriage offer alone will likely contain a hundred or more difficult discussion points."

"I believe I have shown my arithmetic to be adequate to the task."

He shifted uneasily on the bed, but he did not stand. He did not want to take away her feeling of command. "Accounting and negotiating are two entirely different things," he responded.

"True." She paced away from him. "And you will perform all negotiations. But in the end I will choose my husband." She spun back toward him. "If we cannot agree on this, then I shall leave today. Now. No matter what the cost."

He looked at her. She meant what she said. He could see it in the firm jut of her chin, her stiffly erect spine, and most especially in the directness of her gaze. Still, he tried to make her understand. The situation was too complicated.

"You must allow me to eliminate unsuitable gentlemen," he stressed.

If he thought to distract her with that, he was sadly mistaken. She shook her head. "I will choose."

This time he straightened, coming off the bed to eye her from his superior height. "The choices are too great, the histories of each man too detailed." He paused, making sure she understood his next statement. "And many have secrets . . . preferences . . . which I will not tell you." She had to understand that he was unshakable on this point. She had to trust him if he told her someone was unsuitable.

"You must rely on me," he urged. "I swear I will discuss it with you. But there are things I cannot reveal to you, things I have sworn to them—the prospective grooms—not to tell." He paused. "All my girls have been happy with my choices." It was a cheap card to play, and he regretted using it. He did not like bringing his other charges into discussions with Lynette. Among all of them, she was unique. What they enjoyed, how they reacted, meant less than nothing to her situation. But apparently it worked, because she hesitated and he was able to press the point.

"That is why you came to me," he coaxed softly. "Because I know things you do not." Unable to resist, he reached out, stroking her arm. "Trust me."

When she did not react, he let his hand slip away. He would have paced then, moving to ease some of the anxiety that knotted in his gut. But he did not. She looked at him, staring into his eyes with an unnaturally calm, almost cold regard. He had the oddest feeling he was being weighed, his honesty and abilities measured as surely as Lynette had been measured, inspected, and categorized this afternoon.

It took a long while for her to decide. But then, finally, she inclined her head as regally as a queen.

"You may narrow the list to five."

He breathed a sigh of relief, shocked to realize how anxious he had been for her answer. "Then we are agreed," he said, smiling as he took a step toward the door.

She stopped him, reaching out and holding on to his arm. He could have broken free, of course, but he wished to work with her, not against her. He paused, turning back to look her in the eye.

"I will choose from those five?" she pressed. "I will make the final decision?"

He quickly evaluated his options. In truth, he was likely to narrow the field to two, at most three. There were always at least two who were acceptable from his perspective, but never from his charge's. He could probably manage five and still be assured she would make an excellent alliance.

Still, he did not wish to totally concede. He was the instructor, and he needed to keep her under his control. "Three suitors. And then you will choose."

She looked away. He had her caught, and she knew it. He did not have to negotiate with her at all. Indeed, he had never allowed any of his charges this kind of latitude. And yet, strangely, he was not worried. Lynette would make an excellent choice.

"There are things about some men you cannot know. Indeed, you would not want to know. Truly, Lynette, your happiness is foremost in my mind."

She shook her head. "No, your fortune is foremost."

He opened his mouth to argue but held back the words. She was correct, and yet she was also wrong. True, his future depended upon her wealthy marriage. But he would never, ever marry her to a monster—even if it cost him everything he had, everything he'd built from the day he began this unholy business.

He saw her swallow, saw her weigh her choices and make her decision. It was written in her shuddered breath, the firm jut of her chin, and the final squaring of her shoulders.

"Very well. Three choices." Her voice was soft, but no less determined. And he knew she would abide by this bargain.

He smiled, impressed beyond words. Then, to seal their deal, he offered her his hand. "Upon my honor, Lynette, I swear I shall give you as good a choice as possible. I cannot promise any more than that."

She hesitated, staring first at his outstretched hand, then back to his face. "Upon your honor," she echoed. "How worthy is that?"

It was a fair question and, once again, a shrewd one. Still, he bristled. When he answered, his voice was cold. "My honor is the only thing that keeps this particular trade alive. If any one of my brides had not turned out exactly as promised, do you believe I could marry off another? My honor is without question!"

She looked at him, and for a moment humor lit her eyes. "Without question? Oh, I doubt that, my lord. I most sincerely do." Then, before he could react, she grasped his hand. "But I will accept your honor as you have offered it. And I thank you for it."

He shook her hand, all the while staring at the peculiar woman before him. Not a one of his girls had ever acted as she had. And as he turned to leave the room, he wondered if he had handled the situation well. Or if, more precisely, he had been handled by her.

He should be upset by the thought. He should be angry at the possible loss of control over his charge.

Oddly enough, he was not. Instead, he felt invigorated. If nothing else had happened here, Lynette had at last demonstrated her readiness to begin.

In fact, he thought with sudden glee, now he could launch her in earnest.

Chapter 9

She slept naked that night.

Indeed, after her ordeal it seemed fitting somehow that all vestiges of her old life be burned away. She needed no prompting to toss her nightrail into the fire. In fact, she did so immediately after the viscount left her chamber.

The old Lynette was gone. The new Lynette had committed herself to this bizarre course of action.

As the last vestiges of her white gown burst into flames, she vowed that she would become a fire as hot as the one that took her clothing. She would draw men as if they were moths. They would want her. They would desire her. Then one of them would pay dearly to possess her.

And in the end, that man would die, leaving her free.

Free.

The word whispered through her mind, more seductive than any promise the viscount could make.

Free to help her family however she saw fit.

Free of her husband.

Free of the viscount and his hateful plans and cold logic.

Free to do whatever she wanted. Become a teacher or, more shocking still, a doctor. One who did not humiliate patients. One who made health and happiness a priority. One who didn't make them wish to scrub their skin raw trying to erase their memory.

But for now she had to sleep. Curling into herself, she tucked the covers up to her chin and slept.

Until she dreamed.

It was an ugly dream, filled with cold hands, hideous fingers, and the flat, implacable voice of her jailer, the viscount.

"It was necessary," he said. And he repeated it over and over and over until she screamed her hatred aloud.

He was beside her in a minute—in her bedroom, she realized, not in her dream. She could not stop herself from hissing at him to stay away.

He did not listen. He leaned forward, touching her forehead with his fingers. It was a soothing stroke, and yet it infuriated her. She lashed out, hitting him with everything in her. Her strikes were hard, brutal, punishing. And yet they seemed completely ineffective. He blocked her firmly, completely, and gently. Waited until she exhausted herself. Until the anger drained away.

But the fear remained. She did not know when the change occurred. Indeed, she was not a thinking soul at that moment. All she knew was that the anger was gone, leaving behind a mind-numbing terror.

"Do not run!" he commanded, his voice harsh.

She had not even realized she was tensed to flee. His dark command froze her in place as firmly as iron bands. And so she remained still, her body anxious and bitter, her mind seething with a nameless dread.

What would come next? What indignity would shrivel her soul now? Where would she be touched next? She cringed. And then, slowly, she felt something.

A hand.

She whimpered. She heard the sound quite clearly, but only a small part of her realized it came from herself. It was too animalistic. It was too pitiful.

The touch continued. Stroking her brow. Gently. As if she were a child.

"You are safe, Lynette. No one will hurt you."

She heard the sounds but could not understand their meaning.

"It was a nightmare. It is over now. Shhhh."

Then, once, she felt the viscount's thumb reach down and stroke her cheek, wiping away the tears she did not know wet her face.

"It was only a dream."

She buried her face in her pillow, shuddering as a dam seemed to give way within her. Her tears tore at her and her body contorted with each shuddering cry.

"It was only a dream."

"No," she said between gasps. "No, it was real. It was all real."

He didn't answer her. He merely tucked her in

close, holding her as she cried, stroking her hair since he could not reach her face.

"You are safe now, Lynette."

Now she understood his words, but they only made her sob harder. He did everything he could to soothe the hurt. But she knew everything he said was a lie. It wasn't just a dream. It wasn't over. And she certainly wasn't safe. Not now. Probably not for a very long time.

"Don't cry. I am here."

Those, she knew, weren't lies. Those words were the truth.

"You are safe."

She was curled tightly around her pillow, but her back leaned against him. His heat enfolded her, warming her chilled body, heating her aching soul. Perhaps, she thought fuzzily, some words were true. With him, at least, she felt safe.

"Stay," she whispered.

"Of course."

He lay with her all night.

Then, as the first weak rays of dawn filtered through her curtains, she finally stopped crying.

Together they slept.

She awoke alone.

Glancing about the empty room, she realized with horror that it was well past noon. Listening intently, she knew that the viscount had long since left the house. The place felt much too silent, eerily so, for him to be there.

In fact, she thought as she sat up in bed, the whole past twenty-four hours had been eerie. So much so that she wondered which part of it had been real and which a dream. Without a doubt, yesterday's experience had been very real. As was her bargain with the viscount.

As for her nightmare . . . She hesitated. Abruptly, she leaned down into her pillow. Though there was no telltale indentation of his head, she inhaled the scent of bay rum. He had been with her last night. He had held her tenderly as she cried.

He could have merely been protecting his business venture. After all, he had already invested quite a bit of time and money in her. He would lose it all if she did not get a husband. But her heart chose to ignore that possibility. For now, she simply believed that he could be gentle.

Sliding out of bed, she dressed quickly and made her way downstairs. Given the time, she did not expect to meet the baroness here, but she hoped she might find a clue as to her day's instructions. Or rather, her afternoon's plan.

Pushing into the kitchen, she nearly collided with Dunwort, his startled gaze quickly shifting into a wide grin. "Ah, ye be awake. Have a good cry, did we? And do we feel much better now?"

She blinked, taken aback by his frank statement. "Do you know everything that happens in this house?" she asked suddenly.

He chortled. "Not everything. But most." Then he turned around, pulling out a kitchen chair for her. "The baroness is occupied in her afternoon tipplage, so's you've got some time to eat. What shall I make ye?"

Lynette turned, frowning as she deciphered his words. "She is drinking?"

"Aye," he agreed as he pulled out a frying pan. "Always does after the girls see the surgeon. Almost as hard on her as it is on them. Now," he said with a grin, "how about some nice eggs to start off with, hmm? That's wot me mum used to always say. A good egg in the morning can erase a bad night." He leaned in close and winked. "Even if the morning really is the afternoon."

Lynette nodded absently. "An egg would be lovely," she said, but her thoughts were on the baroness. Yesterday, the woman had been cold and cruel. She had returned to being the Witch. Could it be the baroness used that facade to distance herself from the experience? That perhaps she thought a cold tone would shorten the ordeal, and that all the sympathy in the world would merely prolong the agony?

Possible, Lynette admitted begrudgingly. But still, she could not forgive the woman. Not yet. Not until she had put the event more firmly behind her. And to that end, she addressed herself to Dunwort and the two eggs he slipped in front of her.

"Dunwort," she began, her manner coaxing, "how did the other girls . . ." She shifted uncomfortably. "How did they attract their husbands?"

"Wot?" He was busy cleaning the pan, his face carefully averted.

She stood, coming up behind him and dropping her hand onto his arm. "I need to know, Dunwort. Please."

He stilled at her touch, turning slightly to look at her. His eyes were worried, but she returned his gaze steadily, firmly. He would answer eventually; she just had to show him how important it was for her to know.

"That be his task, miss. It's not fer me to explain." Then he shook off her hand, turning back to the pan.

"Now eat yer food. There ain't enough of it to be wasting."

But Lynette did not move. Instead, she shifted, leaning against the wall so she could watch the butler's face. "Were they very beautiful?"

He paused in his washing, looking at her with clear eyes. She didn't flinch from his gaze, allowing him to see the uncertainty in her face. The fear. She had set herself the task of attracting as many suitors as possible, and yet she had no idea how to go about it.

"Aye, they were."

Lynette sighed, already feeling defeat press down upon her.

"But you are ten times as lovely."

Lynette shook her head, returning to her breakfast with a somber mien. Spanish coin would not help her in her goal. "Thank you, Dunwort," she said softly.

This time it was he who pursued her, settling down in the chair opposite. "You do not believe me."

Lynette shrugged. "I am not a fool, Dunwort. I know what is beautiful and what is not. My face and figure are pleasing, but . . ." She paused, searching for the right words. "But they are not that remarkable."

"It be true, yer face ain't remarkable. Though," he added with a grin, "I cain't see nothing wrong with yer figure. In fact," he mulled softly, "ye remind me of the baroness when she was yer age. The hair and body's the same. Even the fire in yer eye. Bit odd, but ye two could be cousins."

She blinked, thrown by his comment. She hadn't thought herself in any way the same as the baroness, but perhaps, when the woman had been younger, before she began drinking—perhaps there were similarities. Certainly in coloring and general body shape. The thought was so strange that she scooped up a bite of egg just to buy time to think about it. Meanwhile, Dunwort continued, his voice firm and specific.

"But it ain't the body nor the face wot catches a man. Never was, never will be." He paused, waiting no doubt for dramatic effect. It worked. She held her breath, her food forgotten as he leaned forward. "Wot catches a man, sure as a fish in a net, is love."

Lynette's chest constricted, cutting off her breath. She was startled by the suddenness of her reaction, the complete and total pain of his statement. Blinking away her tears, she whispered, "But I am not to marry for love."

Dunwort reached out, gently touching her fingers, and she focused on that, his large hand covering hers with warmth. "Not love of the man, though if you can manage that, you'll 'ave him for sure."

She looked up, her vision watery with unshed tears. "Then what?"

"The love of wot yer doing, girl. Of who you are. Inside, yer ten times the woman any of 'is other girls ever was. Yer kind an' gentle. Ye listen to us old folks instead o' thinking ye've got the answers."

"My father's parishioners taught me that, and much more. But Dunwort, I have been listening all my life, and not a man has ever appeared asking for my hand. Or asking for anything, for that matter."

"Aye," he said with a grin. "And that is wot 'e'll teach you." The butler leaned forward. "Six girls he's married off. All rich women, now. Do you know why 'e's so successful?"

Lynette shook her head, completely enthralled. "Why?"

" 'E loves wot he's doing."

She blinked. "Loves selling girls into marriage?"

Dunwort shook his head, frowning. "If that's wot ye believe, then ye're not as smart as I thought."

She set down her fork, looking directly at him. "But that is exactly what is to happen. He has told me so himself."

"Aye. But would ye not 'ave been sold anyway? If ye had stayed with yer family, would you 'ave been able to pick yer man? For love?"

Slowly the truth dawned on her. "No," she said softly. "No. My uncle would have chosen for me."

"Then you would 'ave been sold nonetheless. As would all 'is lordship's girls. That's the way with women."

How could she deny it, when she had seen the truth of it all her life? Out of all her father's parishioners, she could count the happy women on one hand. True, those who had been forced into marriage numbered at least half. But of those who had married for love, many found their choices as evil as the rest. And once married, there was nothing a girl could do to protect herself. No matter the joy that began the union, all too soon the woman became no more than an indentured servant, serving her husband's needs and caring for his children.

"Wot his lordship does is give 'is girls a way out. 'E teaches them how to marry rich. An' wot to do with their blunt once the bugger's died off. That's freedom—when ye's got money and knows wot to do with it. That's wot he loves doing. An' ye should, too."

She shook her head, wishing she understood what was to happen. What was he to teach her? What was she to do? Struggling for clarity, she repeated his words. "I am to love what the viscount does?"

"Naw," Dunwort drawled, his expression frustrated. "Yer t' love what ye learn. The lord God above didn't mean for it to be wrapped in duty or meant for England. I seen more girls suffer in their choices because they didn't know how to enjoy it."

"Enjoy what?"

He reached forward and patted her hand. "Ye'll learn. Just remember wot I said. Enjoy it. Love it, even. An' ye'll be fine." Then he pushed up from his chair.

"Dunwort, don't go!" She reached out, but the butler had moved too far away. "I don't understand."

"Ye will, missy. Ye will." He smiled and pulled at his forelock. "An' now I 'ave chores t' get to. An' ye 'ave yer lessons with the baroness."

Which she did. And Lynette had no choice but to attend. Indeed, the baroness demanded nothing less. Unfortunately, they were tedious in the extreme. Deportment. Dancing. French. All those things she'd once thought frivolous were now the focal point in her life. Only the viscount's book on investment held her interest. And so she read it when she should not have, even getting another book—this one a child's text explaining government—from the viscount's library.

Unfortunately, the baroness did not grill her on the structure of the English government. Instead, she scrutinized Lynette's behavior, her words, even the way she stood or sat or the expression on her face.

"Your opinions are written all over you. Can you

not understand that a woman must hide her thoughts? Men do not wish to be thought idiots."

"Then they should not act as idiots." They were in the drawing room, practicing inane banter, and a more ridiculous pastime she could not possibly imagine.

"Really, Lynette, you are a minister's daughter. Have you not had to sit and listen to stupidities all the day long?"

Lynette sighed. "Of course I have."

"Then why cannot you master it here?"

Lynette threw up her hands in disgust. She was being contrary and she knew it. But she could not stop herself. "I do not understand what this has to do with the getting of a husband. I have no intention of marrying a halfwit. Why should I learn how to converse with one?"

"Good God, Lynette, surely you know by now that one's intentions and reality are vastly different things."

"Of course I do," she answered just as impatiently. "But surely I have some choice in the matter." In fact, the viscount had promised her just that. "You cannot say this banter is how you caught the baron, can you?"

"I?" the woman gasped. "No, girl, I chose for the most ridiculous of all reasons. I chose for *love.*" She spat out the word as if it were bad meat.

Lynette stilled, surprised as much by the baroness's words as by her bitter tone.

"I was a silly girl who fancied herself in love. We married, I might add, with my family's blessing, which goes to show what idiots we all were." She sighed and leaned back against the cushions of her chair. "Lynette, the union was a disaster."

"But why? Did he not love you?"

"Goodness, girl, what passes in a woman for love and what a man feels are entirely different things. A man's love is a thing of the loins. Once that is satisfied, a man's love focuses on position and power in society. That is what I am trying to teach you. How to be a gracious lady. How to maintain your husband's position in society."

Lynette tried to understand, but the questions kept coming. "But if you knew these things, if you did these things for your husband, why was your marriage a disaster?"

The baroness didn't answer at first. Instead, she took her time setting aside her embroidery, standing and crossing to the bottles of spirits she always kept nearby. "In my case," she said stiffly, "my husband had additional requirements in a wife. Now," she said firmly, as she poured herself a glass of sherry, "please say the following phrase in French: Oh, my, sir—you are witty in the extreme!"

So went the rest of her day. They did not stop at dinner. Indeed, if anything, the baroness increased her criticism during mealtime. It made for an inedible dinner and a pounding headache. Added to that were body aches from constantly sitting erect, and Lynette had never been more grateful to see her bed.

It might have been easier if the viscount had been home. Though his opinion on how she might catch a husband could very well add more confusion, she still valued his words more than the others'. She couldn't say why, but what he thought seemed vastly more important.

Perhaps it was because he had successfully launched

six girls before her. Or it could pertain to his gender and position in the aristocracy.

Unfortunately, he had been distinctly absent throughout the day. It was very late when she at last heard him come home. She was exhausted from head to toe, and yet she remained awake, relieved to hear his measured steps upon the stairs, and then counting the seconds until he entered her bedchamber.

She did not have to wait long. A bare ten seconds passed before he opened her door, standing stock still, as if listening to her sleep.

But she was not asleep, so she shifted, turning to look at him. "My lord?"

"Are you feeling better, Lynette?"

She answered without hesitation. "Yes."

"Do you think you will be able to sleep without nightmares tonight?"

She took longer to answer, but when she spoke she was sure. "I should be fine tonight."

"Good," he said on a sigh. "Then rest now. You will begin the Season as soon as your clothing arrives. Take your sleep now while you can."

She blinked, needing a moment to absorb his words. Then, suddenly she was sitting upright in bed, barely remembering to draw the covers up with her.

"So soon?" she gasped, unaccountably torn between excitement and dismay. "Surely there is more for me to learn."

He shrugged, a smile tugging at his lips. He looked tired. Perhaps his tutelage taxed his strength more than it appeared. "My aunt feels your manners are still rough but adequate. Your clothing is all that remains."

"But I cannot begin a Season now! I haven't learned how to catch a husband."

He had been turning away but stopped at her last comment. "How to catch a husband?"

She bit her lip. Had she just said that? Seeing his shocked expression, she realized she must have. "That is the whole point, is it not? To catch a rich husband."

When he spoke, his voice was filled with a rich humor that warmed her. "You need not concern yourself with that, Lynette. I assure you, you will 'catch' a husband."

"But—"

"Enough, Lynette. You are the student. Allow the tutor to plan his lessons in peace." He left her then, softly closing the door between their two rooms.

I haven't learned how to catch a husband.

Lynette's words echoed through Adrian's mind as he walked to his bed. Good God, what an unusual woman she was. He was not sure how, but sometime between yesterday and today Lynette had accepted her situation. More than accepted it, she had embraced it.

That is the whole point, is it not?

He grinned into the darkness. Yes, it was the whole point, but to have her state it so baldly so soon after her ordeal . . . Well, he thought, as he stripped off his tie, that boded well for the coming Season.

Yet something about her attitude disturbed him.

He turned and stared at her closed door. True, he had been the one to close it, but suddenly he realized that perhaps she had already begun closing it. Lynette was a very bright girl. The only thing that kept her bound to him was her ignorance. But in the coming days she would learn quickly, and likely learn very well.

Lord, none of his other girls had even looked at his book on investing until he insisted. But Lynette had not only finished it—in a day, no less—but already taken another. He'd seen it on her nightstand. When had she become so practical? So . . . eager?

But then, what had he expected? Lynette had come to him of her own free will. She hadn't been thrown at him by some desperate parent. Only Lynette had been bold enough to inquire as to whether the baroness—for the letter had perforce been addressed to her—would be interested in sponsoring a minister's daughter for a Season.

So his little Lynette was bright indeed. And practical. And adventurous. What would happen when she learned all she needed to take London by storm? Would he have any control over her? She had already managed to make him promise to give her the ultimate choice of husband. What other concessions would she wrest from him? What concessions would she take whether he allowed them or not?

He settled into his bed with a growing sense of uneasiness. If she was determined upon this course, how would he guide her? How would he stop her if she aimed for her own destruction?

He had seen it before. In Audra. And though Lynette bore little resemblance to his first girl, they were alike in one critical area. When Audra at last accepted her situation, she'd closed him out of her thoughts and fears. She'd no longer confided in him. True, she'd accepted his tutelage, but in the end she made her own way without thought to the cost to her soul.

And of all his girls, she was the one who looked at him with emptiness in her eyes. There was no connection between the two of them, only the bitter loss of innocence.

Though he accepted his failure with Audra, the thought of that coldness between him and Lynette was horrifying. But how could he stop it?

It might already be too late, he realized with a sickening dread. His only hope was to keep her off balance. To push her hard, teaching her more than she could absorb. And, with luck, she would be wed long before she came to hate him.

Sighing, he settled into his bed, the ache in his body in no way comparing to the ache in his soul. Many had accused him of heartlessness, and at times he almost believed it himself. But the truth was that he grieved for each girl, mourning what he had to do to them even as he embarked upon the task. Then, weeks, sometimes months later, he wept at each wedding.

With Lynette, it was different. Their connection had developed faster, ran deeper. He could hold no distance from his task with her. He suffered her every indignity, her every pain, as he had not done with any of the others.

So, if he wept for his other girls, what would Lynette's wedding bring? What type of pain would he face then?

Depressed, he curled his body around a cold pillow and sighed. It did not matter what he felt. Whatever lay before them, Lynette's path was set.

As was his own.

Chapter 10

We will go to the opera tonight. The baroness will choose your gown.

M

Lynette took a deep breath, trying to calm her nerves. She was to go to the opera tonight? He had told her—three nights ago—that she would be introduced to society soon. But she had thought her clothing would take longer to finish. She had thought that she would learn more about the catching of a husband. But she'd only learned more about deportment, not men.

Beside her, the baroness leaned over her shoulder to read the missive, then grunted as she sat down to her morning tea.

"He's rushing you. I told him you were not quite ready, but he's anxious."

Lynette turned to her companion. "You don't think I am ready?"

The baroness shook her head. "You are much too

forward, your manners too rough. Good Lord, girl, you still have hair on your legs." She shook her head, her disgust plain. "But he must rush it."

Lynette frowned, trying to keep pace with the conversation. "Hair on my legs?"

The older woman waved away her question. "You'll find out. This afternoon. I had scheduled you a dancing lesson, but he is in a hurry." She sighed as she took another sip of her tea. "I suppose it's because you are his last. He's anxious to get it over with."

Again, Lynette found herself repeating the baroness's comment as a question. "His last?"

The baroness didn't answer at first. She was busy spreading jam on her morning bread. Eventually she spoke, though her attention seemed distracted. "Marry well, Lynette. The money will finally put his lands in order. Or so he says."

"He has land? Outside of London?"

"Entailed. And a moldering pile of rubbish if there ever was one. But he has been working with it. Doing what he can." The woman looked up abruptly, her light blue eyes hard as they focused on her. "But only if you marry well. With your money, he plans to quit this wretched bride service and become a proper lord." She slanted a look at her charge. "Marry poorly, Lynette, and likely we shall all be tossed into debtor's prison."

Given the fierceness of the baroness's expression, Lynette did not doubt the seriousness of their situation. Especially given the state of the larder when she first arrived.

"All his income has gone into his estate?"

"Aye. And don't forget that when he's showing you off tonight." She rose up from her chair. "Come along. I suppose we should just take care of that hair. I know it sounds odd, but he learned it from one of his foreign friends. Says men like smooth skin, especially on the legs."

"But I don't understand—" Her words were cut off as the baroness tugged on her arm, lifting her out of her seat.

"Don't question. Just endure."

Lynette knew she ought to feel grateful for the distractions the baroness provided. She ought to be thankful that the woman kept her so busy with beauty tips that she did not have time to dwell on the coming evening.

She ought to, but she didn't. Right then, as the baroness ripped hot wax and half the skin off her legs, Lynette was completely miserable.

"Aaaiii!"

"Men like smooth, delicate legs."

Lynette stared down at her reddening flesh. "What are you doing?"

It was a rhetorical question. She completely understood what was happening. The baroness was smoothing more hot wax on her legs. In actual fact, it was quite a pleasant sensation. Smooth. Warming. Delightful.

Then the woman again pressed a sturdy piece of cloth on top of the wax and, without warning, ripped the entire thing off. It took half the skin on Lynette's leg with it.

"Ouch! Baroness, please, is this truly necessary?"

Grunting from her exertions, the lady glared at her. "Do you think I would do this if it weren't necessary?" She leaned backward with a huff, brushing the hair out of her eyes. "Believe me, this has been extraordinarily helpful. Occasionally the suitors like to touch your ankle. You should see their eyes when they realize you have gone without stockings. And that your skin is as a smooth as your . . . as a baby's bottom." She straightened, reaching for more wax. "We've cinched many a deal that way."

"But no man will touch my legs. At least not until after we are wed. Surely it is too soon for you to—Ow!" Lynette huffed, looking down at her reddened legs. Then she frowned as she inspected them more closely. Truly, they did look . . . nicer.

"Be thankful I am stopping at your thighs. That other hair hurts like the devil when removed."

Lynette frowned as she tried to think what other hair the lady could mean. Abruptly, she felt her eyes widen. "You cannot mean . . ."

"I can and I do." Then the baroness relented, placing her hands on her hips as she stared at Lynette. "As I said," she commented gently, "some grooms have particular tastes. But not to worry. We will not do that today. Perhaps not ever." She leaned forward. "But you should be aware of it, Lynette. It is all part and parcel of keeping your husband entertained. Sometimes they like it for variety's sake." She returned to her task, applying more wax with a firm stroke.

"I always thought entertainment was singing. Opera. Parties," Lynette said, her voice sullen. "This"—she gestured to her throbbing leg—"is not at all what I thought."

"This is for *his* entertainment, girl. Not yours." The baroness reached for the cloth strip. "You listen to me. Men like change. They like innovation and different experiences. If you do not wish your husband to look elsewhere for entertainment . . ." She pinned Lynette with a steady regard. "And believe me, you don't. Then you must be a thousand different women. Every night he will want something different. Something unique. This is one of your tools."

"But, still," Lynette began as she gripped the edge of her bed, "you cannot believe that removing hair . . . *there* . . . is necessary."

"Certainly not for a clergyman's daughter. But for one of the viscount's girls? Absolutely. Though not at this moment. Now be silent." The baroness leaned down and Lynette tried to prepare herself for the pain. "We have not yet started on your face."

And so it continued. Lynette began to think fondly of the canceled dancing lesson as she was dumped unceremoniously into a cold bath.

"Cold water freshens the skin," she was told.

Then she was covered in a heavily perfumed oil that made her sick.

"Perhaps you are right. This scent is too strong."

Re-bathed in cold water.

Had her hair tugged and crimped and pulled by the baroness.

"Your hair is too flat. You must learn to lift it by means of pins, ties, glue, if necessary. But get it up!"

And then, finally, blessedly, allowed to don her dress.

"Dress quickly, Lynette. His lordship does not like to be kept waiting."

Lynette nodded wearily. She was already exhausted and the evening had not yet begun. But then she saw the gown.

"What is this?" she gasped.

"Your dress, of course."

Lynette stared, her eyes bulging out of their sockets. "It . . . it . . . it is indecent!"

"Don't be ridiculous," returned the baroness as she held up the slim blue gown. "You picked out the style yourself."

"Of course I did!" returned Lynette hotly. "The design is lovely. But I wanted the gray silk, not . . . not pale blue that any candlelight will show through!"

"Gray!" The baroness pulled a disgusted face. "None of the Marlock women have ever appeared in gray. Not even old Great-aunt Matilda. Come, come, put it on. The viscount will be here soon."

Lynette eyed the thin material with horror. She might as well go out in her shift. The blue fabric was as thin as a poor fisherman's net.

"Do not be difficult," the baroness warned. "It is a beautiful color."

Lynette could not disagree. It was indeed a beautiful blue. Even in the gloomy evening light, the dress seemed to shimmer. By candlelight it would practically glow, drawing every eye to her. Unless, of course, she stood directly in front of a candelabra. In that case, every eye would be watching her naked body.

"Is there not—"

"Put it on," the baroness said sternly. Her face softened. "Trust me. It's perfect."

What choice did she have? Lynette sighed and donned the dress. Her only prayer was that none of her father's parishioners frequented the London opera. If anyone she knew saw her in this dress, she would die of mortification.

She wore no jewelry. Simply the dress, pale slippers, and her hair piled high upon her head. And the cosmetics the baroness applied to her eyes, her cheeks, and her lips.

"Perfect," the baroness at last said, and put away the paint pot. "Now stand."

Feeling more like a doll than a person, Lynette did as she was bid.

The older woman walked in circles around Lynette, assessing her from all angles. "Just remember to keep your mouth shut. A silent woman is a mysterious woman. And men like quiet girls. Unless, of course, you are complimenting their prowess. They adore that. But for tonight, merely smile and be alluring."

Lynette abruptly lifted her gaze to the baroness, but the woman forestalled her.

"I know you have no inkling of how to be alluring. That is Adrian's task. As for my part, I have done all I can."

And with that, the baroness quit the room. For a moment it sounded to Lynette as if the older woman was washing her hands of her charge. Or throwing her to the wolves, perhaps.

She stood in the middle of the room; finally, blessedly alone. She breathed in deeply, but not too deeply for fear of straining the tight fabric of her bodice. Then she exhaled, trying to relax along with the movement.

Not possible.

She was about to go to the opera! It was a centerpiece of the *ton*. A place where the elite gathered to engage in discourse, to plan the affairs of state, to discuss the latest gown style. And likely, she thought with a slight twitch to her lips, to gossip about who was going to marry whom.

And she would be there!

The thought was as exhilarating as it was terrifying. She would be there! In this dress! Practically naked for everyone to see her many faults.

For the first time she wished she had another year's worth of lessons. The baroness could not possibly have taught her everything she would need to know. And worse than that, Lynette now realized she remembered a bare fraction of what she had been told. She would be a laughingstock! They would all be thrown in debtor's prison.

Lynette spun around, wanting to pace the room to ease some of the tension coiling in her belly, but she could not. She might disturb her coif. She could not sit for fear of creasing the Naked Dress, as she had come to call it in her mind. Why, she could not even fan herself for fear of somehow dislodging the cosmetics on skin!

So she stood in the middle of the room and worried.

What if no one saw her tonight? What if they saw her and laughed? What if they were appalled? What if she had nothing to say? Or worse, said the wrong thing? Would there be any bachelors at the opera? Well, of course there would be bachelors, she admonished herself. London was filled with young bucks about the town. But would there be any *eligible* bachelors, ones suited to her purpose?

And what if—

"Good God, you are stunning."

She spun around at the viscount's voice. But before she could speak, she felt her hair tip precariously to one side. She quickly raised her hand to hold it in place but did not know how much force to apply. In fact, as the viscount entered her bedroom, her hands were fluttering about her hair, wondering what, if anything, she could do.

Thankfully, the viscount reached out and grasped her hands, pulling them down to hold before him. "No, no. Your hair is perfect. Don't touch it."

"Oh!" she said, her gaze hopping anxiously from his face to the mirror and back again. "I don't know what to do—"

"Hush," he whispered. "You are perfect. Step back and let me look at you."

She did as told, her hands slipping from his grasp as she moved. Her steps were tiny and her gaze firmly downcast. Despite the viscount's compliments, Lynette felt shy. He was merely saying nice things to bolster her confidence, not because they were true. She worried that with one false move she would shatter the image.

She worried any number of things, but mostly she simply felt strange and awkward, as if her body were no longer her own.

"Look at me."

It took more self-discipline than she expected, but in the end she forced herself to raise her gaze. She saw first Marlock's dark trousers, black and crisp, beautifully outlining the corded muscles of his thighs. Her eyes skimmed over his black coat and snowy white cravat. She saw instead his trim waist and his broad shoulders. A few inches more and she noted his black hair curling around his ear, the locks cut in a fashionable style that she could not name. Finally she came to his face. His lips were curved into a soft smile, but it was his eyes that captured her gaze. They seemed to burn into her. It was just a trick of the firelight, but in truth, it did not matter. His gaze was filled with an admiration that literally glowed.

And it was trained on her.

"What do you see?" he asked.

"You," she whispered. "Only you."

His smile grew, curving upward and drawing her gaze to his lips. "And I see only you." Then he stepped closer, his hand outstretched. She did not even think, but placed her fingers into his. He drew her to the mirror, standing behind her as he turned her to face her reflection. But she did not see herself. Instead she saw him, standing behind her, his hands lightly resting on her arms as his thumbs stroked her skin.

"Do you see it?" he whispered in her ear. "Do you see what all the men will be staring at tonight?"

He reached out and lifted her chin, turning it slightly to the right.

"Do you see the creamy expanse of your skin? Do you see how your breasts are caressed by the fabric, yet still high and full? You are gorgeous."

She felt it.

"You shimmer, and the merest glance from you will set a man on fire."

She blushed at his words. She could not help it. The thought that she, a minister's daughter, could set a man on fire seemed ludicrous. But then his hands stroked her arms, trailing heat along her skin. He leaned even closer, and his lips touched her ear, while his breath skated inside, making her gasp.

"You are the perfect height," he whispered as his hands trailed down past hers to finally rest along her thighs. "Your legs are shaped as a man likes. Strong to grip him. Long to entice him." Then he gathered some of the fabric in his hand, drawing it upward so that it pulled against her skin. "How does this feel?"

She shivered; she could not help it. After this afternoon's waxing experience, her legs tingled at the slightest touch. He clearly knew this because he did not draw the dress higher, but whispered it back and forth across her skin.

"How does this feel?" he repeated.

"As though I am someone else. A stranger in a new body."

"It is no stranger," he said, his head dipping down toward her neck. "It is only you as you were meant to be." His breath heated the skin along her neck and her hair prickled with awareness. "Beautiful." He dropped a kiss just above her collarbone. "Alluring." And then he bit her. It was the slightest nibble, the tiniest taste, but she felt it like an explosion. She gasped, and her body clenched.

"Do you feel it?" he continued. Then he continued along her neck, nibbling, kissing, and occasionally sucking.

"I feel you," she whispered.

"But your body. Is it tight?"

She closed her eyes, experiencing the clench of her belly, the shudder of her breath. "Yes," she whispered.

"Are your breasts taut?"

She didn't answer. She wasn't sure. Then, with a single trailing stroke, he touched the side of her breast, straight out until he flicked the end of her erect nipple.

She gasped as a bolt of lightning shot through her.

"Do you see how this dress shows me that? Do you see your full breasts?"

She opened her eyes, wanting to see what he did. It was only her standing before him. But then again, it was not her. She saw a young woman who seemed to exude sexuality. Her lips were red. Her breasts pointed. Tight.

"Yes," she said. And as she spoke, she leaned backward against him, for her legs would not support her.

"Men like to look at nipples. They like to see a woman aroused."

Again she closed her eyes, luxuriating in the feel of him behind her, supporting her, while his lips played along her shoulder and neck.

"See yourself!" he commanded, and her eyes flew open. "This is the sight of a woman. Look at your lips."

She did. When had she wet them? She did not know, but they were full, red, and glistening with moisture. And her eyes. They were open, wide, and . . . slightly dazed.

"I am beautiful?" she asked, her voice coming out as a throaty whisper.

"Ahhh," he groaned at her words. "You take my breath away."

Then he nibbled upward, kissing her shoulder, biting her neck, and, lastly, wetting her earlobe with his tongue.

"I have a present for you," he whispered.

She shivered as his breath skated along the moisture he left behind. He extended his arms until she was surrounded by him. In his hand he held a jeweler's case. He waited for her attention.

It took effort, so entranced was she by the sight of his dark chin against the white skin of her neck. But in the end she looked to his hands, curious to see what he held. He opened the box. Within it lay two gold earbobs, impossibly long, with dangling blue jewels shimmering at the tips.

"They were expensive, for all that they are glass. But believe me, they will be well worth it." He shifted, lifting out one earring. "Let me put them on you."

Without thought, she tilted her head sideways to give him better access, and she felt his smile against her skin. Then, as he raised his hands, his forearms brushed her breasts.

Again she shivered, and his grin grew wider as he attached the first earbob.

"Close your eyes," he whispered.

She complied and he pressed her head the other way, allowing him to place the other earring. Then the strangest thing happened. He began to kiss her more fully. To stroke her. All along her neck. But with the earbobs brushing against her skin and the heat of his breath warming the stones, she could not tell what was his touch and what was the jewelry.

"I am kissing you, Lynette," he said, though she wondered how he could be doing that and yet still speak to her.

Her response came without thought. "Yes," she whispered.

"I am tasting you." His heat brushed across her shoulder. Or was it one of the blue stones?

"Yes."

"I want you, for you are the most incredible creature alive."

She smiled then, knowing he was feeding her ego, a trick to bolster her throughout the coming evening.

Somehow she didn't care. When he said it, she believed it. And if she doubted, his lips were there, on her body, telling her exactly what she wanted to hear.

She was beautiful. And he wanted her.

"Now, open your eyes."

She did, and was shocked to see that he was across the room from her. The feeling of his lips on her shoulders had come from the earrings, not from him. The rising heat came not from his breath but from herself.

He grinned at her.

"You will be my best girl yet."

She straightened, suddenly flustered.

"No!" he called urgently, stepping forward. "Do not become self-conscious. Lynette, I gave you those earrings so you would remember. Tonight, if you feel awkward or confused, simply tilt your head."

At his urging, she did so, and felt the earbob once again stroke her skin.

"Do you feel it? Do you remember?"

She bit her lip, a slow smile pulling at her cheeks. "Yes. I remember."

"And when you walk, do you remember my hands on your legs?"

At his gesture, she took a tentative step forward. The fabric of her dress slid across her legs, sending a bolt of tingling awareness through her.

"Yes," she whispered, awed and a little overwhelmed by the feeling.

"Then you are ready." With a courtly gesture, he extended his arm to her. She took it easily, almost gracefully, and she was rewarded for her actions.

Straightening her spine, she returned his smile. "Yes," she said softly. "I am ready."

* * *

The opera house was filled with people.

The carriage ride had been close enough. With both the viscount and the baroness sitting across from her, both watching her with steady, inscrutable regards, Lynette had been hard-pressed to breathe, much less relax.

But then she had stepped out of their carriage, taken the viscount's hand, and looked about. Everywhere she turned there were beautiful women, handsome gentlemen, and wealth. Money, riches, and jewels. That was what she saw most.

Thanks to the viscount's whispered compliments, she felt as if she was lovely enough to compete with these women. And when she felt her confidence lagging, all she needed to do was look into the admiring eyes of the young men. They were quite obvious in their comical attempts to gain her attention.

The old men, however, were vastly different. Those gentlemen smiled at her, many boldly assessing her from top to bottom. They gave her disdainful looks. Haughty looks. Still, their stares were filled with a hunger that ate at her confidence. They made her feel dirty, unwholesome somehow. In fact, if it was not for the encouraging smiles of the viscount beside her, she likely would have turned about and run.

But she could not. And so she began a litany to herself. *I am beautiful,* she reassured herself. Then she tilted her head and felt her earbobs tickle her skin.

I am beautiful.

I am beautiful.

I am poor.

That thought slipped like an evil wind below her defenses, pointing out what everyone else could see.

The main difference between her and all the other attendees: except for her glass earrings, she wore no jewelry. Not even a decorative hairpin. Her gown was simple, her slippers plain. Her attire could not have declared poverty more loudly if it were written across her bodice.

How odd, she thought irreverently. She had never realized before just how significant wealth was—the outward trappings, the ostentatious show. As a minister's daughter, she had never felt its lack. A clergyman's child wasn't supposed to adorn herself with finery. Now, for the first time, she saw how important jewels and clothing were in society. Money was written in the very cut of one's coat, in the whisper of silk in a lady's gown, and in the gems glittering from every female throat, wrist, and finger.

They were rich, and she was poor.

For the first time she understood why her father cozied up to the wealthier people in his parish. Now she knew that this was the arena to which her father had aspired. Here were the people he wished to associate with. But to be among them, one had to be rich.

"What are you thinking?" the viscount whispered in her ear.

"That I will never be one of them. Not until I am wed to a man as rich as Croesus."

"You will never be one of them ever."

She stumbled at his bald statement, and she might have fallen had he not been holding her. But before she could phrase her question he continued, explaining his cold statement.

"It is not wealth that is so important, Lynette. It is the power that money brings. Unfortunately, no woman can hold power. Her only influence is through her husband. And your husband will likely be too old to hold sway here."

She shifted slightly, shock and hope intertwined in her voice. "But when I am a widow . . . ?" she asked.

"Then you may use your money to buy an influential husband. But you will never be allowed to wield true power yourself."

She hesitated, thrown by his words, forced to ask the obvious question. "Then why am I doing this?"

He paused, turning so that he looked directly, forcefully, into her eyes. "Wielding power and living comfortably, happily, in your old age are two entirely different things."

At that moment she finally understood his task. He was not saving her from a loveless marriage. He was not handing her the means to control the people who sought to use her. He was merely helping her find peace. A way to be independent enough to seek her own future.

"And do not forget your siblings. Do well here and you can keep them from a similar fate. Your sister can have a real Season, your brother his commission."

She felt a smile tug at her lips. "I am buying your freedom as well."

He dipped his head, acknowledging her statement in the most urbane manner possible. But as he bent, his hand did something entirely different. He stroked her thigh. It was the merest brush, but again her legs felt incredibly sensitive and her skin began to tingle as it had earlier.

"Smile, Lynette," he whispered. "There is someone I especially wish you to meet."

Chapter 11

She was incredible.

Adrian could barely believe his eyes, but it was true. Every time she moved, every time she shifted or spoke or even looked somewhere, all eyes followed her. They watched how she walked, how she spoke, how she simply stood. And when she looked somewhere else, they followed her gaze to see what had drawn her attention.

Lynette was a success.

Adrian felt his gut ease at the knowledge. He had spent the last week dropping hints about town. By now his particular hobby was well known among the gentlemen of a certain set. All he had to do was mention he had a new girl, and many ears pricked up. Mention that this girl was by far his most alluring, most amazing, and, in general, most perfect catch ever, and more than just ears poked up.

But for all the interest he had already stirred, tonight was the most important. Tonight he would see how she functioned in society.

Would she stammer in timid mortification as Suzanne had? Would she boldly assess every man who came across her path as Audra had? Or would she be the queen she was even now revealing—modest, charming, and with an innate sensuality so devastating it made a man's teeth sweat?

Already the gentlemen were lining up, angling for introductions.

"Lynette, may I present to you Lord Winterburr. Lord Winterburr, Miss Lynette Jameson."

Lord Winterburr was barely fifty, worth twenty thousand pounds per annum, and unfortunately in excellent health. Still, he was well worth a look, and Adrian was pleased as Lynette performed beautifully for him.

"Stephen Gibson, Earl of Ashford." The earl was old, crotchety, and ready to die any day. Unfortunately, his previous wife had already run through most of his estate.

"Mark Thompson, Lord Histon." Young, devilishly handsome, and randy as hell. But Lynette, of course, didn't know any of that. All she knew was that he was holding her hand and gazing with devotion at her, his russet brown locks reminding Adrian of a puppy dog. The kind that attracted women like a magnet.

"Brian Strack, Earl of Bonhaven." Brian was well into his sixties, cursed with a perpetual cough, and reportedly worth over ten thousand pounds per annum. He was an excellent candidate. Apparently, the gentleman thought so too—he held Lynette's hand longer than was appropriate, then took advantage of his superior height to peer down her bodice.

Lynette, of course, was blissfully unaware of the man's lascivious intentions, but Adrian saw them and gave Strack a frosty glare. With a respectful bow, the man withdrew.

And so it continued. Introduction after introduction, with Lynette amazing them all.

"Darian Swanson, Lord Rendlen." Rendlen was older, but not in his dotage. His income was highly respectable and, given his lifestyle, Adrian did not expect him to live long. His blond hair and blue eyes made him appear almost angelic, but his appetites were as dark as Satan. Personally, Adrian found him hypocritical, self-centered, and a perfect example of the worst of the peerage. However, the ladies of his acquaintance seemed to think him riveting. Adrian had heard more than one dowager echo her granddaughter's sigh of longing whenever the man appeared.

And Rendlen seemed most particular in his attentions to Lynette.

"Come along, Lynette," Adrian said, a cold note in his voice. "We would not wish to miss the opening."

"Of course not," she returned, her eyes still on her newest acquaintance. "If you will excuse me, Lord Rendlen?"

But Rendlen, apparently, would not release her. He held her hand, drawing it toward his lips as he, no doubt, stroked her palm with his long fingers. "I am afraid," he said in a low, seductive voice, "that I find I am not prepared to release you."

Lynette shifted, her eyes crinkling in merriment. "And why not, my lord? Has your hand cramped?"

"Yes," he returned, "that must be it. I am afraid I shall not be able to relieve this particular malady until you promise to ride with me tomorrow afternoon."

Lynette hesitated. Indeed, so did Adrian. He did not like Lord Rendlen, but the man had a great deal of influence. Any woman who received his particular attentions would capture the interest of more than one hungry bachelor. And better yet, more than one older gentleman would relish snatching a young prize away from Rendlen.

Those thoughts flew through his mind in barely a second. Long enough for Lynette to turn her questioning gaze toward him. Long enough for Adrian to give her a slight nod of approval. He could only hope that Lynette was level-headed enough to trust him when he told her Rendlen was not an eligible candidate.

"Of course, my lord," she said sweetly to Rendlen. "I shall be happy to accompany you."

"Excellent. I look forward to it." The man bowed and sauntered away.

At last, they walked toward their box. It was well placed, far to one side. It was not the best location for viewing the stage, but it was perfect if one wished to be seen. And Lynette was definitely a woman to be seen. In fact, Adrian was a bit surprised by the heady feeling of having her on his arm. It was glorious to know he was the envy of every man present.

She was stupendous, and he could not suppress the pride, the pure male satisfaction that—for now—she was completely his.

And she was also falling, he realized with a shock, tripping over her own feet as she stumbled into an older gentleman.

"Oh, my," she was saying. "I'm terribly sorry."

When Adrian looked up, he saw a happy coincidence. Indeed, here was the very man he had hoped, somehow, to intrigue. And that man was even now helping Lynette regain her balance.

"It was my fault entirely," returned the gentleman.

"Please," said Adrian, as he stepped forward. "Allow me to be of some assistance. Lynette, this is an old friend of my family. Thomas Kirkley, Earl of—"

"Earl of Songshire," she interrupted, slipping into a deep curtsy. "Good evening, my lord. I truly must apologize."

"Little Lynette," crooned the earl. "You are looking quite grown up."

Lynette straightened, her color obviously heightened, her movements more stilted than Adrian had seen all evening.

"Am I to understand the two of you are acquainted?" Adrian drawled, unable to suppress a surge of annoyance. Good lord, he had been wracking his brain for the last week trying to figure out a way for the two of them to meet. And here they were, already acquainted?

"His lordship attended services at my father's church," Lynette answered, her voice high and slightly shrill. Adrian slanted a quick look at her. Her color was elevated, her attitude anxious, and abruptly he cursed himself for not seeing it sooner.

Of course she would meet someone from her father's church. The cleric had practically lived to toady up to the upper class. It was inevitable that Lynette would meet one of her father's parishioners, and he cursed himself for not preparing her for this eventuality.

He moved closer to touch her, to try somehow to reassure her, but he found he was forestalled by the earl, who had both his hands on her arms, smiling as he looked warmly at Lynette.

"My late wife's family lived in the village, and we quite looked forward to your father's sermons every Sunday." He glanced at Adrian and winked. "All that fire and brimstone got her blood moving."

Adrian smiled and nodded, surprised that he had to force himself to stand back and allow Thomas and Lynette to become reacquainted. Songshire was the perfect husband for Lynette. Well-placed in society. Thirteen thousand pounds per annum. Widowed slightly more than five years earlier—long enough for him to tire of being alone and start looking for a replacement. And he was in his late fifties and a gout sufferer. With no known vices or dark peccadillos, he would be an excellent match for Lynette.

Yet Adrian had to clench his hands at his sides to keep from interfering.

"Well, Miss Jameson, I am pleased you were able to contact the baroness. I hope everything is working out as you hoped."

Adrian felt shock stiffen his spine. Songshire had provided Lynette with the baroness's address? Lynette had never revealed how she had learned of the services he and his aunt offered. She had only mentioned that, as a cleric's daughter, she'd heard things not deemed appropriate for her young ears. This information put quite a new spin on Songshire's presence this evening. Especially given the man's obviously proprietary hold on Lynette's arm.

But he could not allow that just yet. It was too soon in the game for Adrian to allow even an old family friend to stake a claim. And so he stepped forward, ready to ease Lynette away.

But again he was forestalled, this time by his aunt. The baroness pushed in front of Adrian and smiled coyly up at Songshire. "My lord," she said sweetly, "what a fortunate happenstance that we should meet today."

"Agatha!" his lordship exclaimed. "My God, Adrian, you are surrounded by beauties." And with that, he bowed over the baroness's hand.

For her part, his aunt blushed prettily, like the veriest schoolgirl, but her speech was still fluent, low. Almost seductive.

"I received your card when Horace passed on. I cannot tell you how much it meant to me."

"And now here you are. With your nephew." Again, the earl's gaze traveled among the three of them, boldly assessing the women.

Beside him, Adrian felt his aunt stiffen. "Adrian has been very kind to an old woman."

"Not old, surely," came the earl's automatic response. But even as he spoke, his eyes lingered on Lynette.

Then, abruptly, the interaction was interrupted.

"Papa! There you are! We were becoming worried."

Everyone turned to see the earl's daughter, the delicate and very wealthy Lady Karen, push rudely into the group and link her hand through her father's arm.

"Come, come," she chided her parent. "The farce has already begun."

"I will be there in a moment," returned her father, patting her arm fondly. "I was just saying hello to some dear friends."

Then it came. The cold stare and the equally disdainful sniff. The woman knew. In fact, likely all the women understood exactly what the Marlock family did for money. They often comprehended more than the men. And that knowledge was apparent in every rigid line of Lady Karen's body as she tried to pull her father away.

"Come along, Father. Geoffrey is quite worried."

She turned her back on them, giving everyone the cut direct. It was expected, and Adrian refused to let it effect him. But beside her, Thomas did feel awkward. Unfortunately, he was being dragged away by his own daughter. He shifted, gave all three of the Marlock party an apologetic look, and bowed as best he could. Then his daughter hauled against her father's arm, and he all but stumbled as they disappeared into the crowd.

Adrian did not move, waiting instead to see how Lynette reacted. To his right, his aunt cursed under her breath. Both she and he were well used to such scenes. It was Lynette who concerned him now.

This, too, was an important part of the first evening out. By appearing with him, and in that dress, Lynette was now thoroughly branded as a Marlock woman. She would suffer such cuts every day for the rest of her life. It was important that she learn how to handle them now.

Stepping forward, he took her arm and gently guided her into their box. He could tell that she was only now understanding what had just occurred. As a minister's daughter, she had been the height of respectability. Likely this was the first time anyone had been openly rude to her, much less given her the cut direct.

And yet she did not seem devastated. Merely subdued.

"Lynette—"

"We used to play dolls together."

He paused. "I beg your pardon?"

"Lady Karen and I. When her mother came to services, she always stayed afterward to speak with my father. Then Karen and I would play dolls."

He did not wish her to, but he knew she had to finish her thought, to say the words out loud. When she did not continue, he completed the thought for her. "And now she will not even look at you."

Lynette looked down at her hands. "Yes."

"She is a spoiled, pampered girl who has no idea what real privation is."

Silently, Lynette nodded.

"There will be many like her, Lynette. Many who do not understand or even want to try. And there will be many who wish to destroy you merely because they can."

He felt her body flinch at his cold words.

"You must find a way around them. You have chosen your course. It would be tragic if you allowed such narrowness of mind to deter you."

She did not speak, but he felt her body still as she considered his words.

"Only you can decide if you are wholesome and good. Only you—"

"And God."

He frowned slightly. She had not spoken of her faith before this. If she allowed the church to rule her thoughts on this matter, they were ruined for certain.

"Yes," he agreed, though his words were cautious and slow. "God. Of course."

He waited, unsure how to proceed. He wanted to touch her, to reassure her, but knew that if she felt sullied, a man's touch could very well end this adventure the same evening it began.

She took a deep breath and lifted her chin. "Then I shall allow God to judge me and not these women."

Abruptly, he found himself grinning. It was as though a great weight had rolled off his shoulders. She had passed the test! Indeed, she had passed the last of tonight's trials. From lascivious gazes to open leers and the cut direct, all that had occurred in the short time it took them to cross from the opera house door to their box. And she had performed through them all with amazing skill and poise.

Good God, she was even smiling as if all the world were at her feet. And indeed, it would be. Very soon. He could not be prouder if she was his own wife.

And with that happy thought, he led her to her seat.

Lynette was in hell.

She wasn't sure she believed in her father's world of hellfire and brimstone. Why would a loving God create such a hideous place? Everyone sinned. Need everyone expect to burn eternally in hell? But for her, hell existed right here. Right now. It encompassed the entire opera house, and it consisted completely of two people: Lady Karen and Lynette's own father.

She did not for one minute believe that her family would condemn her. No, indeed, if she returned home with a rich, titled husband, her uncle certainly, but most likely her entire family would absolve her of any sin, real or imagined.

No, the father with her in hell was the man of her childhood. The man who was all powerful, all seeing, and all knowing. He'd known when she was stealing blueberry tarts and beat her severely for it. He'd seen when she smiled at a handsome street boy with impish blue eyes; he had locked her in her room for three days for that. And when she watched him return from London drunk and broke, he'd glared at her and begun parading her in front of the sons of the rich parishioners—young men Lynette knew to be both spoiled and cruel.

It was only a chance discussion with the Earl of Songshire that had given her any other option. And yet, in her mind's eye, she still saw her father condemning her, ordering her to be a good girl, a helpful girl, a silent, obedient slave to his desires. And beside him stood Lady Karen, equally condemning, as she whispered unfounded gossip into her father's ear and then pointed an accusing finger right at Lynette's breasts.

The very breasts that tingled every time her earbobs brushed against her shoulder.

This was hell.

But Lynette knew how to survive it. In truth, she had spent much of her life hiding her thoughts from her father's parishioners, her family, her father. She simply told herself she was right and they were wrong. But because they were adults and, more often than not, they were men, not a one would listen to her. She had to accept being right in silence. In the end, she would be proved correct.

And usually she was.

But not this time. She couldn't reach for that absolute faith, the certainty of her own position. Because she did not know her position.

Was she sinful, so steeped in shame and degradation that even the most forgiving, most saintly among them would run screaming from the sight of her? Or was what she was doing, what she was experiencing, as glorious as it felt?

She had never been the center of such marked male attention before. Never had she seen such open admiration in men's eyes. She even believed that some of the more foolish among them would leap to the heights of folly on her word alone.

It was a heady experience, having so much power.

That the women disdained her was equally amazing. Uncomfortable as it was, a part of her reveled in it. So much of her life had been spent in invisibility. Perhaps they looked at her askance, but for the first time in her entire life they actually *saw* her.

And there were enough men smiling at her to make up for the women's envious glares. Or so she told herself.

So which was it? Was she right that these feelings, these sensations were as wonderful, as wholesome as singing in the meadow on a summer day? Or had she accepted the devil's temptation, sliding down the black path into the maw of hell?

She didn't know. So she sat, feeling the delicious whisper of her skirt along her legs, experiencing the tightening of her body as her earrings teased her shoulders, and all the while she smiled. It was her angelic smile, the one she put on for her father.

While inside she felt dark. Dirty. Shamed.

If nothing else, that alone told her this was wrong. She couldn't continue. She didn't care what happened to her. Even if her uncle barred the door to her, she would not continue with this plan. She could not.

The decision felt good somehow. Not wholesome

as much as solid. A settling of her future. Come what may, she had made a decision, taken control of her life. And that felt right. With that thought firmly planted in her mind, she focused on the stage, telling herself to enjoy the evening before telling the viscount of her decision.

She managed partially, and in the end she survived. And as they drove home in darkness, she closed her eyes, only too happy to shut out the baroness's sullen grousing about the performance, the gentlemen, the lack of attention paid to older women. Then finally, blessedly, she climbed the stairs to her room, welcoming the silence that wrapped around her. At last she came to her bedroom window, staring out at the night as she pondered her decision.

What would it be like to live out there, on the street? If her uncle truly did bar the door to her, where would she go? What would she do? She didn't know. Yet she was still determined. Even fear of becoming one of the lost women, starving in the streets, did not deter her. It was better than the hell she suffered now.

She turned away from the window, pacing the confines of her room. She had removed her gown and the earbobs, seeing them as part of her problem. She would not fully undress to go to bed, so she paced her room clad in her shift. A single candle burned on her nightstand, and as it flickered in the breeze, weird and terrible shadows danced upon the walls.

She stared at them, thinking of hell and wondering how she would tell the viscount what she had decided. He had put a great deal of money and time into her. Apparently there was even more riding on her excellent marriage for him.

Would he bellow? Would he strike her? She did not think so. And yet she was afraid. Afraid to stay. Afraid to tell him. And afraid to leave.

Hell.

"You are not in bed."

She spun around, facing Marlock where he stood in the doorway between their adjoining rooms. How did he do that? she wondered. How did he slip into her room without the slightest sound?

"You did beautifully tonight," he added. "Soon all the world will be at your feet." He came forward, a warm smile on his face. He was always doing things like that. Reaching out to touch her for one reason or another. To congratulate her. To comfort her. To teach her.

She spun away, her voice tight and urgent. "My lord, we must speak."

He stopped, his hand still outstretched. Slowly he let it fall to his side. "Has something upset you?"

She straightened, steeling herself to simply say it. "I find, my lord, that I cannot continue." Then, before he could speak, she rushed onward, her words tumbling one after the other. "I understand that you have already spent an enormous amount of money on my upcoming marriage. My clothing alone"—she gestured to her full wardrobe—"is worth a small fortune. In addition, the baroness has spent a great deal of time training me."

"Not to mention my time in preparing for your introduction into Society." His voice was low and controlled, and she peered at him, wondering at his mood. His voice gave nothing away.

"Yes, of course," she continued, though more

slowly. "I would offer to repay whatever funds you have expended. But . . ." Her voice trailed away.

"Neither you nor your family have near enough."

"Yes," she agreed softly. "Of course, whatever funds I can manage, I shall gladly give over to you."

He nodded, but that was the only movement. "So," he said, his tone almost casual, "you mean to leave? Without a rich husband? Without a way to help your sister or brother?"

She bit her lip, then nodded, her movement firm and decisive.

"Will your uncle take you back? You have been severely compromised, you know."

"I know." Then she did turn away, needing to hide how much her hands shook. "I shall have to find employment somewhere. At general labor, as you said. I can sew tolerably well. And my arithmetic is most excellent. You said so yourself."

"Yes, I did. But no shop will employ a woman to cipher."

She looked back at her hands, now gripped tightly together. "I was afraid of that. I suppose a governess position—"

"Unavailable to compromised women," he interrupted.

She nodded, knowing he was correct. "Of course," she said softly. "No one wants a fallen woman to teach moral rectitude, I expect."

"No."

She shrugged, wandering toward the window, once again looking out and wondering what it would be like out there. Alone.

Though her gaze remained on the darkened window, her thoughts inevitably returned to the man behind her. He had not moved. Or so she thought. Then she heard him speak, his low tones originating from directly behind her left ear.

"You are quite determined in this?"

She did not hesitate. "It is the best thing for me."

"Why?"

She bit her lip, wondering how much she could tell him. It was hard enough explaining this decision to herself, much less phrasing it in such a way that he might understand.

"Lynette," he continued softly, "I believe I have promised to answer any of your questions honestly, correct?"

"Yes."

"You may also say anything to me. Honestly. And you have my word I shall take whatever you have to say quite seriously. I can see you are upset."

She shook her head. "No. I am determined. Determined that this should end."

"Why?"

"Because . . ." Her voice trailed off, then suddenly the words exploded out of her. "Because it is wrong!"

There. She had said it. She waited a moment, but he did not respond. Indeed, the air was so thick with his silence that she turned around, needing to assure herself that he hadn't quit the room.

He was there. A bare foot behind her, and his expression was so somber, his body so still, that for a moment she thought he was ill. Rarely had she seen him so . . . lacking in animation.

"My lord?"

"Why do you think it is wrong? Is this because of Lady Karen?"

For a moment she was tempted to answer yes. *Yes, because she embarrassed me when she was once my friend. And that hurt.* But that was not the real reason, and above all other things, the viscount required honesty.

"No, my lord—"

"Please call me Adrian," he interrupted. "I weary of the formality between us."

She hesitated but did not argue the point. "Very well, A-adrian." She took a moment to refocus her thoughts. "That an old friend shunned me is painful, but my decision is based on something entirely different."

When she stopped speaking, he merely raised an eyebrow, prompting her to continue. In the end, she stopped struggling with her words. She simply dropped down in defeat on her bed, her words tumbling out as they would without censure from her mind.

"I feel wrong." She gestured to her room and his. "*This* feels wrong."

He nodded, coming down upon the bed to sit near her without touching her. "Feelings are very important. Many soldiers rely on their instincts to warn them of danger. Countless love sonnets have been written to immortalize adoration—"

"I am not looking for love," she interrupted.

Lifting his chin, he challenged her with his dark eyes. "Aren't you? Isn't everyone?" Before she could respond, he waved his comment away. "That is not the issue right now. We are not discussing love. We are discussing how you feel. Can you put a name to it?"

"Wrong."

He nodded, and she was strangely pleased that he took her concern seriously. Her father would have long since ordered her to obey and walked away. But Adrian actually seemed to think about her words. Her feelings.

"Change is always uncomfortable, Lynette. If one becomes used to one pattern, one way of living, then a change from that will inevitably feel unsettling. Wrong."

She pushed up from the bed, needing to pace. "I understand unsettling. This is much more than a change in routine. It is not some childish whim!"

He stood as well. "I never said it was childish. I am merely seeking to understand." He sighed, stepping quickly forward to grasp her hands, containing their anxious movements. "Please, Lynette, try to elaborate. How do you feel?"

The word came to mind quickly, easily. But she did not voice it.

He must have seen the thought on her face, because he squeezed her hands slightly, his words gentle but no less commanding. "Lynette, I have risked a great deal on you. You owe me an explanation at the very least."

"Shameful." The word came out loudly, harshly overlapping his last words. And then she spoke a second time, but in a whisper as her eyes slid away. "Full of shame."

"For what you are doing? Or for what you are feeling?"

She did not want to cry, but the tears came nonetheless. She stared at his hands surrounding hers, but the image blurred. She felt the splash of tears on her skin.

"I see." He did not move, but held her still as he spoke, pressing her hands as if he wished to impress his words on her. "Tell me, is stealing wrong?"

Lynette blinked, startled out of her thoughts. "What?"

"Is stealing wrong?"

"Well, yes. Of course it is."

"And if you were to be caught stealing, you would feel ashamed."

She nodded. "Naturally."

"Naturally," he echoed. "But what if a child was taken away from his parents and raised somewhere else. A village, perhaps, or an island where stealing is acceptable. Indeed, where theft from outsiders was the only way the people could survive. In fact, stealing was so important that the very best thieves were lauded as heroes, given great feasts, and became rulers of the island."

"But that is ridiculous."

He raised an eyebrow. "Truly? I believe some of our coastal towns make a practice of piracy. Luring unwary ships into hidden dangers so they may loot the spoils."

She bit her lip. That was indeed true.

"Now, remember our boy? The one who was taken to live in such a place?"

She nodded.

"What if you caught him stealing. Would you consider him a shameful creature?"

She frowned, beginning to see the direction of his logic. "I would consider the town at fault for teaching him such values."

He grinned, lifting her hands in his joy. "Exactly! So it is not entirely the boy's fault."

"Of course not. He knew no better."

"And therefore the shame is on the villagers, on his instructors." He paused, waiting until she looked directly into his eyes. "Is that correct, Lynette? The shame is not on the boy? But on the villagers?"

She paused, thinking through his words. Mulling them over. Eventually she nodded.

"In the same manner," he said softly, "any shame for your actions or attire should be entirely on me. I am the one who is instructing you."

She knew he'd been heading here, that his logic had been aimed at just that thought, but she shook her head, pulling away. "This is different," she said.

"Why?" he challenged, refusing to move away from her.

"Because I know better. I know the way I feel is—"

"What? Wrong? But how do you know this?" He took a step forward, pursuing her. "It is merely different."

She hesitated, shaken by what he said. And just like that, she was once again in her quandary. Was this the slide to hell? Or was this no more than . . . what? Another way of life?

No, she decided abruptly. "I have lived more than twenty years. I know my own feelings."

"So you know what it is like to give birth?"

She looked up, startled by his abrupt tone. "Of course not."

"And you know the pain of struggling from day to day for food and shelter to no avail. To watch everything slip away no matter what you do?"

She shook her head. Until her father's death, they had lived comfortably enough. And even afterward, there had still been adequate food and clothing. Simply no income.

"Then how do you know this?"

She didn't. And yet . . .

Again he pursued her, stepping closer until she had to tilt her head up to look at him. "You know nothing, Lynette. Not yet. It is all still too new."

She spun away from him, trying to gain some distance, rubbing her temples as she fought to comprehend her feelings, her thoughts, her mind. "You are confusing me."

This time he did not follow, not physically. But his voice did. "Of course I am confusing you. I am teaching you, and part of learning is confusion."

"No!" She was stepping away from him, but abruptly he closed the distance between them, grabbing hold of her arm to spin her around so she looked directly into his dark eyes.

"No what, Lynette? No, you are not confused?"

She stared at him. His eyes were impossibly intense, his expression fierce as he pressed her backward. She landed softly against the wall, and she did not doubt for one moment that if she tried to escape him, she would learn how very strong he could be.

"I am . . . I . . ." She lifted her hands helplessly. "I don't know," she whispered.

"Yes." He leaned in closer, pressing the entire length of his body against her. "That's right," he continued as he ducked his head, inhaling deeply. "You don't know. But I do." Then he pulled back the tiniest bit. "Trust me, Lynette. There is so much more to learn."

Then it happened. She did not know how it occurred, but it happened in an instant. Moments before she had been sure of her course, ready to brave the consequences so long as she lived a moral and upright life. And then, abruptly, her body betrayed her.

She liked the feel of Adrian, hard and lean, as he pressed against her.

Though she no longer wore the earbobs, his mouth was so close to her that his breath teased the skin of her neck. And this time, with only her shift on, she seemed to feel his every exhalation as a physical caress.

It was wonderful.

"Trust me," he whispered again.

Then he did touch her. Not her face, nor her neck, but he skimmed his hands up her sides, beginning at her waist and rising up until he clasped both her breasts in his hands.

She was shocked by the sudden assault. Not because it was painful. On the contrary, even without knowing it before, she had wanted this. She had wanted to feel his hands molding her flesh. She was shocked by her own reactions.

She moaned. The sound was surprising. Horrifying. And so deliciously wanton that she was stunned.

"Trust me," he whispered again as his hands began to move. And she had no thoughts left to analyze. Her breasts were being stroked, rubbed, moved in such wonderful ways.

"This is not sinful, Lynette. This is merely pleasurable. A slow walk on a summer day. A sweet dessert after a bitter meal. This is joy. Do you feel it?"

Her eyes slipped closed and her head tilted backward. If it were not for the wall behind her, she would have tumbled to the floor.

"Do you feel it?" he repeated. And then he touched her nipples.

She cried out at his stroke. She felt as if she had been waiting oh so long for him to squeeze just there. To twist just like that. To bite . . .

To bite!

Her eyes flew open, but that was the only protest she made. Looking down, she saw his bowed head, and what she felt was his mouth. He was kissing her. He was kissing her breasts through her shift. The fabric was moist from his mouth, and it clung to her as he nibbled along the curve of her left breast. Down. Around. And then back up.

To her nipple.

He bit it, ever so slightly, but enough to make her knees buckle beneath her.

Blessedly, he was prepared. He caught her easily, lifting her up before carrying her to her bed. He lay her down gently, and she mourned the loss, even for a moment, of his touch. His kiss. But other sensations were intruding. She felt a tightening lower down. A heat. A moisture.

"I feel different," she whispered. "So . . ."

"You are perfect," he answered. Though his hand continued to stroke her breast, his mouth was at her ear, once again speaking to her, whispering to her, seducing her. "If there is shame in this, it is mine," he said. "Do you hear me, Lynette? The shame is mine."

She moved restlessly on the bed. "But I know better."

"You know nothing!" he exclaimed. With a sudden surge, he lifted himself off her. Grasping the top of her shift with both hands, he ripped it down to her navel. The movement was forceful, powerful, but again, she was not frightened. And as she lay on her bed, her naked breasts bared before him, she knew only hunger, a need that had never before touched her soul.

This was desire. Sinful or not, she wanted it.

And with that thought came another certainty: She could not leave this house. No matter if her soul existed in torment for the rest of eternity, she would remain here.

With him.

Because when he touched her, she could refuse him nothing.

The cool air stoked her heated flesh, and she felt her nipples tighten. It wasn't painful. It was achy and tingly and wondrous all at once.

She opened her eyes, looking at Adrian's fierce expression, seeing his gaze linger, hover, even stroke her naked breasts. But he did not touch her. She wanted him to. She wanted, hoped, desired his hands on her body, but he seemed frozen, suspended above her as he looked and looked and looked.

And all the while her breath came in quick, panting gasps.

"You know nothing," he whispered again. Then he lowered his hands—not to her but to his sides.

She arched, thrusting shamelessly forward, wanting him to taste her again, to do everything and more than he had before. But he did not. He pulled away, stumbling slightly as he gained his feet.

"I want you to read the Bible, Lynette."

Her breath caught, and she lifted slightly off the bed as she looked at him.

"The Song of Solomon. Do not speak to me again until you do so."

And with that he quit the room.

Chapter 12

Good God, she was perfect! Beautiful. Responsive. Intelligent. He wanted her so badly, it had taken every ounce of willpower he possessed to leave her room. If Adrian had so much as touched her again, the Devil himself could not have stopped him from taking her.

How was he going to finish her training? How was he ever going to give her to another man? He did not know. And yet how could he not? His estates, his heritage, his very future depended upon it.

He could not have her. Yet he had never wanted a woman more.

He looked hungrily at the door between them. He should have told her to block it. He shook his head, laughing slightly at the ridiculousness of it all. With all his other girls, he'd had to force them to unbar the door. With Lynette, he wished she would lock it.

No man was this strong.

With a resigned sigh, he closed his eyes, forcibly replacing the image of her upthrust breasts with green, healthy shoots of wheat on his land. He pictured strong homes, new plows, livestock that his part of the marriage settlement would buy. He filled his mind with these things. And when that did not work, he went downstairs to his library to review his ledgers and their pitiful sums.

When he still found himself looking upward, seeing the rosy flush of her skin as he imagined her opening for him, he cursed himself and stormed out of the house.

It was not hard to avoid her the next day. That had always been his plan. She had been introduced into society; the hook had been baited. Now he needed to see how many fish took a nibble.

He spent the day strolling through fashionable gentlemen's clubs, unsurprised when scores of young men begged for an introduction to Lynette. Thankfully, more than a few older gentlemen also made discreet inquiries. Even his dear old friend, Thomas, Earl of Songshire, casually mentioned an interest in furthering his acquaintance with Lynette.

In short, she was every bit the smashing success he had hoped for and required.

But what stunned Adrian was how difficult each little request, each spark of interest, each casual mention of her name was for him. He was mature enough to recognize the emotion. True, it had been some time since he had last experienced it, but for all his other faults, stupidity was not one of them.

He was jealous. Green-eyed, clenched-gut, fist-gripping jealous.

One of these men, one lucky old fool, would be

able to buy Lynette, and experience her glorious abandon every night of his life until she exhausted him into the grave. One of these old, doddering fools would die with ecstasy on his lips.

And that man would not be Adrian.

True, he'd felt a stirring of jealousy with all his girls. Every bridegroom who enjoyed the fruits of Adrian's labors was the object of envy. But he had always contented himself with the money he made. The money that lessened the burden of debt that had crippled him for so many years. The money that rebuilt his lands, that restored his family honor, that would at last restore his own faith in the world.

Sex and ecstasy were one thing; lands that grew green and supported generations with honor and pride . . . that was something else entirely.

Perhaps he was getting too old for this game. Perhaps he was merely tired of the struggle. Or perhaps, he thought ruefully, Lynette was extraordinary.

Whatever the reason, it did not change the facts. He felt a sharp bite of pain every time a new suitor presented himself, but that did not deter him. With every suitor, he swallowed the ache, smiled, and scheduled opportunities for Lynette to further her acquaintance with all eligible bachelors.

Do not allow Lord Rendlen to touch more than your hand.

M

Lynette stared at the morning's missive. She had grown used to the curt instructions, but this one seemed more irritating than typical. Perhaps it was because of their encounter last night. He had left so abruptly, once again issuing orders without explanation.

"You know nothing," he had said. But he never explained. He never taught her.

"Trust me," he had whispered. And when she had, opening herself up to his gaze, to his touch, he had abandoned her without warning. She had lain on her bed in a daze, unable to believe he was simply gone.

Then she had heard his footsteps go down the stairs. That was when she finally realized he was gone. She would get no more information from him, no more . . . experiences that night. And the shock of that realization had torn through her system like a storm.

How dare he! How could he, when she still lay on her bed quivering from a hunger she did not understand?

But he had. He had known what he was doing to her and exactly how to do it so that she became putty in his hands, a puppet to do as he willed.

So, as she'd pulled the tattered remnants of her shift across her breasts, she'd sworn that this would not happen again. He would not disappear like that again. The baroness had often spoken of the power a woman's body wielded over men. Of the ability to keep them in thrall, endlessly fascinated, entertained, and enmeshed.

She would learn that power. She would weave her net about Adrian. Then he would be incapable of leaving her. He would stay with her and do whatever she wished. Answer any questions she asked. Be whatever she wanted.

But first she had to learn more. She had to discover

the secrets the baroness hinted at. She had to learn them and use them.

Looking up from Adrian's curt missive, Lynette smiled as the baroness stomped into the kitchen. Lynette glanced at a nearby clock. Goodness, for the first time since Lynette had arrived at the Marlock home, the older woman had risen late. Apparently, long hours at the opera house did not improve the woman's temperament.

"Good morning, Baroness. Are you feeling well?"

"Harumph!" was the lady's response. She sat down and reached for the tea.

Lynette eyed her, mulling over everything that had gone between them in the last week. From their first meeting in St. James's, to the joyful moments of their friendship, through the hateful session with Dr. Smythe, she reviewed it all.

There was much that she had trouble forgiving, but in the clear light of day Lynette realized that the baroness was as much a victim here as she was. Perhaps more so, since Lynette would eventually escape. She would marry some old codger, then years later, become blessedly free.

But the baroness had not married well. And though she was now a widow, she was trapped here, training young girls who quickly came to hate her, and wholly dependent upon the viscount for her livelihood. There was no escape for the baroness. No eventual freedom. Her only value was in what she could teach the viscount's girls. In fact, all she did, every action she performed, was strictly regulated by her nephew.

He was the one to blame for what went on in this strange household, not the baroness.

Well, then, Lynette thought with sudden resolve, if the baroness was as trapped as Lynette, it behooved them to pool their knowledge and skills. She did not yet know what she could offer the baroness, but she did know what the woman could teach her.

As for how Lynette would engineer their mutual freedom, Lynette did not yet know. But she would learn. Then the viscount would be in for a surprise. Lynette would hold the power. And together with the baroness, she would make changes.

Setting down her teacup, Lynette turned to the baroness. Her expression was congenial, coaxing, but her resolve was firm. "Baroness . . ." she began.

The woman looked up, her eyes narrowed in suspicion.

"I need to learn."

The baroness snorted indelicately into her tea. "Of course you do."

Lynette shook her head. "No. I need to learn how to trap a man." She shifted forward, gripping the table in her earnestness. "I need to learn how to trap the viscount."

She waited, her breath held for the baroness's reaction. She knew there would be one. Resistance, certainly. But, hopefully, a certain gleam of conspiracy, of shared goals, of hope for a better future. She did not expect what came next.

The baroness stared at her a moment, then abruptly burst into laughter. It wasn't a gleeful sound. Indeed, it wasn't even a happy sound. The lady's laughter was loud, harsh, and angry. It left Lynette stunned. But as the bitter humor continued to echo in the small kitchen, Lynette pulled herself out of her shock.

"Baroness," she said again.

The woman raised her hand, stopping Lynette from speaking. "Oh, pray do not try to explain. I thought it would take longer. You being a clergyman's brat, after all. But it seems you are no more immune than the others." She cackled again. "In fact, you have fallen faster than all the rest."

Lynette straightened painfully in her chair. "I beg your pardon, Baroness, but I don't understand."

"Of course you don't. Not fully." She leaned forward, her face harsh in the morning light. "Shall I explain? You have fallen in love with him. With the viscount."

Lynette reared backward. "I have not!"

"Of course, you have. They all do." Then the baroness folded her arms across her chest and regarded Lynette with clear contempt. "Well, it won't fadge. He hasn't a heart, you know. And certainly not one for his girls."

"Of course he does," snapped Lynette, unsure why she was defending the man.

But the baroness continued, her tone becoming more conversational by the second. "It makes sense, really. A man with a heart would find it hard to marry off a young girl to a wheezing old coot. A man with a heart would respond to tears and sobs and pleas." She pinned Lynette with a fierce gaze. "But not him. He hasn't had a true feeling since his parents died and I . . ." She cut off her words.

Lynette could not allow her to stop. She sensed a secret here. In fact, she had sensed some hidden truth between the viscount and his aunt from the moment she had first seen them together. But there had been too much happening, too much to absorb for her to push further.

No more. Now she felt as if her life depended upon the baroness's finishing her sentence. "You what?" she prodded.

The baroness stood and walked to the pantry. "It does not matter."

"On the contrary," pursued Lynette. "I believe it does." She hesitated, choosing her words carefully. "Do you not see that this is unwholesome?"

The older woman spun away from the shelves of foodstuffs, the pain clear on her aging face. "Of course it is unwholesome!" she exploded. "We are throwing young girls to the wolves! What could be more unwholesome than that?"

The words sent a chill down Lynette's spine, but she pushed the feeling aside. "I do not mean your . . . occupation," she said. "I mean the way he treats you. The way he treats everyone." She flicked her finger contemptuously at his pristine missive. "One sentence. Eleven words and a single letter rather than a signature." She leaned forward. "He gives commands as if we were his servants."

The baroness grabbed a small loaf of hard bread, breaking it in half with barely contained vengeance. "We *are* his servants," she snapped.

"Perhaps I am. Dunwort certainly. But you? You are his aunt. You deserve some respect."

"Deserve!" exploded the baroness, her expression torn between hysterical laughter and bellowing anger. "I deserve exactly what I am getting, my girl, and don't you forget it!" Then she threw the bread down on the table, spared one more glare at Lynette, and stomped out of the kitchen.

Lynette sat for a moment, stunned into silence. But not for long. Soon she slipped out of her chair and ran out of the kitchen. She knew exactly where the baroness was headed. Knew exactly what she needed to do.

She barely made it in time.

The baroness was in her upper parlor, pouring herself a stiff glass of brandy. Lynette arrived just in time to grab the decanter and whisk it away, holding it tightly to her chest.

"Give that back!" the older woman shouted.

"No," responded Lynette fiercely. She knew she had to be careful. She had once before come between a drunk and his liquor, and had been lucky to escape with just a dark purple bruise across her cheek. But unless she missed her guess, she was faster and stronger than the baroness. Reaching behind the older woman, Lynette took hold of the tray of liquor bottles. With a hefty shove, she toppled it onto the floor, breaking more than half the containers. Then she rushed forward, slipping between the baroness and the few remaining bottles.

"What are you doing?"

Lynette squared her shoulders. "I will not let you drink until you explain."

"He will kill you for this!" the baroness exploded.

"Why do you feel you deserve such abominable treatment? Why?"

"Give me that bottle, girl. And get to your room!" The baroness tried to appear firm, but Lynette could see the wild panic in her eyes.

"No." She said the word firmly, her demeanor calm, but inside her heart raced. "Why do you deserve such treatment?"

The baroness clamped her lips shut, clearly furious. But her eyes were not on Lynette. They were on the bottle in Lynette's hand and the intact decanters behind her.

Lynette shifted slightly, making her voice more coaxing. "Only tell me what I wish to know and I shall give you the brandy." She hated bargaining like this, using the woman's weakness against her, but she had no choice. If she was to have any hope of success, of changing this household into something better, she had to know the truth. "What did you do to him?"

"Nothing!" The word came out in a hateful burst of loathing and self-disgust. "His parents were dead. He was a child. And I did nothing!"

Lynette stopped, shocked to the core. Could it be true? Could this woman have abandoned an orphaned boy? She stared at the baroness, watching in horror as the woman seemed to fold into herself, slipping slowly to the floor as she sobbed out her misery.

"I tried. By God, I tried. I begged. I pleaded. I even climbed onto a horse in the dead of night. I told him I would take in the boy no matter what he said. But he followed me. He found me and he beat me and he locked me in the bedroom." The baroness took a great, hiccupping gasp. "He never let me out."

Lynette followed the baroness's movements, slipping down onto her knees beside her. "Who?"

"Horace!" She spat out the name like a curse. The baron. Her husband. "He would not take on an impoverished brat, no matter that I was the boy's only living relative." The baroness looked up, her eyes haunted.

"How long were you imprisoned?" Lynette didn't want to ask, but she had to know.

"Thirteen months. One month for every year he was old." The baroness looked away. "By the time I left my room, Adrian had already solved his own problem." She released a short, bitter laugh. "He was better off here than with me. So I let him be."

Lynette stared at the floor. She couldn't think. Certainly, she had heard stories of husbands who were cruel. Indeed, she had spoken at length with many wives who sported bruises of one kind or another. But this . . . It went beyond cruelty. It was horrific. And the damage to both the baroness and the viscount lingered long after the evil Horace was dead.

Shifting slightly, she turned, not toward the baroness but toward a movement in the hallway beyond. There she caught the steady regard of Dunwort, silently watching the pair of them. She wanted to call out, to ask his advice, but he did not remain. He merely shook his head sadly and turned away, disappearing as all good servants should.

Sad and alone, Lynette turned back to the baroness. The woman was still sobbing, tears coming out in great, wracking spasms of grief. Part of her wanted to hand the woman the brandy. Part of her wanted to share the bottle as they both sought oblivion in its depths. But that would help neither of them. So she set it aside, then held the baroness in her arms until the woman's sobs eased.

Finally, when she thought the baroness would hear her, Lynette worked past the lump in her throat to speak. "That is quite a tale."

In her arms, the baroness stiffened, but before she could react, Lynette rushed ahead, knowing the woman misunderstood.

"I know it is true. There is no doubt of the pain it has caused you. But what I wish to know . . ." She didn't finish, but instead lifted the woman's face to look at her. "What I want to know is, why it is your fault."

The baroness merely stared at her, still slightly dazed.

Lynette continued. "Horace was an evil man, and I am glad he is dead. I know," she said with a shrug, "shocking words. Especially from a minister's daughter, but I mean it. Your husband was evil."

She waited a moment, watching the baroness's eyes until she knew the woman was focused on her.

"Horace was evil, but he is dead now." She took a deep breath. "Why do you still need to be punished?"

The smile was slow, but it came as a bitter quirk of the older woman's lips, a self-mocking grimace that showed more clearly than words exactly what the baroness believed.

"Because I am now living on his charity. Do you not see it, Lynette? I failed to house my only nephew when he was but thirteen. And now that I am a poor widow, an old woman with nothing, he has brought me into his home. I have nothing that he has not provided. The food in my mouth. The clothes on my back."

Her words rambled on, but Lynette could tell the baroness was not thinking about what she was saying. Indeed, she probably was not even completely aware that she spoke. Her mind was focused more on the brandy as she scanned the floor for it. Lynette saw her gaze slip about the room, glancing behind furniture, shifting to look behind the two of them, trying to unobtrusively find a bottle she could reach.

But she didn't see any. That was because Lynette had tucked the brandy away behind her skirts, which were even now damp from the spilled liquor. In fact, behind them was likely an unholy mess of shattered glass and mixed alcohol. But Lynette did not care. Instead, she leaned forward, touching the baroness as she spoke.

"This should be a time for healing. For both of you." She paused, trying to capture the baroness's attention. "Does he know what happened?"

Again the bitter laughter. "Of course he knows. I told him. I begged his forgiveness. He does not want healing. He wants revenge."

The baroness now abandoned all subtlety. She shifted onto all fours, ready to search on her knees for her brandy, but Lynette grabbed her hands, stopping her. "What revenge? He has housed you. Fed you. There is no punishment in that."

The older woman looked up, her eyes intent with a manic gleam. "The punishment is you. Don't you see that? You and Audra and Suzanne and all the other girls he has brought here. He uses them to show me exactly how weak and pitiful I am. He does not think I know, but I do. I know." She looked down. "But I deserve it."

"It was not your fault!" Lynette moved again, trying to pull the baroness away from her increasingly frantic search for the bottle. "And what happens to me or any of the other girls is not your punishment."

"Of course it is! He is showing me what a woman can do. With Audra it came so easily. And as he taught her, I watched. I learned." Then she slumped back against the wall, her entire demeanor defeated. "But I am too old." She gestured at the pale wrinkles on her face, the aged skin on her arms. "I cannot do what you do. I cannot entice a man."

Suddenly she shifted, pushing Lynette aside and

grabbing the brandy. Her new position against the wall had shown it to her. Now she gleefully grasped the bottle, tilting it against her lips as she drank greedily. Then, when at last she had to draw breath, she turned back to Lynette.

"It is too late for me. And every day he brings young girls into the household to show me that."

Lynette stared at the older woman. She heard the words, but more than anything else she heard the lies. If nothing else, her childhood had taught her how to recognize falsehoods. Not the ones between people, but the ones people told themselves. How often had she seen two people, both with equal circumstances but one thriving while the other faltered, his life and skills wasted away in bitter failure? Her father always claimed it was God's will, that perhaps one had sinned horribly and the other not.

At first she had believed him. But not for long. Eventually she'd seen something else. Or rather, she'd heard it. The one who failed was always the one who complained. That was the soul who wasted his life and skills, spending his time wallowing in excuse after excuse, listing his stack of grievances for any who would hear. And more often than not, that task of listening fell to her.

But the more she sat and heard, the more she'd understood how hollow those excuses were. True, many grievances were painful, some even an undeniable reality. But that did not change the fact that others had overcome such difficulties. Others had even found happiness.

While the complainer was left with failure and a long string of excuses.

The baroness, apparently, was one of these. Rather than face her situation, she had chosen instead to crawl into a bottle with her life, her pride, and her excuses.

Lynette sighed, wondering if there was, indeed, any hope for the woman. And if the answer was no, then what could Lynette hope to learn from her?

She stood, looking down at the baroness where the woman had collapsed, crumpled on the floor, bottle in hand. She took a moment, knowing that the baroness saw her, slanting resentful glances upward.

"Does capturing a man involve great beauty?" Lynette asked.

The baroness did not respond at first. She chose instead to take another long pull of brandy. Lynette repeated the question, making it clear that she would not leave until it was answered.

"Does capturing a man involve great beauty?"

"Of course not," snapped the baroness hatefully. "Have you not been listening, girl? It requires cunning. Constant change. A thorough understanding of his baser needs."

"It requires intelligence, then."

The baroness snorted. "Aye. Great intelligence." She slanted another disdainful look upward. "Think you have it?" Her words were more a sneer than a challenge, but Lynette chose to accept it as a gauntlet thrown at her feet.

"Yes, I do," she answered levelly. Then she crouched down, catching the baroness's eyes on her level. "Do you?"

The woman reared back as if slapped. "What are you talking about?"

Lynette pressed her point home. "Trapping a man requires no real beauty. Fine. I am not beautiful. Fine. Neither are you."

The baroness looked away, ready to draw again from her bottle. But Lynette grasped her hand, keeping the liquor out of reach.

"You have a choice, Baroness. Teach me what to do, show me the skills I need."

"Or?"

But Lynette wasn't ready to give her the other option. She was still issuing her challenge. "Pick a man, Baroness. Show me how wiles can work without beauty." She leaned even closer. "Make yourself a greater success than any of the Marlock girls. Show me. Show your nephew exactly what you can do."

The baroness didn't even blink. Instead, she lifted her chin to gaze down her nose at Lynette. "Or?"

Lynette grimaced. "Or finish your bottle of brandy and I will do it myself." She stood and walked away. But with every step she took she prayed, silently imploring God with every breath. *Please,* she begged, *please help her help me. I don't know how to do this alone.*

Chapter 13

The baroness chose to drink the morning away.

Which left Lynette many hours of leisure in which to contemplate their conversation. Oddly enough, it was not the baroness's sad tale that filled her thoughts. It was, in fact, something else entirely.

You have fallen in love with him.

The baroness's words haunted Lynette, making her pace tight circles in her room. Was it true? Had she fallen for the man? She would admit to a certain awareness of him. She constantly listened for his footsteps, wondered at his moods, even occupied herself with tiny fantasies about him. About him touching her. About him *explaining* things to her. But was that "love"?

Of course not. But if she did not love Adrian, why did the baroness's next words bother her so?

He hasn't a heart, you know. And certainly not one for his girls.

And that was when Lynette had to admit to herself that perhaps she had developed a certain attachment to Adrian. Not amorous, necessarily. But emotional. Competitive. He angered her. He intrigued her. He frustrated her. He enticed her.

That was all part of his teaching, she supposed. And she would do well to remember that. Besides, he was not a rich man. He was, in fact, decidedly poor, and not what she wanted. She wanted—needed—wealth. To sponsor her sister. To help her brother. To embark upon her widowhood. And Adrian wanted only one thing himself: the money to rebuild his estate.

Thus, after many hours stewing, Lynette decided to rededicate herself to her original task of finding a wealthy husband. And she could start today, with her drive in Hyde Park with Lord Rendlen.

She would have valued the baroness's input on which outfit to wear, but as the woman was otherwise occupied, Lynette had to make the choice on her own. Uncertain what was appropriate, she picked the most demure costume she could find: a dark blue gown heavy enough for the outdoors. Unfortunately, it also sported a neckline much too low for her tastes.

At least it was not diaphanous.

She donned it carefully, then did her best with her coiffure. It was much more simple than the style she had worn the night before, but it still framed her face sweetly, she thought, and gave her somewhat angular looks a softness.

Her hand hesitated over the cosmetics pots, left from last night. Did she dare attempt it herself? She remembered only some of what the baroness had done, and most of it she thought she could duplicate. But did she dare? On her own?

It took a while, but she finally convinced herself that she did not *not* dare. She needed to captivate an eligible bachelor, and if cosmetics were part of the task, then so be it. She opened the pot.

She ended up scrubbing her face clean three times before she found a balance she liked. She had added only the tiniest bit of color to her cheeks and lips: beyond that, she did not want to go. In truth, as she peered at her reflection, she was hard put to decide if she had indeed added any color, or if it was merely the exuberance of her washing that had put a blush on her cheeks. In either event, there was no more time. The knocker was sounding. He was here.

Now she had a new problem. Without the baroness, she could not properly receive him. She thought of rousing the woman, but by Dunwort's last account, the woman was in a drunken stupor and not fit for company. Her only options were to forego the visit or dispense with the formalities.

Since she could not practice her feminine wiles without a subject, she chose to bend the rules of society. Besides, she thought irreverently, her reputation was already severely blemished; what did it matter? She would have to entertain Lord Rendlen alone.

Glancing out the window, she was relieved to see he had brought a high-perched phaeton. Excellent. She could, with all propriety, ride in that vehicle without a chaperone. It was only in the house that she stretched the rules.

She pressed her face closer to the window, inspecting the carriage as critically as she could. It was a handsome equipage, even by her limited understanding. The paint looked sharp, the equipment sturdy, and the tiger—a sturdy boy in his teens—appeared quite stunning in his livery. In short, it was the vehicle of a wealthy man, and therefore fit her criteria.

She turned as Dunwort knocked at her door. "Lord Rendlen waits below," came his deep tones from behind the heavy wood.

Lynette quickly pulled open her door. She saw Dunwort's creased and worried brow. "The baroness?" she asked hopefully, praying the woman had pulled herself together.

To her dismay, Dunwort shook his head. "Not today. And likely not even tomorrow." He sighed. "Ye pushed 'er hard, girl. She may not stop drinkin' ever."

"I know," Lynette said sadly. She grabbed her bonnet, then slipped past him.

Lord Rendlen awaited her in the parlor. He was dressed beautifully, in a superfine coat of darkest blue that perfectly matched his eyes. His blond locks were in a casual disarray that made him look somehow sinful. And when he raised his eyebrows at her solitary entrance, the speculation in his expression added to his appearance of mischief.

Still, the appreciation in his eyes warmed her from head to toe.

"Miss Jameson, you are a vision indeed."

She dropped into a demure curtsey. "My lord," she greeted. "If I am lovely, then it is only because I strove to be worthy of you."

He grinned, and his face became the visage of an angel. "Are we alone?" he asked.

Lynette hesitated, then chose to be direct. "I am afraid the baroness is indisposed."

"How unfortunate," he murmured. But his eyes betrayed no regret.

"I realize that propriety dictates that we miss our ride together . . ." she began.

"Nonsense!" he exclaimed. "We can ride in the park with perfect ease." He stepped forward, his smile daring her into mischief. "It is only in the house that tongues will wag. As we are alone . . ." His voice trailed away suggestively.

"I think," Lynette said in bracing tones, "that we had best get outside then. Where it is proper."

He sighed in regret, then acceded to her request. But as he offered her his arm, he leaned in close to make a scandalous suggestion. "Perhaps, though, we should spend a little extra time on our ride? We needn't restrict ourselves to a bare half hour and remain solely at the park, need we?"

"But that is not proper," she chided, though with little heat. After all, she was supposed to be flirting with the man. She could not do that if she adhered strictly to the rules of Society, could she?

"I am only thinking of the baroness," he offered as he guided her out of the door. "We must give her as much time as possible to rest."

She bit her lip, trying to be alluring. "Perhaps we could remain out a *little* bit longer than is strictly allowed."

Lord Rendlen's eyebrows raised as he guided her to her seat. "Miss Jameson, I adore it when you are naughty."

She smiled, trying to look pretty. "Then I shall endeavor to be more so." She paused, mentally reviewing her words. That was not exactly what she had meant to say, but she could not retract it now. Especially when Lord Rendlen grinned so beautifully at her before springing up into his phaeton.

The first few moments were spent absorbed in his horses. Or rather, he seemed to be absorbed in the animals. She was more interested in how he managed the spirited team. His muscles were strong and sleek, his concentration fierce. Apparently he took his horseflesh seriously. Excellent, she thought, admiring his skill. It would be a pity to spend so much money on prized horses only to mistreat or ignore them.

Moments later, his team settled, he diverted his attention to her. "So, Miss Jameson. You are a clergyman's daughter."

"No," she responded sweetly. "I am myself. My father happened to be a clergyman." She did not know why she said that. She had never before denied her connection to her parents, even obliquely. Now, for the first time in her life, she suddenly wanted to be her own person. Not her father's daughter. Not a Marlock girl. Not even a sister or a confidante or a friend.

She merely wished to be herself. Out for a ride in the park with a handsome gentleman who happened to be rich and titled.

He nodded, apparently accepting her odd statement at face value. "Very well, Miss Jameson. About what shall we converse?"

She turned, giving him her most guileless smile. Then, for effect, she dropped her fan into her lap, giving him a fuller view of her cleavage. It was an awkward movement. She had never used such a ploy before, but the baroness had been most explicit in teaching her the language of the fan. This drop-and-retrieve tactic, she had said, was the most obvious, but also the most effective.

Men like breasts, so let 'em look.

NAME: ______________________________________

ADDRESS: ____________________________________

____

____

TELEPHONE: __________________________________

E-MAIL: _____________________________________

___ I want to pay by credit card.

__ Visa __ MasterCard __ Discover

Account Number: ______________________________

Expiration date: ______________________________

SIGNATURE: __________________________________

Send this form, along with $2.00 shipping and handling for your FREE books, to:

Historical Romance Book Club
20 Academy Street
Norwalk, CT 06850-4032

Or fax (must include credit card information!) to: 610.995.9274.
You can also sign up on the Web at www.dorchesterpub.com.

Offer open to residents of the U.S. and Canada only. Canadian residents, please call 1.800.481.9191 for pricing information.

If under 18, a parent or guardian must sign. Terms, prices and conditions subject to change. Subscription subject to acceptance. Dorchester Publishing reserves the right to reject any order or cancel any subscription.

Lord Rendlen did not disappoint her. He took full advantage of his superior height. Meanwhile, she spoke the words the baroness had told her to say. "I wish to discuss you, of course! I want to know everything about you. I want to know about your horses, your carriages, your favorite pastimes. Everything! What is your favorite food?"

If he was surprised by her statement, he did not show it. Either that or he was too addled by the sight of her half-bared breasts to object. With the help of a few more jiggles and a little feminine coaxing, he was soon telling her all about his hounds, his horses, his favorite beef pie and cream puddings. He gabbled on about hunting and tailors and the benefits of a good watch fob. And all the while she smiled and jiggled her cleavage and took mental note of everything he said.

If she were to marry him, she would need to know his favorite things.

But after two turns about the park, apparently his tongue grew tired. He turned to her, surprise in his expression. "My goodness, I have told you more about myself than most of my dearest friends know."

Again she gave him her sweetest smile. "I am an excellent listener, my lord. I suppose that was one of the benefits of being a clergyman's child."

"Ah," he remarked, as if he understood. He didn't, of course. No one ever realized how much a cleric's job was to simply listen to his parishioners. Lynette doubted, in fact, that her father even understood. He spent more time telling them what to do, whereas she had been required to listen, to hear what they wanted, and understand what they were not saying.

And in all that Lord Rendlen had told her, she had

heard something else entirely. His lordship, although he liked good tailoring and good hounds and good horses, had a taste for something different. She was not sure what, exactly. He did not tell her.

But he had spent a good ten minutes describing a hunt he had experienced some months before, a particularly bloody hunt wherein two of his hounds became so frenzied after ripping the poor fox to shreds, they had descended upon one another. Blood, fur, and spittle had flown every which way. Lord Rendlen remembered the screams of the fox, the growl of his dogs, and most especially the scent of blood. And he remembered it all in excruciating detail.

Which Lynette found unsettling.

But just as she was becoming distinctly uncomfortable with his recounting of the tale, he had stopped himself, turning the conversation to her.

"Now you must tell me all about yourself," he said. "What are your favorite pastimes? What do you learn in the Marlock household?"

Her gaze sharpened at his last question. Though his expression appeared innocent, she could tell he knew a great deal about what she was learning from the viscount. In fact, she had the distinct impression that he knew more than she, and that bothered her.

Before she could respond, he stopped the phaeton. "I thought we could take a walk," he said. Then he gestured to a tree-lined path.

Lynette eyed the pathway critically. There were other couples strolling along it, and there were, of course, many dozens of other vehicles circling the park. She need have no fear for her virtue here. So she gave him another dazzling smile, thinking that she was already growing weary of these sickly sweet expressions, and agreed as prettily as she could.

He was beside her in a moment, helping her down. Then, faster than she believed possible, they were strolling down the lane.

"Marlock told you about me, didn't he?"

Lynette's step hitched noticeably. "I beg your pardon?"

Rendlen patted her hand in an avuncular manner. "Never fear, my dear. Adrian has never hidden his dislike of me. But that never interferes with business, does it?"

She frowned, not completely understanding what he was saying, but beginning to have an inkling. Still, she played as innocent as she could. "I have no idea what you mean, my lord."

He stopped, turning to face her directly. Lynette had enough time to glance around them. Oddly enough, though nearly a hundred people surrounded them in one way or another, not a one of them appeared in their particular stretch of lane. If she closed her mind to the muted sounds of horses and voices, she could well imagine herself alone with him.

"I shall be blunt. Marlock and I dislike one another. I find him hypocritically priggish, and he finds me uncowed by his arrogance and knowledgeable about his faults. However, business is business, my dear, and he has allowed me to see you today. Why? Because he knows I am an eligible party for his particular wares."

His gaze became even more intense, and Lynette felt a dark chill race down her spine. Still, in a world of new experiences, this one was not necessarily unpleasant. So she shifted, returning his gaze frankly. "You mean you are interested in marrying me, and I, in turn, should be interested in your wealth and position in society."

He nodded. "I enjoy the thought of a Marlock woman."

She took a step away, moving slowly and coyly as she sifted through his words. "Are you proposing, my lord?"

He took her arm, drawing her close to his side. "Perhaps," he whispered, and then, abruptly, he angled in for a kiss.

Mindful of the viscount's instructions, not to mention the broad daylight and hundred people nearby, Lynette swiftly drew away. In fact, in that moment instinct took over. She found herself swinging hard, her open hand prepared to slap him with a stinging blow.

But it never landed.

He caught her as easily as if he had been prepared. Perhaps he had been, because he laughed at her reaction. Then, keeping hold of her wrist, he drew her hand up to kiss her palm through its glove.

"Trust Adrian to find a woman of spirit," he said happily.

She tried to draw her hand back, but he would not release her. And throughout it all, she watched his eyes, glittering with amusement while he restrained her.

Abruptly his expression sobered, and his eyes focused with clear intent. "What did Adrian instruct—" he asked softly.

She stiffened, again trying to pull away. "Release me!"

"—about me?" he continued as if she hadn't spoken. "What were his instructions regarding me?"

Lynette ceased fighting. Indeed, it was useless anyway. He was too strong. And at that moment, another couple rounded the bend.

Again, Rendlen moved more quickly than she expected, drawing her hand down to his arm, slipping into the most demure pose imaginable as they once again began to walk. The maneuver was accomplished before Lynette had time to even register the changed circumstances.

But lest she think he had forgotten, he leaned close to her ear, his hot breath stirring the tendrils of hair about her face. "Tell me, Lynette. What did he instruct regarding me?"

"I did not give you leave to use my given name," she said stiffly.

He chuckled, the sound low and almost guttural. "But I have used it nonetheless." Then he drew her closer, using his size and strength to intimidate her. "You must tell me, Lynette. I shall have it one way or another."

She looked up, seeing his height, feeling his power, and, God forgive her, his ploy worked. She was intimidated. She found herself answering his question without volition, her words pulled out of her by his will alone. "He said you should not touch more than my hand."

She was shocked that she had said the words aloud. Never had she meant to give such information away. And yet there was a strange thrill to his domination. A dark power to his looks and his strength. Part of her enjoyed being dominated thusly.

He must have seen the realization on her face. He must have read it in her eyes, because suddenly he was grinning. He released her, letting her gain a bare inch more distance as reward for her disclosure. "Very well, then," he said softly. "I shall touch only your hand."

Then it began. To anyone watching, they would have seemed the most innocent of couples. A man and a woman simply strolling along the paths of Hyde Park. But no one else could have seen what he was doing to her.

He was touching her hand. Not simply. Not politely. Wickedly. He began by stroking her gloved fingers, pinching occasionally, scratching sometimes, and pressing intimately.

"My lord," she said, but he silenced her.

"All I am doing is touching your hand, Lynette," he returned. "Quite proper, I am sure."

Then he unbuttoned her glove. The motion was accomplished with the tiniest flick of his thumb, but she felt shock reverberate through her entire body. Pulling open the tiny indentation around her wrist, he began to touch the sensitive underside. He stroked it. He massaged it. And, once, he wet his finger in his own mouth, then moved it down to her wrist, drawing a long streak of wetness that chilled her skin.

She was reminded of her night with the viscount. Of the way the air had felt across her naked breasts. And she felt her body tighten in answer to that memory.

But Lord Rendlen was not finished. His moistened finger began slipping beneath her glove, pushing forward, deeper into her covered palm. It was the oddest thing. Completely innocent—a man touching her hand—and yet her entire attention was focused on that finger.

All the while, his other hand was busy as well. While one hand probed deeper into the recessed cavern of her palm, the other stroked and pulled at her fingers. Little by little, the two working together managed to tug her glove halfway down. And by doing that, she suddenly found her fingers restricted, held together even as he continued to wet and touch the cupped recess of her hand.

Her face felt on fire and her breathing hitched, unsteady and uncontrolled. In her mind she kept confusing sensations. She felt Rendlen's touch on her hand, and she remembered the viscount's exploration of her breasts. She felt the cool kiss of air on her moistened palm, and she felt moisture gathering between her legs. The viscount had never mentioned the sensation, but Lynette had felt it nonetheless. Her lower regions seemed to be thickening, liquefying, pulsing.

"This is most unusual," she whispered. Then she bit her lip, startled that she had spoken her thoughts aloud.

"Unusual or delightful?" came his whispered response.

She looked up at him, seeing his glittering eyes, his hungry expression. And, as she watched, he at last divested her of her glove.

Suddenly free, her fingers did not clench. They did not even flex. They extended, opening up, offering her palm to him to do as he willed.

"You are most unusual," Rendlen continued. "Responsive. Intelligent. And still so innocent." He grinned. "I like that."

She did not know how to respond. Her thoughts were still on his hand, on his actions as he toyed with the flesh between her fingers, and his thumb stroked an enticing circle on her wrist.

"I have particular tastes, Lynette. Adrian has begun your instruction, and I suddenly find I wish to continue it."

She gasped then, as much from his words as from the sudden brush of his arm across her nipple. She had been so focused upon his hand that she had not expected another assault. But it had been accomplished easily. After all, he had simply adjusted his hold on her arm. Feeling shot through her like wildfire.

"I want to teach you my particular desires. My tastes."

Again he reached out. But this time, instead of a slight brush, he grasped her nipple and twisted it. She cried out in pain and shock. The move had been bold and aggressive—but a single glance around told her they were hidden from all view.

"That was painful, was it not?" he asked.

She nodded, blinking away tears she hadn't known she'd shed.

"But part of you liked it. Part of you is even now throbbing with the beat of that pain. Part of you wants me to do it again."

She looked away, but he stopped her, lifting her chin until she looked directly into his dark blue eyes.

"Part of you wants me to do it again, yes?"

She didn't know if he moved her head for her or if she nodded of her own accord. The truth did not matter. She did want him to touch her again. She did feel the beat of her own heart, pulsing and throbbing in places and in ways she had not expected.

He did it again. She gasped in pleasure as well as pain.

"You could be trained, Lynette. I could teach you."

She continued to gaze at him, the words coming out without stopping. "Yes," she whispered. "I will marry you." Then she blinked. What had she just said? Not more than a few hours ago, she'd had plans for bringing Adrian to his knees. Now she was accepting Rendlen? What was wrong with her?

She had no answer except to realize that revenge against Adrian was one thing, marrying a wealthy lord another entirely. And in point of fact, it had been the entire purpose of her coming to London. She hastened to recover lost ground.

"There are particulars to be worked out, of course," she said.

This time his grin was slow in coming, lascivious in intent, and almost sly as he drew his hand long and slow across her nipple. It was distended and eager for his touch. And she felt every hill and valley of his palm as an erotic torrent of sensation.

"Yes, Lynette. It is the particulars in which I am most interested." He paused as she waited breathlessly, her breasts aching, her body throbbing. She watched his eyes, waiting for him, for the moment he would touch her again. Finally, it happened.

She gasped in reaction even as he leaned closer, whispering into her ear, "I will marry you if you meet my requirements."

He twisted then, moving her once again to his side. Another couple had rounded the bend, and they were no longer alone.

Lynette's body continued to throb, her knees continued to feel weak and insubstantial, and her breasts felt heavy, hungry, and aching for more. But Rendlen did not touch her again. Indeed, he did not even stroke her hand.

She literally deflated at his lack of attention. It was a crushing feeling, akin to the moment she realized Adrian had left her bedchamber. But as her emotions reeled, her reason began to gradually reassert itself. She mulled over their conversation, remembered his words, and felt amazed that she had completed her task so quickly. So easily.

She had agreed to marry Lord Rendlen!

But then, as they neared his equipage, a thought slipped into her mind. She wanted to push it away, but it was a concern that niggled at her, bothering her enough that she could not rest. She knew it would be impolitic to ask. In fact, she knew that he would likely not appreciate the question. But in the end, she decided on boldness. She had to know. Still, she waited until he was about to lift her up into his phaeton to voice her query.

When his hands were on her waist, she looked directly into his eyes and asked, "What requirements will I have to satisfy, my lord?"

He lifted her up, and she scrambled into the seat, but not before she saw an evasive expression settle onto his features. She had seen it on her father's face enough to recognize the look.

"They are a simple matter, Lynette," he said as she settled. He stroked her leg. "But I assure you, you will enjoy the process."

A chill seeped into her blood. He could not mean to enjoy the marriage bed *before* they were wed, could he? She looked down, wanting to see his face, but he had slipped around the phaeton, going to the other side. And when he settled into his seat, his mind was clearly occupied with his horses.

She did not venture to speak again until they were well out of the park.

"What process, my lord? What would you have me do?"

"Never fear, Lynette. I will teach you."

Who would instruct her was not Lynette's fear. She had other more basic terrors to address, foremost among them the worry that he was lying to her. That he meant to enjoy her without ever giving her his name.

"My lord, I trust Viscount Marlock in all these matters," she lied. "Will you explain this process to him?"

At that, Rendlen pulled back on his reins. They were in an alleyway, one of the hundreds throughout London. But glancing around, Lynette could see it was fairly secluded for all that they were in an open carriage.

Then he did the boldest thing of all. He threw up her skirts. Not completely, but high enough that his hand could slip underneath. Lynette cried out, but suddenly his tiger, the small boy who stood behind them, grabbed her arms, holding her still while Rendlen put his hand on her mouth and stopped her scream. Meanwhile, below her skirts, his other hand assaulted her. There was no other word for it. He pressed and moved and stroked her harshly between the legs.

"Adrian will ruin you, Lynette," he hissed into her ear. "You must agree now. This instant. Then we will begin."

Her legs were pushing her backward, her feet pressing against the floorboards as she strove to move away from his hand. It was horrible. It was vicious. It was too much.

But, clearly, he thought this was pleasure.

"Stop!" she cried, pulling free and shoving at him with her hands. But the boy's arms locked around her, tightened painfully across her breasts, restricted her movements.

Rendlen paused, pulling back slightly so that he could look her in the eye. "I will marry you," he promised.

She knew he was lying. She knew it through every fiber of her being. But she did not tell him that. She allowed herself to relax slightly. Ease down her shoulders. And, as much as she hated it, she let her legs drop slightly open.

Then, as the grin began to spread over Rendlen's handsome face, she abruptly pitched forward, simultaneously breaking the boy's grasp on her and using her skull to connect painfully with the man's forehead.

Rendlen reared back, roaring out in pain. Lynette leaped over the side of the carriage and ran. She dashed away, moving as fast and far as she could. She ran mindlessly at first, not caring where she went so long as it was away.

Behind her, she heard Rendlen's curses, but eventually they faded into the background, covered by the noises of London.

It was some time before she came to her senses. Even then, it was to look around in confusion. She was not sure where she was. But she had always had an excellent sense of direction, for all that she had grown up in the country. She found her bearings quickly, rushing as she hurried along the streets until she finally ran straight up the walkway to the Marlock house.

Never before would she have thought to look on Adrian's home as a place of safety, of purity. But she did now. And when Dunwort opened the door, she flew past him, dashing up the stairs to hide in her room, burying her face in her pillows as she sobbed out her pain, her fear, and her confusion.

Chapter 14

Adrian knew something was wrong the moment he stepped into the house. He had spent a long day answering queries, setting up appointments, piquing interest in Lynette. And with each new question, each casual meeting established, his body seemed to grow weaker, more tired, more depressed.

Now it was well past midnight, and he ached from top to bottom. But the moment he stepped inside the house and saw Dunwort's face, his exhaustion fled.

"What happened?"

The large man shrugged. "Don't know."

He quickly scanned the stairs. "My aunt?"

"Drinking. Since morning. She warn't available when Rendlen came by."

Adrian's heart froze inside his chest. *Rendlen . . . ?*

Suddenly he was running through his house. Taking the stairway two steps at a time, he dashed for her room. His aunt he would deal with later. Right now, he had to find Lynette. If that bastard Rendlen had so much as touched her . . .

He slowed just outside Lynette's door, pausing to listen. There were no sounds of crying. No wrenching sobs as from that other night, after Dr. Smythe. But with Lynette that meant little. She was one who would hold in her pain, releasing it only later, in her nightmares, in a torrent of screaming anguish. He did not want to live through another such night.

Silently he turned the latch, letting the door slide open on its well-oiled hinges. She was there, curled on her side in her bed. Her back was toward him, but he could tell from her irregular breathing that she was aware of his presence.

He wasted no time on preliminaries. He walked into the room, coming around the bed so that he could see her face. "What happened?" he asked.

Her eyes were huge. Impossibly so. And though she was not crying now, he saw the telltale splotches upon her pale skin, and the red rimming her eyes. She had been extremely upset. And alone.

Again he silently cursed his drunken aunt. She should have been aware. She should have sent him a message immediately. Lynette should not have been alone during this time.

Slowly, he sat down on the bed. He wanted to gather her to him, to hold her in his arms. If she came to him, he knew things would sort themselves out. But if she held herself still, frozen away from him, then that whoreson Rendlen had ruined her.

And for that, the bastard would die.

But Adrian did not have time for revenge. He only had thoughts for Lynette. Easing closer to her, he rested his back against the headboard, stretching his legs out in front of him, letting his booted feet rest just off the bed. It was a purposely casual pose, close enough to touch her if necessary, but far enough away to let her feel some measure of control.

"Lynette," he said gently, "you must tell me what happened."

"Where have you been?" She did not say it as an accusation. In fact, her voice was very casual, as if they were merely discussing their day over tea. But he did not feel it as such. He felt a blow, as if she had struck him flat across the face.

"I was establishing your position. Interesting potential bachelors. Your schedule is very full for the next few weeks."

She did not seem to react to his words, and he watched her very carefully. When she was silent for too long, he felt compelled to continue.

"You will be attending card parties, a few masquerades, a ball."

He had hoped the last would spark some interest. What girl did not dream of balls and parties? But Lynette did not respond by even a flicker of her eyes. He had to distract her some way. Get her moving and out of her current mood if he ever expected to hear the truth. So, instead of pressing her, he glanced about the room.

He saw a tray beside her bed. It was filled with cheeses, some ham, even a little fruit. Dunwort had created a tempting display, no doubt hoping to lure her into eating.

Obviously the ploy had not worked, for the food appeared untouched. And even though he had eaten a full meal, at the expense of a potential bridegroom, no less, Adrian still feigned great hunger.

"Ah, I see you haven't eaten dinner. Come, join me. I am famished."

Then he leaned over to reach the tray, but her body obstructed him. He could not grab the food with her curled in her current position. He was careful not to touch her while he made his predicament clear.

"Lynette," he said casually, "would you be so good as to sit up and hand me that tray? It has been a long, difficult day, and I would just as soon not go traipsing around your bed only to return back here to eat."

If he said something so callous to Audra, she would likely dump the entire meal onto his head. But Lynette was reared differently. She had been trained to serve from the very beginning, and so she dutifully sat up and passed him the tray.

"My, my," he wondered aloud, "where shall we set it?" He looked around. Before she could make a suggestion, he plopped it directly onto her lap. Then he settled back against the headboard, still careful not to touch her. "Much better. Now we can eat and converse at the same time." He reached out and grabbed a thin slice of ham.

He waited a moment, hoping she would mimic his actions.

She did not.

"Go on, Lynette. Dunwort went to a lot of trouble, you know, bringing up this tray for you. Even when I was sick as a dog with a sore throat, he did not deign to do so much. He said that unless my legs were broken, I could bloody well come down to the kitchen myself." He paused, turning to see if his comment provoked a smile.

It did not.

"You know, he will be quite hurt if he learns you have not eaten at all. Hurt and worried, I might add."

He didn't like using guilt. It was a poor tool at best, likely to backfire as much as assist. But in this case, it worked. Lynette reached out a slim hand and selected a piece of cheese. He had the satisfaction of seeing her delicately place the food in her mouth and chew.

With luck, he could keep her eating as they chatted, long enough for her to eat an entire meal. And as that happened, he very much hoped she would gain the strength to tell him exactly what went on today.

It worked.

He watched her eat, keeping up a constant prattle, describing one gentleman after another. He listed each man's prospects, age, health, family connections, and more. He told her at which rout or party she would see each gentleman, and he acted as if every one of those pre-arranged meetings would absolutely occur.

Of course, in his thoughts he very much feared that his entire plan, and therefore his entire future, was in question. But outwardly he showed no signs of doubt. And as he spoke, he handed her one slice of ham after another. When she tired of the ham, he pushed the cheese on her. He called Dunwort and had the butler bring up some wine. All in all, he did everything he could to see to the health of Lynette's body before turning to her mind.

In the end, she finally relaxed. And long before he thought to broach the topic, she surprised him.

"You need not keep this up," she said. "I feel much better now."

He stopped in mid-sentence, his thoughts scattering. Slowly he lowered a slice of bread back onto the tray. "I see I must work on my subtlety."

She shrugged. "I am a parson's daughter. I recognize such ploys when I see them."

He was silent, regarding her steadily for a moment. "I never cease to be impressed by you." Then he sighed. "We need not discuss what happened if you don't wish."

The offer was out of his mouth before he could stop it. Then, when his mind returned to his words, he nearly choked in shock. Of course she had to tell him! With any of his other girls, he would have coaxed, ordered, perhaps even bullied until he received his answers. It was too important. If she had been raped—

His gut clenched at the thought. But if it had happened, he needed to know. He needed to help her. He needed to kill that bastard Rendlen with his bare hands.

But that had not happened, he asserted firmly. She had not been molested. She was fine, he told himself. And indeed, looking at her now, she remained pale but composed.

"You have to know, don't you?" she asked. Her voice was soft, subdued. But her eyes were trained on him, watching for any lie.

He nodded. "I need to know what happened. But," he added hastily, "I think you need to tell me as well. How else can we discuss it? How else can you put the matter in perspective? Make sure that it never happens again?"

She looked at him, obviously weighing his words, measuring his ability to counsel. And as always happened with her, he found himself holding his breath while she made her judgment. When she finally nodded, it felt as if he had been handed a great prize. And as he was absorbing her gift, she set aside the tray, folded her hands in her lap, and began to speak.

He expected her words to be hesitant, filled with pain and humiliation, for that was what Rendlen most enjoyed. Instead she spoke calmly, deliberately, as if she was reciting her alphabet for a tutor. She told Adrian every detail, every moment of her ride with the bastard. No emotion colored her voice, and she only stammered once: when she tried to explain where Rendlen had put his hand. She waved awkwardly at her lower body, speaking of him lifting her skirt.

Adrian nodded. He was unable to speak past the fury in his mind, so he could not help her supply the words. Instead, he simply ground his teeth and silently swore vengeance. And eventually she finished her recitation, leaving him both furious and relieved: furious enough to choke the life out of the cur who dared lay a hand on Lynette, relieved enough to praise God that it hadn't been worse.

"I will kill him." He hadn't expected to say that. In fact, the statement caught him as off guard as it did Lynette.

"You cannot mean that!" she exclaimed. She leaned forward, grasping his hands when he hadn't dared touch her. "Think what would happen. You would have to flee the country. I would never marry. Your aunt would be destitute. Adrian, please! Say you will not do it!"

She was right, of course. He could no more afford to kill the swine than he could throw away the opportunity to get Lynette married to a wealthy man.

He could not abandon his aunt, drunken witch though she might be, nor could he, in truth, really spill blood. Even Rendlen's blood. But still, the emotion pulsed hard and primal within him.

"Please, don't be foolish," Lynette begged, her brown eyes imploring. "I could not bear being the cause of such disaster."

He looked down, ashamed to the core of his being. "I am the one who should be begging you, Lynette. Begging your forgiveness. I knew allowing you to drive with him was a risk. I knew it, but . . ." His voice trailed away. She was too bright not to force him to continue.

"But why? Why would you send me off with him?"

He sighed. "Because he draws other men. If he approves of you . . ." He hesitated, then pushed further. "If he wants you, then many other men will desire you, too." He looked away, knowing he had to confess it all. "It drives your price higher, Lynette. So I allowed it." Then he looked back, wondering if she would forgive him. If he could forgive himself.

She nodded, and he saw understanding in the slight droop of her shoulders. Truly, she did comprehend what he had done. Likely more than any of his other girls ever had.

She leaned forward, her words urgent. "It is done now, right? I have been seen with him. He has been seen . . . appreciating me." She took a deep breath as she looked directly into his eyes. "I do not need to see him again?"

He nodded, even as he contradicted her. "You will likely see him. You frequent the same circles now." Then, before the fear could rise in her eyes again, he quickly added, "But you need not speak to him nor allow him to touch you again. You are free of him if you wish it."

"I don't ever want to see him again," she said vehemently. Then she squared her shoulders and looked Adrian directly in the eye. "I do not want to, but if I must see him, then it shall be from across a room. I will never speak to him again."

He smiled, pleased with her spirit. Then he shifted awkwardly, knowing that the hardest part would come next. He had to explain what happened, had to tell her that it wasn't evil. That it was possible to enjoy, not such violence, but such intimacy.

"Lynette . . ." he began. He stopped, not sure how to proceed.

But true to form, she was there before him, her expression serious. "You are going to tell me now that I should expect such attacks. That my . . . position in Society leaves me vulnerable to such liberties."

He hesitated. That was not exactly what he had intended to tell her, but she had nonetheless stepped to a logical conclusion. Everything she said was true.

"All women are vulnerable," he finally said. "There are men who will take advantage of that because they can."

"And I am not just any woman anymore. I am a Marlock girl."

He nodded, hating his name and all it represented while part of him rejoiced that she was now inextricably linked to him. For the rest of her life she would be known as a Marlock bride.

"So, men know about . . ." She swallowed. "About my training. They know and will take liberties because of it. Even when those liberties are . . ." She stopped speaking, and he saw revulsion overtake her.

He leaned forward, quickly grasping her hands to hold them tightly between his own. "Lynette, listen to me. Look at me." He waited a moment until she complied. He saw her focus lift off their joined hands to look openly at him. Trustingly. "Do you think you can view your experience with Rendlen dispassionately? Logically? I know it happened very recently, but could you try?"

She nodded. It wasn't a slow movement or even a frightened one, but one filled with determination. She would try to see the event clearly, without the colorings of passion or fear.

"Do you recall why it was so terrible to you? What frightened you?"

She shook her head. "It was hideous," she whispered.

It was too soon, he thought; the experience was too recent for her to analyze, and so he resolved to wait. They could discuss it again later. But she shook her head, continuing before he could stop her.

"He was cold. Rough."

"Did he hurt you?"

She looked up, shock and pain in her eyes.

"I know the memory hurts. But physically, Lynette, did he hurt your body? Was there a great deal of pain?"

She spoke slowly this time, as if sorting through what happened. "Not a lot. Some. Mostly . . ." Her voice trailed away, then abruptly there was shock in her eyes. "Mostly I was surprised. He had been so . . ." Her voice trailed away.

"So what? Was he kind?"

She shook her head. "No. Not kind."

"Intriguing, perhaps? Exciting? He showed you

something new, didn't he? He touched your hand in a way that excited you. And your breasts . . ."

She looked down at herself, and her hands shifted as she tried to explain. "It was like the way you touched me. Only . . . different."

He knew she couldn't explain, didn't understand. So he tried to help her categorize the experience. "It was faster than you expected. More intense."

"Yes!"

"And there was pain. But no more than you could handle. And it was exciting."

Her eyes widened and her voice came out a bare whisper. "Yes. Exactly so."

"Some people, Lynette, have pleasure and pain locked together in their mind. They cannot have one without the other."

She shifted, and he wondered if he was telling her too much, too soon. "Is that how Lord Rendlen is? Does pain feel good to him?"

He shook his head. "No. I believe he is the other side of the coin. He cannot experience pleasure unless he is giving someone else pain."

"You mean me."

He shrugged. "Or any other victim. His mistake with you is that he went too fast. Many women, especially when trained correctly, are unbearably excited by what you experienced. They join with men like Rendlen in bizarre play. But each experience, each search for the greatest sexual moment is linked with more and more pain."

Her eyes were wide with horror, but her mind was still sharp. Lynette clearly understood what he was suggesting, horrifying as it might be. "How much pain?" she whispered.

"Enough to kill, sometimes." He paused, then continued. She might as well know it all. "If you had gone with Rendlen, he would have killed you. Perhaps not today. He was right that he would have trained you well, but in the ways of pain. It would have taken months, likely. Possibly even years. But in the end there is only one thing that could have happened."

"He would have killed me."

Adrian nodded; then he gripped her hands, trying to impress upon her the truth. "There are many men like that, Lynette. And many other perversions as well." He heard her breath catch in fear, but he had to continue. "You are already well on your way, Lynette. If all goes well, you will have many options in your choice for husband."

"And my one task as a wife will be to keep my husband entertained." Despite her brave front, he heard the terror in her voice.

"Yes."

"No matter what he wants."

Adrian shifted uneasily. "Once you are wed, you can always refuse."

"But I will be a second wife. These old men are always widowers, aren't they? So I will likely be his second, and could be completely cut out of my husband's will. Defeating the whole point."

Again, she had cut straight to the heart of the matter. "Yes."

"So I must please him, even after we are married. Until his death, I will have no assurance of safety."

He squeezed her hand, trying to reassure her. "Your marriage contract will specify a minimum amount required in the will. When your husband dies, your future will be adequately prepared for." He took a deep breath. "However, that amount is often minimal. And by the time your husband dies, you will have become accustomed to a great deal more."

"So it behooves me to keep my husband happy. No matter what his interests are."

He could tell the thought frightened her. In truth, it had frightened him many a time, but he was blessed by being born male. He did not face the same choices. Or rather, the same lack of choice.

He gently raised her chilled hands, laying his lips softly against her fingers. "It behooves you to choose wisely. You must make sure that your husband's interests are not dangerous."

She shook her head, not so easily soothed. "But I can never know, can I? Not until I am wed. There are countless women in my father's church who thought they knew the men they married, but after the vows were spoken, after they were bound by God and man, they discovered the truth. Only then were they insulted or beaten or imprisoned within their own homes."

She was right, and they both knew it. Still, he would lessen the risk. "I investigate the bridegrooms very carefully. I will know." He paused. "And many tell me their . . . requirements beforehand. As a way to make sure you are prepared."

She looked at him, and he knew she wanted to trust him, wanted to believe. But her reason would not allow her. "Have you ever been wrong? Ever deceived?"

He felt his body tense. He did not want to admit the truth, not now.

She saw it nonetheless. Breathlessly, she pressed onward. "Who?" she asked.

"Suzanne," he admitted, the name harsh in his

throat. But he swallowed the pain. Then he looked down at the end of the bed, unable to meet her eyes as he confessed. "I did not know. I swear it! Despite everything, I did not know until after. I saw her one day, bruised about the neck. Limping."

He heard Lynette gasp, but he forced himself to continue.

"At first she wouldn't talk to me, but I knew her. I knew how to ask, and in the end she told me it all." He looked up, but not at Lynette. He stared at the door between their rooms. The door that adjoined her experiences to his own. What would it be like? he wondered for the thousandth time, to see that door and know that any moment your husband might come to you. Might beat you. Might try to choke the life out of you as he rutted on you from behind. What would it be like to night after night be faced with that horror?

He could not imagine it. And yet his sweet, gentle Suzanne had withstood it, lived it, and in the end, told him of it.

"What happened?" whispered Lynette. "Is she married to him still?"

He nodded, the movement harsh. "But he is not hurting her anymore. He . . ." He took a deep breath. "He met with some footpads. They beat him within an inch of his life, and then left him for dead."

He heard her soft sigh. "But he did not die?" she asked.

Adrian shook his head. "No. But he is an old man. The night air, the injuries . . . He caught an illness. An inflammation of the lungs." He shrugged. "Suzanne says he can barely lift his hand. She has to feed him broth day and night. He wheezes as he speaks."

He felt her shift beside him. "But he does not hurt her anymore."

Adrian closed his eyes. "No. He does not hurt her."

Both were silent for a time, and Adrian blessed her understanding. Though Suzanne's mother had brought her to him, she was the one who'd chosen to marry with his help rather than trust the boys of her own poor circle. She had been easy to dress and teach, his most beautiful girl in the classical style. Blond curly hair, eyes that made one think of the heavens. She had been delicate. Fragile.

But now when he looked at her, he saw the strength within her, the reserve that had allowed her to withstand everything—his training, her brutal marriage, and now her husband's illness—all with grace and poise. She awed him, and he sincerely wondered if he could have done half as well.

"It was fortunate, then," Lynette said. "About the footpads, I mean."

He turned to her. He wasn't sure why. Only that a note in her voice caused him to search her face. Then he saw it: understanding. She knew what he had told no one, not even Dunwort.

He had hired the footpads. He, in fact, had been standing in the shadows watching as each hired thug beat and kicked and choked Suzanne's husband, just as the brute had beaten and kicked and choked his wife. Then he had called off the men and walked away, leaving the great Lord Brancock to die on the street.

"I could not let her suffer like that," he whispered. "Not Suzanne. Not like that."

Then the strangest thing happened. Before, he had worried about Lynette, wondered if he dared touch her, draw her into his arms to comfort her. Now she touched him. She wrapped her arms around him and bent her head. Her hair fell over his face, its honeysuckle scent wrapping around him in a soothing embrace.

She pulled him closer to her, drawing him deeper into her arms. And he went. Like a child, he pressed his face to her breast and lay there, crying as he had not for years. He had not wept in such a fashion when his parents died. Nor even when Jenny cast him aside in favor of a wealthy protector. And certainly not when each one of his girls had walked down the aisle, entering a marriage of servitude with an old man.

He wept for no discernible reason except that he was in pain. He could not say he mourned his parents. Or his mistress. Or even his charges. He cried without understanding the cause.

Perhaps it was because he had broken his promise to Suzanne. Despite all his efforts, he had not kept her safe.

Perhaps it was because this brutality was the nature of all the husbands who married his girls. Any who would buy a woman such as he could provide would not be a normal man. He would not have typical tastes. He would, of necessity, seek out Adrian and his girls. Which meant that every such husband—even Lynette's—would be cruel or brutal or perverse or, at best, simply insatiable. Such were the men who came for Adrian's charges. Such were the men who bound them in unholy matrimony.

And so Adrian wept, because the truth was that he was not helping his girls. He was selling them in the basest, cruelest, most hideous of ways. Most of the time he convinced himself that he aided his charges.

That after a decade of servitude, they would be free—wealthy widows who could make their own lives.

But was it worth it? Could he know that ten years of perversity would be better than the life they might have chosen without him? Perhaps Suzanne could have become an actress. Maybe Audra would have been content with less, assuming it wasn't complete poverty.

He didn't know, and so he wept. Because now the one woman he most wanted to protect, his darling Lynette, was comforting him, holding him, whispering soft words of compassion. And yet he knew as surely as the sun would rise in the morning, soon she would revile him.

Because soon he would give her to one of those men.

Chapter 15

Adrian woke early the next morning. He did not even remember going to bed and, as he opened his eyes, he suddenly realized he had not. He had slept with Lynette. All night. Indeed, she was still there, relaxed and curled like a kitten against him.

He blinked and rubbed his face, amazed at how rested he felt. Then, listening to the sounds of the hawkers just outside the window, he realized it was still morning. In fact, he realized with a start, it was *early* morning. He had not woken at this time, refreshed; in years.

He knew the reason, though the event was no less amazing because of it.

Lynette.

He had slept so well because of her. He had cried—literally cried!—in her arms, until he had fallen asleep, and she with him. Looking down, he noted that they were both still dressed, his clothing hopelessly creased. Yet, he thought with a tender smile, he had slept like a child. He could not remember such a dreamless, healing night since before his parents died.

The urge to touch her was nearly overwhelming. She rested on her side, one hand tucked beneath her cheek, the other still across his belly as if she had held him to her all night long.

He wanted to kiss her. To thank her for what she had done for him. But he resisted. She had a long, hectic few weeks ahead of her. She needed all the rest she could get. And he did not need to deepen his connection to her.

Already he felt as if her upcoming marriage would tear him apart. How much worse would it be if he allowed himself the intimacy of morning kisses? Of waking caresses? And how would he stop himself from going well beyond the bounds by even his very lax standards?

No, he thought with gut-wrenching regret. He had to leave her. And as soon as possible. Besides, he reminded himself as he eased out of bed, he had something else to do this morning. Something she need not witness.

He dressed quickly, using the time to stoke his fury. It wasn't hard; all he need do was remember Lynette as she was last evening, curled in her bed, shaken and afraid. He recalled everything she had told him, her every experience with Rendlen, delivered in her frighteningly flat tone, and his vision ran red.

He could not do anything to the bastard who had caused the distress. Unfortunately, Rendlen was well beyond his reach. However, his guard against such men, the person Adrian had set to protect against such men, had not been at her post. And for that she would pay.

By the time he left his bedchamber, he was as near to shaking with rage as he had ever been. He found her where he expected. His aunt was seated in the upper parlor, an empty bottle near her hand, her head and body limp in drunken stupor. The stench was hideous. The sight even worse. Bile rose in his throat as he stared at her. He did not know what had set her off this time, nor did he care. He could not afford such a liability in his home.

He stepped forward and gripped her shoulder, trying to shake her out of her sleep.

"Aunt Agatha."

She barely stirred.

"Aunt Agatha! Wake up!"

She shifted. Coughing and sputtering as she came to her senses, she sat up abruptly, peering in foggy confusion about her. Adrian pressed his lips together in disgust as she reached for her bottle. He pulled it away.

There was no liquor left, in any event.

Tossing the bottle aside, he quickly crossed to the sideboard. He frowned as he saw a mess of broken bottles and stale liquor on the floor: another disaster to lay at his aunt's door. Fortunately, the decanter he wanted was still there.

It was an elegant bottle, one of the few remaining from his parents' devastated estate. He thought it might have come from his mother's family, but he wasn't sure. The cut crystal was simple, elegant, and beautiful. And in it he kept the best liquid of all.

Water.

On the rare occasion when he invited potential bridegrooms to his home, he often served them the beverage of their choice—some sort of spirit, mixed strong. For himself, he never wanted anything to fog his mind, so he took water mixed with food dye. Because it came from a cut-crystal decanter, his guest believed it was fine brandy. Adrian knew well how to appear slightly in his cups, when in truth his mind remained sharp as ever.

He poured his aunt a glass of it now: plain water. And he had to stop himself from throwing it in her face. She took the glass greedily, gagging when she realized the contents.

"Water?" she gasped, then cringed as the sound no doubt hurt her head.

"You would be wise to drink it down, Aunt." He did not say more, but his tone must have registered somewhere inside her befuddled mind because she did not protest. Obediently, she lifted the glass and drained it.

He poured her another. By the time she had finished two glasses, she appeared awake enough to hear him. If she was not, he could not find the sympathy to care; she would hear it now whether she was ready or not.

"You began drinking early yesterday."

It was a statement, not a question. Still, he was not surprised when her gaze shifted to the window, narrowing as she realized she had lost an entire day and night.

"I—" she began. But he cut her off.

"I do not care how or why this happened. I care only that because of your negligence, Lynette was nearly raped."

The baroness's eyes grew wide with horror. "What happened?"

"That was your job to know. Instead you chose to drink yourself insensible."

She sat up straighter, fear lighting her eyes. "I could have stopped it?"

He swallowed, part of him wishing to deny the truth. But in his home he was always honest. Even to her. "I do not know. Certainly you could have minimized the damage."

She made to rise, her feet and arms obviously unsteady. "I will go to her."

"She is sleeping. And I have taken care of the matter." His voice was cold, releasing some of his tension onto her because, in truth, he did not know if he had handled the situation. Lynette defied understanding. More and more, he found himself being led by her as much as leading. It was unsettling.

"You are in my home for one reason and one reason only," he continued firmly. "I value your expertise with the girls." He clenched his jaw, angry at the wasted life he saw before him. His aunt was the living embodiment of exactly what he wanted his girls to avoid: a destroyed life because of a bad husband. "You were a handsome woman once."

She shot him a look filled with resentment. "When I was young."

"When you did not drink."

He saw her hand spasm, as if searching for her bottle. But to her credit, she did not move. Not by a shift in her gaze did she betray her longing for a drink, but he knew it consumed her.

"If you cannot perform your duties, you will leave this house."

Once again he saw fear flame in her eyes. It was strong enough that she nearly leaped out of her seat, but her legs were not up to the task. "You would toss me out? Your only blood kin?"

He nearly laughed aloud. Instead, he took a single step forward, his anger more than matching her fear. He wanted her afraid. He wanted her terrified. So he let his fury blaze through him, hoping to sear his words into her brain.

"All blood connection between us was severed when I was thirteen."

"You know that was not my fault!" she shot back.

"I don't care!" he returned, amazed to find himself bellowing. Abruptly he spun away, placing his hands on the table that usually held her liquor. "Did you think you were here because you are my aunt?"

He was silent, awaiting her answer. She did not give it. He turned back to her, staring coldly at her feeble frame. Yes, he realized, she did think that. She honestly believed he felt a family tie. To her.

"Never," he said firmly. "You were never here because of some shared ancestor. My family died years ago. I have none left."

He saw his words hit like blows, and he was glad of it. He stepped forward, wanting his words to hurt, to pound away the illusions she surrounded herself with, to reveal the naked, ugly truth. Finally it would be open between them. Finally it would be clear.

"You are here because you can teach the girls some things. I value your knowledge. And I valued you because of it."

He heard her sharp intake of breath. Good, he thought with cold satisfaction. She understood. Still he pressed his point, making it so plain that even her brandy-soaked brain would not forget.

"You know how to make a woman appealing to a

man. In return, I give you food and lodging and a position by my side." He cast his gaze disdainfully up and down her filthy body. "If you fail one more time, I will happily toss you out and hire a whore instead." He spun on his heel. "Jenny can recommend a good one."

He cast a disdainful eye back on the broken bottles. "One who costs less in liquor."

Then he stepped out into the hallway.

He was not looking where he was going, his thoughts entirely focused on his aunt behind him, so he was startled when he nearly toppled over Lynette standing there, empty food tray in hand. She was dressed, and had probably been on the way to the kitchen when she overheard the argument.

For a moment he experienced a wave of panic. What would she think of him—a man who would toss his last living relative out on the street with no ounce of compunction or remorse? How vile was such a man in her eyes?

Then he shook his head. He did not care what she thought. If such knowledge served to distance her from him, all the better. It would make it easier for her to wed another man. He turned and proceeded down the hallway with barely a backward glance.

She followed him. He was not surprised. Lynette was often tenderhearted, and she would no doubt seek to soften his words. Force him to modify. She would be disappointed. His ultimatum to the baroness stood. She either performed her duties, or he would throw her out of his house like so much refuse.

Without even realizing it, he found himself in the kitchen, searching for his morning tea.

Dunwort was there, pouring the hot liquid even as

he pushed open the door. The older man looked up, his expression carefully blank.

Thankfully, the servant said not a word as Adrian stomped in. And when the door swung open to admit Lynette, the butler merely bowed and disappeared. A good man that, Adrian found himself thinking. Performed his duties and knew when to disappear. A man worth his weight in gold.

"My lord?"

"I thought we decided you would call me Adrian." His voice was curt, his words harsh. But even though he now strove to keep some distance between himself and Lynette, he resented her formal tone. Dammit, he liked the sound of his name on her lips.

"Of course," she said smoothly. Then he heard her put down the tray. Glancing toward her, he saw that her movements were unsteady and somewhat slow. As though she were searching for the right words to say. "Adrian . . ." she began.

He forestalled her. "Do not even try, Lynette. I have issued my orders. She will either obey or not." He lifted his tea, sipping though the brew scalded his tongue.

"Of course," she answered smoothly. He watched from the corner of his eye as she pulled down her own cup and sat beside him. When she reached forward to grab the teapot, he was momentarily distracted by the sight of her arm. It was long. Delicate. Beautiful.

And strong enough to hold him through the night.

She took a breath, and he closed his eyes. He did not want to hear her plead for his aunt. He wanted her to speak to him. To touch him. To continue the soothing caresses she had begun last night.

"Do you truly have no feeling for her?" she asked.

He flinched. Her words made him sound like a monster, but he would not deny the truth. Not to his aunt; not to Lynette. So he lifted his gaze, meeting her eyes with a firmness he hoped she found convincing, because it was the absolute truth.

"No feeling whatsoever, Lynette." He sighed. "Truly, I have tried. But when I look at her, I feel . . ." His words trailed away and he lifted his hands in a gesture of futility. "I feel nothing." His hands dropped back to the table.

"I am not sure I can understand that," she said. "For all his faults, my father will always be my father. Whenever I think of him, I will feel something. Whether anger or love, I do not know. But I cannot imagine . . . nothing. He could never be just another person to me, another soul on God's Earth."

Adrian looked at her and felt the constriction in his chest tighten another notch. "That is good, Lynette. I would not wish you to lose the capacity to feel."

She tilted her head and regarded him. "Is that how it is for you? Do you feel nothing at all? For your charges?" she asked. "For Suzanne or Audra or the others?"

"For you?"

She nodded, acknowledging his question. Then she leaned forward, searching his face as she spoke. "What do you feel for us? Are we merely instruments in your plan to rebuild your estates? Tools you use to good advantage, then discard?"

"I . . ." he began, but then stopped himself. How to answer? Did he tell her the truth? How could he not? "I study you, Lynette. As I have studied and learned all my girls. They are . . . you are my student, and I must teach you valuable skills to survive. The reward for my efforts is money I use to rebuild my home. My family estate."

She nodded as if she understood. "But what of your feelings?"

When he did not answer, she stood, moving to the pantry, where she found bread and jam, bringing it back to the table as she spoke. "When you touch me, I feel . . ." Her voice trailed away, and he saw her gaze grow abstract. Suddenly it sharpened on his face, as if she was asking a question as much as stating a fact. "I feel an intimacy between us."

He nodded. "Such is the nature of what I teach. The sensations I produce in you are new, surprising, sometimes overwhelming. When I give that experience to you, when anyone shares such momentous occasions, a bond naturally develops."

"Yet you say you 'study' me. You 'teach' me." She turned to face him full on. "You do not care for me?"

He shook his head. No statement could be farther from the truth. "Of course I care for you, Lynette. I care for all my girls."

"And love?" she pressed.

"Do not seek to love me, Lynette. I do not share your feelings." He swallowed, pushing his words past the constriction in his throat. "I cannot."

She held his gaze for a moment, then looked down. In her hands she held her bread, covered now with jam. But she did not move to eat it. In fact, she set it back down. She spoke, her tone almost casual, clearly oblivious to how each word cut him.

"I had not realized how hard this must be for you." She lifted her gaze again. "To touch and not to have. To . . ." She paused as she gestured weakly toward her body. "To express love but not feel it." She pushed away from her chair but did not leave. Instead, she stepped closer to him, reaching out to gently caress his cheek. It was the lightest of touches, but he felt it burn.

"I do not envy you your task, my lord. I hope when I marry I will finally restore your estates." She shook her head. "But the cost to your soul has been great." Her hand fell away. "I do not know how you bear it."

Then she left, turning away from him as all his girls eventually did. She walked out of the room while he sat there—his cheek on fire as if she had branded him. And for all the pain, all the confusion that swirled through his benighted soul, one thought remained. One thought echoed in his head.

She knew. She knew what he did and what it cost him. She knew better than him. And when she spoke the knowledge aloud, she cut him as never before. How could she understand? How could she know what he kept hidden from everyone, including himself?

Looking down at the fragile cup in his hand, he suddenly grew furious. Grasping it tightly, he threw it across the room. The tiny cup shattered on impact, sending shards and brown tea flying. And as he watched the liquid slide down the wall, he was reminded of the mess abovestairs: the pool of dried liquor and broken glass near the baroness's feet.

How untidy his life was now. And how sad.

He looked at his empty hands and wondered at what he had become. Was this worse than the debtor's prison he sought so desperately to avoid? Was what he did worse than what poverty daily heaped upon its wretched sufferers?

Did he hurt his girls, or help them?

There was no answer in his upturned palms. Neither was there wisdom in the broken teacup or the dark bottle of brandy in his bedroom. There was only himself, his plans, and Lynette. And an aching emptiness only she seemed to understand.

Taking a deep breath, he fought to subdue his thoughts. These questions often tortured him, especially at night when the darkness surrounded him. But he knew how to deal with them. In fact, it was a simple matter of setting the thoughts aside. He thought of the rich green fields of his estate, and juxtaposed it with wretched memories of prison.

He knew which picture he wanted: the prosperous green fields. And no drunken aunt, empty soul, or too-wise clergyman's daughter would sway him from gaining it. Squaring his shoulders, he looked about him, searching for a rag to clean up the spilled tea. There was no need for Dunwort to see how much his master had lost control.

He needn't have bothered. Before he could even step away from the table, Dunwort appeared, rag in hand. Not by so much as a flicker of his gaze did the man betray surprise at the mess on the floor; wordlessly, he bent down and began to clean.

Adrian meant to stop him. He meant to lean forward and tell his old retainer that there was no need for such servile behavior between them. They had gone through too much together. This was one disaster Adrian should repair himself.

But he did not do it. Indeed, as he watched the older man's capable movements, Adrian realized he did not know how. How did one wash tea off stone?

How did one clean dried brandy out of a braided rug? And how did one function so quietly, so capably in a household so steeped in discord and sin that even the neighbors shunned the sight of you?

He did not know.

He took refuge in what he could do, in words and actions he had memorized from girl after girl after girl. He pulled out a sheet of foolscap from where Dunwort kept it for writing down kitchen lists, and with his quick, bold hand, wrote two sets of orders. The first told the baroness to prepare Lynette for the appointments to come. The second went to Lynette, listing each and every gentleman she was to meet, the time and location.

With that completed, he handed the missives to Dunwort for delivery and quit the house. He had his club and a bottle of brandy waiting for him.

Lynette stared at her list of appointments with an empty heart. In fact, she began to wonder what had happened to the organ. When she checked, it did indeed still beat within her chest, but that was all it seemed to do. It kept her alive, nothing more.

Quitting the kitchen, Lynette went upstairs to see how the baroness fared. She found the woman on her knees, cleaning up the broken glass and spilled liquor on the floor. Lynette helped, and they worked side by side without speaking. Then the older woman left, mumbling something about a bath. Moments later, Dunwort appeared with a missive and handed it over before departing.

The final blow came as the front door slammed and Adrian, too, fled her presence.

Which left Lynette alone, staring at a list of gentlemen, with no thought of what she was to do or how to go about doing it.

She looked at the mantel clock and saw she had many hours before her first activity. Tonight she was to go to a card party and meet a certain Lord Marston, who, it was noted, apparently had a predilection for dogs.

She knew she should search the library for a reference on canines. Indeed, she was fairly certain the baroness would soon appear to quiz her on that very subject. But she did not wish to study right now. She had no desire to learn more about dogs, or to impress an aged peer with a false fascination for creatures she had long since deemed smelly nuisances.

Instead, she wanted . . . She did not dare voice aloud what she wanted. Not even to herself. But the words whispered through her mind nonetheless; she wanted to return to last evening. She wanted to relive each moment as Adrian had fallen into her arms.

She had held him all night. Indeed, she had spent many hours after he slept glorying in the wide expanse of his back, in feeling his heavy weight upon her shoulder, in marveling at how his legs intertwined with her own.

She wanted to return to those moments when her life had seemed simple. Last night the world had narrowed to herself and him. No others. No thoughts of anyone or anything else intruded on their solitude. It had simply been the two of them, without tension—not even the haze of desire that surrounded them whenever he sought to teach her.

It had been peaceful. Healing. She had slept deeply

and easily, waking only when she realized her arms were empty.

But now the night was over, and the morning brought more pain than she could have imagined. Was she supposed to simply return to the way things were before? Before she had held him? Before she had seen how much anguish Adrian hid in his soul?

She could not. And yet what else could she do?

In the end she decided to follow his instructions. But not the ones he had just given her. She chose instead to do something else.

Slipping upstairs, she rummaged through her few belongings, finding her copy of the Bible. It had been a great luxury to have one of her own. Indeed, her family had only the one primary Bible, with which all of them had learned their letters. But she had saved her pennies, skimped where she could on the parish books, and hoarded the tiny gifts some of the parishioners had given her in thanks. In the end, she had bought her own.

Now it lay at the bottom of her satchel, nearly forgotten. When she opened the well-worn pages, she did not turn to her favorite stories. She did not open the pages to Ruth's devotion or Eve's disgrace. She opened to the Song of Solomon.

She had never read the poem before. Her father's sermons had always focused on what he called the great texts: parables of punishment and reward, stories where the sinners were incinerated or turned to salt. But her father wasn't here. So she lay on her bed, smelling the lingering scent of Adrian's bay rum on the sheets, and read about love.

The language was beautiful, the words intriguing.

The first time she read for meaning, seeing the pictures in her mind, glorying with the lovestruck groom, languishing with the momentarily abandoned bride.

The second time she read more slowly, focusing on words and images she was not sure she understood. She frowned over words about myrrh running off the bride's fingers, of dew soaking the groom's hair. And she longed to understand the unfamiliar scents the poems mentioned, the essence of pomegranate trees that intrigued her without explanation.

Then, the third time, she read the entire sequence aloud. She let the words roll off her tongue, and as she spoke she pretended she was reading to someone else. Or that someone else was reading to her. In her mind's eye she saw Adrian lounging beside her, his body relaxed, his mellow voice slipping through the night air to wrap her in a cocoon of sound and sensuality.

That the Bible could contain such beauty astounded her. That she responded so deeply to it relieved her. That Adrian would know of this text, know about its secret power over her, did not surprise her in the least.

It was right somehow that her teacher would know. And as she closed her eyes after reading the last word, she dreamed he was beside her, completing the story, showing her the lovers during their wedding night, teaching her the secrets that her Bible did not reveal, showing her what love between a man and a woman truly meant.

Hours later, she awoke. She came alert with a start, her eyes scanning the room, searching for Adrian. Where had he gone? Wasn't he here just a moment ago? Or had that been a dream?

With a sinking heart, she realized it *had* been a dream. And this was reality: the baroness standing above her, glaring down and holding a scandalous dress in her hand.

"Put this on," the woman said. "Then I shall crimp your hair."

Chapter 16

Lynette's days fell into a monotonous routine. She should have been swept up in excitement, moving from card party to rout to masquerade, but there seemed to be no joy in it. She wore her earrings and her clinging, low-cut gowns. She even learned to move suggestively while following the staid patterns of the current dances.

But Adrian's nighttime visits to her room had ceased.

The first night without him, she was confused. The second she became alarmed. Had she performed badly? By the fourth night she accepted the inevitable. He would not visit her. In fact, he barely spoke to her.

And then, without warning, he was back.

She was applying a light dusting of cosmetics, at which she had become quite adept. In fact, the baroness—a scrupulously sober baroness—had spent many long hours helping her apply just the right amount depending on time of day, type of event, and color of her gown. But tonight, just as she had put the last dab of color on her cheeks, Lynette looked up to see Adrian's reflection in her mirror. His appearance was so sudden and so unexpected that she gasped and nearly dropped the rouge pot.

Only his quick movement prevented disaster. How he was able to catch the tiny ceramic container when she couldn't remember how to breathe was beyond her comprehension. But catch it he did. And as he returned it to her dressing table, he spoke, his voice clipped and devoid of emotion.

"Lord Finton has taken ill. You will not see him tonight."

"Oh," she said breathlessly, "then am I to meet someone else?"

She noted he wore formal garb: dark breeches and coat, alleviated only by the pristine expanse of a snowy white cravat. With his dark hair and brooding eyes, the sight of Adrian in formal wear never ceased to snatch her breath away.

"We are going somewhere else."

She raised her eyebrows. He had not deigned to go anywhere with her lately. She and the baroness had attended every function on their own. Many times, of course, Lynette had caught sight of his dark presence across the room, but they rarely joined company and never, ever spoke. That they were to travel together somewhere was astonishing.

"We leave in five minutes." He glanced dismissively at the elegant gold gown she wore, his perusal taking barely more than a second. "That dress is acceptable."

He left while she remained frozen helplessly before her mirror.

It took some time, but eventually she shook off her stupor. *Wake up, girl!* she chastised herself. But she still could not shake off the tension that gripped her belly.

What was about to happen? What—

She abruptly cut off her thoughts. She thought too much. She dreamed too much. And it always led to trouble. Had not her dreams of the last two weeks only led to a worse awakening every morning? Had not sitting and listening for Adrian's tread in his bedroom only set her up for hours of useless longing?

He did not visit her at night anymore. Dreaming about it only made it worse. He did not touch her as he once did. Wondering if he might now would only make her more distraught when this trip turned out to be another card party or stupid promenade down an equally ridiculous path.

Lynette grabbed her wrap, hurried out of her room, and slammed the door on her speculations. What happened would happen. She would not think about it.

She gasped as Adrian pulled her into a hired hackney and shut the door. They were moving before she had time to realize that the hard seats bruised her bottom and the straw on the floor poked into her slippers. As the carriage picked up speed, she peered into the darkness across from her, wishing she could see him as more than just a dark shadow.

"We are not waiting for the baroness?" she asked, hating the way her voice trembled.

His voice was stilted and curt in the enveloping blackness. "She will not be joining us."

"But where are we going?" Despite her vow to accept what came, Lynette found she could not easily suppress her curiosity. She doubted Adrian would answer. In fact, he remained silent for so long, she gave up hope. Then, abruptly, his voice drifted through the darkness.

"We are going to Jenny's."

Lynette had met so many women in the last few weeks, so many names, that *Jenny* did not at first register. Then, finally, she recalled. "Jenny, your mistress?"

His laugh was harsh. "Not mine. Nor any other man's, in truth. Jenny is her own mistress, even when she plays with the rest of us." The seat squeaked as he leaned forward, and in the weak moonlight she saw the pale outline of his face. "That is what I want for you, Lynette. To learn what she knows."

Lynette's mouth went dry. "How to become a whore?"

He released a coarse laugh. "How to play with a man, entice him, enthrall him, even own him while always, every time, every night, you remain completely and wholly yourself." For the first time in over two weeks, he reached out and touched her, stroking her arm with the lightest of caresses. "It is so easy to lose oneself, Lynette. You must hold tight to who you are."

"Why?" The word was out without thought. Lately she had become so tired, so exhausted by the endless parade of men, that she'd begun to think of surrendering. Of giving up everything to Adrian—her thoughts, her fears, her loneliness. She would let him decide everything for her, and then, maybe, she would find peace. She began to wonder if it were already happening. Indeed, she was losing pieces of herself every day.

"You must be strong, Lynette. You are too precious to destroy."

She tensed as he continued to stroke her arm, her body and mind at war. It was not his words that disturbed her. It was her reaction to him. After all this time, she still longed for his caress. For weeks now he had outlined and explained her various options in husbands. He always made it absolutely clear that the gentleman who gained the privilege of her bed would not be him. And yet, after all that, she still longed for him.

Oh, Adrian. Her pulse leapt at his touch. His voice stirred her as no other. It was all she could do not to throw herself shamelessly into his lap.

But her mind would not let her. Her reason repeated all the things he had said. All that she had decided as well: about the older man she would wed. About the Season she could give her sister, the commission for her brother. About how she would prepare her husband's meals, grace his table and his home, and entertain him at night. The poetry she would read to him. The caresses she would give him. How she would hold him through the night.

She had planned all of this, and then she'd thought about what she would do with her time after he died. She would go to the theater as often as she liked. She would take her family out for ices at Gunters and buy them all the clothing and presents they could want. They would not face this life she had chosen. She had long since decided that.

Perhaps she would buy a place in the countryside and go for long walks alone during which she would never worry about seeing another soul, and would never have to care whether she was dressed appropriately, whether her skin showed to its greatest advantage, or whether some man would take her into a dark alley and do vile things to her.

All these things she would do. And none of them would include Adrian.

"Do you know how copulation is achieved?"

Adrian's voice startled her out of her musings. When she replayed his question in her mind, she was so startled that she did not know how to respond.

He repeated his question impatiently. "Do you understand the mechanics of such a union?"

She shook her head. It took her a moment to realize that he could not see her movement in the dark. Scrambling to gather her wits, she spoke her answer aloud. "No." She swallowed. "No, I do not."

"You will learn tonight."

Again she swallowed, but she still could not think clearly enough to speak.

Adrian continued without pause. "I have narrowed your list of potential bridegrooms to four. I only await the last one's offer, and then you will be able to choose."

"Four have already offered for me?" She was shocked. Stunned, in fact, by the news. Then she frowned. "I thought you would restrict it to three."

He remained silent a moment. Eventually she heard him answer, though the words seemed reluctant. "I decided to allow you more freedom in this." Then his words picked up speed. "Once you have chosen your husband, all that remains is to get the special license and finalize the settlement."

She was startled. "I will not be married in a church?"

His response was quick, his tone cold. "All these

men are less than healthy. They do not wish to waste time awaiting your favors." He paused as if to impress his point. "You would do well to remember that, Lynette. No man will wait long for something for which he has paid dearly."

She looked away, her gaze skimming past his gloomy visage to the equally gloomy landscape outside the carriage window. "I understand," was all she said.

The carriage pulled to a stop. They had arrived.

"Gather your hood about your face. You must not be seen."

She hesitated. "My lord?"

"Adrian," he snapped, correcting her formal tone. Then his words gentled. "I know you are nervous, Lynette, but this is the last place for formality. If you simply obey until we are inside, everything will be revealed." He sighed. "Then you can plague me with questions."

She nodded, doing as she was bid, pulling her cloak tightly about her head and face. Even so, she could not resist voicing her own pique. "I did not realize I was plaguing you, Adrian. I will try not to ask too much."

She made to move out of the hackney, but Adrian grasped her arm, holding her back. "You are not plaguing me, Lynette," he said, his tone harassed. "Try to understand that some lessons are easier to teach than others. Tonight will be . . . difficult for me."

She turned to look closely at him, but in the darkness could see no more than his outline. "Are you afraid I won't understand? I will try very hard to learn quickly."

He shook his head, the movement barely discernible in the darkness. She did, however, hear his chuckle, the sound mocking not herself but him. "That is exactly what I fear."

"I don't understand."

Then he did something he had not done since the very beginning. He reached out and stroked her face. His touch was exquisitely gentle, and she turned into it, unable to resist extending his caress.

He fisted his hand and drew it away.

"Do not let me kiss you, Lynette. Not on the lips."

She looked up, again frustrated by the darkness. "What?"

He grabbed her wrist, holding it firmly as if to imprint his words on her. "You will learn many things tonight. But before we go in, you must swear to me. Swear that if I try to kiss you here"—he reached out and touched her lips—"you will stop me."

His movement was so slow that she leaned into it, aching for the smooth texture of his glove and smelling the scent that was him, on her lips. She closed her eyes to savor the sensation.

"Lynette!" he snapped, his hand abruptly abandoning her.

Her eyes flew open.

"Swear, Lynette. Hit me, kick me, do whatever it takes. You must push me away."

She did not know what to say. All the while, his hand gripped her wrist, the pressure building until she wondered if her bones would snap.

"Swear, Lynette, or I shall have someone else instruct you tonight."

"I swear." She could not have said the words faster. She did not want another instructor. It had to be him. "I swear," she repeated, even more firmly.

Before he could say more, the door jerked open.

"Out ye go," snapped the cabbie. "Oi'll 'ave none o' yer tomfoolery in me carriage. Out!"

Lynette hastily climbed out, followed by Adrian. She did not watch as he paid the man, but instead occupied herself by gazing about her. They were behind a house, a large home in a darkened part of London. But for all the surrounding gloom, the area seemed sedate. Safe. Almost respectable.

Until Adrian caught her arm and drew her inside. There was only scant illumination in the dark hallway: the light of a single candle. But in the brief second it took to gain her bearings, Lynette saw bold wallpaper and a beautiful woman—that was all—before Adrian was enveloped in a flurry of arms and skirts.

"Yer late," the woman whispered. "But I forgive ye." Then she kissed him full on the mouth.

A hot surge of jealousy whipped through Lynette. Apparently, she herself was not allowed to kiss Adrian on the lips, but this strange woman could. And with a great deal of thoroughness.

Lynette narrowed her eyes, barely noting that her hands had curled into fists. But she did not move. Adrian would likely be furious if she interfered, for all that this petite blonde was practically climbing on top of him in the hallway.

She could not remain silent. "Should I wait here, my lord, or go on without you?" Her tone was dry and formal. It was the same tone her father used when conveying moral superiority. And it had not the least effect. She was not even sure Adrian heard her, so occupied was he in supporting the blonde's weight.

Fortunately, the woman heard. She pulled her face away from Adrian's, turning to assess Lynette with an impish grin. "Oh, my," she drawled. "She is a handful." Then she hopped off Adrian to land almost catlike on the ground. But she did not release him, even though he was now gesturing to his charge.

"Jenny, may I present Lynette Jameson? Lynette, this is Jenny."

Though it nearly killed her to do it, Lynette gave the woman a curtsy. It was a short one, sketchily done in the narrow corridor, but it still observed the proprieties.

"Coo, but she is a good 'un," came the woman's response. "Lovely. Good figure. And polite, though it nearly kills 'er to do it." She turned to Adrian, tapping him on the shoulder. "She'll make you a fortune!"

Adrian acknowledged the comment with a nod, but he did not speak.

Fortunately for him, the woman gave him little chance. She led them down the winding corridor and up what clearly used to be a servant's staircase. "Well, I 'ave a treat fer you," she said, her accent smoothing out as she settled in to business. "You can watch Louise. She likes an audience, for all that ye won't be seen."

Beside her, Adrian nodded. "Louise is an excellent choice. Thank you."

"You can watch in here." She opened a doorway and led them into a tiny chamber furnished by an overabundance of pillows and a large, thick mattress on the floor. To one side was a heavy curtain that covered nearly the entire wall. Lynette barely had time to look around before the petite woman was pinning her with a harsh stare. "Whatever ye see, stays here.

One word escapes yer lips, missy, and I'll ruin ye. Mark my words—"

"She understands, Jenny." That was Adrian, stepping forward smoothly. "She will not tell a soul."

Apparently, Jenny did not believe him. She spent the next few moments burning her gaze into Lynette, who could do no more than return the look. Finally, Lynette realized what the woman wanted. With a slight nod, she agreed.

"I will tell no one. I am a minister's daughter, so you may count upon my discretion."

Jenny arched a single, well-defined eyebrow. "A parson's brat." She glanced speculatively at Adrian. "I bet ye have yer hands full with her."

"No more than absolutely necessary," returned Adrian dryly.

Lynette shifted her gaze to him, startled and a bit hurt by the comment, but Jenny cackled. "Tell me another whopper, Addy." Still cackling, she shut the door, leaving behind a single candle hidden in a slight indentation in the side wall.

Lynette looked down, focusing on unbuttoning her cloak in the gloom. When she spoke, she kept her voice casual, hoping not to betray any of her seething emotions. "Was that the Jenny from your childhood? The one who taught you?"

He did not answer. Were she not studiously unbuttoning her cloak, she would have shot him an angry glare. As it was, she had to lean down to unfasten the lowest button.

His fingers were warm on her chin as he lifted her up.

She complied stiffly, not wanting to look at him.

But his touch was firm, and eventually she stared into the dark pools of his eyes.

"You do not like her." His voice betrayed a slight hurt that was startling.

"I-I do not know her, my lord."

"Adrian," he corrected on a weary sigh.

She nodded, using the movement to dislodge his fingers from her chin. She didn't know why she was being so difficult. Indeed, she didn't know why her nerves felt on edge, her thoughts angry, and her body alien. This entire situation was strange, and she felt frightened, edgy, even afraid.

And yet . . .

"She is an old friend, Lynette. I trust her to keep your reputation safe."

She did not look up as she pulled off her cloak. "When did my reputation become so important?"

Suddenly he gripped her, his words fierce. "Everything about you is important," he whispered. He twisted her shoulders, turning her to face him. "We cannot be angry with one another tonight. We cannot!"

He spoke with conviction, yet it was apparent from his expression that he did not know how to correct the situation. Unbearable tension coiled between them, and from his words, he hated it. As did she. But he did not know how to change it.

Lynette felt shame wash over her. Her feelings were confused, her situation untenable. And yet nothing was happening that had not been explained in some part to her. This was not the way to learn, she realized. More than that, this was not the way to get Adrian to explain. So she softened, looking away.

"I am sorry, Adrian. I feel . . ." She shrugged, searching for the words. "I dislike Jenny because . . ." Her voice trailed off as she searched for the words. Eventually, she settled on a half-truth. "She knows so much more than I do."

"It is her profession."

Lynette nodded, knowing he referred to the night's activities, whatever they might be. But in truth, that was not what she meant. Jenny irritated Lynette not because she was so much more worldly than Lynette, but because she knew so much more about Adrian. They had a shared past. A shared love.

Looking into Adrian's eyes, Lynette wondered if anyone could truly understand the complex man before her. The best hope was that a lifetime's experiences might shed insight into his inner thoughts. A lifetime of shared moments that Jenny already had and Lynette would never find. Because, all too soon, she would marry someone else and her time with Adrian would be over.

Because of that, Lynette felt unaccountably sad. And jealous. And bitter with envy because long after Lynette was married and gone, Jenny would still be here. Still greeting Adrian with openmouthed kisses in a dark hallway that led to a bedroom.

Once again, Lynette felt Adrian's hand on her chin, lifting her up so she could look into his eyes. "You do not like her, and yet you extended her your curtsy. You were kind and gracious, and for that I am very pleased. And grateful."

A flush of pleasure washed through her, and Lynette smiled. Their gazes locked, and she felt a tingling in her body. By now she recognized the sensation. It was awareness. Anticipation. But then, abruptly, they heard footsteps, and Adrian broke away.

With a single quick movement, he blew out the candle.

"Say nothing," he cautioned in a whisper. She nodded her understanding even as the footsteps drew her attention.

The sound came from beyond the curtain, which Adrian drew aside to reveal a huge window occupying nearly the entire wall. On the other side was a room decorated in the same style as this one, though with a little more color, a little more workmanship. Many candles burned in wall alcoves. Large pillows filled the floor. Gauzy curtains adorned the walls, including the opposite side of their window, muting her view of the room but not obscuring it.

The footsteps stopped, and she heard female laughter.

Then Adrian distracted her. He was no more than a dark silhouette crossing to her side. He drew close to her and whispered in her ear, "They cannot see you, but if you are loud, they will hear you."

She nodded, not knowing who *they* were. Not sure she wanted to know. She felt his hands on her arms, soothing as he stroked her.

"Relax, Lynette. You are here to watch. I will explain events as they transpire."

She took a deep breath to steady her nerves.

"Think of it as a special kind of theater," he suggested softly.

The show began.

The door to the other room opened, and a small, muscular woman literally danced in. Her head was thrown back, allowing her thick brown hair to fly about her veiled face. Her clothes were as gauzy as the curtains, many layers of veils floating about her in an enticing, almost mesmerizing display. Behind her stumbled two young gentlemen, lords by the look of them. Drunk, by the sound of them.

They were laughing uproariously as they came into the room, but as Lynette watched, she realized they were not quite as inebriated as they appeared. Indeed, they seemed more . . . lustful than drunk. Their gazes glued to Louise, watching with a hungry interest as she twirled and floated about the room.

"Louise is very expensive," Adrian whispered. "Often gentlemen pool their resources, sharing her for a night."

Lynette twisted, her eyes wide with surprise. "Two men with one woman?"

She felt his smile. "It is quite common to have more than one partner. And," he added, his tone becoming apologetic, "your husband will be intrigued by the concept."

"Even if he doesn't outright demand it?" she asked. She already knew the answer.

"Many do, yes. But most women find it easy work—sharing the load, so to speak." Then he turned her back to the display. "Louise always dances first. Indeed, she is extremely talented."

Lynette wondered at the note of admiration in his voice. At least she did, until she began to watch the woman perform. "Extremely talented" was a gross understatement. Louise literally captivated her audience with her movements alone.

But this was not the normal movement of the dances Lynette had been taught. Nor were they what she had seen on the stage. This dance was sensuous, fluid, and very erotic.

Never before had she seen a woman display herself so openly, and yet so coyly. Louise would extend her hand to one of the gentlemen, her bare arm floating toward him, touching him, sometimes even stroking his chest, his arm, his leg. But as he reached for her, she would spin away. Her hips twirled, her breasts skated dangerously close to their outstretched fingers, but the men missed and she danced free.

More than once the girl turned toward the window, arching her back or performing some amazing gymnastic feat. There was no doubt that the dancer knew Adrian and Lynette were watching. There was also no doubt that she enjoyed it, enjoyed showing off.

"See how she loves what she is doing?" whispered Adrian. "It is not just her skill, although that is considerable. There is pure joy in her movements, pride in her body. She is alluring because she loves doing this."

"Dancing?" whispered Lynette.

"Pleasing."

Silence reigned as all four spectators were captivated. But all too soon, the mood changed. The gentlemen were becoming restless, their hands more grasping. Beside her, Lynette heard Adrian's sigh.

"They are young and impatient. Older men enjoy taking their time."

Lynette nodded, storing that information for later, knowing she would need all the skills she could learn to keep her husband entertained.

"Now watch," whispered Adrian. "She will allow them to start disrobing her."

Indeed, as they watched, Louise twirled close to

one gentleman. But this time, as she danced behind him, stroking his chest, he managed to twist around, grasping one of her veils and pulling it free. Louise danced away, still modestly covered, but by one less piece of fabric. Meanwhile, the gentleman raised his trophy aloft. His companion cheered.

Then the other man got his chance, pulling another veil free.

Soon Louise's upper half was naked. Her breasts were not very ample, but what she did have, she used to great effect. The pace of her dancing increased, and she shook her shoulders, making her breasts jiggle. The men seemed fascinated with the display, reaching out to touch or stroke, and once to kiss.

"Men love breasts, Lynette," Adrian whispered in her ear. "We love to see them, to hold them, squeeze them . . ."

"And kiss them?"

"Of course."

As she watched, Louise allowed the men to do just that. Meanwhile, Lynette felt her own breasts grow heavy, her nipples tighten and ache. She wanted to be touched. To be stroked as the men were doing to Louise. She wanted Adrian to touch her.

But he did not. So Lynette continued to watch, feeling slightly frustrated but setting it aside as she watched Louise arch backward, giving one of the men full access to her upper body. He feasted on her breasts, suckling noisily, while her hands undid the man's cravat. In moments, while he nuzzled and teased her upthrust bosom, Louise removed his shirt, spinning behind him to take it from his body.

Lynette gaped in awe at the woman's skill. She had managed to partially disrobe him without the slightest interruption in his actions. And then she had danced away.

But even that was obviously choreographed. Clearly she planned her actions, because even as she spun free of one man, she danced within reach of the other. This second fellow was younger than the first. He was shorter, less muscular, but no less eager to grasp what his companion had lost.

Taking Louise from behind, he pulled her backwards into him, grasping her breasts and pulling at the nipples. Even through the curtain, Lynette could see the dancer stiffen, not in alarm but sensual delight. Unconsciously, Lynette arched as well, leaning backward into Adrian's embrace. He caught her arms easily, holding her steady, but he did not caress her.

Instead he whispered, "Some women like it rough. They like their breasts to be held tightly, to be squeezed and twisted." Indeed, that was exactly what the younger man was doing, and Louise was trembling as she released a loud moan.

"The sounds she makes drive her men wild. She is as well known for her exuberant noise as her dancing." As if to confirm his words, Louise writhed and gyrated in the younger man's embrace, releasing moan after gasp after ecstatic cry. And that only made the men more ardent, more frenzied in their movements.

Then, suddenly, Louise danced away.

"She will allow them to disrobe her now."

Lynette could not take her eyes off the display. She whispered her question. "Completely? She will be naked?"

Again she felt Adrian's smile.

"Completely."

It was as if his words caused it to happen. The men were overly eager now, their intentions obvious. As Louise danced before them, they actively pursued her, moving about the room, cornering her only to have her slip free. But each time they came close, they exacted a cost: they pulled away another of her veils.

Oddly enough, her face covering was one of the first to come free. The men apparently wanted her mouth as well, and occasionally the younger man would grab her not to remove another veil but to kiss her deeply, almost brutally.

The woman allowed it. Arching against him, pressing her body intimately along him, then she would once again slip free.

"See how her lips are red and swollen?" Adrian whispered. "That is why women put color onto their mouths. It is so they look like that."

Lynette nodded, realizing this was exactly the look the baroness tried for.

"There," Adrian continued. "She is naked."

He need not have said so; Lynette could see it and, indeed, could barely pull her gaze away. Never before had she seen another naked woman. And such a woman, as well! Her body was firm and muscular, her breasts high and pointed. Or so Louise gave that impression. Indeed, it was hard to tell as she whirled and spun about the room.

"Louise is getting older," whispered Adrian. "Her breasts are sagging a bit. Her legs are not as flexible as they once were."

Lynette blinked, trying to see what he saw but unable.

"But the men cannot tell, can they?" Adrian continued.

Lynette shook her head. The gentlemen seemed as avidly interested as she.

"Her movements allow her to emphasize her legs and her breasts. See how she thrusts forward. She even holds her breasts high." Fitting action to his words, Louise had put her own hands on her breasts, playing with them while the men watched. But as she did so, she lifted herself, hiding any potential sag.

"She would be popular without such measures, but it never hurts to give the appearance of youth. She does that by displaying boundless energy, Lynette, and great innovation."

At that moment Louise spun toward the window, creating a display for Adrian and Lynette alone. She flattened herself along the glass, arms outstretched, body pressed hard against its cool surface.

Then slowly, simply, she arched herself backward. She peeled herself off the window, top first. Dropping her head backward, then her arms, she arched into a sort of bridge, giving Lynette her first full and complete look at a woman's private parts.

Lynette gasped, unable to stop herself from stepping backward, even as her gaze was glued forward. She looked, saw. It was over in a flash, as Louise continued to draw her body up and over, in effect performing a slow flip to the delight of all who watched.

"Would you like to see more?" Adrian asked.

It was a useless question. Whether Lynette willed it or not, Louise continued. But Lynette did want to see more, to know more. In fact, moments later, she found herself stepping forward, closer to the window to view events more clearly.

Adrian followed. He spoke of the mechanics of copulation. That a woman must be open to receive what a man offered. Her body was uniquely suited to widen, to lubricate, to accept.

Lynette heard his every word, but in a sort of daze. He spoke of wetness, of the smooth glide a man needed, but she did not understand. And when she tried to see what he referred to on Louise, she found the dancer moved too fast to give her a clear picture.

But then she noticed something else. Something about herself. Her own body seemed to be growing liquid. Her lower abdomen was heating, tingling, and in a flash, she thought she did understand. Whether or not she could see it in the dancer, Lynette herself was growing wet.

Then, just as the realization hit her, something else happened. The men grew more aggressive. Apparently, they had grown tired of watching Louise dance. They wanted more. They stalked her. They appeared ravenous. Almost feral.

As Lynette watched in fascination, Adrian fitted himself to her back, whispering explanations into her ear.

"Now she will undress them."

Chapter 17

Lynette scarcely knew what to think. She was about to see a naked man? Or more specifically, two naked men? She twisted, wanting to look at Adrian, but he stopped her.

"Do not shy away now, Lynette. You have come too far."

It was true. She thought briefly of the innocent girl she had been when she'd first arrived at the viscount's home. How far she had come. And now, right in front of her, was the next step—if only she had the courage to take it.

She didn't. At least she did not feel courageous. But she did feel a burning curiosity, and so she leaned closer to the glass.

Adrian continued to explain. He used graphic terms. He spoke of the male organ—the penis. He likened it to a rod or a spade that planted a seed in a woman's womb. He said all sorts of confusing things, but he did not show her one.

Louise did.

The woman continued her seduction, dancing around the men, allowing them to touch her, and while they were otherwise occupied, she disrobed them. Unfortunately, they were not cooperating as much as Lynette would expect.

Instead, they were quite aggressive in their actions, touching her most intimately. The older one even used his hand in place of his male organ, pushing it roughly into the dancer and drawing it out slick with moisture.

"Doesn't that hurt?" Lynette asked, her voice thick and low.

"Did you see how wet she was?"

Lynette nodded.

"That is how you know a woman is ready." He stepped forward, and she could see the frown on Adrian's face. "Funny. I do not believe they have done anything to excite her." He glanced back toward Lynette. "Most men are particularly inept when it comes to exciting a woman."

She tilted her head in confusion. "But you said she is ready."

Again he looked back at the trio. "Like most smart women, Louise has found a way to enhance her pleasure without a man's assistance." He paused as he too watched. "I believe dancing must be her aphrodisiac." He shrugged, turning back to Lynette. "You must find whatever thoughts are most stimulating to you." Then he gestured to the window as he once again slid behind her, this time stroking her arms as he moved.

"Perhaps you will recall this moment in your mind. Perhaps you will remember *it* to grow wet."

She did not know how it happened. Perhaps it was his voice. Perhaps it was his stroke across her arm, so near to brushing her breasts. Whatever the reason, as he whispered the word "wet" she felt a spasm in her lower abdomen. A tightening, and she gasped.

As if sensing what was happening, he pulled away, removing his touch, making his voice colder. "Watch, Lynette. Do not do more. There will be time for the rest later."

She shifted, her eyes pulled wide as his implication sunk in. "Later . . . ?"

He shook his head. "Not now," he affirmed. Then he gestured to the tableau before them. "Ah, she has succeeded."

Lynette's gaze snapped back to the men, watching as the dancer indeed tumbled gracefully backward and stripped the younger man of his trousers. It was another moment before the woman shifted out of Lynette's line of vision, and then, Lynette's shocked gasp reverberated through the room.

There it was.

The male organ.

A penis. Ramrod straight and reddish, sticking up from the younger gentleman's thatch of russet hair. Lynette stepped forward, placing her hand on the window glass as she stared and stared and stared.

"I believe it is young Bert's birthday. Therefore, he will likely go first."

Lynette did not comment. She was too busy staring. Indeed, as she watched, Louise did exactly what Lynette's fingers itched to do.

She touched the rod. In fact, she did more than touch it. She stroked it. She caressed it. She toyed with it. Lynette saw the dancer lick her palm to bring moisture to the organ before grasping it firmly and tugging.

"My God," breathed Lynette. "Doesn't that hurt?"

Adrian's low, deep voice sent a thrill of longing through Lynette as he answered. "Does he look to be in pain? I assure you, he is not."

Lynette spared a glance at the young man's face. Indeed, he was grimacing, his face nearly as red as his penis. But it seemed to be an ecstatic type of pain, and he began moving against Louise's hand.

Then, abruptly, he slapped the dancer's hand away.

The movement was so shocking that Lynette took a step backward, colliding with Adrian, directly behind her.

"He does not want to finish in her hand."

She would have turned to ask him a question, but she could not take her eyes off the events unfolding before her. Where before Louise had been the one in control, now it seemed that the young man was. Surging off the pillows, he grasped Louise by the shoulders, and literally flung himself on top of her.

She went down smoothly, her dancer's grace serving her well despite the man's ardor.

Lynette watched in fascination as he used his knee to push the girl's legs wide and plunged his member inside her.

"Oh!" Lynette cried out softly, not sure if she wanted to turn away or run and protect the woman. But Adrian held her firmly in place.

"Watch. It is all part of lovemaking."

Indeed, as Lynette watched, the dancer arched her

back, moaning loudly as the young man rammed into her over and over again. Lynette was fascinated as he drew outward and then pushed back in. She saw his slim buttocks flex with each thrust while the muscles in his legs stood out like taut cords, and his one free hand grappled with the girl's breast.

"He is hurting her!"

"He is aggressive, but believe me, Louise is used to far worse."

Indeed, Louise somehow managed to wedge one of her arms between herself and the young man, then shoved outward, throwing his arm off her. The movement broke his rhythm, and for a moment he faltered, as he needed both his arms to support his weight.

Lynette thought at first that the gentleman would be angry. After all, the dancer had completely distracted him from his purpose. But then Louise threw her legs around his hips, arching into the young man. Apparently it was enough to put him back in a good humor.

He responded with a cry of exultation as he slammed into her again. Then, suddenly, he seemed to growl. There was no other word for it. It was a guttural cry echoing a shudder that seemed to go through his entire body.

"He has released his seed in her," Adrian remarked, his tone almost casual.

"Amazing," she whispered, awed by what she had just seen. There seemed to be such power in the union. A primal, almost animalistic energy surrounded the couple. Despite what she had been led to believe, there appeared nothing civilized at all about copulation. There was no closing of one's eyes and thinking of England. This was all-consuming.

"Is it pleasurable? To be so swept away?"

She could hear the note of humor in Adrian's voice as he answered. "A man often loses consciousness for a moment."

Lynette could not believe he spoke the truth. But even as Adrian said the words, she could see the young man collapse. Indeed, if she did not know better, she might have thought him dead. "And Louise?" she asked softly, for the woman lay flat on her back, apparently barely conscious as well.

"She knows how to fake it. She did not reach orgasm."

Lynette turned, confused at the new term. But before she could ask, Adrian held up his hand. "It is the term for sexual release. Obviously, young Bert has achieved his."

Then he frowned at the other gentleman, stretched out on the pillows, watching the pair. The other man still wore his trousers, but the firm budge below the buttons clearly indicated an erection. She heard Adrian sigh.

He said, "I sincerely doubt Geoffrey will be able to assist her either." Then he placed a finger beneath Lynette's chin, turning her enough to look into his eyes. "I will have to show you what it is like. And you will have to remember."

Lynette swallowed. "Show me?"

He nodded, equally grave. "I want you to remember the sensations. You will need to find them again on your own." He waited until she gave him a nervous nod, then added, "One more thing."

She waited, not knowing what to say.

"I want you to watch what is happening. Do not look at me. Look at them. Do you understand?"

She did. Or, rather, she nodded as if she did. In truth, she did not understand the urgency in his voice or his firm note of command. A tension seemed to have gripped him, making his voice tight, his tone curt. She did not understand why, except that it had to do with what was coming next.

His anxiety made her nervous. Still, Lynette knew better than to argue, and so she obediently turned her gaze to the glass, voicing her question without thought.

"Where is love in all of this? Does it even enter into the act?"

She heard him pause, half in and half out of his evening coat, his voice a sad whisper in the heated room. "Love certainly helps. A fondness, will lead to sensitivity and awareness of the other person." Then he sighed, and she turned to see him, noting not the emptiness in his voice but the aching sadness that seemed to wrap his entire body. "But if there is love in sex, then I do not know how to find it."

Such was the pain in his tone that Lynette immediately stepped toward him. She wanted to touch him, to ease the ache she knew he felt. She knew because she felt it as well. Dark and empty, like a hole centered in the middle of her chest. But he would not let her approach. He held up his hand even as he finished stripping out of his coat and began rolling up his sleeves.

"But there can be pleasure, Lynette. A great deal of pleasure. And that is what I will show you."

She bit her lip, her hands feeling useless by her sides. "Is that enough?"

He shrugged, the motion obviously forced. "It is all we have, Lynette." And she knew that for him, it was true. He had nothing more. No parents to cherish him, no family to love him, and no woman either. He had only this—the education of young girls—and a dream of a healthy estate.

"Look at Louise," he coaxed, gently touching her shoulders and turning her around. "Do not be afraid. I will not hurt you."

"I know," she whispered. And yet, even as she said the words, the ache in her heart increased, the pain tangible. How did he bear it? This emptiness? Even in the midst of the most intimate union possible between a man and woman, did he still feel this pain?

All the while he kept speaking, his voice conversational as he drew her attention to the mechanics of Louise's work. "She is about to undress Geoffrey. Watch how she fascinates him so he is not even aware of what she is doing."

Lynette turned her gaze back to the people through the window. The young man, Bert, was snoring, his exertions apparently too much for him. The other man, Geoffrey, was more relaxed, though his eyes gleamed with a feral light that Lynette was coming to recognize as hunger. Geoffrey's shirt was gone, Louise having stripped it off, but his trousers were firmly shut as the dancer slipped near, her hips swaying to a beat only she heard.

Left. Right. Turn. Jump. Left. Right.

It must be the heat, Lynette thought dazedly. Though there was no music, she began to feel Louise's dance herself. Then, as Adrian touched her shoulders, she began to sway along with it. With his encouragement, she began to shift slightly. Left, then right.

Adrian stood behind her, wrapping his arms

around her waist as he too seemed to pulse with the rhythm of Louise's dance. "She is enticing him. Do you see it? Without benefit of clothes or fancy steps. She draws him closer even as she takes a step backward."

As they watched, Louise lifted a hip, extended her leg, stretched out an arm. Geoffrey responded, moving closer to her, leaning forward. In fact, he soon appeared to be stalking her as he crawled over the pillows.

Playing the game, Louise slid backward, dancing around him.

Apparently, Geoffrey's patience exhausted itself. Moving faster than Lynette expected, he lunged forward, grasping the woman about her waist and tumbling her to the ground.

And as Louise fell, so did the golden fabric of Lynette's gown. Lynette had been watching the interplay between Geoffrey and Louise, completely oblivious to Adrian, who was releasing the buttons down her back. As she watched the couple before her, he had shifted her gown slowly forward until it slid off her arms and pooled at her feet.

Lynette began to turn, a question in her eyes, but Adrian did not allow it. He merely leaned forward, whispering in her ear.

"Watch."

She did as she was bid. And as Geoffrey squeezed and pulled at Louise's breasts, Lynette felt Adrian release the ties of her shift, tugging it away. Moments later, all her clothing joined her gown at her ankles.

She now stood naked in the warm room. But, somehow, she did not feel tense. She had been sleeping naked for weeks now, and the removal of clothing allowed a cool brush of air across her heated skin. The clothing surrounding her feet also seemed fitting. Though she knew she could kick it away at any moment, the fabric felt like soft bonds, holding her still, keeping her from running.

Meanwhile, Geoffrey kissed and sucked at Louise's puckered nipples. Lynette moaned in grateful delight as Adrian began to pull and knead her own. Louise writhed, her hands roaming freely over Geoffrey's arms, shoulders, and muscular back. Adrian chafed Lynette's back with the fine linen of his shirt.

"Take off your shirt," she whispered.

Adrian paused in the act of nuzzling her neck.

"I have never felt a naked man before," she continued. "Take off your shirt."

At first she did not think he would comply. Then, suddenly, there was cool air behind her, and the telltale sounds of clothing being removed. Moments later Adrian returned, wrapping her in his arms. She felt the heated brush of bare skin along her back.

It was heavenly. She leaned back, swaying slightly and trying to memorize the sensation, feeling the smooth whisper of the skin of his arms, the gentle prickle of his chest hair where it caressed her back and, lastly, the covered bulge that spoke of his desire.

She tensed immediately, shocked by the size of what was behind her. Thank God he still wore his pants!

"Don't be concerned," he whispered. He drew her back against him, holding her close so that she could accustom herself to the feel of him. "I will not take your virginity."

She had not been thinking of that. Indeed, she had

not been thinking of anything beyond the size of him and the smallness of her.

"I will show you, Lynette. You do not know what your body is capable of." Then he bent his head, kissing her neck even as his hands found and cupped her breasts. "Let me show you," he whispered.

She relaxed. Indeed, how could she not? His hands were skillful, knowing just how she liked to be held and touched and teased.

"Do you see what Louise is doing?"

She had not even realized she'd closed her eyes until he spoke. Her eyelids were so heavy, her body liquid as she melted against him. As his hands splayed across her belly, she opened her eyes and looked at Louise and Geoffrey.

Louise had gained the upperhand—literally. She had flipped her gentleman over on his back, feet aimed directly at the window. She stood above him, one naked thigh on either side. His hands stroked her long legs, but his eyes were on her breasts as she straightened her legs and bent over, presenting her buttocks high in the air.

Aimed directly at Lynette and Adrian.

Once again, Lynette got an excellent view of the underside of a woman. It was wet and red and full.

"Yes," whispered Adrian. "That is how you look when aroused."

As Louise presented her bottom to the window, her hands stretched down. Her breasts did, too, near Geoffrey's hands. He wasted no time in enjoying the sight or the situation.

Lynette did not know how the dancer did it, but she managed somehow to keep her focus: allowing the man to fondle her breasts while she undid the buttons along his trousers. Within moments, the fabric was pulled away and a short, thick male organ sprang free.

Adrian said, "Men come in all shapes and sizes, Lynette. But all are most sensitive along the tip and behind."

Because of the angle, Lynette got a full view of Geoffrey's underside as well, quickly revealed as he kicked aside his clothing. She saw the intriguing male pouch that had so interested her when Adrian slept on her bed. Was it weeks ago that she had gotten her first view?

She was about to ask, but the thought spun away as Adrian tweaked her nipples. A hot flash of sensation burned across her thoughts, and she gasped in reaction.

"Dancers are the most flexible lovers," Adrian whispered. "Men appreciate that."

It took a moment to understand what Adrian meant. Indeed, she knew he was speaking to her to distract her from what he was doing, from the way his hands were roving over her belly, spanning her waist, pressing onto her hips. It was an incredible sensation, but it was also overwhelming. Her knees weakened and she whimpered.

"Watch Louise," he whispered.

And so she did, allowing herself to be amazed by the petite dancer.

The woman appeared to be part contortionist as well as a dancer. Louise managed somehow to remain standing, removing Geoffrey's pants while the man fondled her breasts. It was amazing. And it allowed Lynette to see the male anatomy from all different angles while the dancer stroked and fondled.

Lynette's own hands itched to reach behind her. She wanted to feel what Louise felt, to explore Adrian as the dancer explored Geoffrey. But she did not. Her hands pressed against the smooth window as she stared at what went on before her. And all the while, she felt Adrian push her forward, helping her step out of the circle of her clothing as she leaned into the window. Gently he nudged her knees open, spreading her legs as she watched.

She was aware of all these things, and yet completely unaware, her attention absorbed by the sight before her.

"He is enjoying it," she commented as she spared a glance toward Geoffrey's face. It was red, and his breath came in unsteady gasps.

"All men enjoy it," was Adrian's response. But his words came not from a place beside her ear. No, he was kissing his way down her back, stroking her belly with one hand while the other massaged her inner thigh.

Lynette's legs were threatening to buckle from the sensations spinning through her body. She heard her breath as it rasped through her lips, and she twisted to look at Adrian. Again, he stopped her.

"Lean against the window. Look closely at Geoffrey. Do you see how his legs are beginning to tense? See the arching of his feet?"

She looked and she saw, but she did not comment.

"He is coming close. Soon you will see him ejaculate."

Indeed, as he spoke, Lynette saw the man suddenly

jerk forward, pushing through the dancer's hand. A whitish liquid burst forth.

"Is that what happens?" she whispered. It was a foolish question with an obvious answer, but she felt Adrian nod against her waist nonetheless. "But I thought you said men don't like to do that outside of a woman."

Adrian shrugged, the movement communicated to Lynette as his shoulder pressed against her thigh. "Geoffrey is well known for his ability to spring back to life quickly." His words were dry, even laced with humor. She felt him kneel between her legs. "I cannot see from this angle," he continued in a conversational tone. "You must tell me what is happening."

"But—"

"Just tell me what you see." His voice was soft, coaxing, but she heard a note of tension. Or perhaps it was merely thick, as though he yearned for something he could not have. She would have asked more questions, but he was kissing her ankle, stroking the inside of her leg, all the while urging her to speak.

"Tell me," he whispered, just before he nibbled at her anklebone. "It can be quite exciting to hear the act described."

She licked her dry lips, aware that he wanted her to make what she saw alluring. To describe in such a way as to enflame. Her voice, according to the baroness, was yet another tool in the game of seduction. Resolved to try, she looked into the other room.

"There is not much to see, Adrian," she began, her voice low and husky without her even trying to make it so. "He . . . uh, Geoffrey is lying on his back, apparently relaxed."

"Mmmmm," was Adrian's only response, though

his hands seemed to be saying a great deal. They kneaded and caressed their way up her legs.

But thoughts of Adrian's hands inevitably led to a search for Geoffrey's. "He is tugging at her legs. I think he wants her to kneel." She frowned. "But I do not think his organ is ready."

"Ah," came Adrian's soft response. "Perhaps you should kneel as well. That will put you at a better angle."

She froze. If she knelt, she would be astride the viscount. Indeed, she thought with a sudden flash of insight, perhaps this was what they meant by riding one another. She had often heard such jokes, but she never understood them.

"Trust me, Lynette. I will not be harmed."

She did not want to do it. Indeed, it was already awkward, feeling him between her legs, open in a way she'd never imagined—and yet he had accomplished it without her even knowing it had occurred.

"You must watch what is happening, Lynette," he chided. "Come. Bend your legs." As he spoke, he tugged, forcing her forward. Her legs were weak to begin with, and she toppled, landing on her knees.

If she felt open before, it was nothing compared with now. In order to span his very broad shoulders, she had to spread her legs quite wide. But one glance downward and she realized he did not mind. Indeed, he was grinning at her, and she suddenly realized that he seemed quite happy.

"Adrian?"

He inhaled deeply, his eyes drifting shut. "Many men enjoy this scent, Lynette. It is one unique to a woman in heat."

She felt her blush all the way down to her toes, but

he did not seem to notice. In fact, he was leaning to one side, grabbing a pillow to set behind his head. Even as he moved, he was speaking, urging her to look up, to ignore what he was doing.

"Look at Geoffrey, Lynette. What is he doing now?"

She did as she was bid, squinting through the gauze covering on the window as she tried to sort out the bodies. "She appears to be kneeling just as I am. And he is reaching . . ." Her words ended on a gasp as Adrian showed her exactly what Geoffrey was doing. One of his hands touched her left inner thigh, kneading the flesh there, while the other rose in a long caress up her other side. That hand ended between her legs, and stroked and touched the moist flesh there.

Lynette's body spasmed, jerking her both forward and back, seeking deeper contact and then shying away. But Adrian followed, one hand holding her still even as the other rubbed and probed.

"You wanted to know what a woman looks like, did you not?" he asked, his voice low, intense, with a note of predatory hunger. "Now, discover how a woman *feels*."

Then she felt him move his hands, sliding upward, pressing his thumbs deep, widening her, until suddenly she felt them slide inside.

"This is where the man goes. Inside here."

One thumb slid all the way in. Lynette didn't scream. She didn't cry out in pain. What she did was arch and gasp, her legs tensing but not drawing away. Her hands still pressed against the window. Indeed, that was all that held her upright.

"What is Louise doing?" Adrian asked.

Though her eyes were open, Lynette wasn't seeing.

At Adrian's urging, she focused, requiring great effort to speak. "She is . . . moving on top of him." Indeed, Louise was undulating above Geoffrey, moving, teasing, drawing her bottom closer, then farther away.

Suddenly, Geoffrey grasped the dancer's legs, drawing himself upward as he buried his face within her. Even through the glass, Lynette could hear Louise's scream of joy. She arched back, giving her gentleman full access as he nuzzled and . . . and . . .

All thought fled as Adrian's thumbs pushed deep within her, then withdrew.

In.

Out.

"This is what a man's organ does," he whispered. "Do you feel how wet you are? Do you understand how easily a man could slide in?"

Then he did as he described, with his fingers, widening her as he did. Lynette felt her muscles clench in response, fighting the invasion, and yet her resistance was temporary, an involuntary reaction. The muscles relaxed, and she felt as if he were pushing her wider, opening her even more. Impossibly wide. Wonderfully deep.

"What is Geoffrey doing?"

Lynette was gasping, arching and moving without volition, but her eyes managed somehow to focus. "He is . . . his face . . ."

"Ah," returned Adrian. "He is touching her here."

Then Adrian's hand moved. She had not thought a touch could be more intimate than what she'd been experiencing, but suddenly a flash of lightning burst across her consciousness. Her body jerked forward, flattening fully against the glass, but Adrian did not release her. In fact, he continued to stroke her, continued to speak as he touched her in ways she had not dreamed possible.

"A man wants to put himself here," he said. He pushed his fingers deep inside her. "A woman wants to be touched here." With his other hand, he stroked someplace nearer her surface.

Someplace incredible.

Then, suddenly, he withdrew his fingers, sliding his thumbs alongside to the place of lightning. He seemed to play there, and sensation after sensation burst across Lynette. First he pulled her flesh wide, exposing her completely. As if to emphasize what he had done, he blew cool air on her, and this time she cried out in reaction. He moved his fingers around, mixing touch with openness and the caress of hot breath. But it was not enough. Lynette did not know why, but it was not nearly enough.

"Look at Geoffrey, Lynette. What is he doing?"

Lynette did not see Geoffrey. Instead she saw Louise, writhing and dancing while still on her knees, with Geoffrey delving deep into the recesses of her body.

"He . . ." She gasped, unable to finish. Adrian had began to rub, lightly at first, in a circle that was not rough enough.

Then, as she watched, Louise's entire body seemed to clench, jerking. Geoffrey threw her backward onto a pile of pillows. He was atop her in a second, ramming his organ into her while she clung to him, crying out with each thrust.

These things Lynette saw in a daze. She watched in only partial understanding while below her, Adrian lifted his head. She felt his kisses rising along her thigh, and she felt his tug as he urged her lower, closer to his lips.

She went willingly, with no strength to object. Then she felt the brush of his tongue. In the back of her mind, she vaguely thought she ought to resist. But to feel Adrian kiss her, even there, was too glorious a sensation to resist. And so she eased herself a little wider, allowing him full access without even a whimper of protest.

He began on the outside, following the path his fingers had taken. He kissed the top of her thigh; he sucked and nibbled at her folds. And as his hands shifted, helping to support her weight, he spoke, his voice a deep rumble against her skin.

"Is Geoffrey doing this?" She felt his tongue. It went deep inside her, but not as far as his fingers had gone. "Look at Geoffrey, Lynette."

Forcing herself, she opened her eyes. She watched Geoffrey's member push deep inside Louise, ramming in, then withdrawing all red and glistening.

Without realizing it, Adrian was mimicking his counterpart's movements, pushing his fingers within her, withdrawing, then pushing deep inside again. Meanwhile, his mouth moved, conjuring the lightning that Lynette adored.

"This is what the man wants," he said as he continued pushing his fingers inside her, his movements full and hard. Shamelessly, she pressed down. The glass was cool against her breasts, her distended nipples rubbing delightfully as she gyrated.

And all the while, she dazedly watched Geoffrey thrust into Louise.

"But this, Lynette, *this* is what you want."

Then he used his tongue perfectly. The sensations

were overwhelming, flooding Lynette on a tide of delight. She felt her body clench and arch. Something primal took over. Harder. She wanted harder. More, she wanted more.

Suddenly she convulsed, her mind spinning away from her. The explosion of her senses sent her body pitching forward, back. Her legs clenched. Her head reared back and she screamed for joy.

Yet Adrian did not release her.

Dimly, Lynette was aware of Louise, flat on her back but clinging desperately to Geoffrey as he pounded into her. She, too, was crying out, clutching her lover. But Lynette had little comprehension of it; she simply felt Adrian, his hands holding her apart, his tongue continuing its masterful strokes. No longer were his fingers inside her, simply his mouth. Pressing deeply. Firmly. Wonderfully.

Right there! Again, she shattered, though she had not even realized the sensations had receded until they crashed over her again. She struggled, she writhed, she tried to move away.

Still he would not release her. She tumbled backward onto the mattress, and he came with her. He gave her more, sucking more, lapping and stroking and kissing her more.

And more

And more.

This time, everything shattered and the world went black.

Chapter 18

Adrian opened his eyes slowly. Indeed, at this point his body seemed to do everything slowly, but it did not prevent him from gazing up the slender, feminine length of his charge. Lynette, lovely Lynette, lay spread open before him, her luminescent skin still flushed, her body still quivering slightly as she breathed.

God, she was incredible!

He shifted, grimacing at an unusual wetness within his clothing. Good God, when was the last time *this* had occurred? Not since he was still in breeches. Not since before his parents died and Jenny came into his life. But now here he was, flat on his belly in Jenny's establishment, staring at the most beautiful, most responsive woman he had ever met, and he had been unable to control himself. The moment he had felt her tight passage begin to convulse about his fingers, the moment she had screamed his name out loud, he had exploded.

And as she had fought and flailed in her ecstasy, he had clung even tighter, driving them both higher and higher until he felt her convulse about him again.

It had never been like this. He had done this six times before. Six other girls. He had taught them how to experience physical love. How to enjoy themselves. What an orgasm felt like.

Never before had he forgotten himself. Never before had he been so intent on pleasuring the girl that he had ignored education, forgotten any explanation, even ignored his own body and plunged ahead as if nothing was more important than their pleasure.

The two of them.

Together.

Thank God he had been so caught up in intensifying her experience, in seeing just how far he could push her, that he had not ripped off his trousers and plunged into her. Thank God it would have required him to be too long away from her.

So he had exploded in his clothing like a mere boy. Lord, even young Bert had not done so, and this was reputedly his first time.

Lynette shifted and released a contented sigh. He had rolled off her, coming up to gather her in his arms, and now, as she stretched in languid abandon, he allowed himself to feast upon the sight.

Long legs. Full breasts. A glorious crown of hair. A man could do much worse than to spend his days and nights with such a sight.

"Mmmmm," she whispered as she curled into him, playfully resting a hand on his chest. "Is it always like that?"

He wanted to lie to her. He wanted to tell her that her every experience would be at least as wondrous. And he wanted to spend a lifetime making sure it was so. But it was not to be, and so he ruthlessly cut off his longing. He stopped the questions that sprang to his own mind as well. Questions like why he suddenly had these thoughts. Why he wanted something he knew damn well he could never, ever have.

And why the sight of her naked breasts, pressed intimately against him, effortlessly uprooted the image he'd held in his mind for years: the picture of his family lands, rich and green with new growth, his home no longer a crumbling pile of rocks but a beautiful estate. A picture that had sustained him for ages, giving him hope for generations to come.

Yet now, as Lynette shifted innocently against him, that image disappeared as if it had never been.

"I take it from your silence that this was unusual," she commented, her voice dry with humor.

"Unfortunately, yes. Most gentlemen do not—"

"Have your skill?" she finished for him.

He shrugged in reply, and then a noise from the other room captured their attention.

Adrian tilted slightly, narrowing his eyes as he tried to understand the tangle of bodies he saw through the glass. Apparently Geoffrey was at last sated. At least for the moment. But young Bert had awoken from his rest and was attempting to gain Louise's attention. She, of course, had taken full advantage of her respite to curl up on the floor and sleep.

While Bert tried to rouse poor Louise by haphazardly caressing her body and making a sound akin to a mewl, Lynette struggled into a sitting position, cross-legged. Her hair tumbled freely down her back. Her head was canted to one side, and she again watched the occupants of the other room. A slight frown marred her features.

Adrian waited with bated breath, wondering what would come next.

Lynette was a beautiful woman, he thought to himself. Not classically beautiful. Her color was too striking, her body too full for that. But to him, she could not be more intriguing. Her face betrayed her thoughts openly. Honestly. There was no deception in her, and yet her delightful body housed an excellent mind. She grasped events, came to logical conclusions, even reasoned her way out of complex situations all without his aid. In fact, she constantly surprised him, and he often felt as if he had to scramble to keep up with her.

What was she thinking now? he wondered. What delightful surprise lay just beneath the surface? He hardly dared wonder, and yet he could barely restrain himself from asking. She spoke first, however.

"Is your organ as large as his? And that red? Or is it shorter, like Geoffrey's?" She tilted her head again. "His was red, too, so I suppose that is normal."

Adrian groaned. He knew he should have expected this. Indeed, given Lynette's mind, he should have known she would want as many details as possible. Nonetheless, he was caught flat-footed and had no idea how to answer. In truth, he had never measured himself against young Bert or the older brother Geoffrey. As for the color, to be honest, he had never noticed.

Suddenly Lynette was shifting, turning to look directly at him, her eyes sparkling with interest—never a good sign. Adrian schooled himself to be calm and await her next startling pronouncement.

"This is a time for me to learn, correct?"

He nodded, though the movement was wary.

"I have learned quite a great deal," she said earnestly.

He allowed himself to smile. "I certainly hope so."

"But I am not done, am I? I mean, there is a great deal more to understand, correct?"

He raised an eyebrow. "Is there something you wish to know, Lynette?"

Then she flashed that certain expression, the one that told him to beware. She squared her shoulders. "I wish to see your penis."

He flinched. Trust Lynette to put it so bluntly. He looked down at his trousers.

All of his girls had seen his organ, if only for comparison purposes; it was important that they know what one looked like and learn not to fear it. It had taken him three nights to get Suzanne to touch it. But not Lynette. She was staring at him as boldly as a child demanding a treat. Before he could form an answer, she reached out to grasp his pants.

He reacted instantly, catching her hands before she moved too near. It was not that he was shy. However, he was all too aware of his messy state. "Go slowly, Lynette. And pray allow me to . . . clean up."

She stilled, clearly mulling over his words. "Did you . . . while we were . . ." She gestured vaguely toward the wall. "You . . ."

"The word is 'ejaculated,' Lynette. Yes, I released my seed into my pants." He sighed, feeling heat flood his face. "It is not something that happens normally, nor is it something a man wishes to be reminded of."

"But that means you were . . ." She struggled to find the word. "You were interested. When you . . ." Again she made the vague gesture, this time toward her lower body.

He actually grinned, somehow finding humor in the bizarre situation. "I assure you, I was quite interested."

She smiled at him—shyly at first, then with growing enthusiasm. Then again came the shoulders, straightened with pride. "I wish to learn. I wish to see what that white liquid is. I wish to . . . touch it." She hesitated a moment, her posture deflating just the tiniest bit. She tried a coy expression. "May I, please? In the name of education?"

How could he refuse her? Indeed, she would soon have to learn a great deal about the male anatomy. He just had not expected her to be so . . . eager. But a good instructor never allowed an opportune moment to pass. She was interested now. It was vital that he allow her to indulge her curiosity.

"Be gentle, Lynette. It is a very delicate instrument."

"Truly?"

"Mine is," was all he managed before she leaned forward, gingerly pulling at the buttons that fastened his trousers.

It was delicate work, and she was inexperienced. Therefore, as he lay as still as humanly possible, he was treated to an exquisite view of her bobbing breasts as she tugged and pulled at his clothing, naturally rubbing and heating him with her accidental caresses.

It was, in fact, the most erotic thing he had ever experienced. Yet he had to remain absolutely still, doing his best to control his breathing for fear he would frighten her away. It took a while, but eventually she managed to open his pants. Then there was more tugging and pulling as she removed his clothing altogether.

"I wish to see it all," was all she said.

She removed his pants, felt their wetness, explored their texture. She even inspected the garments as she set them aside. Then she turned her attention to him. It was not surprising that he was already growing hard. No man could remain stoic seeing what Adrian saw. Especially as Lynette came closer to him, reaching out one finger to touch his glistening tip.

He could not control himself. His buttocks tightened, and she jerked her hand away.

"I did not hurt you, did I?"

"No," he said, though it took a great deal of effort to keep his tone casual. "Perhaps I should not have said it is a *delicate* instrument. Rather, it is a sensitive one."

"Ah," she said, nodding in understanding. He sincerely doubted she did comprehend, but that did not deter her from further exploration.

She touched his lower belly, feeling the moisture there. Using first one finger, then two, then her whole hand, she rubbed his stomach, exploring the texture of the substance. There was a cloth nearby, which he grabbed and handed to her. She used it to help him clean up, though her movements were slow and intensely stimulating.

"There is a scent," she whispered, her eyes closed, as if she wished to memorize it. He did not answer for fear he might mention it had a distinctive taste as well. She would likely do exactly as he bade, and he knew he would go insane if she began that.

So he remained silent, clenching his teeth as she tossed the cloth aside and slipped her hand lower.

There came a loud moan from the other room.

Adrian had forgotten the trio. Lifting his head, he saw that Bert had managed to wake Louise, but she was a working girl, no doubt tired from her earlier exertions. So rather than continuing to dance and toy with her gentleman, she had chosen the most expedient method of pleasing the birthday boy.

She had simply reached out to clasp the kneeling young Bert in her hand, pleasuring him with a minimum amount of effort. Young Bert was entranced. And so, apparently, was Lynette. She studied exactly what the dancer was doing, narrowing her eyes as she gazed first at the pair, then back at Adrian.

"I want to do that," she said firmly.

He knew it was the next logical step. Knew, in fact, that as Louise began literally pulling young Bert around on his knees, that Lynette would want to attempt at least some form of manipulation of him. And true to form, he felt his body tense in greedy anticipation.

"May I?" she asked.

"I will not be dragged about on my knees."

Lynette glanced sideways as Bert began giggling even as Louise pulled harder, making him hop on his knees in his haste to keep pace with where she led.

"Oh, no!" Lynette gasped. "I doubt I am ready for that. You just lie still while I begin."

Still was the last thing he could be. Nevertheless, he intended to try. She grasped him, her hands firm and tight. And he was so startled he nearly flew across the room.

"Good God! Gently, Lynette! Did I not tell you it is a sensitive instrument?"

She bit her lip in consternation, the apology written in every line of her body. "I am so sorry. Truly, I am. It's just . . ." She glanced through the window. "Louise seems to be holding him quite solidly."

"Well, yes," admitted Adrian. He forced himself to recline once again. "But she began slowly and then built up."

"Ah." Lynette nodded, and Adrian nearly groaned out loud as her hand reached for him again. But this time she touched him with just one finger, gasping in delight as his organ jerked up to meet it. "Gently," she murmured. Then she used that single digit to trace the outline of his member.

She moved so slowly that he was hard-pressed not to react. Indeed, it was torture having her caress him with just her fingertip. She explored it all, starting at the tip. He meant to tell her more, to speak to her about what was sensitive and what was not, but he had not the breath.

She easily discovered the bead of moisture at its opening, touching it, circling around the tip with a child's delight. But she was no child, and Adrian was already having trouble holding still. And yet Lynette never stopped.

Rubbing the liquid all around the tip, she felt the smooth edge of his penis, the clear ridges, even the sloped edge of the head, while Adrian closed his eyes, trying not to experience every glorious sensation but unable to prevent it.

If only she would touch him harder.

But she was afraid to do so, and he could not draw breath to explain.

Exquisite eons later, she decided to explore lower. Still using only one finger, she traced the ridges of his shaft, commenting on the blood vessels visible beneath the skin, exploring the hard pulse that moved his member, and even measuring the girth of him with two fingers.

"I would guess you are most impressive in your size." She glanced through the window. "You seem to compare favorably with those two."

"I have not performed a detailed study," he said on a low growl.

"Well, then, I shall just have to believe that you are certainly adequate to the task."

"Thank you," he returned, unsure whether to be complimented or insulted. He chose instead to be amused. He had never had such an unusual conversation.

Then all thought fled as she abruptly pulled his legs apart, situating herself between them. If she were wearing clothing, her dress would have flounced around her, puffing up slightly as she settled into her seat. But she was naked. Adrian watched her breasts undulate, and his member stiffened even more at the sight.

"This is most interesting of all," she said.

He did not know what she referred to until he felt it. Suddenly she was there, touching, stroking, and finally holding his ballocks. It was a torture he had not expected. None of his girls had ever been so bold. True they had seen, but it was enough to get them to touch his shaft. He had not forced them to do more, knowing they would naturally seek more information when their husbands required it. But not Lynette. She wanted to know all, and so she had positioned herself appropriately, cupping him fully in her hand while he groaned in pleasure.

"You like this?" she asked, her voice filled with innocent curiosity. And then, as if to emphasize her point, she shifted her grip, caressing him as she moved.

His response was a gasp.

"Was that a yes?" she asked, but this time he could hear the mischief in her tone. Still, there was nothing he could do about it. Her right hand came forward, not to join her left but to grasp him about the shaft, holding him carefully but firmly. "Do you like it more than here?"

Both her hands held him, making his head spin with hunger. He could not help himself. He moved. He pushed forward against her right hand, groaning in response. "Yes."

"Yes, which? Which do you prefer?" She alternated her actions, stroking first in one location then the other, and the sensations left him nearly mindless.

Then, suddenly, abruptly, she stopped. Her hands stilled as if frozen, and though it took him some moments to restrain himself, he did at last notice the change.

He opened his eyes. "Lynette?"

She was not looking at him; her eyes were back on the window and the couple beyond.

Shifting, he followed her gaze and nearly groaned out loud. Louise was using her mouth now. Young Bert pumped in glorious abandon.

All Adrian had to do was spare one glance toward Lynette's luscious lips and he knew what she was thinking. He watched as she looked back down at him, her gaze sliding between his face, his groin, and the tableau through the window, then back again to him.

"Is it safe?" she asked.

No, he wanted to answer. *Nothing is safe with you.*

But he did not. He could not, for she would have to learn this. It was his heaven and his hell that he would be the one to teach her.

"Do not use your teeth. Suction is most delightful, especially when coupled by a squeeze."

"And the tongue?"

He hesitated, fearing for his sanity. "Do you recall how I explored you?"

She nodded, and he had the joy of watching her whole body flush.

"I give you leave to do the same."

With a girlish grin, she descended. It was his last moment of sanity for many hours.

They left Jenny's at dawn.

Never had Adrian been more grateful for a carriage, for he could barely walk. As for Lynette, her eyelids drooped the moment they stepped inside the vehicle. At home he sent her directly to bed, whereas he dragged himself to his library to sit and study his correspondence. He knew if he followed her upstairs he would not be able to resist joining her in bed. So he forced himself to attend estate business—though how he was going to read the ledgers, he had no idea. He barely had the energy to open the envelopes.

Five minutes into the task, sleep was the last thing on his mind. He had been scanning his mail, sorting it in preparation to read. Until one letter came to the top of the pile. It was from Audra.

Slitting the envelope, he pulled out the single page. It was a death notification. Audra's husband had died.

Smiling, he performed the calculations in his mind. She was now a free woman, a rich widow at the age of twenty-nine.

He stared at the missive, his grin still in place. At least one of his girls was free now, and earlier than expected! He could well imagine Audra's joy. Would he at last be able to see her smile in truth? A smile that held no hint of canniness or calculation? A smile like Lynette's?

His mind latched on to the image and would not release it. Lynette had the loveliest smile. Every woman was lovely in passion, and Lynette more so than most. But the picture Adrian most remembered was from before, a smile he was not even supposed to have seen.

It had been a moment from her first day here, a time when he had not expected her to be able to manage the affairs of the house, had expected her to flounder as all his other girls had. But she had more than succeeded, and in doing so had given him the first of the many surprises in store for him.

Yet in that first moment, that initial split second when he had been stunned to discover she had managed to not only buy food but also have an excellent meal prepared, she had turned away and smiled. It was not a smile meant for him. It was not a gloating moment of triumph as she well deserved. It was simply for herself, an acknowledgment that she had done well and knew it.

Thus, she had smiled. And the image had burned itself into Adrian's memory, for it, he supposed, was the essence of Lynette.

Her every action, her every thought now came from that place: from the sure and certain knowledge that this was something she had chosen to do. Or so it seemed to him. Even though she had been abused by Mr. Smythe, insulted by Lady Karen, and assaulted by Lord Rendlen, she still somehow managed to keep safe a core within herself, a place that told her she had indeed chosen this life.

And she accepted the consequences.

He admired her. He had never been so sanguine. In fact, he had spent years railing at his own fate, cursing his wastrel ancestors and damning the world in general for being so unfair.

How ironic that he would at last gain his own freedom at the very moment that Lynette lost hers. The moment she said, "I do," he would no doubt be many thousands of pounds richer. The moment she accepted many years of bondage, playing whore and servant to some old man, he would step boldly into a debt-free life.

Unbidden, his hands clenched into fists, crumpling the death notification into a tiny ball. How many years would it be for Lynette? Five? Ten? Twenty? It was not unheard of for a gentleman to defy all medical logic and keep breathing well into his seventies, even eighties. Would she still be able to smile in triumph in twenty years? Would she still be pleased with her choice? Or would she be cursing Adrian's name with every breath in her body?

Glaring down at his clenched fists, he abruptly threw the death notification across the room. He did not wish to see it. Did not want to think about Audra or Suzanne or any of his girls. He wished to think of his estate and his own bright future.

With that in mind, he slit the next missive. It was the last of Lynette's marriage proposals, a discreet letter from her fifth suitor requesting a time and place to discuss the details of his offer. It was this gentleman's earnest hope that the matter could be resolved quickly. If all went as he hoped, the man wrote, he and Lynette could be married within a week.

Releasing a curse he had not used in years, Adrian pushed away from his desk, grabbed his hat, and stormed out of the house.

Chapter 19

A funeral was a solemn affair. Given her father's profession, Lynette had attended dozens of these events. Indeed, if hard-pressed, she believed she could recite the service from beginning to end. But not this funeral. Not this time. Because this was the time and place Adrian had chosen for her to peruse her five suitors. He had explained to her the details of their offers. Indeed, he had been quite cold and logical as he recited the benefits of each man, their lacks, their problems.

One had the gout but appeared otherwise healthy.

One had power in the House of Lords, but it was waning.

One had the most money, but an evil, contemptible brood of children.

He had made a list of each man's attributes, flaws, and finances, and practically thrown the pages at her, as if he wished to end the entire sordid business as quickly as possible.

Hurt by the change in him, his sudden brusque manner, Lynette had gathered up the pages and fled to her room. There, she'd studied each man, memorizing the facts, pairing them in her mind with her thoughts and impressions.

Then, that night, he had come to her bedroom. She had been hopeful, but it was not to speak gently with her. Not to touch her or soothe her fears. He had wanted to tell her, in the fewest possible number of words, about this funeral. He had said all the gentlemen would be here, and she was to make her final selection the next day, before the sun had set.

She would be married a few days after that.

She had stared at him, a dozen questions on her lips, but before one could crowd past the others and be given voice, he'd turned smartly on his heel and left. And for the first time since she had arrived in his home, she'd heard him lock the adjoining door. There would be no more discussion on the matter.

She'd curled into herself in her bed, staring at the window until exhaustion forced her into an uneasy sleep.

Now the day had come. Within an hour, she would be face to face with the five gentlemen who wished to join their lives with hers. Except she knew they wanted nothing of the kind. Joining? No. They wanted a skilled lover and an entertaining servant to the end of their days.

But they wanted her, and Lynette didn't know whether to feel excited, repulsed, or terrified. In truth, she felt numb. The facts and figures about the men in question were a jumbled mass in her mind, none standing out from the others. And yet today—somehow—she had to choose.

"Come along, Lynette. We cannot be late."

Lynette started at the baroness's strident tone. The woman had not touched a drop of liquor since that disaster so many weeks before. Instead, she had been steeped in bad temper, obviously anxious for a drink but restraining. And though her expression remained perpetually sour, her body had started to improve. Her eyes were clearer, her skin rosy. Even her attire seemed better somehow. Crisper. Cleaner. Even in funereal black, the baroness seemed handsome.

Or would if she could simply smile.

Then again, perhaps her dour expression was appropriate to the event, decided Lynette as she glided down the stairs. Adrian joined them at the door, looking as dark and funereal as his aunt. But unlike the older woman, Adrian had seemed to shrink in the last few days. Not in stature, but in his soul. Lynette had no way to explain it, and she had tried many times to understand. She only knew that his eyes terrified her now.

His eyes seemed dead. So dead that they seemed to leach the very breath out of everyone, including herself. Around him, she felt cold and flat. And so empty.

That, too, somehow seemed appropriate. After all, this was a funeral where the widow celebrated newfound freedom while Lynette was choosing her jailer. And what better companions could Lynette have in this endeavor than an old bitter woman, pulled out of her cups to chaperone, and a man who could one night drive her to the heights of passion and the next treat her as so much bad fish?

Of course, she thought with a wild giggle; to cap off the day's entertainment there was herself, a minister's daughter, dressed in a black gown so sheer she might as well be standing in her shift. Add to that the very real possibility that a stiff gust of wind at the burial would strip the gown from her body, and most of the gentlemen would not be watching the coffin, but angling to be the one with the best view of her forthcoming nakedness.

All in all, one could not find better entertainment in any theater in the world.

She was being inspected.

Lynette had long since grown used to the stares, the longing looks from young men, even the haughty, arrogant hatred of the women. But this was new. This was an inspection, not by the men but by the other Marlock women.

The funeral and burial had ended a mere fifteen minutes earlier at the family plot. Guests and widow alike had returned to Audra's home, speaking in hushed tones while everyone looked at everyone else.

Or rather, everyone seemed to be looking at Lynette. Most especially the six other Marlock girls. All six were arrayed in their jewels and finery, all looking at her with catlike eyes, boldly assessing her attributes and apparently finding her lacking.

She recognized the signs. Indeed, she could not have worked with her father for so many years without seeing jealous, tabby-cat women intent on finding fault. And that surprised her. Why the hostility? By all accounts, each one was well on her way to being free. Over half their husbands had one foot already in the grave. Why wasn't Audra, the beautiful widow, the subject of such focused yearning? Why weren't they all clamoring about her, envious of the new life she would soon have?

Instead, they all gathered together and cast their venomous looks at Lynette.

She would have asked Adrian for an explanation. Indeed, she turned, intending to do just that, but he was gone from her side, caught in a group of gentlemen with political leanings. As for the baroness, she sat in a chair to one side, nursing a glass of lemonade and staring resentfully about the room.

Thus there was no rescue as Lady Linston, the fifth Marlock girl, took her by the hand and drew her forward.

"So, you are Adrian's last, are you? We all thought Marie would be, but apparently you just can't keep a good man down." The tiny redhead tittered at her own double entendre as she drew Lynette toward the circle of strikingly beautiful women. If nothing else, Adrian certainly had good taste. Looking about her, Lynette could easily understand how these ladies married well.

They were beautiful, every one of them.

And yet she found she did not like them. Not in the least. Their eyes were calculating, their movements a little too studied, even as each of them moved with languid grace that no doubt drew the eye of every man they passed.

Then she realized with a start that she was jealous of them. Each one had felt what she had, had done what she had done. All with Adrian.

And that, if nothing else, made her angry. Why should she be angry with these women? she chastised herself. They were every bit as much victims in this whole affair as she was. And yet she disliked them. She wanted to bare her nails and shred them to tiny pieces.

"Has he taken you to Jenny's yet?" asked one. "Every time Henry mounts me, I close my eyes and think of that night."

"George hates it that I want to sleep naked. He thinks it's improper! And yet he thinks nothing of dropping his trousers in the library just as I've come in from shopping."

"I was the first one he took to Jenny's," gleefully confided another. "He told me after everything I did, they would name the chamber after me."

Lynette spun around, trying to pair words with faces and names. But for once, her composure deserted her. They had literally surrounded her, their comments coming faster than she could manage, speaking of things she never thought women did.

And perhaps respectable women did not. But Marlock women did, and Lynette suddenly felt completely outmaneuvered and outclassed. What did she know to compare with these women? What did she have?

The circle parted, and the widow Audra stepped forward. Lynette knew Audra had been part of the group from the beginning, but somehow she gave the impression of just now joining them, as a queen entering a room.

Of all the Marlock girls, Audra was the most striking. With raven-black hair and kohl-darkened eyes, she personified exotic beauty. The black gown she wore fit her ripe body like a well-made glove, emphasizing her curves, her tiny waist, and breasts that were full and lush.

This was no grieving widow, but a woman coming into her own.

When she spoke, her voice was low, a seductive purr, but her words cut nonetheless. "Please, please, girls—give the poor child room to breathe. Do you not remember how new all this was? How overwhelming?" Audra extended her arm in a movement that defined grace. "Come, Lynette, let us sit over there and talk."

She drew Lynette away, while the others clustered together and stared from nearby. "My dear, you look quite exhausted. Has Adrian been keeping you up at night?"

Lynette looked away, knowing what the woman wanted to hear and angry that she could not bring herself to lie. So she told the truth, even though it burned in her gut to see the triumphant gleam in Audra's eyes.

"It is my own distemper that is keeping me awake. I find myself thinking a lot lately."

"No doubt. And yearning. And remembering." Audra leaned forward, a possessive gleam in her eyes. "I was his first, you know. He said I taught him as much as he taught me."

Inwardly, Lynette sighed. She knew what she should say. Indeed, she knew exactly what Audra wanted to hear, and it saddened her greatly. Here was a beautiful woman on the verge of a new life, and yet inside she was still clinging to the dubious fame of being the first girl to be debauched by Adrian.

Was that what was in store for herself? Lynette

wondered. Would she someday be leaning over another girl saying: *I was to be his last, you know. But after me, he found he simply could not stop.*

Lynette closed her eyes at the image, trying to force it from her thoughts.

"I was with him for nearly three months," Audra was saying. "And he personally chose every one of my gowns. Ah," she sighed, a look of rapture on her face. "I have missed those fittings. Even now, I dream of them."

Lynette looked away, finally finding enough pity in her heart to say what the widow wanted to hear. "He speaks of you often. I believe he compares every new girl to you."

As expected, Audra beamed in triumphant pleasure, looking about her in a show of graciousness. "Ah, well," she said sweetly, like a monarch bestowing a favor. "That is only to be expected. I was his first."

Then she stood and glided happily away. Lynette watched her go, saw the men follow her movements with their eyes, saw, too, Adrian's narrowed eyes, which found his first charge, then leaped back to his last.

Lynette met his gaze firmly, strongly, but inside her heart failed her. Was what she just said true? Did Adrian indeed compare her to Audra?

Glancing back at the stunning woman, Lynette realized that if he did, Lynette would be the loser. Audra was everything Lynette was supposed to be. Stately. Sensual. And now, by all accounts, a very rich widow. And at that moment, Lynette felt like nothing more than a lost parson's daughter wrapped up in some rather sheer paper.

Lynette would have stood and rushed into the ladies' retiring room, but she was stopped by a slender hand. She turned, seeing the golden beauty that was Suzanne. Slim, elegant, this was the fair-haired beauty Adrian had nearly killed for.

"Do not let Audra upset you," said the blonde softly. "I think she is grieving more than she lets on."

Lynette glanced at the widow, watching her move silently through the people in her home, an isolated creature of such sensuousness that all watched. And yet, for all her beauty, Lynette suddenly saw how alone Audra was.

"It is hard, you know," Suzanne continued. "You nurse a man for years, build your life around his entertainment, grace his bed in constantly new and interesting ways. Eventually it becomes much more than a business arrangement. The transition will be very difficult."

Lynette looked back at Suzanne. By all accounts her husband would not see the new year. Did she look at Audra and see her own future? Would she soon be as alone as the dark-haired beauty?

"I do not think I can do this." That was Lynette, as startled to hear her own words as Suzanne. But then the golden beauty reached out, touching her hands in a gentle embrace.

"Of course you can. Indeed, if you are like the rest of us, you must."

Lynette nodded, knowing it was true. She had committed herself. She could refuse to wed now, but then what would she do? How would she survive? She doubted even a nunnery would take her now. And she had already used so much of Adrian's money.

She heard Suzanne sigh, the sound so heartfelt it

seemed to tear through her. "We all fall in love with him, you know. That, too, is inevitable."

Lynette did not need to see where Suzanne gazed.

"We all wish we were you, right now. Still in his arms. Still being taught what was once so special, so new."

Lynette nodded, now understanding the source of the women's animosity. Indeed, she thought, he must be the desire of every woman. His broad frame, his dark good looks, and the strength and power he emanated attracted her fair sex like a magnet. She knew how glorious he was, how wonderful his intimacy could be.

Yes, she thought as she looked at the other Marlock girls. They would all be jealous of her now. Just as she would be green-eyed with hatred of the next woman he chose to sponsor.

Lynette spoke, unsure why she felt the need to explain but grateful for this woman's kindness nonetheless. "I believe you are his favorite," she said. And though she did not say he had practically killed for her, she thought about it, remembering the pain that gripped Adrian when he spoke of it.

Suzanne merely shrugged. "His latest girl is always his favorite. He cannot afford to feel any differently." Then she reached up, touching Lynette's face with tenderness. "And you, my dear, are his last. You will always remain in his thoughts as none of us ever shall."

Lynette denied it with a single shake of her head. "I am here today to choose my husband."

"I know." Suzanne laughed, and the sound was oddly lighthearted. "That is why I am here. I wanted to speak with you."

Lynette did not ask the obvious question, but Suzanne answered it nonetheless.

"My dear, for all his talents, Adrian is still a man. He does not know that we fall in love with him. He does not realize how hard it is for us to leave him. He does not know, and so he cannot help you."

Lynette looked away. She did not want to think about this. She did not want to remember that soon she would be leaving the Marlock home. Soon she would be married to someone else.

"You have fallen in love with him," Suzanne prompted.

"I have not!" Lynette whispered back fiercely. But in her heart she realized she lied. She had indeed fallen for the viscount. She had, in fact, been deeply in love with him for a very long time. As the baroness had claimed, too.

Why else would she wait up nights hoping he would join her in her bedroom? Why else would his merest look send her to the heights of joy or the depths of despair? She loved the way he spoke, the way he looked, the way he slept until noon, then arose like a bear with a sore paw. And she loved that all she needed to do to turn him back into himself was pour his tea, hand him his paper, and leave him alone for a half hour. Then, she knew, he would smile at her in gratitude and she would sail through a beautiful day.

"No girl can be trained as he does it and not fall in love," reproved Suzanne.

Lynette shook her head—no longer in denial of her feelings but in disagreement with the method. True, her moments in Adrian's arms were ecstasy as she had never experienced. But she treasured as much, if not more, the moments when they spoke, when they shared the tiny details of their day. From the beginning he had challenged her, met her on her own terms, and even negotiated with her as if he respected her mind and abilities to choose her own fate. From the beginning, he had valued her as a person, and it was that which planted the seeds of her love. He valued her. And she valued him.

She loved him.

And yet . . . Her thoughts trailed away. She did not want to finish the sentence. Did not want to acknowledge the question. But it was there nonetheless, and all too soon it surfaced in her mind.

She loved Adrian with all her heart and soul, and yet he was right now preparing to hand her over to another man.

Her chest clenched at the thought, squeezing her heart so tightly that she feared she would die. But she did not. Instead, she breathed her question aloud, not even knowing she was speaking it openly to Suzanne. "Could he not love me back?"

Suzanne's answer was soft, but no less hard to hear. "Has he kissed you? On the lips?"

Lynette spun toward her companion, her eyes pulled wide with hope. "Do you mean it is possible? He could love me?"

Suzanne's expression was philosophical. She shrugged. "I could tell you no. No, Lynette, there is no possibility that he loves you. But you would not believe me. None of us wanted to believe it."

"But . . ." Lynette began. Suzanne forestalled her. "Has he kissed you? On the lips?"

Frantically, Lynette searched back through her memories. He had touched her in so many ways, kissed her in places no other soul had dared touch. And yet, through all that, there had never, ever been contact with her lips.

"No," she whispered.

"And he will not do so. That is the one place he reserves for the bride's husband."

The implication was clear. If Adrian had never broken that rule with her, he had always, from the very beginning, planned to give Lynette away to another man. Despite all their shared passion, every moment of glorious rapture, he had maintained that distance.

He had never kissed her on the lips, therefore he had never loved her.

The pain was unbearable. Unbidden, tears sprang to her eyes. So steeped in misery was she that she did not even bother to wipe them away. All her secret hopes, the fantasies she did not even realize she had built, all came crashing down around her.

He did not love her.

He never would.

She would marry an old man soon and spend the next decade in servitude until she, finally, like Audra, emerged sensuous but cold and alone. She clasped her hand over her mouth to stop a cry of agony.

She did not know when he appeared at her side. But somehow, when she blinked back the tears, she saw Adrian there, his hard eyes on Suzanne.

"What have you said to her?" he demanded, as Lynette struggled frantically to regain her composure.

"Nothing, Adrian—"

"*This* is not nothing!" he said, his voice low and angry.

Suzanne did not flinch. Instead, Lynette saw her rise slowly, almost painfully to her feet. Her expression was sad. "I merely told her the truth. A truth she needed to hear." Then she looked down, and Lynette connected with her compassionate gaze. "Ask her if you need to. Ask her if I am the one who hurt her."

Adrian turned immediately, his expression alternating between alarm, fury, and confusion. "Lynette?"

Then she understood. It was at that moment she fully comprehended what Suzanne had meant when she said that for all Adrian's skills, he was still a man. He was still as confused as her father when it came to emotions.

Suzanne was not the one who hurt her; he was. He was the one who had taught her, who had held her and touched her and teased her. He was the one who had allowed her to fall in love with him. And he was the one giving her away to someone else.

She finally felt it. At last a surge of fury blew through her, a rise of anger that whipped like a gale wind, crushing her tender feelings, leaving her colder, harder, and much, much stronger.

He did not love her. She understood that now.

She lifted her chin, stared directly into his startled gaze, and spoke her words simply. "No, my lord. She did not hurt me at all."

Then she walked away.

She did not speak to him again until they returned home. She went directly to her room to strip out of her funeral clothing as quickly as possible. Unfortunately, as usual, there was nothing in which she wished to dress. So she stood by her window in her shift, staring out into the late afternoon while thinking over everything that had happened.

She came to no conclusions as the sun began to slip lower in the sky. Indeed, all she could do was think the same phrase over and over, no matter how many times she tried to purge it from her thoughts.

She was in love with Adrian.

She heard him come into her room. Either that, or she had at last become so attuned to his movements that she knew where he was no matter what he did. In any event, she knew he was standing in the doorway that joined their two rooms, regarding her with a mixture of anxiety, concern, and confusion.

True to form, he wrapped all those emotions into his sounding of her name. "Lynette?"

At first she could not decide what to do. She did not want to face him, and yet she did not want to let this opportunity slide by. It wouldn't be long now before she had to leave this house, before she wed some other man, and she would always regret not pushing the issue now.

She turned, squaring her shoulders as she faced him, but she did not speak. He interrupted her before she'd even drawn breath.

"What did she say to you? What upset you so?"

She frowned, trying to decide how to broach the subject. Then she shook her head, throwing caution to the wind. She could never choose her words carefully around Adrian. They always became jumbled and confused. She would simply speak and accept what came.

"Why have you never kissed me?"

He had stepped into the room, coming toward her with his arms open, as if he meant to embrace her. At her question he froze, his expression turning wary.

"I do not understand," he said slowly, though his demeanor told her that he very much understood. "I have kissed you hundreds of times."

"Not on the mouth. Not . . ." Her own fingertips touched her lips, and she blinked in surprise at the feel. *No,* she realized suddenly. No one had ever touched her there.

He stepped forward, his expression darkening as he moved. "Is that what Suzanne said to you? Did she ask if I had ever kissed you?"

Lynette shifted, letting her hand slowly drop away from her face. "She told me that you never kiss your girls on the lips. That you reserve such actions for the bridegroom." She looked him squarely in the eye and dared him to lie to her.

He did not, though she could tell he wanted to. She saw it in the way he opened his mouth, then shut it again without speaking. And in the way he shifted his weight away from her, looking down at the floor before finally meeting her level gaze.

"She is correct," he finally said. He shrugged as he tried to explain. "I have never kissed any of my girls. I do so much to them. With them. I need to build some sort of barrier, someplace I cannot go."

"Because it separates us."

He nodded, pain in his eyes. "Because it reminds me that you are not mine to kiss."

She understood now. Probably better than he did. She knew he was a passionate man. No cold fish could ever do what he did, teach what he taught. How easy it must be for him to lose himself in his work, to believe that the woman in his arms today would remain there forever.

But from the beginning she had known she was destined for someone else. That he was only the instructor, not the goal. So he'd created this restriction, this immutable law that even he could not break, a reminder not to his girls but to himself. They were not his.

Lynette felt a tear slip down her cheek. In that moment she realized that she cried not only for herself, for the love that could never be, but for the man in front of her. The man who gave himself body and soul not once but seven times, to women who would leave him. Seven women had walked down the aisle to other men.

"All of them would have stayed, you know," she whispered. "If only you had asked, they would have remained with you."

He shook his head, and she caught the sheen of pain in his eyes. "No, they would not. And if they had, they would have been unhappy."

She understood his implication; still, she had to say it aloud. She had to hear it spoken boldly, starkly revealed in the afternoon sun. "And I?"

He opened his hands, lifting them in a gesture of futility. "I have nothing to offer you, Lynette. And everything to lose if you remain."

She nodded. The movement felt stiff and brittle. Inside, the last of her hopes died, crushed beneath his brutal honesty. He did not want her. He did not love her. Not enough. And now the last of her lessons was over.

She'd never known love could cut so deeply.

"Very well," she whispered. And though she could not lift her gaze to see him, could not even gather the strength to brush away her tears, she found enough resolve to speak. "I shall marry the Earl of Songshire."

Even through the haze of her tears, she saw his reaction. His body recoiled as if struck and his fists clenched spasmodically. Likely without realizing it, he took a step forward.

She shied back, quickly and in fear. If he so much as touched her, she would die. She knew it with absolute certainty. She could not so much as breathe the same air with him or she would collapse into a helpless puddle of pain.

Thankfully he stopped, standing helplessly, barely two feet away from her. He spoke, though his voice was unsteady, his tone uncertain.

"He is not very old."

She nodded. This she knew, but she would rather spend longer with a kind man, a man like Songshire, than a few short years with an ill brute. "I don't mind," she said softly. "He is an old family friend. My family will be pleased, and I hope to enjoy the years we will be together." Certainly she could not imagine living in a household where one member longed for the other's death.

"Lady Karen will be difficult."

Lynette shrugged, thankful at last to have something else to think about, some other problem to focus on.

"It will take some time, but I believe I can bring her around. It will go easier once she realizes I will not come between her and her father." Then she felt herself smile, though she thought her skin might crack with the effort. "She always was possessive."

She saw him nod, but the movement was more of a jerk than anything else. Once again he moved forward, and once again she jumped back, her words rushing in her panic.

"It is my decision, my lord. You promised me I could decide. I want him. I want Songshire."

She saw him stop, drawing back at her anxious movements. Then he waited, standing in silence as he no doubt studied her misery in confusion. And all the while Suzanne's words haunted her.

"For all his talents, Adrian is still a man. He does not realize how hard it is for us to leave him. He cannot help you."

Lifting her gaze, she saw that Suzanne was right. Adrian did not know what to do. He was lost, yearning for what he could not have, eternally trapped in a web of his own making.

"It is over, my lord," she whispered, wanting to set him free even more than she longed for her own release. "I will marry Songshire as soon as it can be arranged. Then you may take your money and rebuild your estates and your life." She forced herself to give him a ragged semblance of a smile. "Perhaps one day you will marry and carry on your family name. And maybe we shall meet, you and I, when I am at a last a wealthy widow and you have your children dancing at your feet."

She could tell he was hurt by her words. She knew as well that he was not even aware of the source of his pain. Yes, she realized, he did love her a little. He did want her. But he was not in love with her and never would be. To him, she was merely a means to his estate. A tool in the grand design of the Marlock fortune.

"Please, Adrian," she finally whispered. "Please leave. Please make the arrangements."

Then she turned her back on him, staring out at the setting sun. Inside her heart, it was already dark.

Chapter 20

"You want what?" Adrian sat bolt upright in his chair, staring across his desk into the Earl of Songshire's eyes. He could not be more shocked if the man had walked in naked.

"Good God, man," returned the earl in amused accents, "I never thought you would be one to cut up stiff on this point."

"But . . . but . . ." Adrian sealed his lips shut. It could not possibly be. This was not a rational discussion.

"But-but nothing," returned Thomas firmly. "You listen to me, boy, I want a Marlock bride and so I shall have one. Why do you think I turned her in your direction in the first place?"

Adrian nodded his head dumbly, looking down at the stack of papers between himself and his guest. "All the particulars have been agreed upon," he said, as if confirming the fact to himself.

"Yes," agreed the earl. "All except one. You must take her virginity for me."

Again Adrian's mind reeled. "You cannot be serious about this."

The earl threw up his hands in disgust. "Look at me, Adrian. I am a fumbling old man. Good God, I haven't the skill or the patience to break in a virgin correctly, much less a parson's daughter." He leaned forward, his eyes intense. "But you do, man. You've made a bloody business out of it."

"I have never taken any girl's virginity!" Adrian snapped, all the while wondering why his hands were clenched, why he wanted to pound his fists into the face of the nobleman who had just made an incredibly generous financial settlement upon Lynette. And by extension, upon Adrian himself.

"Of course you haven't," returned the earl in soothing accents. "But you will now. Because I haven't the patience to do it right." Then he leaned forward, his expression stern. "The young can be so touchy and unpredictable. They take more patience than I have. And you and I both know how a bungled wedding night can ruin a girl forever."

Adrian swallowed, his throat unaccountably dry. "But it is *your* wedding night," he said, his voice hoarse as it scraped his throat.

"No, Adrian. The second time will be my wedding night. Her first time will be with you." Abruptly the man stood, grabbing his hat as he moved. "Do it soon. Tonight, perhaps. I shall get the special license for the day after tomorrow. That should give her enough time to recover." He paused at the door, turning long enough to wink at the younger man. "Then it shall be my turn."

He left, while Adrian remained rooted to the spot, immobile with shock.

Lynette's virginity.

His.

With a sudden spurt of energy, he ran from the room and out the back door. Falling to his knees in the vegetable garden, he cast up his accounts.

Baroness Agatha Huntley knew what day it was. Indeed, the entire household knew. Today was the day Adrian would take Lynette's virginity. The contracts had all been signed, the accounts totaled and closed. Now all that was left was to deflower the girl, watch as the chit whispered her *I do*, and wave as bride and groom rode off into the morning light.

At last Adrian would have enough blunt to set his estate back on its feet. This would finally give him the capital above his debts to start afresh. Dunwort would finally escape the hellhole he called London, for he was set to follow his master into the country. And Agatha would be left to rot wherever she stood.

Yes, Lynette was the last of the Marlock girls. And so Agatha was expendable, because Adrian had made it more than clear that he felt no family connection to his aunt. Her only worth was in her ability to train and escort his women.

The moment Lynette walked down the aisle, Agatha would be cast out like so much rubbish.

Looking down at her hand, she glowered at the cup and the dark liquid held within it. It was cheap brandy, and a more foul substance could not be found in this house. Until now, she had never minded. Bad brandy rendered one insensible as quickly as good. In fact, sometimes faster.

But not today. And not for some weeks. Not since Lynette had issued her challenge.

"Pick a man, Baroness. Show me how your wiles work without beauty."

Those words echoed in her head, tumbled around and around until Agatha had reached for the brandy just to silence the sound. Except she had not drunk, had not touched a drop of liquor since that day. Because the moment she reached for the bottle, she remembered Adrian's words.

"You were a handsome woman once. When you did not drink."

Between Lynette's challenge and Adrian's disdain, Agatha had decided to face her demons. But now they were back in force. Now they were gliding down the hallway all embodied in the form of Lynette.

The girl was beautiful—graceful, young, and warmhearted. She was all the things Agatha had been once. Long ago, before her husband beat them out of her.

She glared resentfully at Lynette's disappearing shadow.

It wasn't fair. How could that girl get everything, while she herself rotted away with nothing? Lynette was the golden child. Lynette would get a rich husband. A respected title. Lord, she even got to be deflowered by the best hand in all England.

Worst of all, Lynette got Thomas: Thomas, the sweet boy who had once professed his love to Agatha, who had once bent on one knee and kissed Agatha's hand with an ardor that would have shocked his parents had they known.

Fool that she had been, Agatha had spurned him. Not harshly. Indeed, she had been most kind. His family would certainly naysay the match to a nameless girl. And she had already given her heart to Horace, a mere baron. God, if she could only go back in time. If she could only whisk herself back to that moment when he had first spoken to her. She would throw her arms around him, do anything in her power to seal their match.

Agatha realized she would have thrown propriety to the winds, purposely compromising herself in his arms and forcing him to do the honorable thing. And he would have. She knew it. Because Thomas was an honorable man. And now he was to be Lynette's.

The thought soured her stomach even as she reached for her glass. She did not drink. Instead, she stared once again at the dark liquid, tempting her as it had not for weeks.

"Pick a man, Baroness. Show me how your wiles work without beauty."

It was a challenge. Issued as bold and brassy as any that had ever been shouted. And up until this moment, Agatha had ignored it. She would not stoop to that level. She would not fight a girl half her age for a man, as if he were some prize at a fair.

But Lynette had Thomas. And Agatha wanted him.

"You were a handsome woman once. When you did not drink."

Agatha looked at the clock. Lynette's deflowering would take place tonight. That meant both the girl and her nephew would be more than occupied.

She frowned again, thinking through her plan. Thomas was a creature of habit. He always had been. In a bare forty-five minutes he would leave his empty house for his club. There he would eat his dinner, smoke his cigars; then, at half past ten, he would return home. Letting himself in by his own key, he would read some Aristotle or some other dead Greek before finally seeking his bed by midnight.

The only reason the man desired Lynette was because she was a novelty. And more than that, she offered the promise of constant change of routine throughout the years to come.

But men never understood their own minds. Lynette would please him for a week or two, perhaps even months, but no young girl had the wherewithall to manage Thomas for years on end. No child still in her twenties understood Thomas well enough to allow him his routine while disturbing it just enough to be daring.

It was not the girl's fault. She simply did not have the history an older woman did. The perspective, as it were.

But Agatha did.

And Agatha would.

With that thought firmly fixed in her mind, the baroness pushed up from her chair, abandoning her liquor in search of other more interesting fare. Tonight she did not want to forget. Tonight she intended to remember. And to make someone else remember how they'd once been together.

She would not stoop to compete with Lynette. She simply intended to show Thomas his mind, assisting the man in getting what he truly wanted.

It was time.

Adrian stared numbly at his grandfather's battered pocket watch. It was one of the few things his father hadn't pawned years ago, probably because the item had been lost for over a decade. Adrian wouldn't have it now if he hadn't discovered it fallen behind a wardrobe. Even then he had stared at it, wondering if he should sell the item.

But the wardrobe had been purchased, not the watch, and so he had kept it. Later, when the last of the rare books had left his home, he had wondered again how much it would fetch. In the end, he had gone to a ball, searching for something to eat, and that was where he had met Audra.

Sometime during that night he'd decided to sell Audra instead of his grandfather's pocket watch. Now, once again, he was staring at the watch, wondering exactly how much the battered timepiece would fetch. Was it possible to sell the item for as much as Lynette? Half as much?

Of course not. Not even one thousandth, but he still contemplated it. He stared at it and wondered and wished and remembered.

He closed his eyes, pain welling up in his heart. He didn't want to do this. He didn't want to take her virginity, to lie in bed with her, to bury himself within her. He didn't want to touch her—because that would make the morning that much harder.

If he cried every time one of his girls married, what would he do when Lynette walked down the aisle? How could he watch the one woman who had ever challenged him, ever teased him, tested him, and overwhelmed him? How could he watch her marry another man?

She had offered to stay with him. Of all his girls, she was the one who had said the words. Or nearly said them. She would stay if only he would ask. She would throw away everything she ever wanted and remain here with him.

He looked around at the pocked walls, the empty shelves, the threadbare carpet. Soon Lynette would have wealth and security for the rest of her life. He could not give her that. He could not even offer her security through the end of the month. She did not know how dangerously depleted he was. How much he had risked on the income from her marriage.

If the arrangement did not go through as planned, all of them would be on the street within a fortnight. Debtor's prison would not be far behind. It would be months before his crop came in. And years before he saw any real return on his investments.

Even with her marriage, he faced long, hard years of backbreaking work.

He had to give her away. His future, his aunt's, Dunwort's, even the people who worked his land, all depended on Lynette's marriage.

But how could he hold her, share a single, glorious night with her, and then send her away? It was unthinkable. So he sat and stared at his grandfather's pocket watch and wished for things he could not have.

He knew he should be upstairs. She was likely pacing the floor, worrying herself into a frazzle at what was to come. She knew what he had to do. Indeed, he had told her, not face to face but in another one of his cursed missives.

Songshire requires that I take your virginity tonight. Your wedding will occur in two days. Direct all questions to the baroness, as I shall be occupied with the final contractual obligations.

M

Dunwort reported that she had read the missive with equanimity. She had not fainted or screamed or cried, not that he had expected such from Lynette. But she had gone pale and needed to seat herself for a moment. Dunwort had given her tea, held her hand, and then, at her urging, gone on about his regular tasks.

Adrian should have been the one to hold her hand. He should have given her the news tenderly, carefully, helping her to absorb the shock and prepare for the no doubt frightening night to come.

He should have, but he couldn't. He couldn't face the betrayal that surely shone in her eyes, the dread that he would have to touch her again, all the while knowing that he would abandon her in the morning.

She would stay with him if he only asked.

Seized with a sudden pain, he gripped the chair, cursing Songshire with every ache, every clench of his belly, every agonizing breath he took. Then, when the fit passed, he stood, resolve in every line of his body.

He would not do this. He could not do this. Songshire would simply have to deflower his own wife.

He was halfway across the room when the library door opened. Framed in the dim hallway light stood Lynette, her hair down, her body loosely clad in one of her sheerest gowns.

Adrian swallowed. This he had not expected. But then again, when had Lynette ever done anything he expected? Anything he planned? Though, even given her penchant for surprising him, he never would have guessed she'd come to him. That she'd stand before him in a sheer gown with no shift beneath.

Good God, he could see her entire body. Her luscious breasts. Her trim waist. The dark thatch of hair at the apex of her thighs. And, of course, her legs. Her exquisitely long and shapely legs.

"Adrian?" she queried softly.

His gut tightened at the sweet sound of her voice. She looked at the gloves in his hands and frowned at him.

"Were you leaving?" she asked.

He wanted to lie to her, but he could not. If nothing else, he owed her honesty.

"I cannot do this, Lynette." His voice was thick and hoarse, his body clenched with pain. He was not sure if it was a mental pain or a physical one. The two were so intermeshed that he could not distinguish one from the other. He only knew he wanted her with an intensity that bordered on insanity. But he could not have her.

"I must leave."

He stepped forward, meaning to do exactly that. But she did not move. She remained exactly where she was, framed within the doorway. And he could not risk brushing past her. Not when she wore that gown. Not if he had to touch her.

"Lynette," he said firmly, trying to put a note of command into his voice, "this will not work."

She cocked her head, smiling at him as if she understood a great secret joke. "What will not work, Adrian?" she asked sweetly. "Are you saying your male organ is damaged?" She glanced significantly down at him, making him all too aware of the visible bulge there. "Somehow I doubt that."

"I have always desired you, Lynette. You know that."

She raised an eyebrow, shocked pleasure on her face. "Truly? I had *not* realized that." She took a step toward him. "I am glad you said so."

"Lynette . . ." he began, his voice strangled.

She cut him off with the smallest of gestures. She twisted her wrist, and with that simple movement pulled the library door shut behind her.

The sound exploded in his mind. "You are supposed to be upstairs," he said. "Preparing." It was an inane statement, indicative of a flustered mind. But it was the best he could think of, especially as he scrambled to keep some distance between them, both physically and emotionally. Talking to her, distracting her in some way, was one of the few, meager weapons in his arsenal.

Again she smiled. "I was prepared. I was waiting." Then she sighed, the gesture pulling her gown tight across her breasts, making them almost shimmer beneath the rose gauze. "And I began to think." She turned slightly, her eyes twinkling with merriment as she displayed herself in profile.

God, her nipples were erect. Adrian's organ swelled to stiff attention.

"I began to think about you, Adrian."

She walked around him. Thankfully, she did not come near enough to touch. Indeed, she cut a wide path around him to lean slowly, carefully, against his desk.

He glanced behind him. He could leave now. She was not blocking his path. But where would he go? How would he run from the image imprinted upon his brain? The picture of Lynette, draped in rose netting, leaning against his desk while her eyes danced a challenge. He could not run from that. Indeed, he very much suspected it would haunt him for the rest of his life.

"Would you like to know what I realized, Adrian? About you?"

He nodded. Indeed, if she had asked him to appear before Parliament stark naked, he would have nodded without hesitation.

"I realized that everyone leaves you."

He reared back as if slapped, but she was relentless. She continued speaking, her words gentle, but like tiny needles slipping deeper and deeper under his skin.

"It began, I suppose, with your parents' deaths. Then the baroness. I suppose she did not truly leave you; she was merely unable to bring you to her home. And then, of course, there was Jenny." Her voice grew a little harsher. It was a bit more clipped, though the compassion remained. "She showed you physical love, but only for a fee, then promptly left you when a better offer came along."

"Jenny cares for me." He didn't realize he had spoken until he felt the pain of the words pushing past the constriction of his throat.

"Well, of course she does," Lynette chided. "Good God, Adrian, we all care for you. But I am speaking of your life."

She leaned forward a bit, her breasts becoming more pronounced with the movement, even as she extended her legs forward, too, showing him the exquisite lines of her calves.

"In the end, Jenny went on to become a famous madame and you cannot afford her anymore."

He could not deny it. Jenny had done excellently for herself.

"And now we come to your hand in all this. Up until this point, everything was done *to* you. But here"—she gestured to the house around him as she continued to slice him with her words—"you became a man. You created the very situation that has pained you so deeply."

At this point, Lynette pushed away from his desk, pacing slowly about him again, forcing him to watch the shift of her body and the slow caress of the fabric against her legs, buttocks, and long, elegant back. He tried not to look. He tried to close his eyes, but still he heard the rustle of clothing against bare skin, smelled the honeysuckle of her hair and the scent that was uniquely her.

"Lynette . . ." he tried again, his voice strangled.

If she heard his plea, she gave no indication of it. Instead, he heard her step behind him, and to his torment, felt her touch him. She began on his shoulders, but quickly pulled close to him, pressing her body against his back, running her hands down his chest, slipping her hand beneath his coat.

"You found women, Adrian. Beautiful women whom you brought into your home. And then slowly, carefully, you taught them."

Her finger flicked his nipple through his shirt, and his legs nearly buckled at the flash of sensation that shot through his body.

"You brought them from innocence to awareness. You taught them all about intimacy—didn't you, Adrian?"

She slid around, gliding sensuously as she rubbed intimately against him, all the while moving until they came face to face, her eyes intense. She studied him.

"You taught them how it feels to be touched." With

that, she took hold of his hands, pressing them to her breasts.

Without willing it, his hands reacted. They cupped her breasts, stroking them, tweaking her nipples while she groaned and arched. Her head dropped back, revealing the curve of her neck to his hungry lips. And before he understood what he was doing, he was leaning forward, kissing that glorious expanse of flesh.

All too soon she pulled away, and his hands fell useless and empty to his sides.

"You taught us all how it feels to be stroked, Adrian," she said as she moved away. "But not a one of us learned how to love." She paused, and her hands dropped away from him as well, falling to her sides. "Because *you* don't know how."

He swallowed, staring at her, feeling a pain he hadn't expected, an emptiness he'd never acknowledged.

"Then each of us," she continued as she walked away from him, "each of those beautiful women you trained, you touched, you became intimate with, each of us left you because that was the way you designed it."

He looked away, unable to bear the sight of her, unable to withstand the hunger her words sparked within him. "It was necessary," he rasped.

"Perhaps. But part of you kept hoping we would love you." She hesitated, as if searching for words. "Or rather, I suppose part of you wanted us to teach you. You wanted us to show you how to love, and then maybe we wouldn't leave you. Maybe one of us would stay." She suddenly leaned forward. "Or maybe you would finally learn how to make it less painful, less hard to say good-bye."

He shifted abruptly, moving away from her, hurrying behind his desk as if the mere placement of furniture between them could stop his thoughts. More importantly, stop the feelings her words conjured within him.

"That doesn't make sense, Lynette. This has always been a business arrangement. From the very beginning—"

"From the very beginning," she interrupted, "you have been hoping someone would love you." She came closer, stepping right up to the desk, leaning over it. "Your parents, perhaps? Jenny? Any one of the Marlock girls?"

Then he said it. He said the words he had never voiced before, never expected to voice, never even believed in before. Or rather, he very much feared he did believe in.

"There is no love, Lynette! There is only lust and hunger." Abruptly, he surged forward, across his desk, grabbing her crotch with one hand, grasping it hard and brutally, with a crude intensity that made her cry out.

She did not jerk away. She did not even flinch. Instead, she reached for him, caressing his arm, his shoulder, until she touched his face.

"*I* know how to love, Adrian. I know what it is."

She took a deep breath, and gradually his grip eased. She reached down with her other hand, gently opening his hand until he released her. Then she pressed their palms together and their fingers intertwined.

"I can show you."

He felt tears blur his vision. Was this true? Was this

what he had been aching for, yearning for all these years? Was this the nameless something she had mentioned on her first night here? That thing she longed for—that *they* longed for—but hadn't found?

"You are meant for someone else."

"I know," she whispered.

He swallowed, but it did nothing to ease the constriction in his throat. "I cannot change that, much as I might want to."

He saw her nod, resignation in her eyes. "I know that, too."

"Then why?" He spun away from her. "Why not spread your legs and have done with it?" He kept his words deliberately crude, cheapening the experience as much as he could. He did not know why he did so, except that he could not let her continue. He could not allow himself to believe this could mean more.

That anything could mean more.

"Because you need to feel it," she answered calmly. "Because you need to know that whatever happens, tomorrow makes no difference. Whether or not I spend the next twenty years pleasuring an old man, it does not affect you or me."

"Of course it does!" he snapped. "It is everything. Your proclaimed *love,*" he practically spat, "will go to him. Your legs will open for him."

"Yes, my body will be his. But you are the man I love."

She could not have hurt him more if she had taken a knife and carved open his chest. She could not love him. She could not feel such a way for him.

"No!" he exploded. He rushed around her, heading for the door. "I will not!" he screamed.

But she was there before him, grabbing his arms, pulling him away from the door. He wouldn't have made it out anyway. He was pushing at the latch, ready to throw the door open as he ran through. But it was blocked, barricaded shut from the outside.

Dunwort must have done it. Dunwort in collaboration with Lynette.

Then, before he could accuse her, before he could bellow threats through the doorway at his servant, she was behind him, pushing between him and the door, her body both a physical and emotional barrier.

"Why not?" she challenged. "Why do you run from it?" When he ceased his struggle she straightened, standing before him without a hint of sexuality, without the tiniest sliver of seduction. Yet he had never found her more tempting.

"Once," she said, "one time, Adrian, let me show you what love is." She reached out, laying her slim hand upon his chest, right above his heart. "Let me show you how I feel." She leaned forward, her whisper skating like fire across his cheek. "Let me be the instructor."

He looked at her then. He saw the tears shimmering in her eyes, but more than that he saw the yearning within her, the need to tell him how she felt. To show him. To teach him.

How could he deny her? How could he refuse the one thing for which he had searched? The one thing she understood he could not even see.

He swallowed, finding his voice thick with confusion and pain. "I don't know what to do," he whispered. He lifted his hands in a gesture of futility, trembling from a hurt so much a part of him that he hadn't even realized it was there.

Not until she'd arrived. Not until she stepped into his arms.

"I do," she whispered, and then she leaned forward and kissed his mouth.

Chapter 21

He did not come easily into her arms. Indeed, thought Lynette, nothing about this was easy. But she wanted to do it. More than that, she needed to do it. As much as her body needed breath, she needed to show Adrian how much she loved him.

Unfortunately, he did not understand. Touch, for him, had always been a matter of stimulation, of arousal and release. He had even said as much to her in that room. In Jenny's place.

"This is what a man wants. This is what you want."

She *had* wanted it, enjoyed it, even craved it. But when it was done, all she remembered were the instructions, the technique of how to feel this sensation, how to produce that reaction.

And when the morning came, she'd been left feeling empty, and he had seemed bereft. It wasn't until now that she understood why. It was because there had been no emotion nested in the movements, no love shared in the touch. And while she had reveled in the explosion, he had remained separate.

Alone.

But not tonight. Not now. This time he would know how a woman kissed the man she loved. This was the nameless something she had ached for, had desired all her life. This love. And if she had to give it up on the morrow, at least tonight she would show him. She would share it with him. And together they would hold it in their hands.

Love.

She began differently than ever before: with a kiss. On his lips. She did not bother with technique. Indeed, since she had never kissed like this before, there was no wisdom in her movements. She merely slanted her mouth across his and brushed her head back and forth.

Their lips rubbed one against the other. Softly. Gently.

Then she licked him.

It was a tentative touch, a gentle stroke, but she felt him stiffen in surprise. He might have even meant to pull away from her, but she clutched him tight, her arms wrapped around his shoulders, her hands holding his head steady.

"I love you," she whispered against his mouth. Then, when he opened his mouth on a gasp, she deepened their contact. She pressed her lips to his open mouth and felt a shudder that went through his entire body. But she did not know what to do next.

He showed her. Tentatively at first, then more boldly, she felt his tongue caress hers. They met halfway, stroking, teasing one another. It was a sweet dance, playful and filled with wonder. She smiled and was pleased when his mouth smiled against hers.

"I love you, Adrian," she whispered again.

She felt his hands clench on her hips. She felt his erection press into her belly, but still his kiss was tentative, his movements uncertain. So she said it a third time.

"I love you." She kissed him again.

This time their mouths met on a frenzy, probing deeper, harder, dueling rather than dancing, taking rather than giving. It was a delightful match, filled with hunger and power, and all too soon Lynette surrendered, opening herself wide, allowing the stroke of his tongue to fill her mouth. She let him feast there, taking what he wanted while she arched in submission, open to his desire.

Then suddenly he ripped away, his breath coming in harsh gasps. He buried his face in her shoulder. Fear made his entire body taut, corded, and immobile.

"I want you," he rasped. Then he took another gasping breath. "I want you too much."

She lifted his face, pulling him upward so she could see his eyes, so he might believe what she said. "There is no too much from the man I love. You have been alone too long, Adrian. Let me love you."

She felt his body jerk in reaction, but he forced himself still. "I will hurt you," he said. "The first time always hurts."

She shook her head. "Not with the man I love. And I love you. Let me give you what you need."

And with that she kissed him again. This time her touch was possessive. She seized his lips, kissing him with demand, letting him feel her hunger and her need.

For *him*.

He shook his head, drawing away as he stumbled backward. "I do not understand," he said.

She followed, pursued him, and finally caught him by his desk. But she did not touch him. He was there, leaning back against the surface, his hands clenching the edge, his head bowed in defeat. She looked at him, her heart breaking.

"Love is not something to understand, Adrian. It is something to be shared. To be felt." Again she stepped forward, pressing her hand to his heart. "Can you not feel it?"

He looked up at her, his eyes haunted. His hand trembled against hers. "I feel you. Only you."

Her sight blurred, washed with tears. "It is a good beginning," she said as she pressed forward, closer to him.

She felt him laugh, a short burst of sound filled with self-mockery. "You are more than I can handle, Lynette. You always have been."

"Never." Then she leaned in toward his heart, using her fingers to unbutton and separate his shirt. "Let me show you, Adrian. Let me tell you what I wish."

She pushed him back as she moved, and he relaxed enough to give her access. She pulled the shirt from his shoulders, and the movement exposed his broad chest to her gaze. To her kiss.

"I wish to spend my life with you, Adrian," she said, and she pushed him down to lie on the hard surface. "I would help you build your home brick by brick, day after day," she said as she kissed his chest.

The soft prickle of his chest hair tickled her cheek, and she smiled at the feel of it. Then she brushed her hands across the glorious expanse of skin, kissing where she willed, kneading the muscles that rippled beneath her fingertips and finally nibbling at the flat disk of his nipples.

"I would bear your children, Adrian. I would raise them and teach them and laugh while you played with them."

Her tongue explored his chest, nibbling where she willed, glorying in every hitch of his breath, every shift of his body. Meanwhile, her hands found his trousers. She was awkward in her efforts, but successful nonetheless as she released the fastenings.

"I wish to wake with you every morning and go to sleep beside you every night," she said. Her tongue teased the whorls of hair around his belly. "And during the day I would listen while you griped about the price of mutton or cursed the weather that was stunting your crops."

She found him, hard and eager as he pulsed beneath her fingertips. But she pulled away, choosing instead to draw off the remainder of his clothing. He tried to help her, his hands clumsy and urgent, but she stopped him, pressing his hands down to the desk, pulling the last of the fabric away by herself.

When she returned to his side, he was not lying down. Instead, he was half upright, his eyes glittering with hunger. "I want to touch you," he said. "I want to touch all of you."

Nodding, she stepped backward. Then she slowly twisted her hands behind her, working the hooks that held her dress from behind. She knew the movement thrust her breasts forward, and she smiled as Adrian's gaze locked on them.

"Your babes would suckle at my breasts," she whispered, and was startled by the sudden rush of hunger that burned in his gaze.

Her dress slithered to the floor. Then, naked to his gaze, she stepped into his arms.

"I would stay with you every day of our lives, helping you, loving you, never abandoning you." She leaned forward, once again finding his mouth with hers. As she dropped soft kisses across his lips, she whispered her last wish. "You would never be alone because I would be with you. Always."

She felt him shudder at her last word, like the forewarning of a dam breaking. And since he needed to be released, needed to let his pain burst free to drain away, she repeated her vow.

"With you. *Always.*"

It was too much for him. Too much for his restraint. There was no bed, but he grabbed her nonetheless. First he clutched her to him, burying his face in her breasts. He suckled there, stroking, kneading, but it was not enough.

Within moments he had reversed their positions. He stood, hauling her into his arms. Still he kissed her, licking, stroking, caressing whatever he could touch, whatever he could find.

And she allowed him. More, she opened herself up to him, arching her back as he took her breasts in his mouth. Laying herself backward as he found her belly. Widening her legs as he pulled open her thighs.

His hands were all over her. His mouth was everywhere. It was frenzied and glorious where he touched her, and she writhed against him when he put his hands inside her.

"Lynette," he cried out, and she smiled, knowing what he wanted, knowing what they both needed.

She was at the edge of the desk, her legs spread wide as he stood between them, stroking her insides, opening her up to his caresses. But that was not what she wanted. So she leaned forward, grasping him with her hands, stroking him just as he caressed her.

"Please, Adrian," she begged.

"It will hurt," he responded, his face twisted in agony. He held himself away.

But she would not let him. Wrapping her legs around his waist, she drew him forward. Suddenly she clenched her legs, impaling herself upon him.

She cried out, the pain as shattering as it was incredible. It flashed through her body like a fire; burning her, releasing her, changing her.

"Lynette?" he asked, and she could hear the restraint in his voice. And the fear.

But she was too breathless to answer. Too focused on the glorious expansion he gave her. The wondrous feel of him inside her, filling her, one with her. It took a while to absorb. But soon she grew accustomed to it.

And she wanted more.

"Lynette," he gasped. "I cannot hold on much longer."

Opening her eyes, she saw it was true. He was sweating with the effort to stay still, his muscles clenched as he stood, frozen in place.

"I want to feel you," she whispered.

With a groan, he began to move. Grasping her hips, he lifted her slightly off the desk, shifting her to a better angle as he pulled himself in and out of her.

She, too, began to move, arching backward, throwing her pelvis forward as she reveled in his every push.

She felt the tension begin. Indeed, it had been coiling tighter and tighter within her since the moment she had donned her dress. But now it was more. This time the tension curled around them both. The tightening felt better, thicker.

She heard his gasping breaths. Knew he was coming close. "Oh, God," she cried out, amazed that it could be this incredible. Awed by the heat and the rhythm and the beat as he thrust against her and in her again and again.

"I love you," she whispered, and then the rush exploded through her. Her body clenched. Her mind spun. And Adrian came with her.

She heard him cry out, felt his body convulse.

He, too, exploded.

She saw it in his eyes. Their gazes were locked together, fused as tightly as their bodies, and when his body released, she saw his eyes fill with wonder. Their muscles trembled, quivering with reaction.

Then he spoke, his word a plea as much as a promise.

"Always?"

She nodded. "Always."

Chapter 22

An hour before sunset, Dunwort returned to move the barricade. They both heard it. Indeed, the sound of a table being pulled away from the door was hard to disguise. How Adrian had missed it being placed there, he had no idea.

"I should sack you!" he bellowed through the library door.

"Yes, sir," returned Dunwort from down the hallway.

"Your only hope is to disappear. Be gone at least a day," Adrian growled.

There was a moment's silence. Then, suddenly, he heard Dunwort speak, his voice quick and light. "The baroness has gone out. There'll be no one here to serve you."

"Then there will be no one to sack!"

Another slight pause, and then they heard Dunwort's running feet, dashing down the hallway. As if from a great distance, they heard his gleeful, "Yes, sir!" before the front door slammed.

They were alone.

Adrian wasted no time. Lifting Lynette into his arms, he strode to the door. He did not release her to open the latch. He did not let her down to climb the stairs, nor relinquish her when he shouldered his way into her bedroom, the nearest door after the stairs.

Indeed, he did not intend to let her go for many hours.

And when, for the third time that night, he poised himself between her legs, he finally found the strength to say the words back. Lowering his mouth to just above her lips, he whispered, *"I love you."*

Then he kissed her full upon the mouth. Below he entered her, using his body to build her passion, to stoke the fire that burned between them; and after the fiery climax, as he collapsed beside her, drawing her into his arms and whispering into her ear, "Always."

Intertwined, they slept. And when he woke, it was daylight. Indeed, it was well into afternoon on the day Lynette was to have her final fitting for her wedding dress.

It was a beautiful gown, he knew. All his girls had beautiful gowns, begun the day of their first fitting, prepared in anticipation of the event to come. And Adrian had spared no expense on Lynette's.

Now she was stirring beside him, groaning slightly as her body protested the night's events. But when she opened her eyes, it was with a smile. And the first words she spoke were the ones he knew he would cherish forever.

"I love you."

She must have seen the anguish in his eyes. Indeed, so close were they now, so intertwined in body and mind, she must have shared the pain that gripped his heart. So she leaned forward, kissing his lips, and he felt the wetness of her tears slip onto his face.

"I cannot release you," he said, his voice thick with anguish. He wrapped his arms around her, drawing her against him, clutching her to his heart where she could never be ripped away. "I do not care what happens, Lynette, I cannot!"

She nodded, and he felt the gasp of her sobs.

"Oh, God," he moaned. "We will go to debtor's prison."

"My plans for my family are ruined," she whispered. But then she lifted his face, brushing away his tears though her own flowed freely. "But we will be together."

He laughed. The sound felt torn from his throat. "Not in debtor's prison, we won't." He held her to him, burying his face in her shoulder as he struggled to retain some measure of control.

There was none. No control. No respite.

And so they came together one last time in a flurry of passion and hunger, but afterward there came no relief.

Only a knock at the door.

Adrian stiffened, and beside him, he felt Lynette's entire body still as they waited in clenched silence.

Again, the knock. "My lord?"

Adrian frowned. "Dunwort?"

"Aye, sir."

He felt a wash of fury seep into his soul. "What the devil are you doing?" His words exploded like a curse.

"A message, my lord. Two, in fact."

Adrian felt his hands clench. "Bloody hell, man, what do I want with a couple of damned messages?"

"One is from the baroness, sir. The other's from Songshire. I'll just slip them under the door."

He watched in amazement as two white envelopes appeared.

The last thing Adrian wanted to see was a note. Any note. But one from Lynette's fiancé was beyond the worst. It sent him reeling directly to hell.

Glancing at Lynette, he saw that she, too, was hurting, her body curled in on itself as she stared at the two white squares.

"Should I burn them?" he asked, praying she would say yes.

She shook her head, and wrapped her arms around her knees.

Adrian stood, hating himself for doing it but unable to stop. He picked up the notes. Coming to the side of the bed, he stared down at the offensive objects. Lynette pulled into herself even more, her head buried in her arms. Her voice sounded hollow as it emanated from deep within her curled form. "Read to me."

He knew she meant the letter from Songshire, but he could not do it. He could not open and read a letter from her fiancé even though it was addressed to him. So he tore open the message from his aunt, frowning as he made out her rushed and hurried words.

"'Beauty means nothing,'" he read aloud. "'Only love. And a bit of canniness in the end. Love, Agatha.'"

He looked up, confused. Looking across the bed, he saw Lynette lift her head, the same expression mirrored on her face. But then he saw something else: dawning hope in her eyes. It showed in her body, too, as she dropped her arms and reached for Songshire's envelope.

Adrian remained confused. "What does it mean?"

She shook her head. "I don't know. What does the earl write?"

"Lynette . . ." He meant to force her to explain, but she was too quick for him. Snatching the earl's missive from his hands, she ripped it open. He watched in terror, hope and fear warring in his gut.

She read and reread the letter to herself. Then she looked up.

Her expression changed slowly, by inches, but the change came over her entire body. One moment she was tense, anxious, and worried. The next, she was smiling. Then grinning. Suddenly she fell on her back while laughter rippled out of her. It rolled out of her in a gale, echoing through the room, reverberating in Adrian's ears.

He did not demand an explanation. Indeed, she was laughing so hard, he did not believe she could give one. As it was, she barely managed to draw breath before collapsing again in another fit of laughter.

He snatched the earl's note out of her hand, quickly scanning the contents for an answer. Then he froze, forcing himself to read the page slowly, making sure he understood every word.

I was somewhat startled to discover that a woman of age can be every bit as innovative as any Marlock girl. Plus, she has the added benefit of shared experiences, a lifetime of perspective, and a heart that withstood the test of time. The contract stands, but for Agatha, not Lynette.

Songshire

Adrian looked up, seeing his love still collapsed in merriment. The truth began to blossom in his mind.

"Does this mean . . . ?" He didn't dare finish the thought aloud.

But Lynette did. Rolling onto her side, she grinned at him. "It means that your aunt has won her bet with me."

His smile faded, but she answered even before he could phrase the question. "I dared her to prove herself. I challenged her to pick a man and bring him to his knees without benefit of youth or great beauty."

Adrian looked down at the missive still clutched in his hand. "Songshire?"

She giggled in response. "You did not know they'd been acquainted for many years?"

His eyes widened as names, dates, and a whole variety of particulars fell into place in his mind. "I believe they grew up in the same neighborhood. But she was poor . . ."

"And he a future earl," she finished for him.

He shook his head. "It cannot be."

Lynette crawled forward, dropping kisses all over his face in her joy. "I believe it is."

At last the full magnitude of their good fortune burst upon his senses. The contract stood! Lynette's settlement with Songshire remained. The money, the provisions for her eventual widowhood, his cut of the agreement, her place in society—it all remained, including the cash that would at last set his finances on their feet. But for his aunt, not Lynette.

He grinned up at her. He was free!

As was she.

Scrambling off the bed, he ran to her side. She shifted, following his movements with a startled look, but he did not care. He reached her in mere seconds, dropping to the ground, heedless of the fact that he was naked and had just skinned his bent knee.

"What are you doing?" she asked.

He did not answer. Instead, he gripped her hand, pulling it toward his chest as he gazed at her, his heart in his eyes. "Lynette Jameson, will you do me the greatest honor of my life? Will you marry me?"

She gaped at him, surprise washing into joy. She cried out. She would have answered immediately, but he stopped her, putting one hand to her lips.

"Wait," he pressed. "There is more."

Obediently, she settled into silence, though her eyes shimmered their answer, and his heart pounded in anticipation.

"It will be very hard. We will not live here. My estate is in—"

"I love the country," she interrupted, using the motion to push away his fingers.

"There is a great deal of work to do—"

"I'm used to hard work. I watched over much of my father's parish."

"The estate is crumbling to the ground. It is dank, dark, and filthy."

"The children will love it."

His body jerked in reaction to her words. Children, he thought with glee. Children!

"But you hate children," he said.

She shook her head. "Not yours, I won't. Your children will be wonderful. Besides, my mother will be a great help." She paused, doubt showing on her face. "There will be enough room for them, won't there? My family? They will be most helpful, and it will be much better than at my uncle's."

"Lynette, it is a huge, moldering pile. If they do not mind the dust, we could use the extra hands." Then he stopped, at last realizing what it could be like. Not only Lynette, he could have a whole family. Filling the old pile of rocks with joy and life again. He gasped, trying to find the words to express his hopes. His happiness. His love. "Lynette, will you—"

But she did not let him finish. She surged forward, crying out as she moved. "Yes! Yes, yes, yes, yes, yes!"

She wrapped her arms around him, kissing his face, his eyes, his mouth, overbalancing him until they both toppled to the ground. He did not care. She was in his arms as firmly as she was in his heart.

"I love you," he said. "Forever."

She grinned. "Forever."

She lowered her head then, intending to kiss him, but they were interrupted. Outside the bedroom, they both heard Dunwort's loud whoop of joy.

"Didn't I tell ye, girl!" came his voice through the doorway. "Ye gots to do it with love!"

Lynette began to laugh, the ripples of her joy flowing into Adrian's body until he, too, allowed happiness to take him.

"Yes, you did, Dunwort," she called. "You did indeed!"

"Now get out of here before I sack you!" Adrian bellowed.

His only answer was another whoop of glee and the sound of footsteps racing down the stairs. The front door slammed.

"At last," Adrian whispered, turning back to his bride. "An end to it all."

"No," she answered as she began to move on top of him, her eyes dancing with merriment. "The beginning of forever."